Lyn Lord

THE
NORTHWOODS
READER VOLUME 3
NORTHERN MEMORIES

CULLY GAGE

D1036379

CONTAINS THE COMPLETE BOOKS OF THE ORIGINAL #2, 6 & 7

Avery Color Studios, Inc.
Gwinn, Michigan

©2002 Avery Color Studios, Inc.

ISBN 1-892384-15-9

Library of Congress Catalog Card Number

First Edition 2002

Published by
Avery Color Studios, Inc.
Gwinn, Michigan 49841

Note From The Publisher

In the continuing consolidation of the Northwoods Reader series from nine books to three volumes, this third and final volume contains the complete following books: Northwoods Reader #2, Tales Of The Old U.P.; *Northwoods Reader #6,* Still Another Northwoods Reader; *and Northwoods Reader #7,* Old Bones And Northern Memories. *People who have enjoyed the Volume 1 and 2 consolidations are sure to enjoy this third volume.*

Table of Contents

Tales Of The Old U.P. - Book #2

Still Another Northwoods Reader - Book #6

Old Bones And Northern Memories - Book #7

TALES OF
THE OLD U.P.

BOOK TWO

Foreword

The stories in this book were originally written so that my grandchildren might know something about the way life was lived in the U.P., the Upper Peninsula of Michigan, at the turn of this century. Then as now it was a lovely land bounded on the north by Lake Superior and on the south by the forests of Wisconsin and the upper shore of Lake Michigan. It was also a hard land demanding much of those who by choice or circumstance found themselves isolated in its wilderness homesteads and little villages. They had to have *sisu*, the Finnish word for being able to endure all evils and yet survive.

Our little village of Tioga, located almost in the center of the U.P., consisted of two little settlements, one inhabited mainly by French Canadians and Indians down in the valley and the other atop a long steep hill where the Finns and Swedes lived. A straggle of houses and log cabins containing other nationalities lined the hill road that joined them. Except for wagon ruts, there were no real roads, but through the valley a railroad and the Tioga River ran, the former our only contact with the outside world. We had no radio or TV and even a newspaper was unusual but we had each other to talk to. Talk was what held the town together. Everyone knew everything that happened down to the slightest detail. It was not gossip, actually; it was the sharing of our lives.

And it was often very interesting talk too, because our forest village had the damndest collection of interesting characters you could find anywhere. I suppose that even cities have them too but in our town they were our close neighbors. Anyway, we cherished and enjoyed hearing about their doings and they helped us to make it through the long winter.

People have asked me if the tales are true. I've always maintained that they are fiction based upon my faulty memories of what took place in Tioga shortly after the turn-of-the-century. If the language is sometimes salty and earthy, it was the usage of the time. We weren't very civilized in Tioga but we enjoyed our struggle for survival because we had a keen appreciation of the absurd. If you find memories and laughter in these pages, let me know.

Cully Gage

Roast Goose For Christmas

Mother was just getting ready to hide the raven again when Mrs. Donegal, Old Blue Balls' wife, came for tea. "Sit down, Emma," said my Mother, "as soon as I get rid of this dratted bird I'll put the kettle on."

When Mother returned, she explained. "I just can't stand that stuffed raven," she said. "It sits on the piano and peers at me day after day til I'm fit to be tied. Unhappily for me, my husband likes it and admires it and insists on having it on the piano. He likes to say, 'Quoth the raven nevermore' and it's his pride and joy. So I hide it back of the door in the kitchen pantry. Sometimes he doesn't notice it's gone for months at a time. And when he does, I just say that the moths have gotten to it and I've got it in a box with moth balls or I make some other excuse."

"I can't abide stuffed critters, either," Mrs. Donegal replied. "Never could. Like having a corpse in the house. But I know all about your stuffed raven because Mr. Donegal sure admires that bird too. Says he's going to have one stuffed if he ever gets a chance to shoot one. I've been a-praying he'll miss. I hope it's expensive to have 'em mounted, Mrs. Gage. Is it?"

"I think John paid a man in Ishpeming twenty-five dollars to do the taxidermy," Mother said. "An awful lot for something that looks like a double-sized crow."

"Oh, well, then I don't have to worry." Mrs. Donegal looked relieved. "Bruce is so stingy he'd never throw that much money on anything, let alone a bird. I haven't had a new coat or dress or hat for ten years. Almost ashamed to come over, Mrs. Gage."

Seeing tears in her eyes, Mother was sympathetic. She knew that her friend had a hard life with a hard man. B.B. Donegal was our school superintendent and he ran his home with the same toughness that he ran his school. His wife and children, his teachers and pupils, were terrified of him. Though we called him Old Blue Balls behind his back, we respected him and worked hard to escape having our hind ends feel his heavy hand or strap. There was no mutiny on his Bounty.

But he was tight as well as tight fisted. He doled out one piece of chalk each week to each teacher and woe to anyone who asked for more. Old Blue Balls had been very poor in his youth and knew the value of a penny. It was part of a million dollars, he said. At home he was just as penurious. The Donegals set a poor table. I remember being invited one evening to eat with them and having hominy, a pickle, and a chunk of salt pork. No dessert! Walter, his son, with whom I played occasionally when he wasn't doing his interminable chores told me later though that usually they had fish and game, for Old Blue Balls was a mighty hunter and fisher, spending most of his weekends in the woods or on the rivers. Walter also insisted that his father was really rich and when I doubted this he took me into the house and showed me a desk drawer full of pork and bean cans each one containing a big roll of bills, even some five and ten dollar ones. And a big tobacco can full of silver. But Walter never had a nickel to spend. Why, I used to have to give him some of my marbles so we could have a game.

When Mrs. Donegal started sobbing about how much she dreaded the approaching Christmas and that never in her married life had she ever gotten a present from her husband, Mother noticed me pretending to be reading *David Copperfield* in the bay window. "Cully," she said, "take those big ears out to the woodpile and bring in some sticks of birch and fill up the kitchen stove. Your father is making pills today so we've got to have the oven hot. Then go over and watch him in the hospital."

That sounded better than *David Copperfield* or Mrs. Blue Balls' woes so I did what she asked. In the early days of this century all the country doctors in the Upper Peninsula of Michigan had to make their own medications. "Some of the concoctions," Dad said, "were wondrous strange." I found him in the dispensary of the old hospital, wearing a white apron, and using a pestle to get the lumps out of a substance he was grinding in the white bowl he called a mortar. When I asked him what kind of pills he was making, he looked at me and grinned.

"Aspirin," he said. "Medicine is five percent surgery and bonesetting, five percent castor oil and calomel, five percent delivering babies, fifteen percent aspirin, and seventy percent humbug. But don't tell anybody I said so."

The pill making was fun to watch. After the lumps were gone, Dad divided the paste into four smaller mortars and then colored each batch differently, stirring them vigorously. Next, batch by batch, he spread the drug on a marble slab, added some flour and cornstarch, and flattened it with a little glass rolling pin. It almost looked like Mother's piecrust. Then he took a scalpel and cut the aspirin dough into little squares about a half inch wide. These he picked up individually and, with a curious rolling motion of his thumb and forefinger, turned them into perfectly round little balls which he put into a wide baking pan and with his forefinger flattened them. Dad sure was deft. He made those pills so fast his fingers just seemed to fly and soon the bottom of the baking pan was covered. It looked pretty with its different sections of red, white, brown, and purple pills.

"Dad, why do you color them differently if they're all the same aspirin?" I asked.

"Ho!" he answered. "That's where the humbug comes in. The placebo effect. Why, I've had patients swear that only the purple pills did them any good. And damned if they didn't."

He was just cleaning up when Old Blue Balls–oops, I mean Mr. Donegal–came in. I'd never seen him grinning before.

"Doctor, if you have a moment, why don't you drop down to my house and see what I bagged this morning. Shot four snowshoe rabbits, two partridges, and a spruce hen. Best

Saturday morning I ever had. But what I'd like to have you see is the size of one of those hares. Maybe it's a cross with some domestic rabbit. Anyway, it's worth seeing." Then turning to me, he said, "And you can come see it too, Cully, if you want."

"Yes, sir, Mister Donegal. Thank you, Mr. Donegal." When he left, Dad carried the baking pan over to our house, put it in the oven, and told my mother to take it out in thirty minutes. "Some physicians don't bake their pills," he told me "but I've found they hold up a lot better if they're cooked. Won't crumble so easily." We walked down the hill to the superintendent's house.

Mr. Donegal led us through the kitchen into the back shed. It was cold in there. Hanging from the pegs of a rack along the wall, all cleaned and skinned, were the carcasses. The biggest hare was at least a third again as large as the others. Dad admired it but opined it was just a big animal, not a cross or mutation. "But you'll sure be having a fine Christmas dinner. That big snowshoe might be tough though. Better cook the fowl with it."

"No siree! No siree!" Old Blue Balls replied. "We're not having any rabbit or partridge this Christmas dinner. We're having roast goose." He took off a burlap bag that covered a huge naked fowl that hung from a nail in another part of the shed. "Remember Doctor? I got that goose the last day of deer season–the same day I shot that Great Horned Owl. Got a deer and a goose and an owl and almost had a shot at a raven like that one of yours on your piano. Ah, I like that north country. Best hunting and fishing anywhere."

Dad was impressed with the goose. "Why, I bet that bird will go almost ten pounds. Some fine eating there, B.B."

"Yeah. The woman is going to stuff it with bread and hazelnuts. We'll have a merry Christmas this year, we will."

Most of the rest of this story I had to piece together from what Walter told me and what Mrs. Donegal told my Mother. On Christmas Eve she stuffed the goose and got it ready for the oven. On Christmas morning they had bacon and eggs for breakfast and Walter and his sister and brother opened their boot socks to find the usual five pieces of hard candy and the usual new book. But then Mr. Donegal surprised all of them. He brought out a large box with a red ribbon around it and presented it to his wife with a real flourish. "Now woman, don't you ever say again that I never gave you a Christmas present. Merry Christmas, Emmy!"

Mrs. Donegal was overcome. "Oh Bruce! Oh Bruce!" she exclaimed with tears in her eyes. Impulsively, she threw her arms around his neck and kissed him. Walter told me he'd never seen the likes of it before. "Oh Bruce," she said again. "Oh, Bruce!" Then shakingly she opened the box. Inside was a stuffed Great Horned Owl.

Old Blue Balls was completely oblivious to his wife's reaction as she stood there frozen in her tracks. "Great Balls of Fire!" he roared. "That's a noble bird if I ever saw one. Puts Doctor's raven to shame. Why you'd swear it was alive the way he looks at you! And that taxidermist did a good job even if he did charge twenty-five dollars. That owl will last for years and years with some careful tending. Merry Christmas, woman!"

"Twenty-five dollars. Twenty-five dollars," said Mrs. Donegal dully as she went to the kitchen.

Old Blue Balls went hunting again that morning–to get up a good appetite for that goose, he said. When he returned at noon he was famished. Taking off his hunting clothes and boots, he plopped himself down at the table. "Bring on the goose!" She brought on the mashed potatoes, and the wild cranberry sauce, and the turnips, and the bread. And then on a big platter she brought in the Great Horned Owl, thoroughly cooked, pedestal and all.

"Would you like to have this carving knife, Mister Donegal?" she asked, holding it firmly and looking him straight in the eye.

I don't know what happened right after that but the next morning Emma Donegal emptied the money from some of Old Blue Balls' pork and bean cans into her purse and took the train for Ishpeming. When she returned that afternoon she had on new shoes, new stockings, a new dress, and a new coat. Oh yes, and also a new straw hat with pink and blue flowers around its brim. She did not stop at her house but came straight to our own and had a cup of tea with Mother. She almost looked pretty the way she kept smiling.

Aunt Lizzie's Mice

In the western part of the Upper Peninsula of Michigan, the year 1915 is still remembered as the Year of the Mouse. Jaques Moreau, the oldest man in town, claimed he'd never seen the like of it in ninety years. We'd had a long warm summer for a change and mice were so plentiful we could get a sackful out of any haystack for our bass fishing whenever we wanted to. But it was with the first frost that they really invaded our little forest village. Out of the woods and fields they came in hordes to nest in our houses and barns and to beget more mice. They scurried across our faces at night. Mrs. Lappinen told Mrs. Niemi that for the first time in her married life, Toivo, her husband, had stopped snoring.

More barn cats became house cats that year than ever before but they soon became fat and satiated and so lazy they'd hardly open a green eye when a mouse ran over their paws. We found mice nests, all full of pink squirming little mouslets, in the damnedest places. Mrs. Olson put on her husband's bearskin coat and got half way to the post office before she put her hand in the pocket and screamed. Two nests were found in the Town Hall's spittoons. The Sears Roebuck catalogs in half the outhouses in town had ragged edges. We shook our boots before we put them on. It was terrible.

We fought back of course. When we flattened tin cans and nailed them over the holes they chewed in our floors, the mice always seemed to find some other way to get in. All they needed was a crack half an inch wide or a knothole somewhere. If we plastered these shut, the mice soon gnawed another opening. Hoping to starve them, our housewives emptied their flour bins into crocks, put their sugar and starch in jars, and their apples and potatoes in sealed barrels. All crumbs and left-overs went into the kitchen stove. Never had there been so many clean houses in our village.

And, of course, we trapped them. Flinn's store was soon out of mousetraps and couldn't get any more but fortunately our family had about nine of them so we did better than most. In our household I was the designated mouse catcher and got pretty good at it before the population reached its peak and declined. At first I had to set all nine traps three times a day and rarely was there a trap unfilled or unsprung. Sometimes I got two at a time. Don't remember how many I caught but there must have been hundreds that I buried in the strawberry patch. Finally the mice became harder to catch and I had to change my bait from store cheese to more attractive fare. The best bait I found, after considerable experimenting, was a paste composed of butter, bran, bread and bacon grease–and licorice spit. I chewed a lot of licorice ropes to get it and can't bear the taste now. Dad said it was the oil of anise that attracted them. Anyway, it sure worked and ours was the first house in town to become mouse-free.

No, that's not quite right. One of the French Canadians downtown, Sieur La Tour, kept his shack mouse-free and it took some snooping by his neighbors before they discovered that his secret was weasel glands. Mice are deathly afraid of weasels so old La Tour trapped a lot of them, carved out their scent glands, and, after squashing them good in a can of tobacco juice, daubed the resulting essence all around the base logs of his shack. Unfortunately, the weasel population was far smaller than that of the mice and La Tour had already taken the cream of the crop so it didn't help the rest of us much.

The other house that had no mice in it belonged to a half-breed Indian trapper named Peter Half Shoes. It was a log cabin with plenty of holes in its moss chinking and dirty beyond belief. A perfect place for mice. And Pete didn't trap them either. He had a secret weapon–his pet skunk Mabel, his love, who slept with him every night. Skunks love mice and, unlike cats, they never get enough of them. They can eat them for breakfast, dinner and supper and still have enough appetite for several midnight snacks. So old Pete's cabin was another one that was pretty mouse-free–though it got a little high when it rained. One of Pete's neighbors tried to rent Mabel for a week but backed out when he learned that part of the deal was that he would have to take Mabel to bed with him. Otherwise Mabel would get too lonesome, Pete said.

Without enough traps, the future of our village looked pretty bleak as the mice begat and begat and the cats yawned and yawned. Then one day some unsung hero invented a new springless mousetrap and most of us found the path to his door. It was quite ingenious and easy to make. All you needed was an old water pail, an empty condensed milk can, some salt and a piece of heavy wire.

You filled the pail about a third full of water, punched a hole in the middle of each end of the little milk can, threaded the wire through the holes and suspended the contraption on the rim of the pail. Then you laid a board up against the pail so the mice could use it as a ladder, and wrapped a piece of bacon around the can to serve as bait. Incredibly the dang thing worked. The mouse would smell the bacon, climb up the ladder, jump across onto the condensed milk can and this would immediately revolve, dumping the mouse into the drink to drown. No work to it. No rebaiting. No setting or emptying ordinary mousetraps and risking your fingers. Just empty the bucket when it got too full. If it got so cold that the water would freeze, you just put enough salt in it so it wouldn't. Eureka! The Perfect Perpetual Mouse Trap!

After the ground froze, most of the mice had established residence in our houses and barns and the little mice factories in the woods and fields had shut down their assembly lines. The new invention soon reduced the mouse population so that our cats became hungry again. The village had been saved.

But I can't resist telling about one small skirmish in the great Mouse War of 1915 and how I contrived a better mouse trap too. One day I was sitting in my Dad's office in the old hospital when Aunt Lizzie, that old troublemaker, appeared and asked him for some poison. "Those mice are just driving me crazy, Doctor," she said. "They scare me silly. I've got two of them in traps but I can't bear to touch them and they've already begun to smell. And I can't abide cats either, even if I could get one–which I can't. They make me sneeze and my eyes water. I'd like some of that strychnine you give trappers to poison wolves for the bounty. I'll pay anything to get rid of the critters."

Dad said no very emphatically and when he suggested that she go rent Pete Half Shoe's skunk Aunt Lizzie left in a ten carat huff. "I was damned if I'd give that old she-devil any strychnine," he told my mother at supper time. "She's buried four husbands already and how do I know she's not setting her cap for a fifth?"

"Oh now, John," Mother replied. "That's not fair. All but the first one were lonely old men and sick when she married them."

"A hell of a way to make a living!" Dad said. "Anyway, I'm not taking any chances of being an accessory before the fact. Why doesn't that old biddy just breathe on those mice? They'd curl up their tails and die in a hurry."

I kept thinking about what Aunt Lizzie said about being willing to pay anything to get rid of her mice. Maybe I could go into business. After all I'd been able to clean all of them out of our house, and the nine traps weren't being used, and I might be able to make enough to buy that old crooked-wheel bicycle of Mulu's. He wanted ten dollars for it which was too much but I had $8.23 in my little iron bank, the one you made your deposit in by putting a coin into the little man's upraised hand and having him put it in his pocket. Let's see. I'd caught more than that in our own house. So I went up to Aunt Lizzie's place on Easy Street. They called it that because it was the only street in town that didn't have a steep hill in it.

When she came to the back door I handed her the business card I'd spent an hour in composing.

CULLY GAGE
PERFESSIONAL MOUSE CATCHER
Satisfakshun Gerinteed
2¢ per mouse

I told Aunt Lizzie I had cleaned out every mouse in our own house and that I could do the same with hers. I said I had nine traps and my own special bait.

She tried to haggle me down saying my price was too high. At first she only offered me a penny for five mice, then a penny for two, then a cent a mouse, but I held fast. The turning point came when a mouse skittered out from under the stove and she pulled up her skirts, screamed and gave in. Aunt Lizzie sure had skinny legs and knobby knees. I went home for my traps feeling pretty good. I'd get that bike of Mulu's yet. I was in business.

When I returned I emptied her two mousetraps, set my own, and looked over the place. There were mouse droppings everywhere and I found a nest with five little ones in one of her cupboard right away. When I disposed of them and asked for my dime she refused. "No, no. I'm not paying for any babies, only for the big ones." Aunt Lizzie was tight. "O.K." I thought to myself, "next time I'll let the buggers grow up."

It was easy pickings at first. By the end of the week I had caught twenty-three mice and had found where they were coming in. One place was underneath the pipe that went from the cistern to the kitchen pump and the other was a knothole in a baseboard. A light snow showed runways going from the house to the garbage pile back of Aunt Lizzie's outhouse. Evidently the mice were going out there to feed during the daytime and back to the house at night to frolic, bed and beget. So I plugged up both openings.

Aunt Lizzie was sure hard to work for. She wouldn't watch me emptying my traps but she was suspicious that I might be cheating on my report. "How do I know you caught six today?" she demanded. When I told her to come see and she refused, I brought a couple of handfuls into her living room and pretended to be about to put them in her lap. "All right, all right. Just mark them on the calendar each day. I guess I'll have to trust you but if I catch you cheating I'll go down and tell your father."

The worst thing of all though was that Aunt Lizzie just kept putting off paying me. When I bugged her about it she first said that she'd pay me after I'd caught fifty. Then when I showed her on the calendar that I had done so, she moved the quota up to a hundred "or until all the mice were gone." Just to be safe I cut off each of their tails with my mother's sewing scissors until she gave me a licking for it. After that I used my jackknife but I kept them in a can back of her shed.

After I reached sixty, the going got hard and I was getting only two or three mice a day, then finally none at all. Still Aunt Lizzie wouldn't pay me. "Your card said satisfaction guaranteed," she insisted. "And I ain't satisfied a bit. There's mouse droppings in the pantry every morning and I can hear them chasing around my bedroom at night. Drat it! I'm tired of sleeping with my head under the covers. You won't get a red cent, Cully, until they're all gone." Geez, she was mean.

But I knew she was right about the mice still being there. I figured there were about three of them left, one who lived part-time in the woodbox that I called Shadrach, another that lived in the walls, called Meeshack, and a third who lived somewhere in Aunt Lizzie's bedroom. I called him or her Abednego and I almost got him with the stove poker once. Shadrach, Meeshack, and Abednego. Guess I heard about them in Sunday School once. Anyway, no matter where I set the traps or what kind of bait I used I just couldn't seem to catch those three. They were smarter than I was. Sure was frustrating.

Having snared plenty of rabbits I made me a tunnel out of birchbark, put cracker crumbs soaked in bacon grease at the end that went against the wall, and had a little noose made of one of the cat-gut sutures my Dad used for sewing up bad cuts. Aunt Lizzie scoffed when she saw it. "You won't catch anything with that contraption," she said. Then she saw me eyeing the cookies she had just baked and spread out on the table to cool. "Now, young man, I'll thank you to leave them cookies alone. I've counted them. They're for poor Mr. Dooley downtown. I hear his wife's in a bad way and likely to die so I think I'll take him some comfort."

"Oh oh," I thought, "so that's how Aunt Lizzie gets her husbands. Cookie bait! She's a trapper too." But I didn't say anything. Just went about my business until I heard her scream and call to me. I found her in the upstairs bedroom standing on a chair. Her wig had fallen off and she was as bald as an onion. I could hardly keep my face straight but then I saw what she was pointing at. It was a big mouse, probably Abednego, sitting on a hat in the hat box she'd just opened. I swear that mouse had the same look of shock that must have been on my face when I first saw Aunt Lizzie's naked pale pate. Actually Abednego looked kind of ornamental on that hat–better than the fake roses. I ran downstairs for the poker but when I returned the mouse was gone. Wow! Was Aunt Lizzie mad! All she could say was "Satisfaction guaranteed! Satisfaction guaranteed!" I got out of there fast. I knew I'd never get my money unless I caught those last three mice. I'd never get that bike!

I waited a couple of days before returning. The old lady had calmed down but my birchbark snare tunnel didn't have a thing in it though the bait was gone. Nevertheless I was more excited than discouraged because I'd brought with me my own new secret weapon. It was Dad's minnow trap, one of those long ones made of wire mesh with cones that projected inwards. Since I'd found a dead mouse in it all dried up, I figured that if he couldn't get out, then maybe Shadrach, Meeshack and Abednego couldn't either. So I pushed some bacon soaked bread through the cone openings and took it up to the bedroom.

Damned if it didn't work perfectly. The next morning I found three live mice in it and Aunt Lizzie said they'd been there all night which was why she had slept downstairs on the couch. "Then them critters just kept squeaking and running around in your cage all night. I couldn't bear it," she complained. "Hardly slept a wink." I was delighted of course and began to dream big dreams. "Cully Gage's Improved Mouse Trap De Luxe"–maybe I could patent it and make a million dollars.

It had one disadvantage though. It was hard to empty without having the mice get away and when my Dad caught me trying with a rope to lower it down our well so they'd drown I got another licking. Had to take the minnow trap all the way to Fish Lake. What would I do when it froze over? But it worked. The dang thing worked.

Though I brought it back to Aunt Lizzie's house I never caught another mouse either in the minnow trap or in any of the other traps. It was clear that I'd cleaned them out. No more droppings anywhere. They were gone. Finally, after two more weeks, I went up to Aunt Lizzie's house to total up the marks on the calendar and to get my money.

The calendar was gone. Aunt Lizzie claimed she had to use it to start a fire that morning and that she'd forgotten I'd used it to keep daily score of the catch. She had a sneaky smile on her face as she said it but it disappeared when I brought in my big can of mousetails and dumped them out on her kitchen table. "Seventy-seven, seventy-eight, seventy-nine," I counted. "Aunt Lizzie, you owe me one dollar and fifty-eight cents!" But once again the old devil refused. "I still ain't satisfied," she said. "I still hear squeaks in the night sometimes. You hain't got all those mice yet, young man. And if you don't like it, sue me!" The dirty old she-devil!

I picked up my things and went home mad as a wet hen and feeling very sorry for myself. I'd wasted a month's hard work. I'd been suckered good. When I told my Dad about it he was mad too but he couldn't help saying that it was a good lesson. There always were some people you couldn't trust, and everybody in town knew that Aunt Lizzie was one of them. Then he told me to solve the problem and to find some way to get paid. "And I'll give you a whole dollar of my own money if you do," he added.

Well, I sure did a lot of thinking and figuring for the next few days until I found the way. What I did was to wait until Aunt Lizzie passed our house on one of her daily evil gossip trips downtown. Then I took my minnow trap full of mice I'd caught behind Flinn's store, unplugged the knot hole and the place under the cistern pipe at her house. Then I let all the mice escape and there must have been eight or nine of them. I grinned when I saw that most followed the old trails right into the house. The next day I did the same thing.

So I wasn't entirely surprised when Aunt Lizzie came to our house and begged me to come back. I told her I wouldn't until she paid me–which she did right there. Better yet, so did my dad.

The first time I rode Mulu's bike I smashed it to smithereens.

Puuko

Puuko was the blackest, biggest, meanest tomcat that ever roamed our forest village. He was also the most amorous. In the ten years of his short life Puuko actually changed the color of our cat population from grey to black. In his prime he terrorized not only every other cat but also every dog in town. Puuko didn't like dogs and most of them made a wide detour around our yard to keep from feeling his claws.

The exception was Pullu, a stupid old hound, who was a slow learner. Day after day Pullu would amble innocently down the sidewalk next to our picket fence. And there every morning was Puuko, crouched in ambush on the upper stringer by the gate post, waiting for his morning ride. He'd jump on poor Pullu and ride him like a jockey down our hill street in a satanic chorus of snarls and yelps. When they got to Mrs. Falange's house Puuko would get off, stalk over to her barn, look over her ten or more barn cats, take care of those who needed it–and sometimes those who didn't–then look for another mutt to ride home. And that was in the daytime when he was still dopey from the previous night's adventures!

"Puuko" (pronounced "Pookoh") is the Finn word for *knife* and it fit that big black he-devil perfectly. Puuko didn't just claw at random; he performed surgery, and every cat in town had been his patient–or paramour. My father, the village doctor, gave him the name after bandaging a long rip on my leg. I'd been milking Rosy, our Jersey cow, and had been a bit tardy in giving Puuko the squirt of warm milk he'd been demanding. Dad admired that long slit–said he couldn't have done a better job with a scalpel. And there was the time when Lempi, our hired girl, made the mistake of trying to sweep

Puuko out of the way with her broom. He swarmed up the handle and slit her arm from armpit to elbow. Puuko, the knife! The meanest damned cat in town!

Even when he was a kitten, Puuko hadn't been a bit loveable. His purr sounded like an internal growl. No one dared pick him up and I was the only person he permitted to pet him–if that's what you can call it. When he occasionally rubbed against my leg, it meant that Puuko was commanding me to smooth his black fur twice–not three times–and perhaps to scratch his ears once.

The family probably insisted that Puuko was *my* cat because on one cold night I had opened my upstairs bedroom window and let him in after suffering through three solid hours of continuous caterwalling. It was a mistake because that tomcat slept in my bed every night thereafter. Except once, for a period of about three weeks, after Puuko's ambition had exceeded his discretion and he smelled hugely of skunk! I slept those three weeks with cotton stuffed in my ears. Actually, Pukko did not spend much of any night in my bed; he was too busy making service calls. It was usually with the first rays of dawn that he returned and sawed hideously away on that cat-gut strung fiddle of his until I gave up and opened the window. No, he wasn't my cat. I was his boy!

All of us respected Puuko but my Dad admired him, mainly because there hadn't been a mouse or rat in the house or barn since he appeared. Indeed, some of the Finns uptown and some French Canadian families downtown used to put out fish heads on their back porches, hoping that Puuko would hang around long enough to take care of their varmints too. He liked hunting rats more than mice; mice were too easy. Sometimes I'd see him up at the town dump behind Flinn's store indulging in an orgy of rat slaughter just for the hell of it, making the rock walls resound with his battle cries. As Health Officer, Dad said the village ought to put Puuko on its payroll. Did more good than Charley Olafson, our constable.

Besides his ability to keep down the rats and mice, Puuko also contributed to our larder, occasionally dragging a dead rabbit or partridge up to the shed door. These we ate gratefully though he always insisted on having the liver. Once he also brought in two of Toivo Lampi's fat hens for our Thanksgiving dinner, payment, Dad said, for the twin boys Dad had delivered ten years earlier but for which he had never been paid.

But the real reason Dad appreciated Puuko was the way the tomcat had taken care of old Aunt Lizzie–no relation–who was the town's busybody and evil gossip, always causing trouble. Puuko made his rounds at night; Aunt Lizzie made hers in the daytime. She was our town's newspaper but all she relayed was bad news, innuendo and suspicion. I don't know how many houses she stopped at to hand out the evil tidbits of the day but ours was not one of them, probably because she was afraid of Dad who made no bones about not being able to stand her. Said if she bothered us he'd give her a dram from the little black bottle on the top shelf–the one with the skull and crossbones on it.

Well, this particular morning Mother was out in the back garden when Aunt Lizzie came to our front door. "Young man," she said, sniffing loudly, "I would like to speak to your mother about an important matter." When I let her in, she marched stiffly into the living room and sat down in Puuko's chair. To my credit, I did suggest that she might find another one more comfortable but she refused. "Go get your mother," she commanded. "She's got to know what you've been up to!" For the life of me I couldn't think of anything

I'd done recently that was bad enough to merit such a visit, but maybe I had. So I let Puuko in the back door.

When my mother and I entered the back door we heard Aunt Lizzie snarl, "Scat, cat!" Then she let out a bloodcurdling scream, bolted out of the screen door, down the steps and up the street, screeching all the way. We knew immediately what had happened. It had happened before.

In our living room, off to one side between the bookcase and the bearskin rug, there was a straight backed, red plush chair that must have been designed by Torquemada for the Spanich Inquisition's torture chambers. No one could sit in the damned thing for more than three minutes without getting a headache. I'm sure we would have burned it up for kindling had it not been Puuko's chair. Besides my bed, there were only two other places in the house that he claimed as his own–the warm spot behind the kitchen stove and that red plush chair. But they were his! Sometimes on a dare one of us kids would sit on Puuko's throne teasingly. He'd come in and stare at you for a moment with those green unblinking eyes of his. When red flecks appeared in them, he'd suddenly arch himself into a huge black monster twice his normal size, hiss menacingly, and snarl his battle cry. No miau, that! It was a terrifying "VVVRRAU!" Finally, he'd give you about two more seconds before swarming all over you, clawing and slashing. The warning sequence was always the same but sometimes it went faster than at others. No, we didn't play the game very often. It was Russian roulette. No one sat too long in Puuko's chair.

Mother was mortified when she told Dad that noon what had happened. "I've got to send Cully up to Aunt Lizzie's house with a note of apology" she said. Dad vetoed that immediately. "No you won't!" he declared. "Let it lie. I don't want that old poison'-tongue making this house into another way station on her daily trouble route. Good for Puuko!" And he gave me a quarter to buy the cat a can of salmon from Flinn's store.

Puuko's greatest admirer, however, was my Grampa Gage–though for other reasons. I remember one special evening that he and I were sitting on the back stoop watching the sun go down when Puuko appeared, preened himself, and sharpened his claws on the big spurce tree.

Grampa lit his pipe and took a long look at Puuko who was stretching his legs and arching his back. "Mr. Muldoon," he said, "some people claim that these damned tomcats have all the fun but they forget that it isn't always easy to be male. It's an awful res-pons-ibility, Mr. Muldoon. Now Puuko there would rather sleep in your soft bed some nights, like if it's raining or snowing. And I'll bet your gramma's garter there are moments that he'd rather just lie there behind the stove a-thinking of warm milk. But does he give in? Does he shirk? No sir, Mr. Muldoon. No sir! Night after night he'll gird his loins and travel the housetops doing his job in foul weather or fair–and getting nothing for thanks but more scratches. Lemme see. I figure there's two hundred odd families in this town, each with two or ten cats apiece. Call it four hundred cats all told, all a-raising their quivering tails in the moonlight and hollering for Puuko to come sing and dance with them all night." Grampa rose to his feet, clicked his heels and saluted Puuko. "England expects every man to do his duty!" he roared.

When Grampa went into the house, Puuko stalked off down the street and I sat there on the stoop wondering if I'd be man enough to be male when my time came.

As the years went by it became evident that Puuko was aging fast. Gray hairs appeared behind the whickers on his face. He spent more time behind the kitchen stove and even returned to by bedroom before midnight. Some nights he wouldn't go out at all. He had sown his black seed with too much abandon for a new crop of jet black tomcats appeared all over our village, each of them full of his former fire. Puuko battled them one and all but from his torn ears, patches of denuded hide and lame left leg it was obvious that the old tomcat was losing more battles than he was winning. Little snatches of plaintive miauing showed that the old devil was hurting in his sleep. Yes, Puuko was getting old. He was just plain worn out. I sure felt bad.

Then an old spinster named Miz Altman moved into the vacant house next door, bringing with her a pure white cat called Melinda. Rejuvenation! I was with Puuko in the side yard when he first saw that white vision. His green eyes widened; he humped his back. And, howling, he made a beeline for her. Miz Altman snatched Melinda up just in time and fled into the house. She was determined to protect her pussy's virginity as vigilantly as she had her own.

It wasn't easy! Puuko stalked her house and yard constantly. He lay in wait in the bushes by the back door. He his under the steps in front. Once when Miz Altman had to take the slop jar to the outhouse Puuko almost got inside the moment she opened the door. Another time when the old lady was shelling peas on the front porch and holding Melinda close behind her, Puuko almost got to Melinda right there in her lap. One night Miz Altman just managed in time to slam shut the upstairs bedroom window when Puuko tore a big hole in the screen. Confined to the house, poor Melinda had to do her dirty in the parsley box.

Frustrated at every turn, old Puuko began to act strangely. He wouldn't eat. He wouldn't curl up on his chair. He didn't doze behind the stove. All he'd do was prowl back

and forth, and forth and back again between our house and Miz Altman's. At night he never came to my window.

The worst part of all, though, were his yowls. They bore no resemblance to the mad housetop singing of his youth. They were single yowls but they lifted the hair on my neck. There was mortal pain in them. I asked Grampa if Puuko was sick–if maybe he was going to die.

"You're damned tooting he's sick, Mr. McGillicuddy. He's love-sick."

That night we had some real trouble. After all of us were bedded down and asleep, Puuko started prowling our roof and porches, really screaming. I'd never heard him so loud. You'd swear there were ten cats in a barrel fighting. He'd grab a high note, shake it, and carry it along the roof peak from one end of the house to the other. Even Grampa poked his head out to tell him to shut up. No one could sleep. Finally I heard my Dad get up and go outside. Then POW! Off went his twelve guage shotgun. I ran downstairs as Dad came in.

I was half crying. "Did you...d-did you shoot Puuko?"

"No dammit," Dad replied. "Couldn't see that old black bugger against the sky. The moon isn't high enough yet. But, I tell you, I'm going to shoot him in the morning if he keeps me awake any longer. He's becoming a damned nuisance. I'm dead tired, being up on that baby case all last night, and I've got another tough day coming tomorrow. I swear I'll shoot that old reprobate before I have my breakfast if he keeps me awake any more." I knew Dad meant it because he was biting his lower lip like he always did when he got really mad.

For a time Puuko was mercifully silent but I knew it wouldn't be long before he'd be raising blue hell again. What to do? Frantically I rushed down to the cellar, got a can of sardines, opened it and started looking for him. He was crouched on the fence, swishing his tail, and looking at Melinda's door. "Here Puuko! Here Puuko!" But he spurned the fish and let out another of his lovesick yowls.

I remember crying there helplessly by the fence until I remembered what Grampa Gage had told me. Then I did something awful bad. I tip-toed over to Miz Altman's house, let Puuko in, left the door ajar, and ran back to my house to crawl shakingly into bed.

Only a few days after this old Puuko died. "Probably had heart trouble," Dad said. "Yeah," said Grampa. "Heart trouble and too much unrequited love."

Grampa was wrong. Sixty three days later, the beautiful Melinda gave birth to five black and white kittens. I felt it was a shame Miz Altman felt she had to drown them. Even if she did warm the water first.

We Took Care Of Our Own

Almost every child in our village went to Billy Johnson's funeral and we took turns tolling the church bells until sundown. Billy was the village idiot though anyone who called him that would probably have gotten a swift poke in the nose immediately. We loved that big gentle man-child. He was the village playmate. He was our own.

I can still see the big man sliding down Pipestown Hill on Arne's long homemade sled with three or four kids on his back, then patiently plodding back up the hill to slide down again and again, and always smiling in that curious way of his. Not a silly smile, either. Not foolish. It was a kind of secret smile of happiness, of contentment. Made you feel good.

Or I can see him in the summertime wading along the beach at Lake Tioga with a child on his back, two others clinging to his legs, and holding hands with two more. Billy never learned to swim but he liked to splash in the water. Or the sight of Billy (after he had helped us fill our berry pails) walking all over town with the daisy chain around his neck that we'd made for him. No one laughed at Billy for this. They just smiled. Perhaps they wished they'd had the nerve to wear a daisy chain. Maybe they even envied Billy for not having to grow up, for having stopped when he was three years old.

Billy Johnson's vocabulary was pretty limited but because he didn't talk much at all it didn't really matter. He would always smilingly say hello when he entered your house or met you on the street and he said it again for goodbye. He also said thanks. His only sentence was "Billy good boy," and that was spoken almost as if it were one word. Sometimes it sounded like a question and when we replied, "Yes, Billy's a good boy," he would echo it as a statement of fact: "Billy good boy!" He could say *yes,* but never said *no,* a difficulty that sometimes led him into trouble as you might imagine. But the word he used most often was "Work?" Everyday as he wandered from house to house he would go up to someone's back door and ask "Work?" And if some chore was given for him to do, Billy was at his happiest. All he asked in return was reassurance. "Billy good boy?"

Since his comprehension was limited we had to tell him what we wanted him to do in very simple words, and to tell him several times, and to show him, and then to tell him when to stop. Mrs. Salmi found that out when she discovered not only her woodbox full of cut birch but also half of her kitchen too. (She'd gone to the neighbors to borrow a cup of sugar and forgot about him.) Billy was no good at weeding something like beets though, never seeming to know the difference between a weed and a beet, but when potato digging time came he helped a lot. Most of our families had him sweep out the barn or pump water for the washtubs or saw wood. Billy was bery strong and he could saw wood all afternoon without tiring but he never did learn to split the chunks. No matter. In our land of "nine months of snow and three months of poor sledding" we needed all the help we would get with our firewood.

Billy had been less than a year old when his father, a miner, was killed. Some cribbing had let go an avalanche of rock upon him. Mrs. Johnson got a small pension thereafter but it was never enough to live on so she worked as the cleaning woman for the Town Hall and the school. She also took in washing and ironing. A hard life but she made do. Mrs. Johnson was a loving woman and very patient with Billy. Some people said she trained him like one would a dog. Anyway he certainly learned to obey anything he understood. He didn't know how to say no. Some little kids at times would command him to sit down, to stand up, to jump but since Billy always did what they asked and always smiled while doing it, such teasings were rare. It was much the same with fighting. If some kid (usually a smaller one who had been beaten up frequently by bigger boys) took a poke at Billy, he never fought back. Just let himself be hit and just smiled or said, "Billy good boy!" No fun, fighting with someone like that.

Despite his obvious limitations Billy Johnson had managed to get some schooling, if you can call it that. Indeed he spent seven years in the first grade under Miss Neeley, another kind and loving woman, and when he got so big there wasn't a chair or desk in the whole school that would fit him, they held a special graduation ceremony complete with a handsome diploma. Not that he had ever learned to read or write or figure or talk. But he could sure sit and smile. Miss Neeley said he was a calming influence, that just having him around made her work much easier. She missed him when he graduated.

I would guess that after leaving school Billy spent most of his time roaming our village playing with the little children or the dogs or cats and doing the chores of most of the houses in town. But then suddenly Mrs. Johnson died in her sleep. Dad said he had a hard time filling out the death certificate. Over work was the disease, he said, and Billy's mother had died of it, but no doctor would use that on a death certificate. So he put down "cardiac arrest," and let it go at that.

What to do with Billy? Only one person, Aunt Lizzie, suggested that he be "put away," be sent to the insane asylum in Newberry, if they would have him. Unanimously we agreed that such a course would be outrageous. We couldn't do without Billy. Suddenly we realized that he was one of the threads that bound us together. He had been the playmate of every child in town. He had done chores in every house in town. He was our own. No, we wouldn't send him away!

So for two years we passed Billy around from home to home usually for about a month or two at a time and we always made sure that he lived in one that had love and little children. Billy was no trouble at all. Didn't eat too much, always washed before and after meals, always said thanks. He really helped a lot and when it was some other family's turn to have him, everyone hated to see him go. Yes, we took care of our own. Or was it that Billy took care of us?

Only once was there any trouble. When Billy was living with the Niemi's, their oldest daughter with her four children came back from Detroit after the marriage had broken up. Billy had to move right away so Miz Altman, a retired school teacher who lived in the house next door to ours, took him in until other arrangements could be made. She too was a loving person and Billy filled a hole in her life that even her white cat could not. When it came time for Billy to move on she wouldn't let him go. "It's not fair to the poor boy," she insisted. "He needs a real home and I'll give it to him." So she went on the train to Marquette, signed the papers and formally adopted him. A few people gossiped a little about it, her being a spinster lady, even though she was old enough to be Billy's grandmother but we agreed that it was the best thing for Billy. It must have been for he even learned a new word. It was Mama. Miz Altman loved to hear it and lavished seventy years of repressed affection on him. She wasn't too possessive either. She let him wander from house to house doing chores and playing with his little friends.

Some said she was too permissive and didn't check up on him enough, and that was why the accident happened, though really it was Fish-eye's fault if it was anyone's. Fish-eye or Fishy was a French Canadian kid about eleven years old who was always getting into trouble or making it. Shorter than the other boys his age, he was the village dare-devil, climbing to the top of the biggest trees, tip-toeing along the upper girders of the railroad bridge over the Tioga River where it crossed the gulch. He'd do anything on a dare.

Anyway, Fish-eye and two other boys and Billy climbed through the barbed wire fence that protected the old mine pit back of Pipestone Hill. In our town this was the ultimate of all forbidden things. Everyone of us had been warned a hundred times never to go there, to keep away from *that* place. The walls of the pit were very steep and the water in it must have been hundreds of feet deep. It was scarey even to think about looking down into that great hole. Yet there was one flat place reached by a narrow winding route where you might be able to get to the edge of the water. The boys told Billy to sit down just inside the fence so of course he did. Then they made their precarious way down to the flat place. Fish-eye announced that he was going for a swim and couldn't be argued out of it. So, taking off his clothes, he dived into the icy water and swam around a bit, taunting the others to join him. Unfortunately he soon got some terrible leg cramps that doubled him up as he was swimming back to the ledge and in terror he cried "Help! Come help me!"

Billy heard him and obeyed. Billy good boy! Fish-eye got out all right but Billy did not.

Almost every child in our village went to Billy Johnson's funeral and we took turns tolling the church bell until sundown.

The Sinner

Old Man McGee was trying to remember the Ten Commandments as he put the morning coffee on the box stove and laid out the hardtack. "Now put your mind to it, McGee!" he said aloud. "What are them 'Thou shalts'?" Though he screwed up his brow and scratched the white mop of his hair, nothing came except "Thou shalt...not make...any grave image" and that didn't make much sense so he knew he had it wrong. It was hard to think before breakfast when your brains, like your feet, still felt frozen.

The old man poured himself a cup of coffee and put some hardtack in it to soak a bit so he could chew it. He was still thinking painfully. Yes, it was tomorrow, according to the notice in the post office, that the big revival

meeting was being held in the Methodist Church. The Reverend Cleophas Jones was coming again to the village. Ah, he was a good one. Full of hell and damnation, his sermons were! Nobody, no, nobody could really lay it into sinners like Reverend Jones once he got heated up and started hollering. McGee felt the excitement crawling up his spine. The whole town would be there, maybe even a few Catholics unless Father Hassel scared then out of it. A real doings!

But then the old man winced, remembering what a fool he'd made of himself the year before at a similar revival meeting. The whole damned congregation had laughed at him. He could see it yet. There he was a-kneeling on the ledge with the others and the organ playing and the preacher a-standing over him yelling at him to confess and be redeemed. And he couldn't think of a damned thing to say except that he'd once shot a deer out of season. Hell, there wasn't a man in town couldn't have said the same thing. That's why they laughed so hard. "No sir, McGee. You've got to do better than that! You've got to kerlect yerself some real sins this time," he said to himself, gingerly chewing the hardtack in the corner of his mouth where a few teeth still remained. "Thou shalt not...What was that rhyme you learned at yer mother's knee, McGee? How did it go?"

Gradually the words came back to him and he said them again and again.

> "Have no other Gods but me;
> Unto no image bow the knees;
> Take not the name of God in vain;
> Do not the Sabbath day profane;
> Honor thy father and mother too;
> And see that thou no murder do;
> From vile adultery keep thou clean;
> And steal not; though thy state be mean;
> Bear not false witness–shun that blot;
> What is thy neighbor's covet not."

Old Man McGee went through the list. He thought for some time about number three. He'd sinned plenty on that one with all of his goddamns but it would be no better than saying you'd poached a deer. As for the Sabbath, well, he couldn't think of how he might have profaned it, and his father and mother way back in Scotland had been dead for many a year now. Not murder. He didn't have anything against anyone. Adultery? Who would have an old coot of seventy-eight years–even if he could do it! Now stealing was a possibility, and bearing false witness–that meant lying–that wouldn't be too hard to do. But coveting looked like the best bet. No trouble with coveting–wanting something some other person had. "Start coveting, McGee! Covet like hell!" he commanded himself.

But the saying of it was harder than the doing. The trouble was that he didn't want anything. He had a tight log cabin and plenty of winter wood. Smoked fish and the carcasses of nine rabbits and one deer hung frozen in his shed. "How about the taters, McGee?" he asked himself. "Maybe you kin covet some potatoes?" but when he opened the trapdoor and looked down into the little dirt cellar he saw three burlap bags full of them still untouched. Plenty to make it through the winter what with his big slab of salt pork, lots of flour, sugar, salt and coffee. McGee scratched his head. No covets there! Why he even had some biting money in a pork and bean can, enough to buy anoher pail of Peerless Smoking Tobacco, and then some. Didn't need another pipe. Couldn't buy a better corncob pipe than the old blackened one he was smoking right then.

It being time to do his duty anyway, the old man put on his clompers (lumberjack boots) and went to the outhouse. Maybe he could find something in the Sears Roebuck catalog he could covet. That was always a good place to do some figuring–especially in the summer with the sun coming in the door and the flies a-buzzing round. But this winter day it wasn't so good. He let himself down on the hole gingerly and felt the cold boards trace an icy circle around his rump as he thumbed through the catalog from back to front. Wagons, no! Had no horse. Tables, no. Scythes and sickles? If he had them he'd be conned into helping someone make hay. No. Pumps, pots, pans. Nothing there. The cold was crawling up Old Man McGee's back. Ah, the Ladies Underwear section. McGee tried his best but all he could see was underwear. Didn't feel a danged twitter. Discouraged, he went back to the cabin and talked to himself.

"Well, sir," he said. "Looks like you just got to go out and do some stealing, McGee. Reckon stealing's a fair to middling sin. Nothing great, I s'pose, but bad enough so tomorrow they won't laugh when you tell 'em you done it." Again he winced, remembering what had happened the year before.

It wasn't as easy as he thought it would be. On his way to the post office and then to Flinn's store, he didn't see a thing worth stealing except a sled and that had three Forchette kids on it. Nothing in the post office either except the revival announcement which he read again. "Gotta have something to say when Reverend Cleophas Jones calls you up tomorrow night, McGee," he admonished himself. "Gotta have something to say!"

There was plenty to steal at Flinn's store even if there wasn't anything he really wanted. Nevertheless the old man had stashed away in his coat pocket three dried apricots, a box of animal crackers and a handful of nails before M.C. Flinn was at his side.

"I'll thank you to empty out your pockets on this counter, Mr. McGee," he demanded, coldly sucking air between his teeth and rubbing his hands. "Let's see. The nails will be eighteen cents, the box of animal crackers fifteen, and the apricots are two cents a piece, sir. Total forty cents, sir! Or I'll call Charley Olafson and you'll spend the night in jail, sir!" Old Man McGee fumbled in his watch pocket for the folded dollar bill that he always carried there so he could always feel rich and gave it to Flinn without a word. The storekeeper scraped the collection into a paper bag and handed it to him. "Don't need your business, Mr. McGee. Don't need your business. Don't come back."

On the way back to his cabin, McGee gave it one last try. On a big bank of snow outside Miz Altman's gate he saw a shovel. He went over to it and was debating whether to steal it then and there or to wait until after dark when Miz Altman came to the door. "Mr. McGee, I see you eyeing my shovel as though you wanted to borrow it for a bit but couldn't bring yourself to come up to the door to ask. Why of course you can borrow it," she said kindly. "Better yet, why don't you take it and keep it this winter. I've got a better one in the shed. Maybe you can fix that splintered handle for me and bring it back next fall. Help yourself, Mr. McGee."

The old man doffed his cap and thanked her as he picked up the shovel, but under his breath he said to himself, "A fine sinner, you are, McGee. You've got two better shovels in yer own shed. Sure tough trying to do some decent sinning in this here damn town." He went down the hill, carrying the nails, the animal crackers, the shovel, and trying to chew sidewise on a dried apricot. "Got to think of something to say, McGee! Got to think of something to say!"

The evening of the revival meeting finally arrived. It had warmed up a bit, to ten below, and a steady procession of people converged on the church, their footsteps squeaking on the snow. Five or six sleighs and cutters sat in the shoveled space outside the carriage shed while the horses that had pulled them, heavily covered with blankets, steamed as they ate their hay. Inside the church about fifty people shivered in the lamp-lit pews despite the red glow from the sides of the two pot-bellied stoves. A murmur of conversation suddenly came to a halt as the revivalist and a woman strode up the aisle and stood behind the pulpit.

"I (pause) I am the Reverend Cleophas Jones, minister unto the heathen and the damned, and this is my wife, Mrs. Cleophas Jones, who will grace us on the organ." As she went over to the antique to limber up the foot pedals and try a few honks, we looked him over. A gaunt scarecrow of a man! The Reverend Cleophas looked us over too with firey eyes that had the impact of a blow. Few of us could meet that piercing gaze without looking down and feeling guilty. Finally he broke the electric silence. "Play, woman, play!" he roared with a voice that shook the rafters, and the old organ boomed out with "When the Roll is Called Up Yonder, I'll be There." When only a few of us sang the words, he abruptly stopped his wife. "Sing, you sinners! Sing!" he commanded us in a terrible voice, his face livid with fury. We sang hard.

I still remember the texts he used because I looked them up afterward. There were three of them, all from Deuteronomy, and they scared the hell out of all of us. "The Lord shall smite thee with madness and blindness." (Deuteronomy 28:28.) "And thy carcass shall be meat to all of the fowls of the air, and unto the beast of the earth, and no man shall drive them away," (Deuteronomy 28:27) and "The Lord will smite thee with the botch of Egypt, and with the emerods, and with the scab and with the itch whereof thou canst not be healed," (Deuteronomy 28:27.) It was the botch of Egypt that hit us the hardest.

Deuteronomy was just for starters. The Reverend Cleophas then painted for us a picture of the damned in hell so vividly you could smell the brimstone burning, and feel the devil's hot pitchforks piercing your bowels. He let out screams of mortal terror to show us what we had coming to us, screams of agony that raised the hair off our guilty scalps. There were devils in us, he said. The same red devils who would torture us in Gehenna unless we repented our evil ways. Oh, I can't remember or recapture the terror of the scene as that gaunt madman beat us with his words of fire.

Suddenly he was silent for a long time and when he began again his voice was soft and cajoling. "Now, friends," he said. "I know you're saying to yourself that your sins are small, small sins, not really bad enough to go to hell for. Or that you've only thought of sinning and never really did it." The Reverence Cleophas gestured to his wife who came through with a mighty burst of sound from the organ. Again silence. Then he gave us a shot from the second barrel of his mouth cannon. "It's the devil in you!" he thundered, "who is thinking those thoughts. He's got you. He's taking you away. Down, down, down!" And we were back down in hell again burning, burning, burning!

Suddenly he was on his knees beside the pulpit praying for our rotten souls, asking The Lord to chase out our devils, begging Him to let us see The Light when we came forward to confess. The organ boomed out "Gathering in the Sheaves." "And Lord, when I, the servant, goeth down among these poor sinners to lay my hands upon their evil heads, let them come forward to confess their sins and repent. Amen." Then he was roaming among us, up one aisle and down the other, laying on hands and collecting the first batch to kneel on the long ledge before the pulpit. The organ played "Come to the Church in the Wildwood. Come! Come! Come!

All of those selected came willingly, though as in a daze. All but Old Man McGee. His refusal infuriated the Reverend Cleophas Jones and he worked McGee over pretty bad, imploring, threatening. Finally, he got down on his knees and asked the whole congregation to join him in singing "Come, Come, Come!" to the old man huddled there on the front pew. Finally McGee gave in and let himself be led up to where the other chosen were kneeling. "Halleluja, Halleluja!" They were all mighty proud that Old Man McGee had seen the error of his ways, and was going to confess and be saved. Old Man McGee having been the most reluctant sinner was called on first. There was a long silence and the revivalist had to really lay it to the old man before he finally spoke.

"I once shot a deer out of season," he said miserably.

Christmas, 1919

O f the seventy-five Christmases that I have known, the one I remember most vividly came shortly after my fourteenth birthday. The holiday season had begun very well, mainly because I had escaped having to take part in the Christmas program at church and school. Because my voice had changed, I no longer had to wear those damned angel wings that the boy sopranos wore at those affairs. Instead, since my younger brother, Joe, had to put them on and sing the solos, I kidded him unmercifully. Besides, there was new snow and the rabbit snaring was very good in the poplars down by the lake. Freed from school, every morning I'd ski down through the maple grove, then down the field and through Beaver Dam Swamp to bring back a snowshoe hare or two. I got so many that year I remember having to take them around to the neighbors.

But it was good at home too. Mother brought down the big box of Christmas decorations from the attic to be sorted out and restrung as needed. We would spread all of them out on the kitchen table, the red and green balls, the yellow lemons, the white icicles, the little blue fairy boats and silver stars, all of them incredibly fragile since they were of

blown glass and very aged. My brother and sister were not permitted to handle them but I was, and so I gloried in my responsibility. Their jobs were to string the popcorn after I had popped it in the box stove and to prepare the loops of cranberries to be hung from the branches of the Christmas tree, jobs that once had been mine, and very tedious ones, with much pricking of fingers. The only ornaments they could sort were the little tin candleholders, each with a little spring that

opened up its jaws when depressed. We used to chase each other around the table trying to pinch each other with them.

Then there was the making of presents for our parents all done in great secrecy up in the bedrooms. I remember that this was the year I made a calendar for my Dad, an undertaking that seemed to go on interminably, for I had gone to Flinn's store and for ten cents had come back with four yards of wrapping paper, the kind that the meat came in, brown and shiny. I spent hours cutting it into 365 squares with a day and date on each square and a little message of cheer. By the time I got to August, my brain had dried up so that I was writing things like "I don't think it will rain today" or "A long time to Christmas." As I recall, I never did finish the daily gems though I did assemble it and gave it to my mother to put in Dad's stocking. Which was probably just as well for I doubt that he ever looked further than the first week of January.

For my mother, who hated the long winter, I had prepared a sheet of birch bark full of violets that I had with some foresight pressed in the pages of an old Sears Roebuck catalog the spring before. I forget what Joe had made but I remember helping my sister Dorothy with the cross-stitching of a hot pad when she cried with frustration, being only seven years old.

Although Joe and I had long since discovered the fraudulence of Santa Claus, Dorothy had not and so we entered into the conspiracy enthusiastically. Yes, those little marks in the dust on the baseboard of the great pot-bellied coal stove in the living room were the footprints of the Brownies, the little elves who spied on children when they were naughty. "No, Sis, that stuff about Santa coming down the chimney and into the stovepipe is all wrong. Dad leaves the back door open on Christmas Eve and he comes in that way. Yeh, we've heard the sleighbells and if you listen you'll hear them too. So you'd better be good!" Dorothy's eyes would get wide and a delicious shiver would run over her. I remember my envy.

And of course we all left notes under the stove for the Brownies, notes that were always gone the next morning when we came down in goosepimples to dress by the warm glow that illuminated the brown isinglass. Each note always made affidavit of our virtue, whether we had been good or not, and contained one request, no more. We had long been told that Santa looked with disfavor on greedy little children. That year Dorothy's was for a doll cradle, Joe's for a pair of skis all his own, and mine was for a shotgun.

Oh, how I wanted that first gun! I ached in the bones for the hunger of it. If I got it, it would mean that my father recognized that I was no longer a child. Friends my age had them. With a gun I could shoot the rabbits and not just have to snare them. I could shoot partridges too, maybe even a deer if I cut the shell three-fourths across. Oh, how I wanted that gun that year. When I hesitatingly suggested my desire my father had only grunted unfavorably, and the year before when I had asked for it in the notes placed under the stove, all I found on Christmas morning was a Daisy air rifle with a pump so weak the pellets often would just leak out of the muzzle. I was fourteen now and there was no Santa. Yet perhaps. Perhaps.

So I was very good those last weeks before Christmas. I pumped the water tank full to the brim everyday without being reminded. Not only did I keep the woodbox by the kitchen range full of birch and kindling, I also split up a huge pile and stacked it against the barn.

The horse and cow were fed lavishly and fresh lime was spread under new straw on the stable floor. I rubbed neatsfoot oil on the harness until it gleamed. I even cleaned out the chickencoop. I was good beyond belief. I didn't even fight with Joe, my brother.

Until the day before Christmas, when everything went wholly to pot! It all began at the breakfast table when Dad told Joe and me that we would have to get the Christmas tree this year because he had too many other things to do. I was overjoyed to have the responsibility. Maybe Dad was really beginning to think I was grown up enough to have that gun too. Whoops!

You might be wondering why we would wait so long before putting up the tree, but our father was always afriad that the fifty or so real candles on it would set the house afire, so he wanted a fresh green tree to minimize that real danger. Always we had three buckets of water under the Christmas tree as an extra precaution, and the tree was always taken down promptly the next day. But oh, those flickering candles turned the old bay window and the living room into a fairyland. "Now make sure you get a good tree," Dad said as we took the handaxe and left the house. "Eight feet tall and even all around. No dead branches. Get a good one."

Joe and I made our way down the ski trail to the swamp which was full of birches, balsam and spruce. How carefully we combed it, sizing up tree after tree. I even chopped down a thirty foot spruce because the top of it looked extra good, but when it was down there were too many flaws. *This* Christmas tree had to be perfect. We covered that swamp, my brother and I, and were getting kind of discouraged when suddenly in a little clearing both of us yelled at the same time "There it is!"

Unfortunately, as it turned out, we weren't looking at the same tree. Mine was a blue green spruce covered with brown cones, perfectly shaped and symmetrical. Joe's was a balsam, also a fine one.

We argued. Lord how we argued. "You're a dumbhead." You're a double-dumbhead!" I pleaded with him but Joe was stubborn. I called him stupid and lots of worse names. I pulled the rank of my age and finally took the axe from him and chopped down my spruce whether he liked it or not. Whereupon we fought until both of us were weeping. "OK," I said, "You bullheaded bugger. I'll drag my tree up the hill all by myself and you can do what you want with that measly scarecrow of a balsam. I'm not helping you."

Actually, I wasn't sure I could drag that spruce out of the swamp and up that long slope all by myself, and I was certain that Joe couldn't haul his, but I did it somehow, having to rest several times. At the top of the hill I looked down and there was Joe, just a little way up from the swamp, lying exhausted beside his tree, so I knew I'd won. But a half hour or so later, there the kid was in the side yard, putting up his balsam beside my spruce in the snowbank by the front steps, whimpering with fatigue, the stubborn little devil.

My father must have had a hard morning because when he returned at noon, and caught us hollering at each other and fighting savagely, he swatted both of us hard and told us to get into the house. The noon meal was ominously quiet and after it was over Dad said, "Well, let's go out and I'll hear your arguments and we'll pick a tree." I began reasonably enough but Joe did not, and within two minutes we were fighting again, slugging and biting and scratching and crying. Dad was furious. "All right, boys. We'll have no Christmas tree this year!" He picked up a trunk in each hand and dragged both trees back by the barn and threw them on the manure pile. We were devastated.

We were also confined to our rooms for the rest of the day, eating our supper from trays brought up by our silent mother. Dorothy sneaked up the stairs once and called us bad, bad boys–which didn't help either. She said that Santa wouldn't put anything in our stockings. I didn't have to be reminded. I'd blown it. I wasn't mature enough to have a gun. Merry Christmas! Although I was fourteen, I sobbed in my pillow and hated that bull-headed brother of mine. Merry Christmas!

That was a long, long afternoon and a longer evening, because in our house we opened our presents on Christmas morning. As I said, we had to stay in our rooms. Mother came up once to give me a hug and tell me, as she had always done, not to come downstairs on Christmas morning until we heard her play Stanley's March on the piano. She said that tomorrow would be a better day, but I was desolate. No gun. Probably no presents. Dad was mad at me still. And not even a Christmas tree! In vain I listened for the rustling of things being wrapped and unwrapped in the kitchen below my room, sounds that had always been there on Christmas Eves. Once, only once, I thought I heard the slight tinkle of sleighbells but decided I must be mistaken. I'd even spoiled Christmas for Dorothy. No Christmas tree. No Santa for me anyway. I wept myself to sleep.

Suddenly it was morning and Joe and Dorothy were in my room tugging at the cover. "Merry Christmas, Merry Christmas. There's the piano. Hurry!" I fear I did not hurry leading them down the stairs, dreading to face that limp stocking and the tree-empty room and the look on my sister's face.

Then there we were in a room filled with a glory of color and flickering flame. And Dad, sitting in his old chair, with that crooked grin on his face. Not one Christmas tree but two–side by side in the big bay window. A balsam and a spruce. And my mother smiling through her tears. And a shotgun in the corner by my stocking.

Forest Fire

W e'd never had such a dry spring and early summer. Usually May and June were our wettest months but this year only a few brief sprinkles had fallen, not enough to do any good. The forest floor crackled underfoot, it was so dry. Lake Tioga was down three feet and the Tioga River trickled through rocks that none of us had ever seen. The trout, usually scattered through the streams, were now concentrated only in the alder lined beaver dam pools. Indeed, the whole U.P. was a tinderbox ripe to break into flame. All of us knew that sooner or later some fool fisherman would leave his little coffee fire undoused or one of the trains would dump its ashes or send its sparks into the brown weeds along the right-of-way and then all hell would break loose.

Our little forest village of Tioga was especially vulnerable. Not only was it bordered on the north, west and south by woods full of leaves and downed branches but each house was surrounded by long uncut grass about a foot high, grass that due to the drought was already brown. (This of course was long before the age of the rotary mowers that now keep our yards green.) Unless the owner cut it with a scythe or had the cow graze it overnight it was more of a hayfield than a lawn. If a fire got going in the Buckeye west of town and we had a strong west wind, the flames would roar down our entire hill consuming every house in its path.

That was why all of us felt uneasy when we awoke on the morning of July 30th to find the sun a red ball in a gray haze of smoke filled air. Your nose stung with the acrid smell of wood smoke; your eyes watered. And there was a wind from the southwest, not very strong yet but then it always blew harder as the day progressed. Yes, there was a forest fire and it wasn't too far away, perhaps seven or eight miles distant on the far end of Lake Tioga.

All of us knew that sometimes under the right conditions a forest fire could run faster than a horse especially in jack pine where it would leap from the treetop to treetop in a crown fire. We were glad that there wasn't too much jack pine west of town until we remembered the long belt of old spruce slashings that ran north from the lake to the mine. Lord, they were so dry, they'd explode! Once those old cuttings get going we wouldn't have a chance. Also, there wasn't enough water even to put out a grass fire. Due to the drought, half of the wells uptown were dry and for weeks people had been hauling washwater in barrels up from the lake on lumber wagons or going to the spring for drinking water. What to do? Take what valuables we could to the north side of the lake? Get on the afternoon train? Pray?

Even before Pierre La Font, who had been fishing for pike, ran up to my Dad's house with the news that a big fire was roaring along the south edge of the lake, some of our men were assembling at the Town Hall, each with a pail, a spade, an axe and two burlap bags. Some men, but not enough! Charley Olafson, our huge constable, night watch and deputy sheriff had his big silver star on his chest.

"One more man and I've got enough for the first crew, Doctor," he told my father, "but you'll have to round up another dozen at least for back-up when these get pooped out. We'll take three boats up to the dam and either try to hold the fire at Goose Creek or at the Huron River. If we're lucky and the wind holds from the southwest maybe we can do it, but I want the boats so if we get cut off we can go out on the lake and not have to chance it in the bush. If the fire gets over the Huron I don't see how anything can stop it, Doctor. Gad, I wish I had one more man right now. Oh, there's Simonen. I'll get him."

John Simonen had just come out of Flinn's store with his weeks groceries. A short, wiry but very strong man, he made his living cutting pulp and trapping. None of us knew him very well. He was a loner, living by himself in the old Niemi homestead south of town. Never went to church or any of the school doings. Never went to the saloon. Not much for conversations either. He'd shown up in our town about ten years before and since he seemed to want to be alone, we let him. Besides, he padlocked his shack whenever he left it and we took that as an insult. No one in our town locked their houses.

Charley Olafson went over to the store. "Simmonen, you come with us now. Big fire up the end of the lake."

"No!" said John Simonen. "No, I no go. I too busy."

The big man grabbed him with one hand and lifted him into the air, then hit him on the side of the head. Not too hard. Just enough to make his eyes cross. "What you mean, you won't go? I'm the law. I say you go or I put you in the cage. Which you want?"

All of us kids knew what he meant. Inside the west wing of the Town Hall was our town jail consisting of a large cage made of latticed strap iron. Inside its iron door was a cot, a water pitcher and a slop jar. We'd often peered through the window to observe some drunk who'd been causing trouble sitting on the cot, holding his head in his hands. That was the cage.

John Simonen nodded his aching head. "OK" he said. "I go."

Charley Olafson turned to one of the kids and asked him to take Simonen's groceries back to the store and to have Mr. Flinn keep them for him. Then, followed by a mess of us kids, the twelve men carrying their gear walked down to the lake and got into the three rowboats Charley arranged to be ready for them. We watched them leave, four to a boat, two men in the middle each pulling an oar, until they disappeared in the haze. You couldn't even see the point around which they had to go. Too much smoke.

When the men got to the dam and disembarked, Charley ordered one man to row up along the edge of the lake to see how close the fire was and then to come back fast. "We got to know how much time we got before she hits us. Just hope we have an hour, maybe two." Then he stood on the dam and looked over the situation.

The Huron River that flowed out of the lake was plenty low but in most places, except for the deep pool below the dam, it was about thirty feet wide. Enough water for the pails and shallow enough so a man could wade through it to the east bank if he had to get out in a hurry. About three hundred yards downstream it narrowed where the river ran through a notch in the hills but above this the west side was mainly a dry swamp full of brown bunch grass, brush and maybe thirty dead tamaracks. Evidently beavers had downed them some years before when they had a dam at the narrows. You could see the dry beds of some of their old canals down which they'd dragged their birch and poplar logs.

"Jeez!" said Charley. "First thing we got to do is chop down those tamarack snags before we start the backfire. They're the worst for shooting sparks and brands of any tree. We've got to keep the fire from jumping the river and with this wind those tall tamaracks will shoot off so many embers we won't have a chance. So cut 'em down!"

As the men started chopping, Charley went down to the narrows. "Oh, God," he said to himself. The hill ridge was covered with jack pines, with pine needles and leaves six inches deep. It was one huge torch just waiting to be lit. No chance to do any back burning there. Those jack pines would explode. Probably make a crown fire, maybe even a fire storm if the upward draft from the blaze got strong enough. For sure if the fire climbed up the ridge into those pines it would jump the river. Somehow it had to be stopped short of the ridge. Charley went a bit further south. "Not too bad there. Mostly swamp and we can burn that over. No, it's at the edge of the ridge where we got to stop it," he said to himslef. He returned to his crew just as the boatman returned. "We've got about an hour, Charley," the man said. "She's a big one and coming fast but mainly along the edge of the lake. Not too far back."

That was good news. It meant that it might be contained in that corner of the river and the lake. Might be! Most of the dead tamaracks were down so Charley had the men start burning the swamp with one man across the river on the east bank watching to see if any embers came down there. Like the others, he had his pail full of water and wet spruce branches in the burlap sacks to beat out any chunks or sparks that came down. And a spade to cover up the hot ashes or embers with dirt.

They started the back burn of the swamp about twenty feet out from the base of the narrow's hill and then set little fires all along the south and west. The dry grass started burning immediately and the fire was soon sweeping across it. Billows of smoke arose and in a few minutes the whole swamp was ablaze all the way to the river and the dam. The man on the east bank called out for help and Charley sent several men over to put out little spot fires, beating them into submission with their fir-filled wet gunnysacks or shovels. The cutdown tamaracks were still burning fiercely with flames ten feet high in the stiff breeze but fairly soon the rest of the swamp area was a blackened smoking desert. Charley ordered each of the men to throw a few pails of water from the river on the worst of the burning fallen trees. It did little good; just gave the men the hotfoot and covered them with ash.

That part being under some control, all but the man on the east bank and another to keep watch over the burned swamp followed Charley to the hill at the narrows. After putting out some little fires that had crept back toward the higher ground from where the burn had started, the ten other men began to make a fire lane at the western beginning of the jack pine ridge.

"We've got to do some digging here, boys," Charley said. "Chop all the brush and bury the leaves and the needles under dirt. Got to have a strip about ten feet wide that's pretty bare so we can maybe burn up to it."

It seemed impossible to put a ring around that western part of the hill. Not enough time and the smoke was getting worse. All the men had bloodshot eyes into which their sweat ran stingingly. Their mouths, their throats were parched. Often they drank from their water pails or threw water over their hot faces. Sometimes they lay facedown ont he ground to get a breath or to fill their lungs with bottom air that had no smoke in it.

All were terribly tired and the forest fire hadn't even shown up. "Each man clear ten feet by ten feet and then we'll take a break," said Charley and he shoveled furiously himself, helping each of the others in turn. When the first hundred feet of the fire lane had been cleared, he told them to quit while he went back to check on the first burn. It was OK so he had the two men who'd been watching it join the others.

Suddenly a burst of laughter came from the exhausted men. John Simonen was lighting his corncob pipe. He'd worked just as hard as the others, maybe even more so, and yet there he sat in all the smoke puffing away. "You're crazy, John" Matt Laitala said. "You're nuts!" but he said it admiringly. Matt went back to his jacket and brought back a pint of booze, passing it around. "A little snort right now is good for a man," he said. Each one, including John, took a careful swallow, not too big a one, before handing it to the next man. They were comrades and the feeling revived them.

"OK. Now we go on," said Charley. "Each man take twenty feet more and clean it up. That should do it." Somehow they finished the strip.

"Matt, you come with me and we set fire to the next swamp beyond," the big man ordered. "And you others, you get your pails full of water and soak your bags good and put 'em behind and along the cleared strip. Then take a rest. Maybe we can make another lane and burn it out between."

While Charley and Matt were gone, two high school kids showed up. They'd hiked along the shore to see if they could help and they brought not only sandwiches but the welcome news that the back-up crew would be arriving within the hour. The men and boys were beginning work on the second firelane when Matt came running. "Come quick," he said. "We got to clear the other side of the hill or she'll climb and get into the pines."

The other swamp was ablaze when they got there and the smoke was awful but again somehow they managed to contain it. This time however, they had to fight the face of the onrushing flames at the edge of the hill, throwing dirt, beating the flames down with their wet sacks, stomping the hummocks. Finally, incredibly, they prevailed but their clothes were full of holes, their eyes bleared; their faces blackened by ash. They were so tired, they sagged. Charley Olafson was in no better shape. He was shaking but his voice was firm. "Well, boys," he said. "We've done our damndest. If that fire goes on the far side of that swamp we've just burned we're sunk but with the wind beginning to shift to south I don't think so. We'll corner the bugger right here. Fill your pails and take a five. Only wish we had a bigger lane or another one but I'm pooped and so are you. Let's go soak in the river. Wish that other crew would get here."

Just as he spoke, a big hill about a mile away burst into flame. Great masses of smoke, blown by the wind, drifted over the lake. Under them could be seen tall trees, orange with fire, shooting off burning branches or toppling. The men could hear it coming. There was a roaring, crackling sound punctuated by crashes. Bleary-eyed, but fascinated, they watched it come down the hill. Rarely did it make a steady advance but first one river fork of fire flowed in one path, then another in another, then both met and joined, devouring everything inbetween. Suddenly the swamps the men had burned and their firelane at the narrows seemed terribly small and inadequate. They looked at each other and then at Charley.

"Looks bad, doesn't it?" he said. "But I've seen worse ones. That fire's not very wide and it's blowing into the lake mainly. She's not going to get anything to feed on when she hits our back burn. Let's go widen our lane at the narrows and we'll fight'er there. If we can keep it from getting in those jack pines on the hill she'll burn herself out."

All fatigue forgotten, the men grabbed their shovels. "Wait a minute, wait a minute," Charley roared above the noise. "Look! If the pine hill goes, everyone drop everything and head for the boats. And don't any boat leave till it's full or I'll choke the guts out of you. Hear me?" They heard. And they chopped and shoveled and scraped like madmen in that hot and smoke filled air. Half a mile away now. They scraped some more. When one man went down from fatigue and smoke someone flung a pail of water over him then told him to fill the pail and hurry back again. Somehow the lane was widened to fifteen or twenty feet, though now they staggered when they liften their shovels.

"OK, quit! Quit now," Charley yelled. "Go soak yourself in the river and your sacks too, then come back and we'll fight the bastard all along the lane. Rest a bit. The worse is coming."

They watched it, felt its coming in the heat on their faces and hands, smelled it coming in their dried up noses and burning throats, tasted it in the windblown ash. They saw the fire divide with one branch flowing to the edge of the blackened swamp by the dam, then later another river of fire creeping its way to the other charred swamp. And they, twelve utterly tired men and two boys, in the middle, waiting and waiting for the fire to come to them. Two deer came first, then a coyote passing within a few feet of a man before bounding down to the river. Then a skunk, waddling slowly, and a scurry of mice. Everything was fleeing–except the men.

Charley walked along the thinly positioned men with no sign of panic. "Now remember," he said. "Your job now is to beat out any fire that jumps the lane. That's all. If you get it quick you can kill it. If your water runs out, shovel dirt. Don't put the water on the fire. Use it to soak your bags and use them. If you get too many flames to handle or if fire gets behind you, just holler and I'll be there to help–or someone else will. We can do it! I'll tell you if we have to head for the boats." His voice was husky and he coughed a lot saying it.

Suddenly the fire was in front of them with flames licking up the trunks of small trees, turning the reddened branches into gray ash before they fell to the ground. The very earth was afire; the heat was unbearable; it was hard to keep your eyes open; it was harder to breathe. Frantically, the men ranged the hillside beating out the bits of fire that flared in the leaves behind the lane. Twice Charley had to help out when too many spots of flame appeared in one man's territory. The big man flailed his bag and smote his shovel madly, almost with the strength of the insane. "We're getting'er boys. We're getting'er! Keep it up! Keep it up!" He helped John Simonen put out a burning stump. "You're a good man, John. A damned good man. I'm sorry I had to tunk you this morning. Keep it up!"

Wordlessly John pointed to the right. A little spotted fawn was ringed by the advancing fire and was staggering in the smoke. Suddenly John Simonen dashed through the flames, grabbed the fawn and brought it in his arms through the ring of fire again, gave it a slap to send it on its way to safety, then ran to throw himslef into the river to put out his burning clothing. "Oh, you damned fool. You damned fool!" Charley muttered hoarsely. "Hope the bugger drowns." But he was too busy smotheirng flames to care too much what happened. And he was surprised when after a few minutes John reappeared to start furiously fighting the fire again by his side. Charley noticed that John's hands and face were burned some but neither mentioned it. Too much to do. Too tired to talk.

That was when the back-up crew arrived and took over. They had plenty left to do but the fire had been turned back on itself. The original twelve men, utterly bushed, gathered at the dam, too tired to get into the boats. They lay there in the shade of the spillway for some time before washing down with river water and some sandwiches. No one spoke. Then John sat up and filled his corncob pipe. "Any of you boys got a match?" he asked. In spite of their fatigue and burns, every one of those grimy, black faced, dead faced men had to laugh.

From that time on, John Simonen belonged. He had helped save our town. The men with whom he'd fought that terrible fire befriended him, fed him in their homes, took him with them to the saloon or sauna, even fishing and hunting. They found that he wasn't really a loner, just a lonely man who had never known how to join a group. Somehow, it wasn't just that he had carried out that little deer in his arms or that he had worked harder than any of the others or that his face and hands had got burned pretty badly. It was that remark of his: "You boys get a match?" Grace under pressure; humor in hell fire. We liked a man who could say that.

Halloween

It wasn't fair! It wasn't fair to spoil Halloween with a curfew! Halloween was our night of nights and we planned for it all year long. When the village elders announced that every kid in town would have to be in the house after the church bells rang at 7:30, we were incredulous. They can't do that to us! No monkey business on Halloween? No tricks? Why, it was as bad as abolishing Christmas. In vain we protested to our parents. We said we'd rebel even if Charley Olafson put us in jail, and we got lickings for saying so. No, the curfew was real; the church bells would ring at 7:30 and every kid would be in the house or in bed. How we hated the old folks! Couldn't they remember how it was when they were young–if they ever were?

Yet in a way we couldn't blame them. The year before we'd had the best Halloween ever. Hardly a window in town had not been soaped; hardly a doorknob had escaped anoitment with cow manure. Some of the bigger kids had taken Flinn's delivery wagon all apart then reassembled it on the roof of his store. The smaller ones had made the night hideous by running their spool ratchets on the windows or by knocking on the doors and then caterwalling insults at anyone who answered. Way back then in the early years of this century, trick or treating was unknown. It was all trick and that was treat enough for us. We raised bloody hell!

And it wasn't just that we'd made a pretty clean sweep of dumping over every outhouse in town. Or that we even had dumped over Salo's four holer with the doorside down and Mr. Salo still inside holding his shotgun loaded with rock salt. You could hear him hollering a mile away until his wife got him out and fell in the hole doing it. No, I guess they put on the curfew because we collected almost every gate in town and stacked them up so no one could get into the school the next day. There was a pile of them forty feet high at each door; front gates, barnyard gates, pig pen gates.

Why, we worked our tails off almost all night doing it. You should have seen how it was next morning with the pigs and chickens and cows and horses running all over town and people trying to find them and their gates and putting up their fallen outhouses and scraping soap off their windows and cleaning their doorknobs. Wow, were they mad! Old timers like Eric Saari said it was the best Halloween our town had ever known. Eric probably said that because we missed his shack with our devilment. Too far out, and besides he didn't have an outhouse. Just went down and did his duty in the swamp. Said he wasn't no chicken to be cooped up when he had to go. He was one of the few who escaped our monkey business.

Anyway, it was a sad and frustrated bunch of kids that trooped home from school to be jailed inside our houses on this particular Halloween night. Except for three of us–Fish-eye, Mullu and me! We weren't sad; we were just scared by the enormity of our plan and the consequences that would ensure if something went wrong and we got caught.

We'd planned it the afternoon before in one of our secret places in the grove. Mullu and I would swipe eight clotheslines and knot them together and bring them to the side of the school below the open bell tower. Fish-eye would crawl through the school's basement window carrying two more clotheslines and make his way up the two main flights of stairs then up the ladder into the bell tower, fasten a clothesline to the bell lever, then throw the other end down to the ground. We'd join it to the rest of our line and drag it up to the top of the little hill behind the school. And then we'd ring the bell like hell.

That was the main plan. Fish-eye perhaps had the hardest job but he was always a little crazy anyway and feared nothing alive or dead. Also, since he usually slept alone in the cow shed, there being nine kids in the family, he could get away and come back without being noticed. I'd chosen Mullu because he was so big and strong and tough. Without him, ringing the bell with that much clothesline might be too hard to get it booming in the night. Also his parents were usually in the saloon or somewhere else. They were rarely home.

If Fish-eye or Mullu couldn't ring the bell by themselves, then I would join them, but if they could handle it, then I was to hide in the bushes by the school and be the scout. We knew that Old Blue Balls, our school superintendent, and other men would be there as soon as the bell started ringing so my job was to run and tell the other two when to quit and head for home. I didn't particularly like that assignment. Old Blue Balls always scared the hell out of me. Why, he'd kill me if he caught me–or almost, anyway. Also, I would have the hardest time getting out of the house and back again. My room was an upstairs back bedroom and the boards of our backstairs creaked and shrieked with every step so loudly that anyone in the living room would be bound to hear. Moreover, my parents rarely went to bed before eleven o'clock and our rendezvous was for ten.

My only chance was to climb out of the window, drop five feet onto the roof of the entry shed to the back door, then jump down another seven or eight feet to the ground. I figured I would handle that without killing myself but how was I to get back in again? Putting up a ladder would surely give me away. It was a problem that I solved by getting the rope that had once been our swing and hiding it under my blankets. I would tie knots in it and by anchoring the top end to my bed be able to climb back, I hoped. I also had nailed a couple of spikes into the sides of the shed to help me get over the edge of its roof. If all failed, I'd sleep in the barn with Rosy, our Jersey cow, and try to sneak in the house to pull in the rope before my parents awoke. It was sure chancey! The only thing that kept me going was the feeling that we had to raise hell for all the kids in the world.

I was sent to bed early, even before the church bells rang, because I'd argued too hard with my dad about the unfairness of it all. "It's time to bring a halt to this Halloween vandalism," he said firmly. "It's gotten out of hand. Be good to have a quiet Halloween for a change." I got a swat on the hind end to speed me up the stairs.

It seemed to take forever before the alarm clock got to nine-thirty and I could get out the swing rope, tie the knots and fasten it to the bedstead. Because there was light in the living room windows, I knew that my parents were still up so I had to be very quiet when I climbed out on the roof of the entryway dragging the end of the knotted rope behind me. The jump was not too hard and soon I was with Mullu and Fish-eye bringing with me all of my own family's four clotheslines.

Mullu had only three–all from Old Blue Balls' backyard, he proudly said. Fish-eye had two clotheslines joined together with a big rock at one end. He had unlocked one of the basement windows in the school before he'd gone home so all was in readiness. Huddling there in the dark and talking in whispers we reviewed our battle plans. Mullu was to join the seven clotheslines together and lay them on the ground all the way to the little hill. Fish-eye was to enter the school, fasten the end of his two lines to the bell and then heave the other end with the rock on it over the edge of the school roof. Mullu would join Fish-eye's line to all of the others. I was to find the best place to hide in the bushes near the front door. Next, we would all meet on the hill then to see if they would need me to help with the pulling. I prayed that they would.

Again we rehearsed the sequence and decided it would be best to ring the bell five or six times, then wait for a few minutes, then ring it again and again until I, as the scout, ran up the hill to tell them to quit and get the hell out of there. As the two of them hauled on the clothesline very carefully to make it taut high above the schoolyard, I went back to the school to see if the ropes were visible. No. They were high overhead once they were tightened. I returned and told Mullu and Fish-eye just to try to get one soft bong before I went back to my bushes.

Lord, it was the loudest bong in the world! I lay on the ground there in the darkness absolutely petrified. Bong, bong, bong, bong, bong! Then silence. Then bong, bong, bong again. I heard a man come running up to the school door around the corner from where I hid and the rattle of a key in the lock. Bong, bong, bong! And then I heard Old Blue Balls' terrible voice. "Stop it!" he roared. "I'll tan your tarnel hides so you'll not sit down till spring. Stop it this instant!" Bong, bong, bong, bong, bong went the bell. I could hear Old Blue Balls running up and down the stairs in the darkness hollering till he made the walls vibrate. And the hair on my back too! Oh, he was mad! Another silence and then another bonging as the superintendent emerged. "Got to get a light! Got to get a light! That young devil's hiding in there somewhere pulling the bellrope."

Two other men, one with a carbide bullseye lantern, ran up to meet him. To my horror, one of them was my father and the other Charley Olafson, the night watch and jailor. I buried my nose in the dirt like a worm, as I heard Blue Balls explain. "There's a damned kid in there who's been..." Bong, bong, bong, bong, bong! "Who's been ringing that damned bell. You know how the bellrope runs down those holes in the three floors from the belfry to the basement. Well, when I searched one floor, he must have run down to another and started ringing it…" Bong, bong, bong, bong, bong!

I was even too scared to grin, being no more than fifteen feet from where they stood talking. Then they made their plans. Charley and the superintendent would start at the basement and search all three floors one by one as my dad guarded the back door and the fire escape. Bong, bong, bong! There under the bush I groveled in terror as my father passed not four feet from where I lay. It was time to quit. Shakingly I ran in the darkness around the other side of the school and up to where Mullu and Fish-eye were still heaving at the rope. "Lemme have one good pull!" I said breathlessly and in all my days I've never known such satisfaction as when that old bell boomed over the valley. Any more would have been a vulgar indulgence so, after shaking hands and hugging each other, we parted and went home. The silence was deafening.

It took me a couple of tries before I made it up the rope and into my bedroom. I had just untied the knots and hid the rope in an old sweater in the closet when my father returned. I could hear him talking to Mother in the kitchen and the clink of a spoon against a bowl as he had some bread and milk. I also heard him mention my name and the room seemed suddenly full of alarm bells. "No, John," my mother said, "Cully's been here all the time. You know how hard he sleeps. Why he didn't even hear all that bell ringin, or he'd been down here asking what it was for." Nevertheless in a minute or two the steps of the backstairs squeaked heavily as my father looked in my room to see if indeed I was in bed. He knew me! I sure was in bed and I made my breathing nice and easy-like until he went away. When I finally did go to sleep, I was reciting over and over again that old poem we had to memorize in the fifth grade about "Curfew shall not ring tonight." It had been a good Halloween after all.

The Tank

It was seven o'clock and time to get up for the boy had just heard his father open the back door under his bedroom, to go out on the stoop and blow his nose. A mighty blast, that. The neighbors could set their watches by it. Dad didn't believe in handkerchiefs except when we had company. He took his nose between thumb and forefinger and blew it free. Said that a rich man put in his pocket what a poor man threw away. Anyway it was time to go down to  breakfast. Maybe there'd be another piece left from the blueberry pie we'd had for supper.

After breakfast it was chore time. The boy went to the woodpile and chopped some kindling with the dull double bitted axe. He enjoyed that kindling job, especially if the chunk was of white cedar. One good blow and the chunk fell apart cleanly and then it was easy to split off the smaller pieces. He liked the smell of fresh cut cedar as he carried the kindling and some previously split maple to the woodbox by the kitchen stove. His next chore was the carrying out of yesterday's ashes. Getting some pages of the *Chicago Tribune* from the pantry, the boy spread them out under the stove, opened the ash door and removed the steel container, spilling some gray ash. It was too full because the day before had been washday and the stove had been burning all day. Carefully he folded the *Tribune* and poured the spilled ashes into an unfilled corner of the container, then took it out to the ash pile back of the outhouse. A cloud of grey dust arose as he emptied it but it didn't hurt his nose like the ashes from the coal stove did when he did that chore during the winter months. The boy was glad that it was summertime. He didn't have to go to school and after he'd done his chores he could play all day.

The next job he detested. He had to pump water into the old oak watertank upstairs. His was the only house in town that had running water in the faucets; all the others had to draw up pails of water from their wells. Maybe that was easier than all the pumping he had to do everyday. The boy went up the backstairs to see how far down the water level was. Oh, oh! Almost empty. Phew, that would mean 800 strokes of the pump handle down in the kitchen, an eternity of pumping. After pumping 200 strokes the boy's arms began to ache so he went upstairs again. Lord, he could barely see the water. Someday, when his folks were gone, he'd take a brace and big and bore a hole in the kitchen ceiling, make a float and run a string over some spool pulleys by the tank then down into the kitchen right by the pump, put a weight on the end of the string and make marks on the wall to show how full the tank was. A good idea but his father would give him a good licking if he ever tried it.

Two hundred thiry, two hundred thrity-one, two hundred thirty-two. The boy's arms ached. Four hundred seventy-seven, four hundred seventy-eight; his arms were getting paralyzed. If they fell off, his folks would be sorry but he wouldn't ever have to pump that damned tank full again. Maybe there was another leak in the old wood tank. He checked but no, no leak. Four hundred ninety-nine, five hundred. The boy went upstairs again. Now he could see the water level. The tank was half full. Someday he'd get a steam engine to run the pump like they had at the mine. "Nuts, I'll do the rest of it later. I've got other chores to do."

Rosie, the Jersey cow, had been kept in for a few days because of a sore leg but it had healed and the boy let her out of the barn, opened the big swinging gate, and followed her up the street to the gate that blocked the lane through the grove to the big pasture field. Rosie walked very slowly swinging her bag back and forth and she knew where to go. Impatient, the boy slapped her on the back but it didn't do any good. Just hurt his hand. Cows always took their time. You couldn't hurry them. He thought of just letting Rosie find her way to the pasture by herself but then he remembered his father's admonition. Don't let her stay in the grove or she might eat some of the blue aconite berries in the woods and die. So the boy followed her down to the field and waited till the cow began to grab and munch the grass.

Returning, he cleaned out her stanchion, putting the mess around the rhubarb this time for the boy loved the rhubarb and sugar plum pie his mother baked. Soon the sugar plums would be ripening all over the forest clearings. They were fun to pick too. You could strip them off the big bushes a handful at a time with no stopping. Just had to watch out for the bears who loved them too. They boy could almost smell that pie with the pink juice leaking through the fork holes in the crust. He went into the house and pumped again. One hundred more pumps, two hundred more to go. It was time to clean the horse's box stall. The boy didn't mind doing it even though the ammonia smell of the manure was rank. Billy was his horse, his love. "I wish Dad didn't have to use him on his morning and afternoon calls so often. Maybe, this afternoon I can have him all to myself and ride him down to Lake Tioga or up to Rock Dam if he isn't too tired out." The boy scraped the box stall clean, scattered lime over the floor and put down fresh straw. Then he dug a few carrots from the garden to put with Billy's oats in the feed box.

What next? "Oh, yes, the tank. Have to finish pumping it before Dad gets back." But the boy couldn't bear to tackle it just then. Instead, he went to the chicken coop and gathered the eggs, brown ones from the Rhode Island Reds and whites ones from the Leghorns, finding four of each. One white one was huge, a double yolker. "Bet that made her holler," he thought. The boy hefted the burlap sack in which the broody hen was hung. She didn't squawk or move. "Still broody. No sense taking her out now. Maybe tomorrow." Since one of the nests was getting pretty thin, he put some more straw in it, then filled the feeder with scratch feed and put fresh water in the pans. His father had asked him to check to see if the coop needed cleaning. It did all right. The winter's leaves and straw were caked in layers on the floor and the place smelled pretty strong but cleaning the coop would take almost a day's work so the boy just put some more straw over the old stuff. Besides it looked like it might rain maybe and you couldn't finish cleaning it when all the hens were in there with you. Feeling a bit guilty, the boy got some haywire and patched the hole in the chicken wire fence where the skunk got in one night and also the upper hole where the partridge had killed itself the fall before during the Mad Moon when they went crazy.

The boy felt tired so he returned to the house and went down to the cool cellar with a glass and a spoon, using the latter to push back the thick cream from the big bowl so he could dip out the milk. Then he got a big cartwheel sugar cookie from the jar in the pantry and sat down with his milk on the back stoop for his midmorning snack.

Back to work at the pumping! Six hundred and one, six hundred and two, six hundred and three. Would he ever get done? He climbed the backstairs again. Jeez, it would take 150 more strokes at least just to bring the water up to the upper plank that was kind of rotten. His father had said never to have the water level so it touched that place. "I ain't big enough to have to do all this pumping, I'm only ten years old going on eleven," the boy said to himself resentfully. "Why did Dad have to take a bath last night after mother used to much water for her washtubs? It wasn't fair. At 698 strokes the boy had to quit. Couldn't even get two more. He heard his mother filling the teakettle and begrudged the act. Filling that kettle meant ten more pumps probably, and he told her so. "Well, Cully," she answered, "why don't you quit for a while and bring in a cake of ice for the icebox instead? We're about out. And have another cookie to take along."

The icehouse was a fairly large square shed behind the barn. It had doubled walls with the space between them filled with shredded charcoal from the old kilns. In the old days, they used the charcoal in the big stone furnace by the waterfall to melt the iron ore into pig iron, the boy remembered. And he also recalled with pleasure how his father had taken him down to Lake Tioga when the men were cutting the ice the winter before. How two men with a long crosscut would saw out the four by two foot chunks of blue ice, fasten big tongs and then have a horse pull the ice blocks up a snow ramp and onto the empty sleigh. And the boy also remembered how the next day his Dad had taken him back down to the place and they had caught a lot of lawyers (ling; landlocked cod). Not much fight to them even though they were about two feet long. They froze right away in the snow. His mother never liked to cook lawyers because, even though dead, they kicked around in the frying pan as though they weren't. Just reflex action, his father said, and they were fine eating. Good to have fresh fish rather than smoked ones for a change when the snows were deep on the land.

The boy unlocked the big heavy door to the icehouse and swung it open. Very cool in there but he got up a sweat uncovering the sawdust from a long chunk and prying it loose with a crowbar, then sawing it into three pieces. The house icebox, if empty, always took two of these smaller blocks. You didn't have to make the cut all the way through with the saw–just go down about three inches then put the axe blade in the cut and hit it hard with the crowbar. He liked the way it split open and left some chips of ice for him to suck. Cool on the tongue! The boy put one of the three chunks back in the icehouse and covered it with sawdust and shut the door tight. Then came the hard work of getting the chunks–must weigh

The Tank

25 pounds apiece, he thought–into the wheelbarrow. Pretty heavy but he managed it. The boy sat down and sucked some more ice before wheeling the iceblocks over to the barn well about fifty feet away. You always had to wash down the chunks so they'd be free from any sawdust or dirt before putting them in the icebox in the house. That was the rule!

Getting water out of the barn well was more fun than pumping but it took a certain knack. You first had to unwind the rope from the windlass and hang it in loose loops from the circular stone wall bording the well so that it could fall free. Then you took the bucket and dropped it, open end down, into the dark water below. If you did it just right, the bucket would fill up instantly; if you didn't, you had to try and try again. Then you turned the crank on the windlass around and around until the bucket broke the surface and came up where it could be reached. There was a tricky moment then, too. The crank handle had to be held with one hand while you grabbed the bucket with the other at the same time. Sometime the bucket slipped and down the pail went again, the windless handle revolving so fast that it would break an arm if it hit you. But the boy enjoyed the challenge and soon the ice cakes were clean enough to take to the house and put them in the zinc lined chambers of the ice chest.

The boy was pooped and so he sat down for a time at the edge of the sandpile, noting dully that his little brother had messed up the play iron mine he'd constructed the afternoon before. He was too tired to care much. But the tank had to be filled before noon and the eleven-thirty train was whistling down in the valley so the boy started pumping again. Seven hundred fifty-two...seven hundred eighty-five. Upstairs the boy went again. Yeah, almost full at last. Fifty more strokes should do it.

Somehow they got done just as his father entered the kitchen door. "Cully," he said. "I'm tired. Unhitch Billy from the buckboard and feed and water him. He's tired and hungry too. I trotted him back all the way from Halfway so I could be sure to get here in time for dinner. Now, water him good before you give him the oats." The boy went back to the barn well and it took three pails before Billy quit drinking and could have his oats.

The family was almost through dinner when he boy sat down to the table. He felt almost too tired to begin to eat but once he did, he found he was very hungry. Or at least until he heard his father say, "Edyth, after you do the dishes, open all the faucets. I just heard that this morning the new steel water tank I sent for is down at the depot and Marchland will be bringing it up soon. I got Charley Olafson and another couple of men to help bring it upstairs and install it after they tear out the old oak tank."

The boy was suddenly too tired even to taste his apple pie.

He Hung Himself
To The Maple Tree

Dad was feeling very good as he finished the last bite of cheese that went with the apple pie. A good supper. "Madam, you have acquired merit!" he said to my mother as he settled himself down in the big Morris chair and lit his evening cigar. It had been a long hard day. As the only physician in a forested territory as large as the state of Rhode Island, he had spent the morning traveling via freight train caboose to Sidnaw and back, the afternoon making house calls via horse and buckboard, and soon it would be time to go across the street to his office in the old hospital for another three hours.

That's why he was so irritated when he heard a knock at the door. "Another wart! I'll give him short shrift. Why can't they wait till office hours!" He was biting his lower lip as he opened the door. It was Gervais Lafollette, a big French-Canadian kid from downtown. One of his eyes was swollen shut and there was a big purple and red bruise on one cheek. Dad gave him his short shrift. "So you've been fighting with the Finns again. Well, you go over and sit on the hospital steps and I'll come over when I've finished my supper. You ought to know better than to come at this time!" Dad slammed the door.

But he hardly had time to light his cigar again when Gervais opened the door. Didn't even knock. "No, no, Doctor. Not me. Not me. It's my father. He's hung himself. Come quick. He said he was going to hang himself and he did. Ma mere, she say run up and get the doctor. Please!"

When Dad returned about an hour later he went to the wall phone in the front hall, cranked it a couple of times, then said to the operator, "Millie, call Father Hassel and the undertaker and tell them they'd better get down to Lafollette's place as soon as they can…Yeah, suicide…Hung himself."

Dad went back to his Morris chair and smoked his cigar for awhile while Mother and I waited expectantly. He was thinking hard. Finally he spoke.

"Well, I suppose I might as well tell you. News like that sure travels fast. Millie had already heard it and the body was still warm when I got there. Anyway, I guess it was Pierre Lacotte who found him still kicking a little and let him down from the chain-fall but he was dead when I got there. Evidently, Lafollette had tied the noose-rope to the chain-fall, raised an old ladder against the maple tree, tied the chain-fall to a limb and cranked it up, put the noose around his neck, then kicked over the ladder."

"What's a chain-fall?" asked my mother.

"Oh, it's like a block and tackle sort of, except that it uses a chain. You can lift a ton with it using just one hand. I suppose he stole it from the mine shop that time they had the break-in after the mine shut down. Anyway, it worked. Lafollette's dead as a doornail. Wonder what his wife and kids are going to do now? Not that he ever took very good care of them at that–always drinking and fighting and screwing around.

"How old was he?"

"Let's see. Oh, yes. I delivered his first boy, Gervais, the year of the big storm. He's the one who came to the door to get me. Let me see. Gervais must be fifteen. Oh, I'd say Lafollette must have been thirty-five or thiry-six."

"What a shame!" said my mother.

"No," replied Dad. "He was a no good just like his father and his grandfather before him. Grandpere Lafollette spent time in prison for killing a man. I just hope Gervais breaks the chain but he's always fighting so I don't know. Sure got a bad beating this afternoon. From Mullu, he said."

"How did Mrs. Lafollette take it?" Mother asked.

"Well, when I went up to the house she and the kids were sitting at the kitchen table eating bread and meat. She had a scarf over her head and used the corner of it to wipe her eyes every so often but she wasn't carrying on like so many of these French women do when somebody's died. Lacotte, of course, had already broken the news to her. She kept saying over and over again, 'Raoul, he always say he was born to be hanged.' She told me he was very drunk, that they'd kicked him out of Higley's saloon and that he was probably going to the barn to get the bottle he always kept hidden there. I asked her if she'd seen the body yet and she said no, that none of them had been down to the barn. I told her not to. Lafollette wasn't fit for any wife or kids to see. Tongue hanging out, eyes bulging, and blood from his nose all over his face. Gruesome! I told her to wait until after the undertaker had fixed him up." Dad fell silent.

"I feel sorry for his wife and children," Mother said. "They've always been poor. what will they do now?"

"I asked her if she had any money," Dad answered. "She said there wasn't a penny in the house so I told her the Township would take care of the funeral expenses and I'd see that she got an order up at Flinn's store for groceries to tide them over. Got to find some work for Gervais though. Wonder if he's big enough to load pulp? Anyway, I left a ten dollar bill on the table for her."

They buried Raoul Lafollette two days later. Father Hassel, our village priest, refused to follow the many suggestions that Lafollette be put to rest in the Township cemetery rather than in the Catholic one. "Though the poor dark soul never came to confession in his whole life, he's still one of ours. Dig his grave in the west part. That's unconsecrated ground that's never known holy water." And Father Hassel said a low mass for him. Few besides the family attended.

The word went around that no one went to the burial except the graveyard diggers and the undertaker, Ed Stenrud, and that just as they put the cheap pine coffin in the hole Ed asked them if someone couldn't say something good about the deceased before they covered it. There was a long silence before one man spoke. "Well," he said, "they claim he was good at snaring rabbits."

One afternoon, a few days later, Father Hassel came to our house for his weekly game of chess. Or for the glass of whiskey Dad always had ready for him. The two men liked each other and it was a chance for good civilized conversation. They also liked to beat each other and the games were played intensely with the prize being one of Ed Stenrud's cigars. The undertaker always sent each of them a box every Christmas. "Ed's a good businessman," Dad said.

So I wasn't surprised when he asked me to go down to the ledge in the cellar and bring him three cigars. "One for the pot and two for the whiskey," he grinned as they sat down at the chessboard and arranged the pieces. I got a book and went over to the baywindow to read but Dad would have none of it. "You clear out, Cully. You know the rules. Go help your mother. Haul in some wood."

But after I carried in some wood for the kitchen stove, I tiptoed up the back stairs carefully avoiding that third creaking board from the top and quietly went into the front bedroom. Because there was a register in the middle of the floor, it was a good place to listen. I'd heard lots of interesting things through that grating.

At first it was mostly chess talk about gambits and the Queen's Knight to the Rooks fourth and other moves or strategies I didn't understand. Then Father Hassel, after a silence, asked Dad if he'd signed the death certificate for Lafollette yet.

"Yes, I put down as suicide-strangulation but I haven't mailed it out."

"You haven't? Well, I'll take that pawn, Doctor. And may I ask why haven't you." The priest's voice was elaborately casual.

"You've just made a mistake, there, Father. Check!"

"Maybe you did too, Doctor. Higley told me Raoul Lafollette was far too drunk to be able to climb that ladder and fix the noose and the chain-fall. Of course, he may have sobered up. Just the same though it couldn't have been more than an hour after they kicked him out of the saloon."

I heard Dad clear his throat before he spoke. "OK," he said, "if you want to trade bishops it's all right with me. But Father, people don't bleed from the nose when they are hung by the neck. And Raoul still had a bottle in his pocket with an inch of whiskey in it when I examined him."

"And a man about to hang himself would have emptied it. Makes sense," the priest replied. "Now why did you make that move, Doctor? You're up to something. Caveat! Caveat!" They were quiet for a time.

Dad broke the silence. "Now that's an ingenious move, Father, but I'm not going to let you suck me in. Not like last time. I'll just counter by moving my Queen over here, sir. Did

Higley also tell you that Nurmi had been to the saloon looking for Raoul and with blood in his eyes? A short time after Raoul started home?"

"Yes," said the priest. "He told me that. Higley didn't know why Nurmi was so mad but I do. His daughter's three months pregnant and she's hiding in the house of one of my parishoners. Do you think…?"

"Can't tell about these Finns, Father. They can go really berserk. And Nurmi had an uncle who hung himself. A religious fanatic, he was. A Holy Roller. Now Father, you know you can't get that rook out of the corner."

"Oh, yes, I can. Just wait a minute. And while you're waiting, Doctor, there was another very angry man on the scene too. Lacotte! When we carried Raoul into the barn to lay him on the hay till Ed came with the hearse to get him, we saw the carcass of a young steer hanging from the rafter. All skinned out and with one hind quarter gone and the hide lying in a corner. Lacotte was furious though he tried to hide it. But I don't think he was surprised to see it. Just mad. Purple in the face."

"Hmm, I heard last week someone had stolen Lacotte's big bull calf just like they did last year. So you think then that…?" Dad's voice trailed off.

"I think I've got you, Doctor. Check!"

"Oh no, not yet you haven't. I'll just bring the bishop back to protect my king and I'll trade you my bishop for your queen any time. By the way, Father, did you find a billfold on the body? Higley said Raoul had a lot of money on him. Claimed he had got it by selling his rifle and also having been paid for working the jammer down at the loading dock. Any man who sells his rifle in this country could well be contemplating suicide."

"That's right," said the priest. "Deer meat and potatoes don't make it through the winter. But maybe Raoul left his billfold in the house on the way to the barn."

Dad sounded scornful. "Fat chance of that," he said. "No matter how drunk he was, a man keeps the money. Besides when I went up to see his wife she said they didn't have a penny in the house. Now, Father, you're the one in trouble. Check!"

There was a long silence before Father Hassel spoke. "You wage psychological warfare, Doctor," he said. "I'm finding it hard to concentrate. If what you said is true, then why would his wife put ten dollars in the poorbox when I administered the low mass. I know she did because there wasn't anything in it beforehand and I checked it right after the service. And no one else went near it. You're right. I am in trouble, Doctor! No amo te, medicus!"

"Check!" Dad's voice was triumphant. "I've got you on the run, Father. I gave her a ten dollar bill. Is that what she put in the poorbox?"

"No, it was two fives. So she must have been down at the barn and..."

"Check again, Father," Dad said. "I suppose you also saw that Gervais had been beaten up pretty badly, and that his mother kept a scarf over her head. French women don't wear scarves indoors, do they Father? Unless they have good reason? Check! By the way, I also learned that Gervais lied too. Mullu, the kid who he said beat him up had been up to Ewen visiting his uncle that day. Why did they lie, Father? Maybe you can ask them that the next time they come to confession."

"Before you say 'checkmate,' Doctor, I'm surrendering. You win and here's one of Ed's cigars for your pleasure. I would appreciate, sir, just another small shot of that very good whiskey." They were quiet for a time. Then the priest spoke again.

"Well, Doctor," he said. "I must be going back to my supper and my ugly housekeeper. That was a very good, though somewhat complicated game. I shall skin you next time, sir. But before I go, may I offer you a bit of Latin for your spiritual guidance: 'Si finis bonus est, totum bonum est.' Do you know what that means, Doctor?"

"Yes," said my dad. "It means all's well that ends well. I'll send out that death certificate tomorrow. Thank you, Father.

The Privy

It was on Midsummer's Day that Leif Larsen decided to start building The Perfect Outhouse. Leif had been thinking about it for almost a year. Now that he was 75 and retired from building log cabins and saunas, he had to have something to do. Handling those big logs had gotten to be too much for him and besides he'd had his bellyfull of people who became impatient with his slowness and careful craftsmanship. They didn't understand that it took time to do a job right. People said that Leif Larsen was the best log butcher in the whole U.P. The term was not derogatory; it was high praise. Any man could put up a shack but only a few log butchers like Leif could build one that a man could be proud of all his days.

The old Norwegian had everything ready for his project. The fall before, after the sap was out of the trees, he had selected and cut the logs from a thick stand of white cedars in Beaver Dam Swamp. Ten feet long they were and with no taper to speak of, each had a butt diameter of seven inches. Only in a very thick swamp could you find such uniform cedars, a swamp where they had to grow straight and tall to see sun. After felling the trees, Leif had peeled off the bark with a draw-knife and now in the early summer sunshine they gleamed white. Next to the log pile was a stack of boards, fresh pine lumber with no knot holes, and besides this was a smaller pile of flat rocks that Leif had hauled all the way from the shore of Lake Tioga in his wheelbarrow. All was ready.

He got out the plans he had drawn to scale on sheets of shelf paper the winter before and studied them as he sat on the chopping block. Not that Leif needed to look at them for he could see vividly in his mind every bit of his intended masterpiece. Seven by six feet and seven feet tall it would be. Hardwood floor and shingled roof. A two holer. Leif had been undecided for a long time about the latter. All you really needed as you sat there on your throne in the warm summer sun, with the blue bottle flies buzzing around, was just one hole.

Olga, his wife, would never be joining him as he did his duty. Too shy and besides they never had to go at the same time. So why two holes? Well, for one thing it was the custom. One hole for a man to crap in and the other for pee. If you used the same hole for both, then the front edge of it would get soggy from the drip. Besides, it was better to have that second hole for the wood ashes and water so you could stir them up with a long handled shovel and reach every corner of the pit. The ash lye would keep it smelling sweet. Leif wasn't going to have any stink in his perfect outhouse. No sir! So it would be a two holer. The best two holer in the whole U.P.

The first thing Leif did was to get some string and stakes and measure out the corners and the pit. Out of the house came Olga with her arms akimbo and her tongue working hard. "Leif! What you doing now? You no put outhouse there. That's no place so close to house. Put back by old one by woodpile." Leif's back stiffened.

"No," he said. "I put it here where everybody can see how I make it so good. Why hide?"

She pleaded with him in vain. She pointed out that it would be much nearer to the well than the old one was and that being closer to the house wouldn't save any snow shoveling in the winter because he'd have to keep the path to the woodpile open anyway. Why have to make two paths? She argued that there was always a big snow drift forming there in the winter. "You can't keep the path open there like you can the other one."

But as only a Swede is more stubborn than a Dutchman, and only a Norwegian more bullheaded than a Swede, Leif had his way. As he started digging the pit, Olga began to weep for the first time in their forty years of married life. "I tell you one thing, Leif, I no use your outhouse, no! I not going have everybody in valley seeing me to take crap there. No! I use old one."

"I but old one down, Olga!"

"OK", I use slop jar!" Leif kept digging.

His wife had a point. The Larsen's house was built on a minor hill at the edge of our big one and it overlooked the entire valley. Like so many others, no shade trees blocked the view. Many have wondered why so many of the farm houses in the U.P. sit there starkly in clearings devoid of any trees. They simply don't understand our hunger for all the sun we can get and our hidden fear of the encroaching forest. Clear a piece of land and in ten years its edges will be full of little poplars and spruce. Ten years more and they will half cover the place. Olga was right. Not only from the road to Lake Tioga and the Copper Country, but also in plain view of all the houses in the valley, Leif's perfect outhouse would be clearly visible. He wanted it that way.

I will skip over most of Leif's labor for it took him all summer to complete his project. The work went slowly but careful. The logs had to be measured, cut to size, and then with axe, saw and chisel, fitted together so tightly that no caulking was needed. The ends were dovetailed and the bottom logs set upon a stone foundation. A box of cedar boards enclosed the pit so no dirt could fall in.

On the inside, each corner held a long cedar post thrust deeply into the ground so that even fifty kids couldn't dump it over on Halloween. An enclosed wood ventilator box ran upward from the pit to a screened opening under the eaves so there would be no smell or flies when you sat in place. Making the holes and hole covers alone took a week's work, cutting, beveling and sanding. When Leif tried to measure Olga's legs to make sure the holes would be just far enough from the floor she kicked him. It took half a day in the swamp to find just the right kind of cedar roots for a coat hanger and for the paper holder. No Sears catalog for this outhouse. Roll paper, the best!

The door gave Leif some trouble. After he had it put together and in place, it just didn't look right when it was open. Sort of spoiled the symmetry. So the old Norwegian built double doors like those on the church, each one with a long window in it so he could see out over the valley when he sat on his throne. That took care of that!

As you can imagine, once the news got around that Leif was building The Perfect Outhouse, he had a lot of company. All of us admired real craftsmanship and day after day one man or another would be up there on the hill watching him work or arguing religion. You see, Leif Larson was the town athiest, though he called himself a free thinker. He didn't believe in Heaven or Hell at all and he opined that maybe there was a God but he hadn't seen him yet. As for going to church, Leif didn't. He said that the first time he'd been there they threw water on him and the second time they saddled him with Olga and he supposed that the next time they'd take him out, put him in a hole and throw dirt in his face. He liked to argue, Leif did, and people used to egg him on to see what outragous things he would say next.

After the roof was on and shingled, Leif walked down to the valley to take a look. No, it wasn't quite right. Pretty good but not perfect! The cedar logs were already getting gray from weathering. Should he varnish them? No, varnish always flaked off when it froze. So Leif used paint instead, bright yellow and white and blue, Norwegian colors, alternating on each log. Yah, that was better. Nobody could miss seeing it even though they were half a mile away. It sure stood out fine, there on the hill.

About the time Leif finished the painting, an old friend, Anders Lundberg, a Deacon in the Lutheran church, came up to pass the time of day and once again to try to make Leif see the error of his ways. "Nice job, Leif," he said admiringly, "but you not make outhouse; you make little church, yah. You religious down deep."

After Anders left, what he'd said troubled Leif and made him angry. "OK, they want church, I give them church!" And grinning a bit to himself at the sacrilege, he put a little steeple on top of the outhouse. And it did look better. It really did look like a tiny church on the hill when the doors swung open.

Although he should have known what would happen, Leif was unprepared for the storm of protest that swept our town. Olga wouldn't speak to him, nor would his old friends–except to give him hell. "Take it off; take off that steeple or we will," they told him. You could almost feel the ostracism developing that our town always used when one of its folk had done the unforgivable deed.

Nevertheless, the next morning Leif went out to see his beautiful outhouse and use it for the first time. Everything was done and done right and it shone in the sun. But as he sat there on the fur lined hole, nothing would come. He pushed hard and harder but nothing. Three times that day he went back and tried again to no avail. It wasn't just that maybe he had really built a church. It was that he couldn't bring himself to pollute perfection.

That evening Leif drank a bottle of whiskey, soaked his outhouse with kerosene and burned it down.

The Balloon

My father, Dr. John Gage, was the only physician in a large wilderness area. Tioga with its six hundred so-called souls was its largest town but there were several scattered hamlets and many isolated cabins or homestead farms that he served. Most of those in them were Finns from the old country but some were French Canadians, Indians, Swedes and assorted other nationalities. They had come to the U.P. to work in the mines and pine forests or on the railroad. When the virgin pine had been cut and the iron mines closed, they were stranded. Somehow they survived.

They liked and respected my father not only because he would come to them day or night, whether or not they could pay for his services, but because he was tough and fearless, the ultimate virtues in that rough land. They had heard how, when all the others had fled, Dr. Gage had gone to an isolated lumber camp full of smallpox and had stayed there three days and nights, tending the sick and dying. (Dad hated smallpox with a passion. He never could stand the smell of burnt sugar because he said it was just like the odor of a man dying from smallpox.) And they knew how their doctor, with Jim Johnson, the deputy sheriff, had put on their old clothes walked up the Northwestern Railroad track to meet an armed murderer who had escaped from the prison at Marquette. Pretending to be section hands and carrying only a pick and a shovel, they had captured the escapee and brought him back in handcuffs.

Our people also remembered how when Maggi O'Rourke went insane and was screaming and cursing and waving a butcher knife threatening to cut the little doctor's throat if he came near, Dad had calmly walked to the door and said, "Maggie, if those people are bothering you, I'll send them away and then give you something so you can sleep." That same knife was in our kitchen cabinet when I was a boy and it was indeed very sharp.

Yet my father had one real fear. It was of fire, house fires or forest fires, especially. He'd seen too many horribly burned men, women and children trapped inside their one door cabins when the stove pipes, too full of creosote, had caught fire and exploded in the middle of the night. And he had seen the terrible holocaust of a crown fire racing fast along the tops of pitch-filled jackpines. Dad loved the forest and the desolate aftermath of a big burn always affected him deeply. Once he took me trout fishing on Blaney Creek and pointed to a large area of charred snags. "See those, Cully. Two years ago they were young white pines, all about fifteen feet tall. I think I know who did it too. La Seur! That old French devil sets forest fires each year on these plains just so he can have better blueberries. Hope he doesn't get sick."

Everywhere Dad went in the woods, he put up *Prevent Forest Fire* signs. You could almost know where he went fishing or partridge hunting. He gave talks to the school kids and got a conservation man from Down Below to train a selected group of men in fighting forest fires. As Township Supervisor, he arranged to have shovels, axes and pails stored in our little tin covered firehouse in the event that a forest fire might threaten the town. Even at home, Dad never discarded the match with which he lit his pipe without making sure it was out and then breaking it in two to be sure. Sometimes even in the middle of winter when it was way below zero, he'd let the house fires go out in the stoves and clean the stove pipes of their soot and creosote. Yes, he was scared of fires.

I started this tale planning to tell you how we celebrated the Fourth of July in Tioga early in this century and I guess I got to talking so much about my father because he played an important part in the experience. Every year he got a big wooden box full of assorted fireworks and put on quite a show once it got dark and the townspeople and their kids lined up along our picket fence to watch the display.

The Fourth of July I remember best was in 1914 when I was nine years old. It began when the sun came up over the valley and the church bells rang and every shotgun in town went boom. Then came the sporadic rattle of firecrackers as the kids went into action. They had saved the money they got from selling arbutus to the passengers or trainmen on the Milwaukee and St. Paul Railroad; they had stashed away every cent they'd received for doing errands or odd chores. And they had blown all of it at Flinn's store on cap pistols and rolls of caps, or torpedoes, snakes, but especially on firecrackers.

The latter came in assorted sizes from the big four inchers called yellow jackets to packages of very tiny ones whose fuses were so intertangled that most of us just set fire to the whole package at once and revelled in the banging and crackling that resulted. Always there were some that were duds and these we touched off individually. If they had no fuses, we bent them in half, made a cut on the bend, and they'd go off without a bang but with a satisfactory whoosh. We called them squibs.

The standard sized red firecrackers were about an inch and a half long and made a good loud bang when we touched them to the burning brown punk. Gad, that was fun! Even toddlers barely able to walk were provided with a spool on the end of a long stick into which a firecracker was inserted and lit by their parents. Some of the girls used the sticks and spools too, screeching when the explosion came, but not us boys. That was sissy stuff. Often we'd light a cracker and throw it into the air, but usually we lit it on the ground or a crack in the sidewalk or porch. If we had been wealthy enough to buy a three incher, we'd hide it under a tin can with just the fuse sticking out and enjoy seeing how high the can would be shot into the air. Or we'd pretend to be iron ore miners and put a large firecracker into the side of a sandbank to see how big a hole we could blast. Sometimes we'd join the fuses of four or five firecrackers together, light them and run.

The torpedoes, little balls of powder covered with paper and having a cap inside, we'd have to throw hard on a rock before they exploded and often they didn't but wow, were they loud! Made your ears ring. The snakes were for sissies. You'd light a little white tube and it would elongate, twisting along the ground as it grew. Then if you touched it afterwards, it would collapse into ashes. We called them "snakes in the grass." Some of us also bought a few "son-of-a-guns." These were round circles of explosives about as big as a quarter. We put them on a flat rock, then ground them under our heels. This set off spurts of crackling fire in every direction. Only the kids who had shoes, and not many of us did in summer, tried these son-of-a-guns or spit devils.

By ten o'clock in the morning, the hound dogs could come out from under the barns where they'd been hiding, for most of the ammunition had been shot off. Only a few intermittent bangs could be heard as the kids salvaged a firecracker or two. It was then that Dad set off some of the giant firecrackers he'd got in the box of fireworks. They were huge red things, about ten inches tall and two inches in diameter with a square wood base. Dad would light the long fuse then run and hide behind a clump of maple trees. What an explosion! The biggest boom in the world! Kids from all over town would come running to see him shoot off another. The only thing comparable was when Ed Stenrud, our undertaker, once put a half stick of dynamite under his garbage pile and blew it to hell and high water. By noon the town was quiet again.

In the afternoon all the townspeople and their kids traipsed down to the beach at Lake Tioga about a mile away. There they heard speakers patriotically praising our country and its ideals, and heard our makeshift band play the *Star Spangled Banner* and *My Country Tis of Thee*. A Spanish War veteran told of his war experiences in Cuba in a faltering voice that no one heard clearly; American flags waved everywhere.

Then we watched the birling matches in which two lumberjacks got on a big pine log and began rotating it with their spiked boots. By stopping suddenly, one of them tried to dump the other one into the lake. Next came the drilling matches. A huge granite boulder was attacked by three-men drilling teams of miners. Two of them with huge fifty pound sledges hammered the long drill while the third turned the drill bit after every tenth slam. Clang, turn, clang! Which team could get the drill down into the rock all the way to its white band first? It was exciting and we always wondered what would happen if the sledgers missed. Finally, there was the greased pig let loose for anyone to catch and take home. Great hilarity!

But the best was yet to come–my father's fireworks. To us kids it seemed as though it would never get dark enough to start them but finally about the time the moon came up, Dad set off the pinwheels on the pillars of our porch. Every inch of space along our picket fence was occupied by people or kids, sometimes three deep. Then came the Roman candles. How proud I was when I was old enough to wave one in a circle and shoot the red, yellow and green balls of fire high into the air. Next came the skyrockets, placed carefully in their troughs, and trailing sparks to great heights over the schoolyard before they exploded and discharged their display of colored lights. "Oooooh!" yelled the crowd.

Red flares were then set alight and in their glow my father soaked tight balls of shredded excelsior in kerosene. Now was the moment or moments–the fire balloons. Holding the tissue paper upright, Dad lit the excelsior in the ring below it. Ah, too bad! The damned thing caught fire and burned right there on the ground. He tried again with the second balloon and the same thing happened. One big flare and the balloon was ashes. The crowd groaned with disappointment. There was only one more. But this one did not burn. It swelled until its five foot length was filled and slowly it rose as the people cheered. Up, up it went and then catching the breeze at about a hundred feet, it floated east down the street with many of the screaming kids following it. Finally they lost sight of it over the dark trees where the old stage coach trail to the Copper Country used to run.

Dad then passed out sparklers to all the kids still at the fence and after a bit we went to bed. It had been a fine unsafe and unsane Fourth of July.

The only trouble was that next morning we awoke choking with wood smoke. The worst forest fire we'd ever had was roaring east of town. Probably began where Dad's balloon came down. Anyway, it was called Doctor's Fire from then on.

THE BALLOON

The Crow That Talked

It was in a bar in Hancock that Nikki Sippola first fell in love with a bird. It was a yellow and green parrot, a nasty dispositioned but lovely critter who when it felt like it would say "No crackers!" or "Who the hell are you?" or "What? What?" as well as some other profane and vivid expressions taught to him by the customers. One of its sayings, which I can mention because it was spoken in Finnish, was "Saatana pelike-da–buscan housu." Nikkin never told us kids what it meant but he laughed every time he spoke of it, so it must have been choice.

Nikki spent two days and all his month's drinking money watching and talking to that parrot. Much of that money went for peanuts and popcorn for the house rule was that anyone who talked to the parrot and had it respond was supposed to feed it or have his drink taken away and poured down the drain. Nikki spent more of that drinking money for bird feed than for beer. Completely entranced, he finally asked the bar tender how much he'd sell the parrot for. "Maybe I give you fifty dollars?" Nikki didn't have fifty dollars but he wanted that parrot more than anything he'd ever hungered for in his whole life–more even than for a canoe or for a rifle or for even Lempi, his wife.

The bartender laughed. "For fifty dollars you might get a canary. I wouldn't take five thousand for the bird. It brings in more trade than anything I could do. Made fifty dollars on peanuts alone last month. The parrot eats some and the customers eat some and then they get thirsty and have to drink more beer. Fifty dollars? You're crazy, man!"

Noticing how disappointed Nikki looked, the bartender said, "Why don't you get a young crow and teach it to talk? I seen one once up at Hibbing who was pretty good though not like old Bill here. It could say, "What? What? What?" and "Dammit!" and some other things. Fact is, that's what give me the idea to buy this parrot. I hear though that crows are harder to teach than parrots and that you got to get them young, just before they leave the nest."

"I can get a young crow I think," said Nikki, "but even if I did, how'd I go about learning him to talk?"

"I dunno for sure," answered the bartender. "Old Bill here was talking when I got him but he's learned most of his dirty words at the bar. You just got to catch him when he's about ready to talk and then say something simple over and over. And if he does say something even if it's not just quite right, you give him something to eat. But he's got to be hungry. I don't know what crows eat."

"Hell, they'll eat anything," said Nikki, "specially if it's rotten. Corn for sure and maybe worms or bits of rotten meat. That's no trouble." He was getting enthusiastic.

"Well, let me know how you come out," grinned the bartender. "I may need a spare bird if old Bill get sick or dies. And I'll pay you fifty bucks for your crow if he can talk."

"No, you don't!" Nikki replied. "Five thousand, mebbe!"

By the time spring came and the crows returned, Nikki had his cage ready. It had taken many hours of gathering and peeling straight willow shoots, then nailing them onto the frame of a box four by four by four feet. A crow needed a big cage, not enough to fly in of course, but large enough to get around in. Then there had to be a door and a substantial perch where the crow could sit while Nikki taught it to talk. And a feed pan and water can.

"Why you no wait till you catch your crow?" asked his wife Lempi. She was highly dubious about the entire project. "You not going to keep that cage in my house. Out in the barn maybe OK." Lempi kept the cleanest house in town. A perfectionist. People opined that maybe she was that way because she'd never been able to have children, a great sorrow to both her and her husband. Indeed one of the reasons Nikki was so interested in having a talking bird was that it would bring kids to the place. Nikki always liked to have us around and Lempi often brought out a cinnamon roll when we dropped by. But we had to eat it outside and not bring any dirt into her spotless kitchen. She was a cleaner, Lempi was. Why she scrubbed her floors with lye water sometimes three times a week and Nikki had to leave his boots on the porch or, if it were snowing, on a rug in the summer kitchen before entering the house. There'd be no dirty bird in her house.

The crows returned the tenth of April that year and Nikki spent a lot of time in the woods locating where they went to roost at night and studying their habits. He also practiced calling them. He'd always had the gift. You just had to squeeze your neck muscles and make a sound like clearing your throat only louder to make a good caw. But now he learned that there were a lot of different kinds of cawings. Three short sharp caws meant danger; it was a warning to all the other crows. One single long caw meant that everything was all right. Two caws, the last with an upward rise in pitch, seemed to mean that the crow had found something interesting and was inviting other crows to join it. But there were other sounds as well, especially after they had gone to roost: little gurlings, cooings, and even some sounds like those made by a human baby. Nikki practiced imitating all of them. "Maybe I've got to learn crow talk first," he thought. "Maybe if I imitate the mother of the crow I'm going to get, it may imitate me and then I can start teaching him."

About the middle of May the crows began flying eratically, the males pursuing the females all over the skies. They'd suddenly rise, then plunge downwards. From his blind, Nikki watched their courtship. One bird actually turned a somersault after soaring abruptly, then falling. On the tree limbs or occasionally on the forest floor, he watched the males spread their black tails, curve their necks and strut along with their wings drooping. No cawing then, more cooing than anything else. The female was less active but finally she would begin to respond when he came close to her, touching her bill to his, and fluttering her wings. Often two or three other crows would sit above the love pair on a branch watching the show and giving the two-caw call that meant there was something good going on. Quite a performance!

Shortly after the mating, the birds began their nests. Nothing fancy, and mainly assembled from branches and twigs and grass, they seemed almost thrown together in the crotch of a branch high up in a large pine or maple tree. Almost the size of a squirrel's nest. Somehow, Nikki was able to locate four nests altogether but two of them were over four miles from town on the south shore of Lake Tioga. The closest one was back of Mount Baldy and it was in a medium size maple that looked climbable once you got to the first branch about twenty feet up. Moreover it had a limb parallel but lower than the one holding the nest so Nikki felt he could slide along it to see what was inside or to get the fledgling.

He built a good blind nearby and dragged an old ladder out to the tree one night shortly after the nest was completed, then blazed a trail so he could find the tree in the dark if he used his miners carbide head lamp. He didn't much relish climbing up there in the darkness and wouldn't do it unless he had to but he had to get that young crow.

Once Nikki saw that the female was sitting on the nest he kept away from the area for more than a month fearing that he might disturb the hatching. Then, when he did return, he went to the blind before dawn to watch the young birds being fed. So far as he could tell there were only three of them, one larger than the others. "He's the one for me," said Nikki.

Finally after long waiting he saw one of the little crows stand up and walk a few feet out on the limb before returning to the nest. It was time! When Nikki began to climb the ladder what a torrent of cawing arose. Crows from everywhere seemed to swoop around him. One grabbed his cap and dropped it to the ground. Another clawed his face as it swooped by. So that night, Nikki put on his headlight and climbed the tree and got his crow, the biggest one in the nest. It didn't protest; just huddled in his hand as he put it in the bag and when he opened the cage door back in the barn and set it in a sort of a nest he'd prepared in a corner, the crow promptly went to sleep. Wasn't hurt a bit.

The next morning Nikki looked it over. The little crow was about six or seven inches long and not quite feathered out. And it was hungry. Its beak seemed almost bigger than its head and it squawked as Nikki fed it bits of worms and little balls or corn meal mush. Nikki imitated the squawking and tried to give the bird its food only after it made some kind of sound. By the end of the week he could hold the crow as he fed it. You could almost see it grow.

Nikki named the little crow Akkari (Oscar) after his brother-in-law although Lempi's brother was dumb and Akkari was bright. Indeed it was a quick learner. Nikki only had to dip its beak in the water pan once to teach it to drink and by the end of the first month it would answer back when Nikki made some cooing or cawing but only if it was hungry. That was no problem because at first the little crow was always famished. It would eat almost anything Nikki put before him: peas, berries, household scraps, chickenfeed, but it preferred meat scraps or worms. After every rain Nikki picked nightcrawlers in the garden for Akkari.

By the end of August the crow was full grown and had acquired a few words. Nikki had tried at first to teach it the Finnish word "Mitta?" but that failed so he settled for its English equivalent "What?" which more or less resembled a caw. Akkari picked that up fast. For a time, whenever Nikki said anything, the bird would ask "What? What?" It really sounded like it wanted to know. Akkari sure got some bits of nightcrawler when he first said it.

The next word the bird learned was "Hello!" perhaps because all of us kids used to say it so often when we'd visit the Sippolas. It wasn't quite right, being more like "Allo!" but it was clear enough. The bird's first sentence was "I come back"–again perhaps because Nikki and all of us said it to the crow when we'd leave him and give him food to carry him over. It sounded a bit slurred but you could understand it all right. Akkari also learned some other words and phrases that I forget but what I remember most vividly was his laughter. First, he'd give a shrill whistle and then say, "Ha!...Ha, ha, ha, ha!" It almost sounded human and anyone who heard it couldn't help laughing in return.

Anyone, that is, except Lempi. Nikki's wife couldn't abide that crow even if it was in the barn. She was jealous of the long hours her husband spent with the bird. "You getting so you don't talk anyone else!" she complained. Besides, she was appalled at the bird's dirtiness. Nikki did his best to keep the cage clean, putting fresh burlap bags on the floor everyday and washing them in the creek behind the house. He was always glad when I brough him some of our old newspapers for the same purpose. But Lempi was right. Crows are almost as bad as geese. What goes in one end usually comes out of the other and soon the barn was smelling pretty high. "And you, too, Nikki," said his wife. "You start smelling like crow too. You wash again." Nikki took a lot of saunas during those months.

The Sippolas had a big fight when fall came and the nights got cold. Nikki wanted to bring the cage into the house but Lempi was so angry all the time he didn't even bring it up. Instead, at first snowfall, he brought the cage into the summer kitchen and had it out with Lempi. Oh, how she raged and raged. Oh how she argued! Nikki tried to explain that he was making money, big raha, that in the spring when the bird had learned a few more words and especially to say, "Akkari wants peanuts!" he would sell it to some bar owner for "thousands of dollars, Lempi!" She was not convinced. "Sometime I wring its neck like chicken!"

"You do that and I bust you in nose good!" he answered. "We keep akkari over winter in summer kitchen, not in house."

And that's the way it was. Nikki had his way for once but it was a hard winter. The summer kitchen, a shed off the real kitchen, was usually never heated in the winter. It was used only on the hot days of summer for cooking, baking and heating the wash water in the copper boiler. Many of our houses had summer kitchens; they kept our houses cool, but in the winter they were only for hanging up bacon, deer carcasses or smoked fish. No one built a fire in the summer kitchen's range during the snow months.

But Nikki did and it came hard at times to wake himself up two or three times at night to fire up the stove again so his crow would stay warm enough. And, as you can imagine, he had to work pretty hard to keep the smell down. Lempi never entered the room without holding her nose and all in all she made Nikki's life pretty miserable that winter.

It was in the middle of April when Nikki got up very early one morning to go netting trout in Goose Lake. There was still a big sheet of ice in the middle but a ring of open water could be seen along the shore. By setting an illegal gill net in the shallows of this ring, you could usually come back with a sack full of trout. But you had to get up before dawn, before the game warden did. Nikki arose and dressed ate a bit, and then cleaned out the crow's cage, put clean newspapers down, and was on his way.

Unfortunately, he didn't close the cage door tight enough. When he returned that noon Akkari was strutting around the tablecloth on the kitchen table and Lempi was gone. She did leave a note: "No more! I go my sister's house in Marquette and I no come back so long you have that dirty bird."

Nikki was deeply hurt by her leaving but he was also defiant. "OK, if she go, she go. I make it OK." He brought the cage into the kitchen and put it by the window on Lempi's chair. Cooking wasn't so bad though he got awful tired of bacon and eggs and liver sausage. No homemade bread. No cinnamon rolls. No pie. No dinner pail all fixed when he went to work.

And somehow, everything got pretty dirty. Nikki would sweep the floors and try to put things away but the dishes piled up. Washing his clothes was a terrible chore and they never really got clean. Why, he didn't have any time to do anything but take care of the house and that damned bird. Moreover Akkari hadn't learned any new sayings except "Shut up!" Nikki had tried his utmost to get the crow to say "More peanuts" to increase his salability but all he got were the same old words or that damned whistle and laugh. Maybe that's why it learned "Shut up!" Nikki would say it so often. Lonesome and troubled, sometimes Nikki almost hated that damned bird.

It wasn't till the middle of July that Nikki decided that living alone wasn't worth it so he went down to Higley's saloon and offered to sell Akkari. He told Higley how much trade the parrot had brought into the bar in Hancock and how it would liven up the place. Higley just laughed. "How much you want for that damned crow?" he asked.

Nikki started at a thousand dollars and ended up offering the bird for fifty. Higley just laughed some more. "Nikki," he said finally, "I wouldn't take that damned crow of yours if you gave it away. I got enough dirty birds at the bar every night as it is. NO!"

Because ot was impossible to get away and go to Hancock just then, or to Ishpeming or Marquette, Nikki found a farmer up beyond the old furnace who would care for the crow free. Besides, the man had a kid who had often come to see and talk to Akkari like the rest of us did. So Nikki, feeling bad, took the cage and the crow to its new but temporary home. In the fall Nikki would take the bird up to the Copper Country or somewhere and get a bunch of money. Meanwhile he could at least visit it once in a while.

The house sure seemed empty with both Akkari and Lempi gone. Nobody to talk to. Not much to do. So finally Nikki wrote Lempi, asking her to come back. This is what he wrote. "Dear Lempi: You win. I get rid of Akkari. You no see him again. Come home." He even signed it "Love, Nikki."

Lempi came up on the afternoon train next day and the whole town was glad. "I lonesome for you too, Nikki," she said as she hugged him. Although he had cleaned the house very hard, she did it all over, happily. And she baked him bread and cinnamon rolls, even a blueberry pie. It was like old times–very good. And it was very good to hold her in his arms that night with a cool wind blowing in through the open window. Nikki slept better than he had for months.

Until shortly after dawn, when Lempi shook him and pointed to the window. There on the sill was Akkari. "I come back," the crow said. "Hello, hello!" And then it gave the shrill whistle and laughed.

Nikki pulled the covers back over his head.

A Boy And His Horse

Half the people in town were down at the depot that afternoon in the summer of 1913 when the salesman from Green Bay drove my father's newly purchased Model-T Ford out of the boxcar and off the ramp. It was the first automobile most of them had ever seen and they ooh-ed and ah-ed when the motor started. The salesman was there to give Dad directions for cranking it ("always keep your thumb tucked in or you'll break your arm!"), for setting the spark and throttle levers on the steering wheel, and for using the clutch and brake pedals. "Let the clutch out easy, Doc," he advised, "or it'll stall or jerk like an unbroken broncho. It's a knack."

After demonstrating the complicated process several times, he had my father try it. Then finally up the hill street they came, a rabble of yelling kids streaming behind. I'd never seen my father so proudly triumphant. When my mother came out to observe the glorious vehicle with its shiny brass radiator, wood-spoke wheels, and leather straps tied to the headlights, Dad almost burst with the glory of it. "No more damned horses, Edyth," he said still shaking from the vibration. "They say this shebang can even go thirty miles an hour. Why I can make calls in half the time."

Dad had some trouble learning to drive but he kept at it. Whenever he put on the brakes, he also pulled back on the steering wheel as though it were reins, sometimes even roaring "Whoa!" Possessed of little mechanical aptitude, he often gave the engine too much spark or too little throttle and so getting the Ford started usually took a good ten minutes. He even had difficulty putting the top up and the isinglass curtains in place when it rained. Those early tires were always getting punctured or suffering blow-outs which meant jacking up the axle, taking the tire off the wheel and vulcanizing and patching it right there. No spare. It was a most complicated procedure for my father and he almost wore out the Owner's Manual reading and re-reading it.

But how proud and delighted he was to take us out for a drive even though it was usually just up and

down our street. There were no gravel roads then, just wagon ruts outside our village limits. Dad navigated them when he had to but they were not for pride or pleasure. When she went with him, mother would put on her brown duster robe and fasten a veil over her hat with long hatpins. When we met a horse and wagon, Dad would squeeze the rubber bulb on the horn as a warning, then come to a complete stop to let the rig by. Horses were terrified of the sight, sound and smell of the first automobile. Often when my father parked it outside our house, farmers would drive up their teams to have their horses smell it. Then they'd ask Dad to start the engine while they held their shying nags tightly. They didn't want any runaways when later they met us on the road.

At that time there were no garages or filling stations anywhere in the whole U.P. Dad would have a barrel of gasoline sent up on the train and this would then be hauled to our barnyard to be set up against a bank. To fill the car tank, we'd first have to strain the gasoline through chamois cloth into the pour can and we had to make sure that the wheel cups were always full of axle grease.

Dad also had to be his own service man even unto grinding the valves. When major repairs were needed such as overhauling the engine, he usually got an old Cousin Jack (Cornish) miner who had repaired the big machinery in the mine's engine house. They'd put a chain hoist onto a big limb of a maple tree and lift the engine out of the car so they could work on it. Sometimes the town blacksmith had to make a new part. All in all, owning a car in 1913 was no small deal.

Despite the envy of my friends, I hated that automobile with a passion. Indeed, my father almost had to force me to ride in it. At first he thought it was because I was scared of the noise and speed but I wouldn't even sit in it when it was silent and unmoving. Then he thought it was because I was sick and he gave me calomel and castor oil. Only after some weeks did he discover that my reluctance came because I was afraid he would sell Billy, the horse I loved so dearly. He did sell Prince, our other horse, almost immediately and I was glad of that. A mean critter, a kicker and a biter. Once that black devil cornered me in the box stall and I had to flatten myself along the wall under the long feedbox so he couldn't get to me–a long and terrible half hour. Until Dad bought the Ford he always kept two horses and kept both of them tired out, making his house calls all over the countryside, summer and winter no matter what the weather.

Oh how relieved I was when he told me he wouldn't sell Billy, that he needed him when the car broke down (which was frequently) and also that he would have to have some means of transportation during the spring break-up when the dirt roads become impassable.

To Dad, Billy was the spare horse and he had originally bought him both for that purpose but also because he wanted my mother to have a horse she could ride. My mother was a gentlewoman, city reared, who in her youth had done a lot of riding, side saddle of course. I used to love to see her on Billy, with that little derby pinned to her brown hair, galloping down to Lake Tioga and back on a fine summer's day. She rode him well. By the time I began to ride Billy however, arthritis had set in and she no longer could do it. But she encouraged me and bought me a real western saddle with a horn on it that I could hang onto while learning to ride. By the time I was twelve I was galloping everywhere with confidence and ease.

A Boy And His Horse

Let me tell you a bit about Billy. A pure white gelding, he was not a big horse, as horses go. Dad said that he had raced in his early years and I believe it because he could never resist turning on a burst of speed automatically whenever anything went past him–even a train. Billy could jump too. I'll never forget how he took off over a big log that had fallen across one of the old logging roads–so smooth and easy–and then how he looked at me over his shoulder as if to say, "Nothing to it!"

Most horses are pretty dumb but Billy wasn't. In fact, he almost seemed to have a sense of humor enjoying the little tricks he played on me. Always when I put on the saddle blanket and then the saddle and started to tighten the cinch straps, he'd swell up his belly thereby insuring that the saddle would slip and dump me off when I got on. Then he'd whinny in delight. I swear that when I first took him down to the lake to have a drink and he went down on his knees while I went over his head into the water, he grinned and whinnied almost a horse laugh! Again and again when I tried to put on his bridle in the winter months, Billy would play a game with me, clenching his huge teeth tightly so I couldn't insert the cold bit. Not that it was too cold either for I always warmed it first by putting it inside my shirt but I'd always have to sweet talk him, stroke, currycomb or brush him all over before he'd open his mouth. Yet once, when I foolishly galloped him across the railroad tracks down by the depot and he caught a hoof in the rails and fell upon me breaking my leg in two places, Billy stood there until help came. He stood over me with one foot in the air, fearing to put it down lest he'd step on me.

How I loved that white horse! Not just riding him along the forest trails but also caring for him. Never did it seem like chorework; it was always a labor of love. Climbing up into the loft and throwing down the fragrant hay that still held the smell of summer in it, scooping out a more than generous helping of oats from the bin (and being careful not to have a mouse in the bucket), I'd watch him eat with great pleasure. I always warmed his water in the winter. Even cleaning out the stable was a privilege, not a duty, and now in my old age when I use horse manure to make the compost I need to attempt to grow *The Perfect Potato*, I think of Billy. Always I had fresh straw for him and I brushed and currycombed him until he shone. When I brought him a carrot or apple from the house, he'd nibble it daintily from my hand and nuzzle my pockets to see if I'd brought along a sugar lump, the long kind that the old Finn women used to suck their coffee through from the saucer.

And I talked to him, sharing my hurts and hopes and dreams.

Finally it became apparent that Billy was growing very old. It was painful to see him trying to get up on his feet in the morning. His nose was getting grey. I couldn't bear to urge him to gallop anymore for he tired so swiftly. Sometimes I'd get down and lead him rather than ride the forest trails. Billy didn't eat as much and he ate very slowly. There also seemed to be a film over his eyes, and he became lame. No longer when I'd go down to the pasture to call him would he come charging up to me at the fence whinnying. Instead, I'd have to go to him and pat and stroke his sides before he seemed to recognize me enough to follow me back to the barnyard or stable. It was heart breaking to see my friend plodding heavily and painfully up the lane.

Then one morning I overheard my father telling my mother that he'd have to do something about old Billy. "He's no use to us and Cully doesn't even ride him anymore. Maybe I'd better shoot him to put him out of his miseries. Or perhaps I could get someone to lead him down to the slaughter house and have them take care of it." My mother protested, saying that I would never forgive him if he did such a thing, that it would be better just to leave Billy in the pasture until he died. Dad just grunted and I remember how once when I was very young, he made me wallop against a sapling a wounded rabbit he'd shot–until it died. "I want to teach you, Cully, that it's not unkind to put an end to suffering," he'd said when I weepingly obeyed him.

Watching Billy in his last days was a bad time. The bottom seemed to have dropped out of my world. I couldn't eat, and it was hard to sleep. One moonlight night I crept out of my bed and walked down to the pasture to see if old Billy was all right, then slept in the grass beside him until dawn came.

Dad didn't have to shoot Billy nor was he taken to the slaughter house to be sledged between the eyes and have his throat cut. One night we had one of our terrible U.P. thunderstorms with almost continuous flashes of zigzag lightening and rolling crashes of unbelievably loud thunder reverberating over our granite hills. The next morning I found Billy dead in the pasture. With a burn streak going down his mane to his legs, he had been killed instantly by lightening.

I dug his grave myself, nine feet by six, and five feet deep, an undertaking that took most of the day. Then I rounded up some of the kids who too had ridden him and with great effort we finally managed to put him into the huge hole. Then I sent them away and covered Billy with all the flowers I could find in the pasture, mainly daisies and Indian Paint Brush, and shoveled the earth over him, weeping so hard I could hardly see.

Sixty some years later, I still ache, remembering.

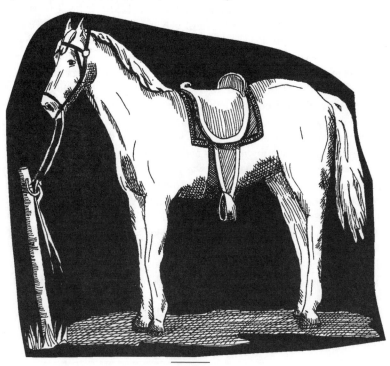

The Wake

During the winter months there wasn't much for a man to do in the evenings except to go to bed–which is why there were so many kids in Tioga. Oh, you could grease your shoepacs, put a new handle on the axe, boil your traps, empty the ashes or reread the Sears Roebuck catalog for the tenth time, but there was little fun in that. No place to go and nothing to do. The dog days of winter.

Nevertheless, there were five men in our town who had found a way to get away from their wives and children once a week on Saturday night. They had a sort of club, the Last Man Under the Table Club, which met in the back room of Callahan's store to play poker and empty a keg of beer.

It wasn't much of a store that the Mike and Dinny Callahan brothers operated. Little on the shelves except pork and beans and other staples. No meats. Just coffee, sugar, Peerless smoking tobacco and Red Man snuff; boxes of dried prunes, apples and apricots; a barrel of crackers and a big wheel of yellow cheese made up most of the inventory. But Callahan's stayed open until nine at night every day of the week, and being located next to the post office it attracted enough business to keep the two bachelor Irishmen afloat.

Behind the main part of the store was the room where the Last Man Under the Table Club had its fun, and behind this was a smaller room where Ed Stenrud, our undertaker, kept his coffins and caskets and did his dirty work. Sort of a spooky place but it was alive and full of hilarity when the five regulars slapped down their cards, made their bets and drank till they were thoroughly polluted.

They were a motley crew, those regulars. First there was Dinny Callahan, the store keeper, who had started the club some years before. So long as Dinny was half sober, he kept the sessions lively with his thick Irish brogue, laughter and song. But he was one of those unfortunate souls who couldn't hold his liquor very well. Four mugs of beer and perhaps a shot of whiskey and Dinny's eyes would begin to glaze; five mugs and he would slowly slide off his chair and pass out. Dinny was always the first man under the table.

Didn't make any difference. The others, without a glance, always played on. Occasionally, after half an hour or so, Dinny would revive enough to enter the game again but one more mug and he was blotto till morning.

The other four players were Laf Bodine, the red headed trapper we called King of the Poachers; Paddy Feeney, our blacksmith; Bill Maler, logger who had a homestead down by Lake Tioga; and Untu Salmonen, a big Finn who pumped the handcar up and down the railroad tracks maintaining the right-of-way. To all of them, these weekly poker sessions were the highlight of their lives.

They played straight draw-poker with deuces wild. Paddy, the blacksmith, was the banker and with five white chips or one red chip for a nickel and a blue chip for a dime, no one ever lost or won very much but they had a high old time. Actually, the game was just an excuse for getting thoroughly drunk, the traditional U.P. Saturday night spree. One keg of beer and perhaps a bottle of rotgut whiskey from Higley's saloon was usually enough to do the job. If they had hangovers the next morning, well that was the price you had to pay. You ought to get drunk on Saturday night.

But all good things come to an end and after seven years the Last Man Under the Table Club died a sudden death. Here's how it came about. The last session was much like all of those that had occurred before, but perhaps just a little louder and gayer because there were two bottles of rotgut instead of one to go with the keg. Laf, filling a long shot inside straight, warwhooped and pounded on the table. Untu with only a pair of threes and his six bet bluff was called by Bill Maler holding only a pair of nines, so he did a war dance around the big table, yelling with triumph. Dinny, the storekeeper, kept losing steadily as usual and kept drinking more and more so he could bear the taunts of the others. "Here's to the Irish! They always lose! Have another snort, Dinny!" Paddy wouldn't drink to that but instead started singing a sad song or two in honor of the ould sod.

It was about midnight when Dinny passed out and slid under the table. The other four played on, wondering who'd be the next to join him. Then Bill had a great idea. "Let's give Dinny an Irish wake," he proposed. "Let's get one of Ed Stenrud's coffins out of the back room and put Dinny in it until he sobers up." A burst of laughter greeted the suggestion and the deed was done. They didn't use one of Ed's fancy caskets but settled for the pine box Ed used for poor folk. Putting it on the floor beside the card table they continued their game, each one putting a blue chip in the pot for Dinny and taking a snort for him too. Finally, realizing that they were all getting shaky and wanting to see what Dinny would do when he came to, they stopped drinking and began putting on a mock wake. "Ah, Dinny was a fine man but he couldn't handle likker. It just made him sicker!" Great guffawing and pounding of knees! Someone got a candle from the back room, lit it and put it near the coffin. Laf played preacher and gave forth with a long sloppy sermon about our dear departed. More laughter, more suspense, more snorts. When would the bugger wake up?

Laf's talking of Kingdom Come reminded them of Sammy Hall, the old drinking song, and all joined in tipsily.

> "Oh, my name is Sammy Hall, Sammy Hall, Sammy Hall,
> Oh my name is Sammy Hall and I hate you one and all,
> You're a gang of muckers all. Damn yer hides!

Oh I killed a man, tis said, so tis said, so tis said,
Oh I killed a man tis said, that I hit him on the head,
And I left him there for dead. Damn his hide!

To the gallows I must go, I must go, I must go,
To the gallows I must go with my friends all down below
Saying Sam, I told you so. Damn their hides!

Oh, the preacher he did come, he did come, he did come,
Oh, the preacher he did come and he looked so very glum
As he talked of Kingdom Come. Damn his hide!"

Dinny at last began to stir in the coffin. They began to wail loudly and keen and mourn. "Ah, poor Dinny. He was a good man, a brave man, he was. Let's drink to Dinny. Too bad he died! Let's sing another song for Dinny, poor soul."

Suddenly the little Irishman poked his head up out of the coffin, took a shocked look around and then went back into the box again. His four comrades laughed so hard they could hardly sing the last verse of Sammy Hall:

"There was Nellie in the crowd, in the crowd, in the crowd
There was Nellie in the crowd and she looked so very pourd,
That I told her right out loud: Damn yer hide!"

Suddenly Dinny, by that time cold sober, jumped out of the coffin, punched Untu in the nose and Paddy in the eye and, grabbing an axe furiously drove them from the room. Then he smashed the coffin and the card table and two chairs before he sat down to nurse his wrongs, as any good Irishman would and should.

That was the end of the Last Man Under the Table Club but not the last of the tale. As you can imagine, the news of what happened spread joyously the length of the town before noon next day and most of the townspeople enjoyed it hugely. Nothing so exciting and hilarious had happened in Tioga for years. One person who did not find it at all amusing was Father Hassel, our Catholic priest. Still shaking from the experience of the night before, Dinny had come to him early next morning to confess his sins, and afterward he told the priest what had happened, that he really thought he was dead until he heard them laughing. "Ah, my son," said Father Hassel. "Once again I find that Our Dear Lord works his wonders in mysterious ways. You haven't been to confession for eleven years and I'd about given up all hope for you. I trust you will be at church come next Sunday, my son." Dinny promised that he would.

Then Father Hassel sent word to Paddy Feeny that he wanted to see him. When the blacksmith came the priest gave him billy blue hell. "Sacrilege! Sacrilege!" he roared and he told Paddy that his only chance of escaping eternal purgatory was to keep the churchyard and graveyard mowed and tidied up for two years. They needed it.

As for Dinny Callahan, no one had ever had such a mad on for so long a time as he brooded over what they'd done to him. The Irish have always cherished revenge. No one plays a dirty trick on an Irishman without paying for it. Unfortunately, all of the other members of the club were a lot bigger than Dinny and better fighters, too, as he found out at the post office when Untu innocently said, "Hi, Dinny, how are you?" hoping to make amends and perhaps get the club started again. Dinny interpreted the greeting as asking if he were still dead and laid into the big Finn, fists flying. Untu grabbed Dinny by the neck and threw him out of the post office door, then slugged him hard when he tried to fight some more. No, thought the Irishman. Some other way had to be found to get even.

Finally, he set out some traps in the swamp back of the slaughter house and caught four skunks, one for each of his tormenters. After the carcasses got ripe enough, and after slitting their stink glands to be sure they stunk enough, Dinny spent half a dark night dropping them through the holes of outhouses.

It wasn't enough, but it was something. Erin go braugh!

The Old Tailor

Who's he? Old Fabian, our tailor.
He makes the whole town proud of him,
Oh how he walks and carries eighty years.
You'd think his tailor's yard was in his coat,
The way he holds himself. Some say
He held a general's rank in Finland,
And had to flee when Russia took her freedom.
Whatever was his past, for twenty years,
He's worn that old brown derby helmet-like,
And marched, stiff-stepping down the hill to church.
You see that path he's shoveled from his house?
It's like him. Why, on his knees,
Beside his tailor's iron and dog-eared *Bible*,
I've seen him, heard him speak to God;
And though the tongue was strange, the tone
Was that of a proud soldier making his report
To the superior officer. He makes us proud.
Too proud perhaps, for but a week ago
To our back door he came, another man,
Old, broken, bent. I'd never thought to see him so.
Our cook translated: "He has no wood.
He says he's had no fire for forty hours
And it's been twelve below. He's had not work.
The people tell him that he does things wrong.
He blames it on his eyes." She paused as he began,
Faltering, to speak again. The grutturals
Grew weak and trembling. Suddenly he wept.
It's hard to sit and watch a brave man cry.
'He says he's never had to ask for anything
From anyone before, but now he's old and sees not good.
And can you give him something he can do
In trade for wood and food? He hasn't

Eaten much, he says, for many weeks.'
When cook informed him what we told her to,
The old man said, 'I t'ank you.' and his
Hand crept to his head in effort to salute
In his old manner…but it failed.
He'd lost too much to manage it, you see,
Too much of his true self. And that's
The only tragedy of age. He'd conquered it
And kept himself intact until that day.
Now though he still goes marching down the street
As if in step to drums we cannot hear.
I fear the memory of that last defeat
Walks with him.

The White Wolf

Seventy-five years ago there were many wolves in the U.P. though now they are almost extinct. All of us who lived in Tioga had heard them at night, usually in the deep of winter, when a wolf chased a deer out of the Buckeye and down through the big maple grove that covered the north side of our long hill. Their yapping and howling made the night ring with a wild eerie sound and we could almost follow the course of the pack as it pursued its quarry. Children shivered in their beds until the howling grew faint and finally was lost over the hills.

As children, all of us were fearful of wolves and needlessly so for in all the history of town, not one single person had ever been harmed by them. But we had heard the story of Little Red Riding Hood and the Finn kids had listened to their elders telling how, in the old country, they used to take a family dog or two with them on their sledges when they had to go cross country and that when the wolves attacked, the driver would throw out a dog to keep the wolves busy while whipping his horse so he could make his escape.

It was all nonsense of course. Timber wolves are either afraid of man, or more plausibly, they can't stand his adominable scent so they avoid contact with people if they possibly can. Rarely did we ever see one in the forest when hunting or fishing though we often saw wolf tracks in the snow or found the remains of a deer they had killed. Occasionally one of our deer hunters shot a wolf, or a trapper caught one or poisoned one, but not very often.

The possessor of a wolf skin coat was greatly envied. Indeed, if I remember right, there were only two such coats in Tioga. One was owned by Vic Toulon who had inherited it from his grandfather, a full blooded Menominee Indian. That coat was no beauty after all those years. It was mangy and moth ridden and held together in front by shingle nails and a loop of haywire but Vic was sure proud of it. The other coat, in contrast, was a beautiful garment, admired by all of us. It belonged to the best fur trapper in town, Eric Sippola, and the lustrous skins it was made of were from wolves that Eric had trapped or shot himself.

Our people couldn't understand how Eric managed to catch so many wolves until our blacksmith once gave away the secret, saying that he saved all the parings from the horses' hooves for him. Eric had told him that this particular bait overcame the wolves' intense cautiousness. Once the secret came out, other men too began to trap a few of them but it was still difficult work. You had to do it just right.

First, you had to boil your traps in a soup made of wild cherry bark and handle them with new or newly washed canvas gloves when you made your set at the base of a tree whose roots were spread far enough to leave a narrow hole between them. Then you put the hoof parings deep in the hole and one or two traps were placed and hidden in front of it. Eric always set his trap so that its pan was flush with the surface of a little indentation where a wolf would most likely put its right front foot if he tried to get at the bait. Then the trap was covered with sifted moss and leaves so it looked right natural. You had to know your stuff to catch a wolf.

Unlike the other Finns who lived on top of the hill, Eric's cabin was down in the valley, near the slaughter house. He was a nice man, about 35 years of age, and a bachelor. When some of us boys would go down to see him or the skins he had tacked onto his shed, he would give us a piece of hard cinnamon toast and tell us trapping stories. Since all of us did a little amateur traping for biting money, we appreciated the lore he shared. He told us how to catch a weasel with a rat trap nailed to the bottom of a sapling; how to bury all but the tail of a sucker at the edge of a lake and then put your trap where a mink would have to step when it tried to dig it out; how to skin a skunk without getting stunk up too badly; how to stretch a muskrat hide over a round-ended board. Yes, we learned a lot from Eric and we missed him a lot after he shot the white wolf and then himself.

Stories about that white wolf had been around for two or three years. It roamed the area east of the old Hayshed Dam where the upper Tioga River tumbles through a gap in the granite hills. Rough country, completely wild and uncut, with rocky knobs, tangled alder swamps and a few lakes or streams. Except for some landlookers employed by the lumber companies, few people ever entered that wilderness. One of those who knew it well was Eric, who for some years had put a trap line through it all the way to Hell's Canyon in the Huron Mountains. He'd built a little overnight shack at the canyon so he could make his rounds every two days to check his traps.

At the post office one evening, Pitu Marsellies claimed that he had seen a white wolf, an arctic wolf, up by the Hayshed Dam and some of the other men were scoffing at the tale when Eric broke in. "That's right, Pitu," he said. "I seen that white wolf too, yes, three times I seen him, once close enough to see that he had pink eyes. An albino just like that white deer Laf Rafferty shot and brought to town four years ago. I tried last year to trap him but he's sure cagey. I'll get him this fall when the fur is prime. Bet that hide would go for a hundred dollars!"

And that fall, Eric tried hard, almost neglecting his traplines. Once getting a glimpse of white, he followed the wolf track in the early snow for two days, studying the wolf's habits. Probably rejected from the pack because of its color, the white wolf was a loner and a roamer. The track led all the way from Summit Lake to the headwaters of the Dead River and back again. Following it, Eric found where the wolf slept at night on top of a hemlock hill, where it caught and ate a rabbit, where it had crept up on a partridge and grabbed it just as it took off, where it followed a porcupine but decided not to tackle that ball of quills. Because of a deformed toe, the track of the white wolf was unmistakable.

One night, sleeping beside the trail, Eric had heard the white wolf's solitary howl, a deep throated tone that rose quivering in pitch a full octave, and was sustained there a full five seconds before coming down. Eric had often heard the wild music of a wolf pack in full cry, barking, yapping and yowling, but he had never known a howl like that of the white wolf, lone and lorn, there in the wilderness. The trapper put another log on the fire and felt for the gun under the blanket. But the howls gradually grew weaker and the time between them lengthened. "He's headed north now," said Eric to himself. "Maybe I can cut across and get on his trail...No, don't want to lose it."

Eric did his utmost that fall to trap the white wolf but failed, and when the deep drifts of winter came he had to give up. About the middle of March, however, he took up the quest again for wolves are hungrier early in the spring than at any other time and are more easily caught. At the same time he would go after beaver. Because of the daily thawing in late March, snowshoeing is so difficult that only at night, when the snow freezes hard again or early in the morning, can one walk without the terribly hard labor of lifting wet snow with every step. It is probable that Eric was snowshoeing after dark when he fell off a granite cliff onto some jagged rocks and broke his left leg in two pieces, one that pierced the skin.

We can't be sure what actually happened, but a timber cruiser for Silverthorne Lumber Company, who stumbled upon his body by sheer chance while looking for a lost forty of virgin pine, had this to say: "I was going south along the ridge when I come across snowshoe tracks, maybe two, three days old and heading right for the cliff. Curious, I followed them and seen where the poor bugger went right over it. I go round and back to the bottom of the hill and, Jeez, what a mess of blood and thrashing around marks in the snow. Must have hurt him bad! And there was a wolf track I crossed before getting there, a big one. Well, I follow up the track where the man had crawled, leaving a trail of blood. How far? Mebbe four hundred yards and it must have took him two days of hell and you know, that wolf track was in his trail off and on. Probably knew the man was crippled bad. Finally, I seen Eric there in the snow with his head half blasted off. A mess. But before he shot himself, he got the wolf. Just one shot and right through the backbone, not fifty feet away. A white wolf. An albino."

Apil Fool On You, Emil

In our little forest village of Tioga, April Fools Day was taken seriously, almost religiously. All day long you had to catch someone else and avoid being caught. Even the little kids would go to the window and cry out, "Hey ma, there's a robin. Come see!" though there were still patches of snow on the ground and the maple trees were just beginning to fill the sap buckets on their waists. Hell, the crows had just started to come back.

No one loved the day more than Emil Olsen, our town's practical joker. All year long he was always pulling some trick on someone. Why once he even greased the grave digger's shovel and laughed uproariously when the clods stuck to it instead of covering the casket. But April Fools was his day of days and his favorite victim was Eino Tuomi, his best friend and neighbor. Every year when the evening mail was being "disturbed" (distributed) in our little post office, Emil would be there in the anteroom telling all the tricks he'd played on Eino that day. "Oh, for stupid! Oh, for dumb! Eino, he fall for anyhing I do!" And then he'd tell how he put a horsehair in his pipe or salt in his sugar bowl, or glued the pages of the Sears Roebuck catalog together in his outhouse and nailed his barn boots to the floor. And more. Oddly enough, Eino never resented the tricks. He just said patiently, "You crazy, Emil. You nuts!"

But I'd better tell you something about these two characters so you can understand and appreciate how Emil finally got his comeuppance. Both had been hard ore drillers and had worked together for many years in the Oliver Iron Mining Company's deep Tioga mine

until it suddenly shut down. Evidently the management had robbed the supporting pillars of ore that held up the overburden a bit too much. Anyway one afternoon when I was playing in the sideyard, a monstrous roar occurred, our new cement sidewalk cracked and the house shook. A great cloud of dust obscured the sun. "Cave in! Cave in!" All the people along our street streamed out of their houses and started running toward safety for they knew that the whole west end of town had been undermined. However, as things turned out, only an area about the size of a city block had collapsed but what a huge gaping hole remained. For years, we kids used to go gingerly to the edge of that hundred foot deep pit and wonder where the two men lay who had been buried in it.

Anyway, the mine shut down never to reopen and Eino and Emil were too old to hunt for work elsewhere so they stayed, eking out a precarious existence on tiny pensions and their own hard work. Perhaps an account of how they managed it will show you how our people survived hard times.

After the mine closed, Eino and Emil moved into two log cabins that had been abandoned. They were well built, snug structures of square hewn logs, warm in winter and cool in summer and they sat side by side across the street from the cave-in pit. Eino always had two old chairs in his front yard and it was there that the two old men would sit on a summer's day smoking their corncob pipes and arguing. Always arguing. Why they'd even argue about which bird would fly off the telephone line first.

Eino, the Finn, was a small but wiry man with a soft voice but Emil, the Swede, was a huge fellow with a voice like a bull. You could hear him bellowing all the way from Flinn's store. At first, I thought they were mad at each other, but instead, they were great friends, almost inseparable. They had evolved a symbiotic way of living that really worked. Eino had a barn behind his house and kept a cow; Emil had a chickenhouse and a big garden full of potatoes, rutabagas and cabbage which both helped till. They shared everything and we never saw one without the other. Why, when Eino's cow had to be serviced by Mr. Sulu's bull, they both held the rope that led it, almost hand in hand. Didn't bother them a bit when the usual bystander made the usual bawdy remarks about their mission. (I always hated that job when I had to take Rosie, our Jersey cow, to the Sulu's bull. It was interesting once I got there, but oh, how everybody kidded me along the route. "Wassa matter, Cully? Why you no do it yourself?" (Stuff like that.)

So they had milk and butter and eggs and occasionally they stewed a tough old rooster all day and night on the kitchen stove. Or if the gods were good, they had real meat from a young steer they'd raised instead of the usual illicit venison. Once Eino traded a calf for two of Delong's young pigs but the bear got them before they could be butchered. Besides berries, the only fresh fruit they ate were apples they had picked from a tree at one of the abandoned houses. And they had fish, of course, fresh trout or pike in the summer and smoked or marinated for the long white of winter. They didn't fish much with hook or line for the trout though. Instead, as they showed me once, they'd take a stick of dynamite, a blasting cap, and length of white fuse, put it on a raft in a promising beaver dam, light the fuse and run like hell. Then they'd scoop up all the trout, suckers and chubs, put them in gunny sacks and dump them uncleaned, guts and all, into the marinating barrels in their cellars. Almost every family in town had dynamite after the mine closed. Very useful in making a new outhouse hole or getting rid of a big stump. We kids used to have fun throwing chunks of ore at a blasting cap trying to get it to go off until once one did and Nicky Johnson lost an arm.

For the necessaries, the two old men had to have some biting money and that came from odd jobs or the thirty dollar pension checks that came to them each month. I was up at M.C. Flinn's store once when they came there to have the checks cashed. Emil, who could neither read nor write, always got red faced when he had to put his mark (X) on the check and when Mr. Flinn wrote "Emil Olsen, his mark. M.C. Flinn, storekeeper" under it. They always bought the same stuff: a pail of Peerless smoking tobacco, two dozen circular disc of black rye hardtack, a bag of korpua (a dried toast flavored with cinnamon), coffee, sugar and salt, a chunk of salt pork, and a half slab of bacon. Once a year they bought a sack of flour and some baking soda for their pancakes. Like all of us, they made their own maple syrup, so all in all they ate well and lived well. Nobody thought of them as being poor, nor did they.

On the afternoon of the last day of March one year, I had been selling copies of *Grit* up and down the street to my regular customers and somehow had an extra copy left, so I thought I'd give it to Eino who could read fine. I'd done that before and was always rewarded my having them tell me stories of mining in the old days or hearing them argue over something in the magazine. I could hear them hard at it by the time I got to Flinn's store. With a brace and bit, Eino was drilling a hole in the telephone post beside his house and Emil was giving him hell.

"Oh, for dumb!" he was yelling. "You no get any sap from telephone pole. It dead wood. It got no roots. Eino, you crazy dumb!" The little Finn was not bothered at all. "Oh, yah, I get sap. Best sweet sap. More sweet than maple tree give."

"No!" roared Emil. "Look, dummy. Hole is dry. Pole is spruce, dead spruce. It no give sap, stupid! Oh, for dumb!" Eino, unperturbed, took a length of elderberry stalk out of his pocket, slit it in half, scraped out the pith to make a little trough, hammered the spike into the hole and hung a pail from it. "Sure, Emil," he said. "No sap now. It come at night. You see in morning I get pail full." They were still arguing when I left, but I heard Eino say, "I make pancakes tomorrow for new syrup. You come eat my house, Emil. Bring eggs. I got sour milk."

According to the way Eino told the tale at the post office that next evening, on his way to breakfast, Emil had stopped at the telephone pole, put a finger first in the sap pail and then in his mouth. His face red with fury, he charged to the chair where Eino was sitting. "You sunabits, Eino, you peed in sap can. I going bust you in nose!"

Eino didn't get up. "Apil Fool, Emil! Apil Fool. Old Eino, he not so dumb!"

Summer Romance

My two girls, Cathy, 16 and Susan, 14, were bellyaching as they sat miserably on the front steps of their grandfather's house.

"Ugh! What a dump to be stuck in," said Sue. She was almost crying. "We've been here a whole week with five more weeks to go," she wailed. "Don't know about you, Cathy, but I've had it up to here. I want to go home. It's not fair for Dad to drag us up to this dead hole in the woods just because he was born and raised here and wants us to know what it's like to live in a little town. Live in one? Die in one, if you ask me."

Cathy nodded. "I feel the same way. There's nothing to do around here except walk up to the store, walk down to the post office, wash the dishes, or try to make conversation with Grandpa when he isn't sleeping on the couch. I'm fed up, too. No, it isn't fair!"

"It's easier for you than for me, Cathy. You at least can write Tim everyday…."

"And never get any answer." Cathy was angry. "We've been here six days now and no mail at all. Maybe he's fooling around with that dumb redhead while I'm gone. The least he could do is send me a note. Oh, I hate men."

"Well, I don't," said Sue. "That's part of what's wrong. There just don't seem to be any boys up here. Not our age anyway. There must be some of them hiding in the bushes somewhere, probably covered with moss. Even down at the beach where we go swimming you only see little kids. Haven't they got any older brothers or do the natives up here leave as soon as they can shave? Wouldn't blame them, at that. I want to go home."

Cathy had been thinking. "Hey Sue, how about this? Let's have a heart to heart talk with Dad and tell it to him straight–that we just can't stand being up here any longer, that we're sick of it, and want him to take us home. We're old enough now so that if he wants to come back with Mom to do some more fishing, we can take care of ourselves."

Sue was not impressed. "Not a chance," she said. "He still thinks of us a little kids. But if all of us, and I mean John too, say we want to go back and keep talking about it, maybe we won't have to stay here so long. Hey, here comes John now." She pointed up the street to their younger brother.

"Hey, John, come here." The boy came over and sat on the steps with his sisters as they explained.

"Nope, not me." he replied. "I don't want to go home. I'm having fun up here. Jeez, we've sure been having fun playing Duck on the Rock. You put one rock on another big one and choose up sides and then one guy knocks it off…"

"Knock it off, yourself," Sue said in exasperation. "Maybe you're having fun but we sure aren't." She began to cry a little. Sue could always turn on the tears when needed, but John wasn't impressed.

"Nope. No you don't. Bawl yer head off, but I'm staying here. You know what they've got down in the grove? They got a big cable they found up at the old mine and it's strung between two big trees and you climb up one of them and sit down on a seat that's under a pulley and wow, what a ride! Scary! Really neat! I'll show you where it is sometime–if I have time. Gotta get my ball now. Nope. I'm staying up here as long as I can." He left them, whistling.

"Well," said Cathy, "Let's face it, Sue. We're stuck here for the rest of the summer. Wait…I've got an idea. John! John!" she called.

Her brother came to the door. "Whatcha want?"

"Who are you going to play baseball with–and where do you play?" Cathy asked her brother.

"Oh, there's a bunch of us kids. There's a men's team here that plays against other towns each Sunday and they practice against us kids on Saturday, tomorrow. We thought we'd get ready for them, do some batting, and practice on fly balls and grounders. They got a diamond up there by the old mine. "Bye."

"Wait a minute, Bullet Head. How do you get there? Any big kids on your team?"

"Yeh, my friend Davy has a big brother, Jimmy, who plays with us, and there are a couple of other high school guys. I already told you–it's up by the mine. You know, by the big tall building with the wheels on top. Up there. I gotta hurry."

"Wait, we'll go with you," said Sue.

"Oh no you won't. I'm going by myself. Don't want any big sisters tagging along. Nuts to you." And John ran up the street.

The two girls looked at each other. "OK," said Sue. "Let's go looking." They giggled all the way up to the mine. The diamond was just a cow pasture with gunny sacks for bases. No bleachers. So they sat demurely on a rock and watched, occasionally applauding a good hit or catch and whispering to each other that there really were two or three possibilities, "that short blonde one over there and the one with light brown hair who looks like he's part Indian."

That evening after supper the girls cornered John. "Who was that short blonde guy, the one who fell down when he stumbled on the bag?"

"That was Tommy. He's a character. Always saying something to break us up."

'Who's that neat one that hit the ball into the creek?"

"That's Jimmy. Davy's brother. He plays basketball too. One of the guys has a rope hanging from a tree branch in his yard–must be twenty feet long–and Jimmy can climb that thing using only his hands."

"Did any of the guys ask you what our names were?"

"Naw."

The next afternoon both girls skipped swimming to watch the practice game between the boys and the town men's team. Again they were the only spectators and again were ignored despite their applause for the one weak hit made by the younger players. A rout. Moreover, these efforts seemed to have been completely in vain. Nothing happened the rest of the week. Jimmy and Tommy never appeared. Nor any other boys. Several times each day Cathy and Sue spent hours carefully dressing and grooming themselves before walking up and down the hill street. Each afternoon they swam in the lake, lay as attractively as possible on the beach, or paraded back and forth across it. No boy even remotely their age showed up. Just a lot of little kids, six to ten, all of whom John seemed to know well. Sometimes on their jaunts Cathy and Sue would occasionally encounter a pair of high school girls who stared at them impassively when they tentatively offered a friendly smile, then giggled after they had gone by. Utter abominable misery, day after day. The girls constantly begged us to take them home.

As usual it was Cathy who first faced up to the situation. "I guess Jimmy and Tommy or any of the other boys our age aren't going to come to us. We're just going to have to go where they are." she said to Sue.

"If you ask me, they're hiding under some rock somewhere, the cockroaches," said Sue. "We'd have to overturn every boulder and beat every bush around this lousy town to find even one and then he'd probably run away. Nuts to 'em. Let's just take off and hitchhike home, Cathy. I just can't stand it another minute."

"Listen, Sue. You know we're stuck here and besides, I've got another idea. Maybe what we've got to do is work through their little brothers and sisters. Make friends with them and maybe they'll show us those rocks where the big guys hide." Cathy grinned.

That's exactly what my daughters did. They promised John that they'd be good to him for once, that they'd make chocolate fudge or popcorn or cookies for his friends if he could get them to come down to Grandpa's porch after supper. The bait worked. By the end of the week a motley group of little kids, boys and girls alike, were coming for their snacks and having fun chasing one another around the yard, chattering and laughing on the front steps. Cathy and Sue presided with skill over these nightly gatherings, learned all the kids' names, got them to talking about themselves (and their older brothers) and answering a thousand questions about how it was to live and go to school in a real city.

Every evening the two girls were queens holding court. To the village children they were glamorous creatures from another world, yet who were really interested in them and how they lived. The word got around–Cathy and Sue weren't a bit "stuck up." They were friendly and they were fun. Indeed, so many kids began to show up that Grandpa began to grumble at the noise and chased them all away when the clock struck nine.

It didn't take much of this before my daughters were never able to be alone even when they wanted to be. We began to call them the Pied Piperettes for rarely could they get more than a block from the house on their walks before an entourage would begin to assemble. When they asked about Sliding Rock or Mount Baldy or the old iron furnace by the waterfall, there was always a group of youngsters to lead them there. Sue and Cathy even visited some of the boys' hideaway shacks in the grove to dutifully admire the piles of stones stored up as ammunition for fights that were sure to come. Together with the kids they scratched their names on Writing Rock up on Mount Baldy and marvelled at the ski jump the older boys had constructed.

When Sue and Cathy mentioned that they wished they could get to see the bears at the dump they were told marvelous stories about how the bears came to town in the fall to raid the apple trees, and what happened next. Sue and Cathy even learned how to swing from birch saplings on the edge of the hill, to eat raspberry tucks and nibble wintergreen leaves. Then one day, Davy, John's special friend, asked them to come up to his house to see his pet skunk. When they did, there were Jimmy and Tommy sharpening a scythe on the grindstone. My daughter Sue managed to ask Davy a lot of questions. How had and who had caught the skunk? (Jimmy had when it got tangled in the chickenwire.) Who had de-scented it? (Old Pullapin with a jackknife.) Before they knew it all of them were talking as though they had always known each other, Jimmy and Tommy included.

When Sue and Cathy got back that afternoon they were higher than steeples, laughing and jabbering secretly with each other, completely triumphant and very happy. That evening I noticed that there were older boys on the edge of the porch when dusk came to our village.

The remaining weeks of that summer went by very swiftly for all of us. Even today, many years later, the two girls remember that period as one of the best times of their lives. Tommy and Sue, Cathy and Jimmy were together every hour they could manage. I don't know what they did or didn't. All I know is that every morning the girls shampooed and set their hair in rollers, washed and ironed their dresses for the evening, laughed and giggled constantly or whispered to each other whenever I came by. They refused to go with us to our old hunting cabin; they didn't want to go swimming at the beach.

About dusk Sue and Cathy disappeared completely and when they returned about midnight they were always radiant. Their mother told me not to pry—as though I would have. I knew they thought that they were in love. Thank heaven it was about time to go home. I think my wife worried a bit too obviously once because Sue felt she had to reassure her. "Mom, Jimmy and Tommy are so darned shy, it's painful. All we do is talk and talk and talk. They keep asking us all about what it's like back home or telling us how someday they're going to escape and do great things. Or we go exploring. Things like that. Don't you and Dad worry. I tell you these boys are unbelievably shy. Terrible!" Sue had collected the scalps of half the boys in her high school but she told us she had never met any like these from the backwoods.

Finally it came time to depart. The morning before we left, and quite accidentally, I overheard the two of them talking in the bathroom. "I cried myself to sleep last night," said Sue. "I can't bear to go now. I love Tommy, I really do. And you know he hasn't even kissed me yet, Cathy. I could have killed him last night, he's so awkward and shy. Have I got bad breath or something? But I'll get him tonight even if I have to wrap my arms around him and throw him to the ground. Darn him anyway!"

"I know. I know," Cathy responded. "Jimmy's the same way. They've been in the woods too much or something. But we've got one more evening together. Only one. Only one!" I could hear both girls weeping.

Cathy and Sue were on edge all day. I did not dare do my usual teasing about their hair dressing and primping and when I insisted that they pack their bags so we could get an early start the next morning they turned on me in a fury. Hour after hour they got touchier, nastier, and all through the supper meal they were withdrawn and surly. It was therefore with some appreciative amusement that I saw and heard them suddenly change into gay bubbling spirits once Jimmy and Tommy came through the gate to get them.

For the first time the two couples walked away hand in hand. A last evening together with moonlight flickering down through the maples over the sidewalk. I tried to remember what it was like but couldn't. So wishing them well in their kissing I finished loading the car. Couldn't get to sleep though, so I was down in the kitchen having a midnight bowl of cornflakes when they burst into the house, right on the stroke of twelve according to our previous agreement, Sue from the back door and Cathy from the woodshed. Both were rubbing their mouths and when they saw each other doing it, they doubled up in a fit of uncontrollable laughter.

It was years later before I found the reason why. Both of the girls had indeed gotten their farewell kisses but both of the boys had been chewing snuff. I used to chew it too when I was their age. Made me feel tough and manly. Gave me courage.

Bears, Bears, Bears

No account of life in the old U.P. would be complete without some mention of bears. I dare say there wasn't a single one of the inhabitants of Tioga who had not seen or encountered them repeatedly. Every fall they raided our gardens and apple trees. Every year someone had a pig taken by bears. That was one reason that old Mrs. Murphy always kept her Paddy pig in her bedroom every night. When we picked blueberries or sugar plums, bears were picking them too so we always kept a wary eye out for some big black shape in the bushes. Not that they were usually dangerous, but it wasn't wise to surprise them.

Most bears have poor eyesight and hearing though they possess an excellent sense of smell, so if the wind is blowing away from them, they often did not know you were there until you were too close for comfort. Finally, getting that whiff of human scent, they sometimes would stand up on their hind legs trying to locate you before they padded silently away. A huge animal in maturity, sometimes weighing over 500 pounds, an erect black bear twenty feet from you, is a scary sight. Lots of big white teeth too in that red mouth. Generally, they'd run away, far faster than one would expect, yes, as fast as a horse could run. Watching a bear run up a hill is quite a sight. It gallops along swiftly with its front legs passing between the back ones, crashing through the brush and getting over the crest in no time at all.

Although bears are included in the group of animals called The Seven Sleepers, they do not truly hibernate, as Mulu Ankinen found out one afternoon early in March. He'd been snowshoeing across country to check out a beaver pond where he could set some traps and under a big windfall lodged against a granite outcropping he saw the black back of a sleeping bear. Thinking it was still hibernating, he poked it with a stick and out it came with a tremendous growl. Mulu turned and ran, of course, but it's hard running on snowshoes. He fell and lay there playing dead while the she bear sniffed him all over. Finally, she turned and went back to the den and Mulu, shaken by the experience, returned to town. The next day, armed with his deer rifle, he retraced his steps and shot her where she lay. A big sow bear with two little cubs barely eight inches long.

Bears have their young in February and March and the cubs nurse the mother until spring, even as she sleeps. They remain with her for about a year and a half, but then are driven off to fend for themselves. I've said that bears were not usually dangerous but this is not true of a mother bear with cubs. Most of the bear maulings of humans is done by sow bears with young. I almost got in trouble myself one time when I tried to take a picture of a cub that had climbed up an old pine stub. I never saw the mother but I heard her growl before I ran.

Arvo and Arne Mattila almost got it too when they found three young cubs playing and boxing each other on the shore of Lake Tioga. After some trouble and a lot of squealing, they captured the cubs, put them in a burlap sack, and started to take them to town thinking they might be able to sell them to the zoo on Presque Isle in Marquette. But the mother bear, hearing the squalling, showed up and made for the two Finns. Just in the nick of time, they managed to jump into their boat and row toward Flat Island and what they though was safety. But bears are good swimmers and the she bear dived into the water after them and the gunnysack that held her yelping young.

What to do? Arvo and Arne didn't want to be caught on that little island with a mad mother bear, so, counting on the bear's poor eyesight and hearing, they rowed like the devil in a big circle downwind and back to the mainland. They said the mother was still swimming toward the island when they got ashore. I don't know what happened to the cubs. Arvo and Arne brought them over to our house to show my dad and ask his advice. (He told them to take them back to their mother, but I doubt if they did.) Anyway, the cubs sure were fun to watch once they'd gotten over their fright. About three feet long and weighing maybe forty pounds apiece, they frolicked and tumbled all over our yard and at the bread and honey we put out for them. Almost human.

Marcel Pitou said that once he had been chased up a birch tree by a sow bear and that when it climbed up after him, he was able to kick it hard in the nose with his boot. He'd heard that a bear's nose is its Achilles heel, the most sensitive part of its body. Anyway, the bear went down the tree, hung around at its base for a whle growling, but finally went away.

Stories like these did not bother most of us who spent a lot of time in the woods. We respected bears but did not fear them. Indeed, they feared us and would always avoid us when they could. Perhaps they disliked man scent almost as much as we were repelled by theirs. When they had crossed one of our paths along the river, they left a rank odor that would linger for hours where they had passed. I remember vividly how once when Grampa Gage and I were driving Billy and the buckboard up an old logging road to go trout fishing, the horse had stopped suddenly with ears back and white eyes rolling, backing and filling and refusing to go onward until Grampa got off the rig and led it. Bear smell! Moreover, four hours later on our return trip, Billy did the same thing at the same spot.

A solitary animal, often nocturnal, you rarely saw more than one bear at a time but old man Takkinen claimed he once saw seven of them in a group one October, just before they paired off and mated. He said they were sniffing and some of the males were cuffing each other. After mating occurs, the males always go their own way. Never did anyone ever find two big bears in the same den.

Occasionally, however, especially when there had been a poor crop of berries, we saw several bears at the town garbage dump at the same time but even then the biggest one would chase the others away until it had had its fill. They didn't fraternize at all. They walked by their wild lone.

Many of the townspeople, especially the women and kids, however, were very afraid of the critters. Once when we had a half grown bear up a clump of maple trees in our front yard near our front porch, my Grama Gage almost went crazy with the fright of it. She locked her bedroom door, pulled down the curtains, and then spent most of a long afternoon peering along the edges to make sure the bear was still in the tree. "Why don't you shoot it, John? Why don't you shoot it before it jumps to the porch and breaks through my window?" she asked my father. Instead, Dad got a plate of sardines and put some in the crotch of a lower branch which the cub came down to eat before it took off down the street with a posse of barking dogs and yelling kids in pursuit.

Dad liked bears but that didn't prevent him from shooting a big one once when deer hunting. Its glossy black hide and head he had made into a rug. We never used it on the floor but had it hung over the unused door into the back hall stairway. As children we used to poke its glass eyes and shiveringly put our fingers into its snarling mouth when we felt brave enough.

Most of the bears that our townspeople killed were raiding our apple trees or private garbage dumps. The township picked up all the garbage once a year in the spring but by fall each house had its own pile of cans and stuff by the barn or outhouse so the bears had good pickings. Usually they came by night and we'd go out the next morning to see the mess they'd left, and their footprints. The latter looked almost like those of a huge man. You could see the five toes and the heel but it was wide, not as narrow as a man's track. Bears walk like a man does but on all fours, putting the heel down first before the toes. We could tell how big a bear was by his prints. One huge bear left footprints as big as a dinner plate in our garden dirt one fall and Dad estimated its weight as being over 600 pounds.

The biggest bear I ever saw came out of the brush and entered the big pool under the old Rolling Null logging dam on the west branch of the Tioga. I was no more than a hundred feet downstream flyfishing for trout when it appeared, so I froze motionless as it proceeded to catch some big redhorse suckers. The bear would thrash around in the water, then suddenly poke its head under and come up with a big one in its jaws. Then he'd sit down in the water, hold it in both fore paws and eat it like a stalk of celery. Because I was downwind, that bear never knew I was there. It was an enormous animal and I could feel the hair on my neck tingle when once it turned and looked directly at me. Also, I was sure relieved when, after dining on three big suckers, it loped away. I swear that bear was eight feet long with muscles on its muscles.

Few people appreciate how powerful bears are. One of our French Canadians, Raoul Decroix, sure did. One fall, just before he was ready to butcher a two hundred pound hog, a bear broke down the pig pen and made off with it. Raoul got his rifle and trailed that bear two miles before he lost the track in a swamp. None of us could figure how that bear could do it. How did he hold that hog? Surely not in his mouth. On three legs, holding it with the fourth?

Another French Canadian, Pierre Toulouse, told of watching a bear run down a crippled deer and break its neck with one mighty swat of a forepaw. I know that bears can kill deer for I saw one eating on a deer carcass up by Brown's Dam. Of course, it's possible that the deer had died from disease or something else for bears like carrion of any kind. Maybe that's why they smell so bad.

Arvo Mattila had a camp up at the junction of Blaney Creek and the Tioga. It was well built of heavy logs and had a good roof of boards covered with sheets of galvanized iron. No one had been in it all summer. When Arvo went there to take supplies for deer season, he yelled, "Vandals! Der's been vandals here!" for half the roof was stripped off, the door was hanging ajar, and a mattress had been hauled out in front. Inside was an incredible mess. Cans and bottles and frying pans were all over the floor. Chairs were broken. The stove pipe was wrecked; the table was overturned. But vandals had not done it. There were bear tracks and claw prints everywhere.

I myself witnessed a big bear overturn a huge and solid pine stump, break it off from its tough roots and haul it ten feet away to get at the grubs or ants that infested it. Five men couldn't have done it even with crowbars. Bears seem to be especially fond of red ants. An old Indian who lived down by the tracks told me "It's dere pepper. Dey need it when dey been eating rotten meat." Bears also like honey and seem impervious to bee stings when robbing a nest. They eat the bees too.

More bears around our village were killed by the Finns than by those of other nationalities, perhaps because their folklore had many tales of evil spirits assuming the shape of the bear, or of men who had been turned into bears by some sorcerer. Bears are hard to hunt because they travel far in the forest and are always moving. Also, in the winter they leave no tracks in the snow because they're asleep. In the spring and summer their fur is often mangy and you have to wait till early fall when it is prime enough to make the bearskin caps and coats that the Finns wore so proudly.

Some of them ate the bear meat and I have too. It is very dark, almost black, and you have to be sure to get rid of the fat or you'll gag on it. Meat from an old bear is terribly tough and tastes like boot leather but that from a half grown cub is quite palatable, having a taste that is halfway between beef and pork. We usually parboiled it before roasting. Pan fried bear steaks usually went into the outhouse hole.

Under their black hides, bears have a heavy layer of fat and this was often rendered down by our people to make bear grease for our boots. It was an excellent waterproofing agent when rubbed hard into the leather but it smelled terrible. My friends, however, didn't seem to mind it at all. Nor did Alphonse Valois who used it to keep his unruly black hair smoothed down. When he asked Arminda Paquette for a date, she put it eloquently, "Non, non,

Alphonse, you stink like a bear!" He did. When he left the anteroom of the post office, he left his odor behind.

I guess that's about enough about bears. Except for one tale that Slim Jim Vester, our town liar, used to tell. He said he'd taken his horse and buckboard up to the Granite Plains after blackberries. "I allus take my gun along," he said. "Those bear, you can't trust 'em come berry time. Well, I'd got my ten quart pail half full when up comes a big old he bear aslavering and grunting. Wanted my berries. So I ups and shot him right in the ear three, four times. Fur didn't look so bad so I took my pail and rifle back to the buckboard and went bac to skin 'im out. Big hide; Mister. Tried lugging it by the tail but it keep ketching on every bush so I ups and puts it over my back and shoulders. Waal, I hadn't got more 'n fifty yards when a big old sow bear comes out of the bushes and blocks my way. I says Howdy and starts walking polite my way again. You know what, Mister? I had to screw that old sow bear four times afore she let me pass."

That's enough about bears.

Twenty-seventh Letter
Of The Alphabet

Tom Helet and Mary Modine were born twenty minutes apart on the same day of the same year in houses that sat side by side on our village hill street. From that beginning, their lives were entwined for eighteen years. As babies, they played on the floors of both houses while their mothers shared gossip over the morning coffee cups. Until they went to school, the boy and girl were inseparable companions and they remained that way through first grade. With entrance into second grade came the cruel jeers that enforced the first law of childhood: boys play with boys and girls with girls. Tom felt the social pressure first and was outraged when Mary came to his assistance and yanked at the hair of the other boy with whom he was fighting. He didn't appreciate her help. "Leave me alone!" he yelled at her. "I'm not going to play with you no more! I hate you."

But she wouldn't let him alone. If he walked up the street, she tagged along. If he played in the yard, she appeared. The more he rejected her, the more she sought his attention, any attention, good or bad. It was always bad. In school they competed furiously, taking turns having the better report card. Always Mary chose Tommy as her partner whenever this was possible. She always managed to sit near him and made his life miserable. Finally, he hit her a good one. It was a mistake because, bigger than he was, she beat him up. What was worst of all. Mary teased him unmercifully about his ears which did

stick out a bit. "Elephant ears! Elephant ears! Jug ears! Hi Jug!" The latter became his nickname and soon was adopted by everyone–even occasionally by his mother–and every time he heard it, Tommy hated Mary with a passion. He used to daydream about putting her in a wire cage

with legs and hands tied and only her neck sticking out. And then he'd put in some rats and watch gleefully as they chewed her up.

Only once had he really gotten some revenge. In the fourth grade the school put on a program at the Town Hall on May Day. They'd set up a May Pole with paper streamers coming down from its top, each held by a boy or girl who skipped and sang as they circled and wound the streamers about the pole. Though the dance had been practiced thoroughly and well, Tommy disgraced himself by giving Mary a good kick in the butt as she passed him in the final round. She screamed and socked him and the whole program was a disaster. He got a good licking when he got home.

To get away from her, at least in school, Tommy went to the principal and asked to skip the fifth grade, saying it was too easy and that he was bored. Surprisingly, his request was granted and for a month Tommy had some peace. Then Mary was promoted too, finagled a desk just in front of his own, teasing him more than ever. Once, when he dipped her pigtails in his inkwell, she didn't tattle to the teacher but told her mother who told his mother and Tommy got another licking.

In the seventh grade, Tommy had discovered that girls had legs and that Mary had pretty ones. He hated himself when he found himself looking at them. Once at a party where they played spin-the-bottle, Mary had kissed him so enthusiastically, he kept thinking about it even when he was trout fishing. And, for the first time, Tommy didn't burn up the valentine she sent him but hid it in one of the books in his bedroom.

It was in his junior year in High School, though, that he surrendered. Mary had seen him practicing some waltz steps on the sidewalk one afternoon after school and offered to teach him to dance not only the waltz but the foxtrot and two-step as well. "We've got a victrola, Tommy," she said. "My mother's gone to Ishpeming on the train and there's no one home. I can teach you." Somehow he let himself be persuaded. The session went better than he'd expected but that night Tommy didn't sleep well. The insides of his arms kept remembering how Mary felt when they held her.

The lessons continued, almost every other day, until he felt confident enough to ask her if he could take her to the Junior Prom. She refused. "No, Tommy. All the girls have decided to go as a group but if you want to sign my program when we get there, I may save a dance or two for you." He was furious. "What the hell do I care? What the hell do I care!" he told himself over and over. "I'll dance with the other girls, and to hell with Mary!" But when the time came and he found that her program had only one empty space for his name, for the last dance of the evening, he took what he could get, and didn't dance with anyone else. Just hung around in the corner with the other stags, glowering at each of her partners until his turn came. It was a waltz that seemed to end almost before it began. The two of them could have danced on forever. Almost like floating, he thought, floating with the prettiest girl in town in his arms. Tommy walked Mary home with the moonlight flickering through the maples overhead but when they stood there in the doorway, uncertain and awkward, he could not get up nerve enough to kiss her goodnight. Instead he bolted and ran away, walking the streets for an hour shivering with delight. He felt immensely tall, as though his head were brushing stars.

The next evening Tommy asked Mary to come with him to see Orion's Belt in the sky. They took the back road over to Mt. Baldy where they sat for a long time on Lover's Rock holding hands. When finally Mary said it was time to go back, he told her the tale of the twenty-seventh letter of the alphabet. It was called the sodoredo, he said, and he scratched its name with a piece of quartz on some shale. It looked like a short bar ringed on each end with a circle. It was Chinese, he said, the only Chinese letter in the alphabet. And then Tommy told her a wild imaginative tale about the ancient Emperor Tang who was utterly bored and unhappy because he had seen everything and done everything. "Find me a new pleasure or off with your head!" was his command to Ko-fu, the chief counselor. "You have one month only. Begone!"

Fearing for his life, Ko-fu journeyed to the far reaches of the empire seeking the new pleasure but in vain. Finally, when the month was almost up, he went into a great forest to hide and was starving when he met a poorly dressed, but beautiful, young woman sitting on a log sucking a chicken bone. "Food! Food!" Ko-fu cried. "No," said the woman. "I am starving too, You can't have my chicken bone but you can suck on the other end of it if you wish." Ko-fu did so and finally their sucking lips met. An electric shock traveled up his spine. "Hai, Hai!" he shouted. "I have the Emperor's new pleasure!

After he tried out the chicken bone on his five hundred concubines, the great Emperor Tang was so delighted he decreed that all the chickens in China were to be reserved for the Imperial Court, and all their bones for the royal lips alone. But the people soon discovered that they didn't need a chicken bone to perform what they called the sodoredo, that all that was required was a man and a maid with their lips touching.

It was then that Tommy kissed Mary for the first time. Over and over again they practiced making the twenty-seventh letter of the alphabet until the moon was overhead and they were exhausted. On their way home, Mary asked Tommy why he called it the sodoredo in his story. "Oh," he replied. "There's a forest bird that always sings 'sol-doh-re-doh'. Somehow every time I hear it, I think of you." Tommy whistled the notes. It became their secret call to each other.

Their senior year in High School sped by as swiftly as that last dance of the Junior Prom. Tom and Mary were together constantly. They wandered the old logging trails as well as our hill street hand in hand, caring not who saw them. They got up at dawn to cook a little breakfast together at one of their special places along a stream or lake. They studied together but did not sleep together. Tom brought Mary daisies with all petals removed except one. They collected minerals and wildflowers, birds and stars. Not once did they have a lover's quarrel. It was a year of unutterable delight. It ended too soon.

As that last idyllic summer after graduation came to a close, Tommy made preparations to go to the University of Michigan in Ann Arbor. He would have to get a part-time job for board and room but had enough money to pay the tuition. The last weeks were full of sweet agony for both of them as the separation came closer. They swore the ancient vows of eternal fidelity. They made plans. After he got his degree and a job, they would be married and have children and live happy-ever-after. Mary would wait for him. He would hitchhike home for Christmas. There were tears in their twenty-seventh letter of the alphabet. They were not to see each other again for more than half a century…

As Tom Helet drove his big car northward toward the Mackinac Bridge, he was not thinking of Mary Modine. After all, fifty-one years had passed since he'd been in the U.P. That chapter in his life had long been closed. Shortly after he had left to go to the university,

Mary and her family had moved to California. The letters between them, at first so full of yearning, had gradually petered out. She had married and so had he. No, the reason for his growing excitement was that he was going home, home to the old U.P. to start a new life. Retirement had been hard on Tom, not because of financial reasons–there was a big pension and royalties from the two inventions–but mainly because he felt lonely and useless. His wife had died three years before and two weeks of visiting his daughter and grandchildren up in Maine had been one week too long. Though his son was stationed in England, Tom had no urge to travel. That was why, when the letter from Reino Bissola arrived at his New York condominium offering to sell him the old family home in Tioga, Tom decided to buy it and spend the rest of his days in the land of his youth. The old house had been left to his sister who had sold it to Reino. It was in good condition, Reino wrote, but needed painting and a new roof. Good! Give him something to do. And he could hunt and fish again. Tom sent a check to hold it, made tentative arrangements to sell the condominium, packed his clothes and was on his way. On his way back to Tioga and the U.P.!

Suddenly at the end of a long stretch of road, he saw a shimmering silver structure that almost seemed to be floating in the sky, the Mackinac Bridge. Soon he was on it, the tires snarling on the gratings, with a glimpse of a huge ore-carrier floating down below. Exhilaration rippled up Tom's spine. There's the U.P.! Going home! Going home! Clear lakes and streams! Clean air–and the spruce and balsam and birch of his boyhood! Fifty-one years–but now he was back where he belonged. Tom even found it hard to stop for gas. Go where the wild goose goes! Go, go, go! All the doubts about the wisdom of his decision faded away. He took the old road on which he'd hitchhiked so long ago rather than the newer U.S. 2 even though the gas station attendant said the latter was much more beautiful since it ran closer to Lake Michigan. No, he was retracing his steps, erasing them. At Trout Lake he bought a pasty and a bottle of ketchup and sat on a little side road under a big hemlock tree as he ate it. Tom though about Mary for the first time. She had baked him a pasty for the other trip fifty-one years before, and he had eaten that one under a hemlock tree too. Yawning, he dozed a bit there in the sun before going on. It was good, very, very good to be going home.

At McMillan he turned west on M-28. Again he thought of Mary when he saw signs telling of the Tahquamenon Falls, the place they had once decided they would see on their honeymoon. Might be worth a side trip someday, he thought, but now the urge to get to Tioga grew strong within him. The forty mile stretch of absolutely straight road through the barrens west of Seney passed swiftly and soon he saw Lake Superior at Munising. Refueling there, he was amused to hear people talking with the old U.P. accent, prolonging their vowels, saying 'hunt-ting' and 'fissing.' Tom grinned remembering how hard it had been to get that U.P. flavor out of his own speech. Now he would have to learn it again.

He did not remember the highway at all from there to Marquette. There were magnificent stretches that ran along the dunes at the very edge of Lake Superior. There were great hills over which the road swooped into jackpine plains. Finally, he saw the first hills of home, those great granite domes dusted with fir trees, the oldest rocks in the world, people said.

Almost before he knew it, as he turned a hill curve, there was the valley of the Tioga River and the Frenchtown settlement near the depot. But the depot was gone. Up the hill street he drove, his eyes misting as he saw the old house sitting in the big yard. Tom parked the car in the barnyard. The barn was gone and a garage had taken its place. The three apple trees were still in the backyard but they were huge and needed pruning. No outhouse. The big spruce under which he had played in the sandpile as a child had disappeared but the rhubarb patch along the walk still looked lush. Reino had written that the key to the back door would be in the same place–on the ledge above–and it was there, though he'd momentarily forgotten you had to put it in the keyhole upside down. He entered.

Except for the windows, the kitchen was completely strange. No huge range with its woodbox. No pump from the cistern sat on its drainboard. The kitchen cabinet with its large drawers for flour and sugar and utensils no longer stood between the windows. Instead, everything was modern chrome and white. The round kitchen table at which the family had eaten so many meals was gone. Tom was a stranger in a strange room in a strange house. He opened the door to the pantry and closed it quickly again. Exploring further, he found a new bathroom where a closet had been and that the dining and living rooms had been merged into one. The big bookcase and piano were gone. Only the bay window was the same. Suddenly feeling very tired, Tom sat down in a comfortable but strange chair, closing his eyes so he could be for a moment among old memories. He wished he had a stiff drink to lessen the disappointment and loneliness that swept over him.

Finally, Tom shook himself and faced the situation. "No, you can never go back to what you knew fifty-one years ago," he said aloud to himself, lighting his pipe. "So you go forward. You can do anything you want to with this old house once you buy it. So why don't you go up to Reino's house and complete the deal?" After a few more moments, he did so.

Although they were just sitting down to the table, Reino was glad to see him and insisted that Tom have supper with his daughter and her husband. A really warm welcome. Almost like old times eating on an oil-cloth covered kitchen table with happy talk and laughter. It was going to be all right after all. He was back home again. As Tom wrote out the check for the house and signed the papers, Reino said, "Yah, they always come back to the U.P. as soon as they can. Too bad you had to be away so long, Tom. Oh, by the way, did you know that your old sweetheart Mary came back too? About a year ago, she came and she's also living in her old house. Her husband died and her family's grown so she came back too. This is a good place to grow old, Tom. Good huntting and fissig yet. I take you up the Tioga tomorrow, eh? Show you around, eh?"

So Mary had come back too. Tom felt no particular emotion. Indeed he was a bit surprised that there was none. Too long ago! Too many years between. Nevertheless he somehow felt comforted and less lonely. She would be fun to talk to anyway and so would Reino and there would be others. Plenty of things to do. The old house did not seem quite so strange when he returned to sit in the big chain again.

Tom did not sit there long. Up he got and combed his hair and beard. "Gad, what an old man you are!" he said to the image in the mirror. "But she'll be an old woman too." He crossed the yard and knocked on Mary's door.

A complete stranger, a matronly grey-haired plump woman with eye glasses, opened it. "Yes?" she said, and it was only when he heard her voice that Tom knew it was Mary. "I'm Tom Helet," he replied awkwardly. "I've come back too." A look of shock and disbelief came over her face but she invited him in. "Sit down, Tommy, and have a cup of coffee with me. It will be good to talk over old times and get caught up with each other."

The conversation did not flow easily. They found it hard to look at each other. Mary told the story of her life and he told his. Neither seemed particularly interested though they were both very polite. Too polite. After the coffee and cookies were gone, she went to the door with him. "You must come back again, Tommy. Any time." As he turned to leave, he noticed tears in her eyes. "It's been a long, long time," he said, "but it's good to be back."

He crossed his yard and had nearly reached the back door when suddenly he heard her whistle. It was the sodoredo, the sound of the forest bird, the twenty-seventh letter of the alphabet.

Nothing But The Truth

In that land and at that time with few newspapers and no radio or television, the thing that kept us amused and going was talk. Everything that had happened, was happening, or might be, was constantly discussed in exhaustive detail, spreading from house to house, uphill and down. In such a situation, the person who could tell a good story was prized but only so long as he stuck to something at least vaguely resembling the truth. Slimber Jim Vester was the best story teller in the whole town. Hell, he was the best one in the whole U.P. but he got little honor in our village for he was a congenital and practiced liar. He lied for the love of it.

It wasn't that Slimber Jim stretched the truth, but that he stretched the lie–and without shame. The delight of his life was to find some innocent and then to lead him on and on into an outrage of absurdity as he told his tale. Slimber would lie to anybody but he preferred young boys or traveling salesmen. They were more gullible. He burnt me plenty when I was young, not just once either, but many times. Trouble was he looked and sounded so honest and sincere, what with that shock of white hair and wide innocent blue eyes. Also, he always started off so nice and easy and plausible and the story he would be telling was always so interesting you kept forgetting he was the town liar and couldn't wait for him to finish it. I suppose it's hard for you to understand, not knowing Slimber Jim, but perhaps this sample might help.

With a couple of other kids, I was sitting down in the waiting room at the railway depot passing time till the evening train came in. As usual, there were five or six of the town's unemployed men sitting there talking by the big pot bellied stove. It was either there or Higley's saloon and Higley always booted out anyone who didn't have drinking money.

If I remember right, they were swapping deer hunting stories and a couple of traveling salesmen were listening to them lie when in with his old hound dog came Slimber Jim to stand by the stove facing the salesmen. We kids nudged each other and snickered. We knew what was coming but the old man just stood there benignly, nodding his head in complete belief no matter how wild the tale, and stroking the hound at his feet. Didn't say a word until one of the salesmen turned to him and asked if the hound were a good hunter.

"Well," said Slimber, "I can't rightly say yes and I can't say no. Old Grabber here does fair on rabbit give him a trail smoking hot, but for partridge he ain't worth a damn. Well, you can't say that either. If he sees one in a tree, he'll bark some but he don't look up much. Just keeps his nose down snuffing."

"Does he point game?" asked the salesman.

"Naw. Oh, he's got some pointer or setter or springer blood in him, I s'pose, cause he'll freeze a little when he sees a partridge on the ground but he ain't half as good as an old horse I once had."

"A horse that pointed partridge?" The salesman was getting taken.

"Yup. Come by it accidental, but he sure could point pats. Tell you how it happened. Every fall, when partridge season come around, I used to hitch old Joshua up to the buckboard and we'd mozey up them old logging roads back of the dam on the Tioga. Lots of popple there. Good spot for pats, hey Joe?" One of the other men nodded. "Best place around here," he said.

"Well," the old man continued. "We'd be driving along slow like and when I'd see a partridge in the road or in the bushes long side, I'd naturally pull in the reins and then get off the rig and shoot'im. Well, I do that ten, twelve times, day after day, and pretty soon old Joshua, when he see a partridge, he stop by hisself knowin' I was going to stop him anyway. And, of course, he'd be a-looking at the bird so I could tell whereabouts it was at. Could see'em better than I could."

"But a good pointer will lift his leg too. Don't suppose your horse would do that?"

"Hell he wouldn't! Joshua just got to stopping quicker and quicker and waiting for me to shoot and pretty soon he'd stop fast on three legs and wave the other one at the bird, he did. Damned smart horse, old Joshua, but not worth a damn on ducks. And he never would retrieve. At that he was better than old Grabber here. And he didn't have fleas either. Don't like fleas. Ain't been able to abide the sight of 'em or lice either. Ever have lice, Mister? No? Well, don't you get a room at the Beacon House up at Ontonogan. I crotched me a mess of 'em there once."

"Thanks," said the salesman. "I'll remember that. How I missed getting them sleeping in some of the Godforsaken hotels on this route I'll never know. How do you get rid of lice if you get them?"

"Well," said Slimber Jim. "It ain't really too hard, you know how. You get one of them fat, two-sided combs with the thin tines and you just keep working your head over, day after day. Better learn how to nick 'em between two fingernails like this. If you hear 'em make a little pop, you've got 'em. Got to be quick when you get 'em off the comb though. Some of them old graybacks are sure quick legged. They'll be back in yer hair before you can spit. Not too hard to get rid of them but don't try to drown 'em by washing your head. They can swim better than you can. They can't jump though–not like them flea lice I got from Lulu Belle. You happen to know Lulu Belle, Mister?"

"No, can't say I ever knew anybody by that name," said the salesman.

The old man nodded. "Probably not," he said. "She catered more to old men anyway. They didn't mine her wooden leg or the fact that sometimes she was lousy. Used to work out of Green Bay, she did. Come through here maybe once ever two months or so, her and that fleabitten poodle she slept with when she couldn't find her an old gaffer to make happy...."

"You said something about flea-lice," interrupted the salesman.

"Yup," said Slimber. "Dunno how it come to be, but Lulu Belle's lice and that damned poodle's fleas, they crossbred somehow. Made flice. That's what we come to call 'em hereabouts. Big critters, half an inch long half flea, half lice. Ruined Lulu Belle's trade once they started spreading. You got to watch out for them crossbreeds, Mister. They got the worst parts of both–like the time I mated that there blue heron with a duck. Anyway them flice are blue hell to get rid of. Only one way to do it." Slimber paused, filled and lit his pipe.

"I'm afraid to ask," said the salesman swallowing hard. "How do you get rid of flice?"

"Well, sir," said Slimber. "There's some folks say you can poison 'em and others like to snare them. You sure can't comb 'em out. They jump too good. Had a helluva time till I started studying their habits. Found they feed only on dogs by daylight. Didn't really bite me any time. It was their crawlin' around that bothered–and coming back to sleep in the hair of my crotch at night. Coming back single file. Damned near drove me crazy."

"Well, old man, how did you get rid of them?"

"Waited till after dark and they were bedded down. Then I shaved off all the hair from one side of my crotch, set fire to the other half and stabbed 'em with an ice-pick when they come out of the sugarbush."

"Pardon me," said the salesman. "I've got to take my medicine." He opened a bag and took a long swig from a bottle. There was a long pause before he spoke again.

"I think you mentioned, sir, that you had once crossed a blue heron with a duck?" The salesman's voice was respectful.

"Yep. You like chicken meat, Mister? White or dark?"

"I guess I like the dark best. Specially the drumstick."

Slimber Jim put out his hand. "So do I, Mister. Best part of the bird, I say. And that's the worst part of a duck. Not enough drumstick to pick at. Well, sir, I figgered anyone could raise a duck that had good fat drumsticks would make a million dollars. I was living up in a shack by Mud Lake at the time and I tamed me the horniest old blue heron you ever did see. Skinny as a twig he was from screwing every hen heron or thunderpumper around and not finding time enough for fishing. So I give him some of the fish I caught and pretty soon he'd eat it outa my hand, sociable-like.

Well, when you're up in the bush long enough, you keep thinking about beef meat and chicken drumsticks and such after a while and I got the idea to catch me a duck, which I did, and put it in a cage with that old heron hopin' they'd mate. Well, they did, though that old blue heron he has to get down on his knees to get the job done. Them eggs were like none I ever see, Mister. Shaped lopsided and you could hear that she mallard a-yelping every time she laid one. Nine of 'em hatched out too and they growed fast. Funny looking critters they were. Had the long legs of their old man but a short neck like their mother. Full grown, they stood maybe three feet tall. Well, maybe a mite under that, to tell the truth, but they was sure a big awkward bird. Couldn't fly either but Lord Amight, you ought to see them run and jump. Used to jump up and roost on my shack every night. Hell to feed at first cause they couldn't peck up anything on the ground without falling on their face, what with that long legs and short neck and all."

"Were they good eating?" asked the salesman. "Have big drumsticks?"

"Can't tell you, Mister, said Slimber. "Never could catch the buggers. Every morning, they'd lay out a warwhoop and jump down off the shack, then run and jump around the clearing with their mouths open catching flies. Fed on' em mainly, they did. Cleaned out all the mosquitoes and blackflies and deerflies for three miles around. I could sit outside there by the shack and never have to swat once. Never had it so good. Cleaned them flies up too good cause they kept having to go further and further to feed and when they come back home at night to sleep, they wuz so frazzled they couldn' jump up to roost and then the foxes got 'em. Well, all but one." Slimber paused and emptied his pipe in the pot-bellied stove.

The salesman was silent for a long time, but finally he bit. "What happened to that one?" he asked.

"Well," said Slimber, "that one, he was the best jumper of the bunch. Choked to death on a woodpecker." The salesman grabbed up his bags and fled into the night.

Cully Gage

"Cully Gage" was born December 1, 1905, the son of an Upper Peninsula family physician and his wife. It could be said that he was a "child of the forest", for as a very young lad he loved exploring the forests with all of its' trails and trout streams. He was familiar with nearly every acre of land from Champion north to Lake Superior.

The name Cully Gage is the pen name for one of the most common, genuine, sincere and down-to-earth men it has ever been our pleasure to know. He explained to us that as a boy, the Finns called him "Kalle", their word for Carl or Charles, and his middle name was Gage after his "marvelous grandfather". His given name is Dr. Charles Gage VanRiper but inside he has always been "Cully Gage".

After spending the early years of his life with the people he writes about and when civilization beset him, he took the train from his home town to Marquette where he enrolled at Northern Michigan University. He studied at Northern for two years and then transferred to the University of Michigan in Ann Arbor where he earned his Bachelor of Arts and Master of Arts degrees, subsequently teaching in the high schools of both Saline and Champion.

From childhood "Cully" had been plagued with a frustrating speech problem and determined to conquer it, he enrolled at the University of Iowa where he completed his Ph.D. and not only found a surcease to his own difficulties but also a new and challenging field. He returned to Michigan and began teaching at Western Michigan University in Kalamazoo.

In 1936 he established the Speech Clinic at Western Michigan University providing help and correction for many "faltering tongues". He has authored numerous text books dealing with the cause and correction of speech difficulties. "Cully" worked very closely with many of his students helping them overcome the anxieties of hesitant speaking. Many of his students have not only lived in his home but have also helped him plant pine trees at more than one cabin site. They were introduced to the serenity of the woodlands and streams of the northland by this fine man.

Now in semi-reirement he shares two beautiful worlds: the "forest child" has a 122 year old farmhouse in downstate Portage where he has large organic garden and is striving to produce his Perfect Potatoes. He has developed a beautiful park on the land surrounding the house and 30 foot pine trees planted as seedlings grace the area. He also maintains a special retreat in the Upper Peninsula of Michigan. His wife Catharine, their three kids and nine grandkids all share in his feelings for both where carpets of pine needles and love abound.

For all who know and admire Cully Gage, that certain twinkle of mischief in his eyes will always be present and his stories of early life in the great Upper Peninsula will provide hours of entertainment and reminiscing.

We wish to take this opportunity to thank Cully for sharing his stories of those great people and events which were such an integral part of his early life in the land he loves so much. By allowing us to record them on paper they will be remembered and enjoyed forever.

Avery Color Studios, Inc.

Sue Krill, the illustrator, is the daughter of Cully Gage. She is the mother of four children, teaches flute, aerobic dancing and, although she has long been painting, these are her first pen and ink sketches. Although now a native of Grand Haven, Michigan she too loves the Upper Peninsula and has managed to visit there every year of her life.

STILL ANOTHER
NORTHWOODS
READER

BOOK SIX

The Inheritance

In my other Northwoods Readers I've told several tales about Eino, the swarthy little Finn and Emil, the big blonde Norwegian who lived happily in Tioga long ago. Here's another one about those two old bachelors who lived in houses next to each other up by the old mine.

First of all, I must tell you about how they managed to live so well despite being seventy years of age and long unemployed. Both had little pensions of $30 a month from the mining company for which they'd worked for many years. That may not seem like very much now, but then a dollar was worth twenty times what it goes for today. Besides, they didn't need much biting money because they shot a lot of deer in season and out, caught trout and pike all summer, and they had a common garden that produced all the potatoes, cabbage and rutabagas they needed. Emil had a chicken yard and coop behind his house, while Eino had a cow and cow barn, so they had all the milk and eggs they needed. Emil did the canning of meat, apples, and berries; Eino did the baking. No, they may not have had much but they had enough, and they shared everything together. Neither had a care in the world. Life was very, very good.

Or it was until one day Emil got a letter from Norway. "It's a registered letter," Annie, our postmistress told me when she asked me to notify Emil, "and he has to sign for it up here in person. Tell him it looks important."

I heard Eino and Emil arguing long before I got to their houses to find the two old buggers sitting on empty nail kegs on Eino's porch, playing checkers on a third keg between them. "Yump!" shouted Emil, "Yump, you dumb Finn. Why don't you yump?"

"No," said Eino in his quiet voice. "I no jump. I no so dumb. If I jump then you jump two, three times. No!"

Finally I got their attention and told Emil about the registered letter waiting for him up at the post office. "Annie says it's from Norway and you should come get it right away."

The old Norwegian scratched his head. "Who from?" he said. "My father, mother they die long ago. No brother. One sister I write to three time and never hear back. Maybe she dead too." He sure was puzzled.

So was my father that afternoon when Emil and Eino came to him. Emil waving the letter and explaining and asking, all in a confused jumble that Dad couldn't make head or tail of. "You sign paper for me, Doctor, eh? Paper saying me Emil Olsen. I got no pastor for say it. No Norwegian church here. Swede Lutheran but I don't go. Hell with Swedes! Maybe I get money, eh?" He opened the letter and showed it to my father.

Dad shook his head. "Emil, I can't read Norwegian and I can't make any sense about what you're trying to tell me. I suggest you take your letter over to Leif Backe's house in Halfway and have him translate it into English, then bring it back and I'll see if I can help you."

After the two men left, Dad shook his head. "Lord, the problems our people bring me!" he muttered. It was true. Since many of our villagers were first generation immigrants and were literate only in their own languages, Finnish, French and others, whenever they were faced with any kind of legal document they came to my father for advice because he was educated and because they trusted him completely. He had examined contracts for pulpwood, notices of jury duty, sales agreements, oh a lot of other things. Not that he ever played lawyer, he always referred people to Tim Clancy in Ishpeming if the problem needed more than just explaining.

This is the letter's translation that Emil and Eino brought back to Dad the next day:

"As executors of the estate of Knud Olsen, deceased May 2, 1915, we are seeking to locate one Emil Olsen, nephew of said Knud Olsen. According to our information, he never married nor had children and there seem to be only two possible beneficiaries, a niece and nephew. Aud Olsen, now deceased, of Tronheim, Norway and Emil Olsen who emigrated to the United States of America about the year 1870. A letter found in the effects of Aud Olsen, gives the address of said Emil Olsen as being of Tioga, Michigan, U.S.A., and it is to that address this letter is being sent.

In order to be certain that you are indeed Knud Olsen's nephew and beneficiary, it is necessary that you provide the following: 1. The names of your father and mother; 2. The date and place of your birth; 3. Statements from your pastor and/or mayor that you are said Emil Olsen. Upon receipt of the above information, providing that it is satisfactory, we shall send you the bank draft of your legacy."

After reading the translation Dad said, "Well, Emil, it looks like you're coming into some money. I'll write you out a statement saying that you exist. We don't have a mayor but I'm township supervisor and that should be good enough. I'll write it on official stationary and stamp it with the township seal so it'll look official." This is what Dad wrote:

"I hereby certify that Emil Olsen, formerly of Trondheim, Norway, has been a citizen of this village of Tioga, Michigan for at least twenty years. I know him well both as an employee and as a medical patient."

He then signed his name and embossed the letter with the Township seal. (I remember that embosser very well. Working like a stapler, I'd stamp out a lot of circles from store paper when Dad was on his house calls, then cut them out to serve as play money for our poker games up in the hayloft. Yes, even at the age of ten we boys had already learned not to try to fill an inside straight.)

So Emil mailed his letter with the enclosure to Norway and nothing much happened for two months. Meanwhile, he and Eino lived their good life getting ready for winter. They cut ferns and bracken and hauled many loads of leaves to the cow barn for bedding; they made wood, lots of it, enough to last till spring. They smoked thirty pike they'd caught in Lake Tioga and hung them from the rafters of Eino's summer kitchen. Potatoes and rutabagas were dug and stored in the cellars. Eino made a big jar of sauerkraut. Then they went hunting to get venison for canning when the autumn approached snow time. Every bit of it was fun, more fun than work because of the companionship felt by the two old friends. Life was very, very good.

Oh, there were a few times when Emil wished the money, if any, would come. "Maybe I get enough raha to buy a horse and wagon," said Emil when the two old men got tired of hauling the maple saplings they'd cut on Keystone Hill. And there were times when they wished they could have a drunk from the bottle of whiskey they were saving for New Year's Day. But, for the most part, they just forgot about the inheritance. Let the winter come. They were ready for it. It's a good feeling that few people from Down Below can appreciate.

Then the letter came. In it was a bank draft for 35,000 kroner. About five thousand dollars. A fortune! Emil Olsen was a rich man.

He was also a very troubled man. "Now what I do?" he asked my father. "Kroner no good this country." Dad told him to take the bank draft to the Miner's National Bank in Ishpeming where for a fee they would cash it into dollars, and then to establish a checking account and a savings account. When Emil didn't know what they were, Dad tried to explain but it was obvious that the old Norwegian didn't understand.

Emil didn't sleep much that night because he kept fingering that letter under his pillow to make sure it was there. During breakfast with Eino the next morning he asked, "Eino, you got any money? I got dollar fifty, not enough to go Ishpeming on train. I pay you back. You come with me, eh?"

Eino went down to his cellar and came back with a ten dollar bill from the graveyard money he'd saved long ago. "O.K., Emil. Here enough pay round trip maybe. But you pay back. Coffin money." A lot of our old folks in Tioga had some anxiety about a proper burial. They didn't want to be shoveled naked into the cold ground. Unlike his friend, Eino had always been a lookaheader.

Neither of them had been on a train for many years so they enjoyed the ride, but when they got to Ishpeming they were lost. Finally Emil asked a passerby where to get to Miner's Bank and was told to find the Indian statue horse trough and go north across the street. That was easy but it was a good thing Eino was there because Emil couldn't read the big sign, being illiterate in English even after many years.

When the big Norwegian presented the letter and bank draft to the teller she called the manager who asked if he wanted to deposit it in a checking or savings account. "No," said Emil. "Cash. I keep all money myself, yah." The manager told him that was unwise, that he might be robbed or lost it, that a bank account was as good as gold, but Emil was stubborn. He'd heard that banks sometimes failed. "Give money," he said, "twenty dollar bills, yah."

Now five thousand dollars in twenty dollar bills made up quite a packet and to keep enough of them for other customers the teller had to include five one hundred dollar bills and twenty fifty dollar ones. One of the latter was kept by the bank to cover the costs of the currency exchange but all the rest were counted out and put in a canvas bag labeled with the bank's name. To make sure he wasn't being cheated, Emil made the poor teller count them a second time. "Eino, you watch and count too," he whispered hoarsely. Finally they left the bank, Emil looking pregnant with the money bag under his sweater. They still had two hours to spend before the next train home.

Robbers? The thought had never come to Emil before but every man he met on the street of Ishpeming looked as though he might be one. The money sack kept trying to slip out of the front of his sweater. He had to buy a belt to keep it in place, though like most of the men in the U.P. he'd never worn one. They held up their heavy pants with suspenders, usually red ones. He needed new suspenders too; those he wore were linked to the fasteners with haywire. But that meant he'd have to open the bag to get money and he sure didn't want to do that on the street, not with all those suspicious characters coming by. Often looking behind to see if they were being followed, they made their way to Voelker's Saloon and there Emil stationed Eino to watch for robbers while he went around the back to open the money sack. Then, giving one twenty dollar bill to Eino, and keeping another in his pocket they went to Bradstad's department store where he bought a belt for fifty cents and two pairs of scarlet suspenders, one for himself and the other for Eino. The belt worked fine! He still bulged in front but the money was secure, so the two old men returned to the saloon. "We buy only two beers, Eino," Emil said. "No get drunk till we get back to Tioga." Riding on the train later he told Eino how once when he'd worked in the woods all winter up by Big Bay he'd come out with over two hundred dollars pay only to get drunk and find himself the next day without a penny of it. That wasn't going to happen this time, no sir.

When the train butcher (I don't know why they called them that but they did) rolled his cart down the aisle between the red plush covered seats monotonously chanting, "Candees, seegars, oranges, sandwiches, bananays," Emil bought two oranges, two bananas and two cigars. When you're rich you can live it up! It had been many years since either of the two old men had tasted such fruit or smoked anything but Peerless in their black corncob pipes.

They were still smoking their cigars when they got off the train at Tioga's station. "Seegars, eh, Emil?" said Francoise Vervaile when he saw them. "Got lots of raha now, I see, yes." You borrow me one dollaire for beer, maybe, for celebrate?" Unwisely Emil gave him the money. How had the village known so soon about his inheritance? Of course, everybody in Tioga always knew everything that happened to anybody and immediately. Still it was a bit unsettling. Emil didn't like the way Francoise looked at his bulging sweater either. Not that he'd ever stolen anything; no one in Tioga ever stole because everybody would know but just the same, he'd better find a good hiding place for the money. Worry wrinkles crept across the old Norwegian's forehead.

After a supper of venison stew left over from the night before, Emil went back to his house to think, an activity to which he was unaccustomed. Pulling down the window shades, he spread out all the money on the table, tried to count it to make sure, but soon gave up. Too much! Somehow he would have to find a place to hide it, but where? Should he divide it? Made no sense to have it all in the same place so someone could steal it all at once. What would he put it in? Jars? He didn't have enough empty ones. They were all full of fruit and meat. Maybe Eino would have some or he could buy some. Yah, he could buy all the jars he wanted now. Should he bury them in the garden or in the cellar or in Eino's cowbarn? Emil's head ached from all the thinking. Finally he put the money in the canvas sack, tucked it under his pillow, and went to bed, but that was too lumpy so he moved it to the bottom of the blankets. No, someone could come in and lift them and take the raha without his even waking up. Finally he put the sack between his legs at the crotch and went to sleep, a very restless sleep.

In the morning the bag was still there when it was time to go over to Eino's house for breakfast of blueberry pancakes with maple syrup, blueberries they'd picked together in July month, and the syrup they'd boiled down in April. That had been fun. Now he could buy them without any of the work though it really wasn't work. The coffee was weak because they'd had to be careful. He'd go up to Flynn's store and buy a whole pailful and they'd have coffee so strong that it would leave a fuzz on the tongue. Now he could have anything he wanted. Lots of raha now! He patted the money sack he'd brought along, not wanting to leave it in his own cabin even for a moment.

"Eino," he said, as they smoked their corncob pipes afterward, "You my best friend. I got too much raha now. I give you half."

"No," Eino replied. "That your raha, Emil. I don't want. I got enough for me to make it through win-ter. What I need raha for?" That set off a long argument, another enjoyable one, but Eino could not be persuaded. "You always dumb Finn," Emil roared, "I give you free and you no take. You crazy!"

Having decided to put his money into jars and to hide them somewhere, Emil and Eino went up to Flynn's store to buy them, but that presented another problem. Emil didn't want to carry the money sack up there and he didn't want to leave it in his unlocked house. Back then in Tioga no one ever locked his house lest he insult his neighbors. Indeed neither the front nor the back door even had a lock. Finally Emil put on his old packsack with the money bag in it, after taking out two twenty dollar bills for his pocket, and up the hill street they went. The news of his inheritance had preceded them, for every person they met had to stop to congratulate Emil on his good fortune. "How much you get Emil? I hear you millionaire now, eh?" "You-sta go buy Flynn's store, Emil?" "Want to buy horse and wagon, Emil, for carry groceries?" They were genuinely happy for him but they also wanted to know if he'd gotten "stuck up," now that he was rich. That's the worst thing you can be called in the U.P. Any stranger who moved to our village was immediately and carefully scrutinized for any sign of condescension, and if it were there even in the slightest degree he was ostracized. Each of us was as good as anyone else, not better. Emil passed the testing. "Yah, I get a little money from mine uncle but no so much," he lied.

Even Mr. Flynn had heard the news. "Mr. Olsen," he said, rubbing his hands uncon-sciously, "Instead of climbing the hill, I can send my delivery man by your house each day if you want something. You can charge it and pay once a month." That was the first time any-one had called him Mister and Emil kind of liked that, so besides the Mason jars he also bought a whole ham and a can of peaches to stash in the packsack atop the money bag. "We going eat high on hog, now, Eino," he said. "Anything you want, Eino?" Eino said no.

While at the store Sulu Kangas looked surprised to see Emil buying the jars. "Why you can now, Emil? All berries gone and apples too." Emil told him he'd just shot another deer for the winter and had to put it up. Nevertheless, he knew that everyone in town would hear about it and think that he was going to hide his money in the jars. Things were sure getting complicated and that damned money was making a liar out of him.

As they boiled potatoes and fried a slice of the ham for dinner, Emil asked Eino for ideas about where to hide the money. It was a-worrying him, he said. He just couldn't be lugging that money bag everywhere all the time.

Eino wasn't much help. Every suggestion he made was rejected for one reason or another. Oh, how they argued. Finally Emil asked, "Where you hide graveyard money? Maybe I hide same place." Eino told him he kept it in his mattress. "Oh, for dumb!" Emil shouted. "Mattress first place robber look." So it went on and on.

All the rest of the month was miserable because Emil wouldn't leave his house, although he'd bough padlocks and hasps for both doors and hid the bag under the flooring of his cellar. That didn't allay his anxiety much because he always kept tearing it up to see if it was still there even if he'd only gone over to Eino's house. When Eino told him he was going nuts about that money and should forget it, Emil put his fears to a test by digging three holes in the garden, then replacing the earth and smoothing it down. The next morning it was evident that someone had been there. "Nah," said Eino when he looked. "That's no robber been there; that's a skunk been hunting grubs and worms. They always go for fresh holes." But Emil wasn't convinced. "There robbers here," he said.

No, it wasn't much fun, that money business. Eino began to go to Higley's saloon for a beer or two alone and to other places too. When deer season came, Eino had to hunt by himself and deeply resented having to lug the buck home without help. "Why hunt?" Emil said. "I buy you steaks, pork, maybe even chickens. I got lotsa money."

"Damn your raha," Eino replied. "Deer meat better, not so fat, I like walking woods too. You going money nuts, Emil." The fine fellowship was disappearing. There was anger between them although unspoken. Rarely did they play checkers together after Emil insisted they do it only at his house. Sometimes a day or two would go by without even a meal together. It was wrong, all wrong. Both were lonely and unhappy, and even their arguments were only half-hearted when they did occur.

One of them wasn't. It occurred when Eino insisted that Emil go to Ishpeming and put the money in the bank so he wouldn't have to worry about being robbed all the time. He could get out the money any time he wanted. Made no sense to keep it all in the house. Keep a hundred dollars only for spending, then go get more when he needed it. The old Norwegian grew purple with fury. "No!" he roared. "I no give bank my money. Banks go bad and I lose everything. No! No! No!" Though they argued long and hard Emil wouldn't give in. There's nothing as stubborn as a Norwegian–except perhaps a Swede.

"Then spend it and get rid of it," Eino advised. "That money got you and me in jailhouse. Spend it!"

Well, that was an idea. Emil had come to realize what a curse all that money was. It was spoiling the fine life he and Eino had lived together for so many years. He was tired of worrying day and night. Get rid of it. Yah, that made sense.

So Emil and Eino went on a spending spree the likes of which Tioga had never known. At first it was easy. They bought a case of whiskey and a keg of beer at Higley's but soon got tired of drinking it by themselves. More fun drinking at the saloon. Then they bought new mackinaws, sweaters, long underwear, many socks, boots, mittens, always getting the best but hating throwing out their old ones. Five pails of Peerless tobacco they purchased and six fancy briar pipes which bit their tonges so much they went back to the old blackened corncobs that they'd smoked for years. They got new jackknives but put them away because their old ones felt better. The new axe and crosscut saw weren't any better. A box of canned soup, a big tub of lard, a big bag of Pillsbury flour cluttered Emil's kitchen. Two slabs of bacon hung in Eino's shed though they still had half a one left from before. Emil bought a huge box of chocolates that they didn't even open. The maple sugar they'd boiled down in April was sweeter. One evening, they counted the money Emil had left and were appalled to find that it still totalled four thousand dollars.

"We got to buy big stuff," Emil said. "We never get rid of money this way. What we buy, Eino?" The old Finn gave it a lot of thought.

"How about horse and wagon and sleigh for carry wood and hay?" he suggested.

"Yah, yah, that's good," Emil answered. "And then we hire someone build horsebarn with hay loft and bins for oats and bran for cow and bags corn for chickens." He was enthusiastic again, Eino thought, more like old Emil.

So they hired John Untilla, Mullu's father, to build the barn and when it was finished they got a young horse and wagon and sleigh from Fred Hamel. For paying cash, Hamel threw in two tons of hay and five bags of oats too. They only hitched up the horse once before deep snows came, drove it down to Lake Tioga and back, and then put it up for the winter. That gave them more chores to do with feeding, throwing down hay from the loft, and shoveling manure but it would be good to have a horse in the spring when they could go way up the river fishing trout.

They counted the money again. Finding that there were still more than three thousand dollars left they were depressed. At night they pored over the Montgomery Ward catalog, even the ladies underwear section, but found nothing they wanted. One afternoon they went on the train again to Ishpeming, visiting all the stores but the only thing they bought were two big banana splits at the Chocolate Shoppe and two beers at Voelker's saloon. It sure was hard to get rid of raha!

Remembering they'd often wished for a boat they could put on Lake Tioga to fish for northerns, they offered Reino Kangas one hundred dollars for his. No, he said, I sell you boat for twenty dollars, that's all it's worth. Our people in Tioga were too honest. So they had boat that they'd pick up next spring season after breakup.

Eino suggested buying land, maybe two forties of spruce and balsam, but Emil demurred. "When all money gone, how we pay taxes?" he asked. Eino agreed.

One of the good things that came from all this frustrated spending was that Emil had lost his fear of being robbed. Indeed, sometimes he wished someone would rob him. He tore the locks off his house and left the money bag invitingly on the kitchen table, but of course no one took it. No, the damned money bag was still there and so was the compulsion to get rid of it. It was evil. It had almost ruined their friendship and might again. "Dig a hole and drop it through the ice on the lake," said Eino one day but Emil had a better idea. "No, I give it away. I give to poor."

That too wasn't easy. First of all, there weren't many of us in Tioga that by our standards could be called really poor. Though they often had little biting money, they had warm cabins and plenty of stuff in the basement they'd canned along with the potatoes they had dug. They also were very proud as the two old men found out when they tried to give them money. Katy Flanagan chased them halfway down the street with her broom when they tried to put a twenty dollar bill in her hand, despite the fact that she had four children and a long-gone husband. Others too refused to take any money and showed clearly their feelings of being insulted. In fact, the only one who accepted any was Pete Ramos who immediately headed for Higley's saloon to spend it.

The next thought that hit them was to throw a helluva party for the whole town on Midsummer's Day in June with pasties, beer and red pop for all. They'd hire an accordion band from Ishpeming for dancing and entertainment. But Tioga had no place big enough to hold nine hundred people. Where would they get the tables and benches? OK, they'd have a picnic down at the beach at Lake Tioga. Exploring the possibility, Emil and Eino went to Ishpeming's two bakeries. "A thousand pasties? You crazy?" was the response they got. Then they thought of making a long trench by the lake, filling it with charcoal and baking the world's largest pasty. How many jugs ketchup? How many jars pickles? In the end, the logistics were obviously beyond them. No, that wouldn't work.

Desperate, they came to my father for advice. He heard them out. "You mean you want to give away two or three thousand dollars? You sure?" Yes, they answered. That damned money was wrecking their lives. They didn't need it or want it. "Then give it to the churches," Dad said. "And to the library which hasn't been able to purchase a new book for twenty years."

"That good idea!" said Emil, and Eino agreed. "But I no give any Norwegian raha to Swede Lutheran church. Mine uncle Knud, he turn in grave. Catholic church, OK; Finn Lutheran, Methodist OK; yah, even Holy Roller church back Finntown OK. Library, OK too. Yah, good idea!"

So it was done. Keeping only two one hundred dollar bills for their mattresses, they divided the rest of the money five ways and distributed it to the astounded recipients. How the tongues of Tioga waggled! Father Hassell preached a sermon in their praise; so did the other pastors. The Library Board gave them a citation. They were heros in the town, though privately everyone thought they'd gone nutty in their old age.

Finally the money was all gone. Emil and Eino built a bonfire in their backyard and burned the money sack while passing a bottle of whiskey back and forth. Then they resumed their lives as they had led them long before, as though nothing had happened. A good life, yah! Two good friends together.

But on Midsummer Day when I was up at the post office Annie asked me to tell Emil that his pension check had come and another letter too. The other letter was from the lawyer in Norway. "Dear Mr. Olsen," it said, "We have discovered further assets of your late uncle and are therefore enclosing a bank draft for 15,000 kroner to conclude the settlement of his estate."

Thanksgiving 1913

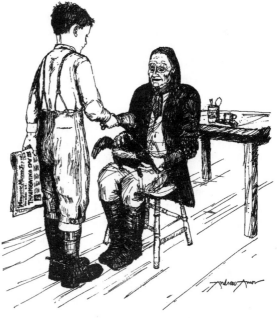

Clomp Clomp–Plop Plop; Clomp Clomp–Plop Plop. That was the familiar sound made by the hooves of old Maude as Mr. Marchand drove the horse up our hill street every morning and evening bringing the mail bags to the post office. And that was the way our days went by in the little sleepy village of Tioga in the early days of this century. Like Maude, time never galloped; it just plodded along.

Perhaps that was why we made such a big thing of our holidays. We needed something to anticipate and something to remember. December brought Christmas, January, New Years Day. With February came Valentine's Day, followed by St. Patrick's Day in March when our Irish fourth grade teacher, Miss Feeley, told us about the Kings of Ireland and pinned bits of green ribbon on us. Then came Easter, May Day, and in June Midsummer Day, the latter celebrated mainly by the Finns and Scandihoovians. The Fourth of July was one of the best ones with parades and fireworks, but August and September were barren months. Labor Day had not yet been invented. October's highlight was, of course, Halloween with dirty tricks (but no treats), and the dumping of outhouses. Finally, came Thanksgiving.

Thanksgiving in the forest village of Tioga took up most of a week. In school we always had a program about the Pilgrims which our friends and parents always attended. One year, as I recall, I was chosen to be John Alden in a skit about the Courtship of Miles Standish, a role I sure hated because I wanted to be one of the Indians. When the time came to perform I was so petrified being up there on the stage I forgot my lines and stammered miserably as I proposed for the shy Miles that Priscilla (Elsie Hebert) should marry him. "Why don't you speak for yourself, John?" Priscilla asked coyly and the audience broke out in great gales of laughter. But the show went on. The Indians and Pilgrims gnawed on the corn we'd colored yellow and munched brown paper drumsticks before we closed by singing "Over The River And Through The Woods."

Not many of the people in Tioga had ever eaten a turkey or even viewed one, though my own family always did on that important feast day. Nevertheless, they fed well on what they had, perhaps an old rooster from the chicken yard or a couple of ducks shot earlier and frozen in the back shed, or perhaps only a choked rabbit that had been snared in Goochie Swamp. But Thanksgiving meant having all you wanted to eat for once–even second helpings. It was also a day of thanks, thanks that we had survived, thanks that we had escaped the calamities that happened to others in our town. With the thanks, too, there was always a little prayer–that we'd be able to make it through the win-ter. (In Tioga, we never said winter. We always put a little pause between the syllables–as we did in saying hun-ting. The U.P. has a brogue all its own.)

No one looked forward to Thanksgiving as much as did my father, the village doctor. Dad really loved to eat–perhaps because he had almost starved when putting himself through medical school. Why he never got fat, having three big meals each day, I do not know for he stuffed himself at each one. Two of those meals always included pie with a chunk of sharp cheddar cheese. Dad like any kind of pie but his favorite was venison mince meat pie. That mince pie was always the high point of our Thanksgiving feast. Oh, the turkey was fine, the mashed potatoes and rutabgas O.K., the oysters on the half shell very good, but it was that venison mince pie that was the zenith of the whole meal. Only that brought the compliment of compliments: "You have acquired merit, Madam!" Woe to any patient that came to the door when Dad was eating his pie.

I suspect that my Mother's anticipation of Thanksgiving was not that great.She had to do the cooking, set the table with fine linen and the fluted Haviland dishes, then afterward cope with a mountain of pots, dishes and pans. Nor did she particularly care for mince pie. This I could not understand when I was a boy for, like my father, I loved it beyond measure. Indeed, it wasn't until years later, just after I was married, when I raved about my mother's marvellous mince pie (and had shot my deer for the venison) that I understood. My new bride wrote my mother for the recipe and here it is:

> 4 pounds of venison; 2 pounds beef suet; five pounds diced apples; one pound dried figs; one pound pitted dates; four pounds golden raisins; four pounds dried currants; one cup candied citron; one cup candied orange peel; one cup candied lemon peel; eight cups beef broth; four cups boiled cider; two cups apple brandy; two cups dark rum; two cups molasses; four cups light brown sugar; two cups currant jelly; four teaspoons salt; four teaspoons ground cinnamon; two teaspoons ground nutmeg; one teaspoon ground cloves; one teaspoon mace.

> Brown venison (half-inch slices) on bothsides in frying pan then transfer to large pot, cover with two inches of water and cook over low heat for three hours. Cool, then dice meat finely. Also chop up apples, figs and dates and add

to kettle. Also the suet. Chop up the citron, orange peel and lemon peel and stir thoroughly into beef broth, cider, brandy, molasses and rum, adding salt and spices. Simmer for two hours uncovered until thickened then can in sterilized jars. This makes eight quarts, enough for eight pies.

My lovely new bride took one look at the recipe, snorted, and bought a jar of mincemeat at the corner grocery, telling me in no uncertain terms that she would never be the saint my mother was.

It was a fine U.P. day, that Thanksgiving of 1913. New snow had fallen overnight; the sky was very blue and there was a lot of cold sunshine. Fine day for a feast! But suddenly at breakfast my mother dropped the bomb. "John," she said to my father, "what kind of pie would you like to have for dinner?"

"He gave her an incredulous look. "Why venison mincemeat pie, of course. What else?"

"I'm sorry, John," my mother replied. "All the mincemeat is gone. I used the last jar of it to make a pie that you could take to deer camp, remember? I was sure that you'd get a deer as you always do and had planned to make new mincemeat when you brought it home. But you didn't."

Dad was stunned. "No mince pie? No venison mincemeat pie on Thanksgiving?" He was outraged.

"No," Mother said quietly. "I canned sixteen quart jars of it last year but it's all gone. You can have blueberry pie, apple pie, pumpkin pie, wild blackberry pie, and I even have a quart of the sugarplum-rhubarb that you always like…."

Dad got up from the table. "No mince pie? Lord, if I'd known that I would have shot one of those does. Thanksgiving and no mince pie! No. I don't want any other kind of pie." He stalked out of the house biting his lower lip as he always did when furious.

By the time it was almost eight o'clock and time to start doing my chores, but as I passed through the kitchen Mother stopped me. "Cully," she said, "I'd appreciate it if you'd go down to the cellar and bring up jars of pumpkin and cranberry sauce that are on the left hanging shelf. Remember when we picked them in the bog last September before the first frost came?"

Yes, I remembered those cranberries. Those little red and white globules were fun to pick out of the gray sphagnum moss. Unlike blueberries or wild raspberries, they filled up a pail in a hurry. After she thanked me Mother asked for some more help. "Cully, please take these tweezers and pluck the pinfeathers out of the turkey. I'm pressed for time even though we won't be having dinner until two o'clock. That big turkey will take five hours roasting, I'm sure. Meanwhile, I'll make your father a pumpkin pie. Once it's before him, I don't think he'll be able to resist it." Taking a big scoop of flour from the big bin of the kitchen cabinet, she sifted it on the tin-covered counter top.

Plucking those damned pinfeathers wasn't much fun. Plain tedious, it was, and I felt relieved when Mother took the tweezers from me to finish the job. "Now, Cully, remember to keep the woodbox filled and take the horse a sugar lump and put some molasses in the cow's bran pail before pouring in the hot water from the reservoir on the range. Oh yes, and put out a chunk of suet for the whiskey jacks, the Canadian Jays. It's Thanksgiving Day for them too. Oh Cully, you're a fine helper. Don't know what I'd do without you."

So I did my chores, throwing down fresh hay for the horse and cow through the holes in the loft, putting down new straw in their stalls and giving old Billy not only the sugar lump but an extra scoop of oats. Then I took scratch feed to the chickens in the coop behind my father's hospital. There were only three brown eggs that day from our little flock of Rhode Island Reds. They never laid very well once the snows came. I brought in some new firewood and swept the front porch.

By noon I was finished and the wonderful warm smells of the kitchen sure set me to hungering. Famished, I begged Mother for a cookie but she wouldn't let me have one. "No, Cully," she said. "You'll just have to save your appetite for the turkey and trimmings. Go out and play for an hour or two."

Knowing that my friends would be eating their own dinners at that time I decided instead to go up to see my friend Pete Halfshoes, our resident full-blooded Ojibway Indian. Dad said he was older than my Grampa Gage but he sure didn't look it. His long hair was jet black and there wasn't a wrinkle on his coppery brown face. I sure like Pete Halfshoes. He'd served in the regular United States army, had fought in the Spanish-American War and had been an Indian scout in the expeditions against the Apaches. Walking with him in the woods was a revelation. He knew every animal track and forest sound and smell. Pete had a curious way of walking in the woods that I tried to imitate but couldn't, seeming to walk on his toes rather than on the balls of his feet. He didn't walk; he glided silently. But he liked me, I think, though, of course, he never said so. Pete never talked much.

When I got to his house, Pete Halfshoes greeted me as always by holding up the flat of his hand to which I responded in the same way. He was having his Thanksgiving dinner, eating pork and beans out of a can with a spoon. Nothing else was on the table but a cup of tea, a piece of korpua, and a handful of dried berries in a saucer. Thinking of the huge banquet that awaited me at home I was so upset I almost cried. It wasn't fair! It wasn't fair! When Pete broke off a piece of his one korpua and handed it to me I could hardly swallow it. This old Indian was sharing his meager food with me as had his ancestors with the Pilgrims of that first Thanksgiving Day. I left hurriedly. It wasn't fair!

How vividly I recall that Thanksgiving dinner of 1913. With the big brown turkey before him there was Dad at the west end of the long oval table sharpening the carving knife with the round file. Mother was opposite him pouring her tea from the gleaming silver teapot. Across from me was my little brother Joe, aged three, banging his silver cup on the highchair. Dorothy, then only one year old, was sleeping in her crib behind my mother and between the box stove and Aunt Rebecca's sea shell cabinet. On the south wall of the dining room hung the huge wolf skin while above the door the deer head with its huge antlers presided. The table with many dishes on the white linen tablecloth was full of promise.

But there was something terribly wrong. Usually such a meal was filled with gay conversation, teasing and laughter, but that day there was none. Mother was too exhausted to talk much, Dad was still biting his lower lip thinking of the mince pie that was not to be, and I was thinking only of Pete Halfshoes and his can of pork and beans. When Dad passed me my plate heaped high with turkey, stuffing, and a lot of other things I felt I could not eat a single bite of it. But I did, of course. We Gages had to eat everything on the plate whether we liked it or not, and besides I was very hungry since I'd had my breakfast many hours before. Nevertheless, every single mouthful made me feel terribly guilty. It wasn't fair!

No one took a second helping except my father, and I think he did so only to postpone the challenge presented by the pumpkin rather than the mince pie. Having consumed his big drumstick (Dad always got the dark meat), he carved himself two big slices from the thigh, ladled the brown gravy onto a mound of stuffing, toyed with his Waldorf salad, ate two more oysters, and then, as my mother watched, forked up the tip of the pumpkin pie tentatively. "Not bad, Madam!" he said as he ate all the rest of it. "Not bad!" Patting his bulging vest, he left the table to take a siesta on the couch in the living room. Mother gave me a wink. All was well!

But it wasn't! While I helped Mother with the dishes I couldn't get Pete Halfshoes out of my head. Then came the terrible thought that I should steal the other drumstick and take it up to the old Indian. No, no, no! I couldn't do that! It would be stealing and we Gages didn't ever steal, nor lie, nor cheat, nor shoot does. I vividly recalled how only two years before, when I was only six, that I'd come back from Flynn's store with a pocketful of dried prunes I'd swiped from the open keg by the candy counter. When I innocently offered one of the prunes to my mother and she found out how I'd gotten them all hell broke loose. What a lecture! What shaming! "Gages never, never steal!" she told me. "I'll not tell your father. He'd spank you too hard but promise me you'll never do anything like that again." I promised. Then she unscrewed the bottom of my little cast iron bank, took out a quarter and sent me up to Mr. Flynn with it along with my apologies.

Despite that promise I just felt I had to steal that drumstick for the old Indian, my friend. So after my mother had gone to her bedroom to rest from her long labors and Dorothy was still sleeping in her crib and my brother Joe was building little houses out of dominoes, I sneaked into the pantry, twisted off the big drumstick, wrapped it in newspaper, hid it under my shirt, then went to Pete's cabin.

I found Pete there with his pet skunk on his knee, stroking her white striped pelt. When I pulled the package out from under my shirt and opened it I blurted, "This is for you, Pete. Happy Thanksgiving! I'd have brought you a piece of mince pie too but we didn't have any mincemeat this year because Dad didn't get his buck." I could tell that the old Indian was touched though, of course, his face didn't move a muscle. "You good boy, Cully," was all he said.

It sure seemed like a long way home overwhelmed as I was by the enormity of my good deed. I was a thief. How I dreaded the coming of suppertime! And when it did come I was rigid with shame and fright as my mother put the carcass of the turkey before my father. He gave it a hard look. "Where's my drumstick?" he roared. "Where's the other drumstick? If the dog's gotten into the pantry again I swear I'll shoot the bugger." It was time to take my bitter medicine.

"No, Dad," I said trembling. "It wasn't the dog. It was me. I stole your drumstick."

He couldn't believe his ears. "What?" he roared. "What did you say?"

Somehow through my tears I managed to tell him about Pete Halfshoes eating nothing but pork and beans from a can and how bad I felt and how unfair it was for Pete to have so little when we had so much and that was why I stole the drumstick.

Mother fave Dad a fierce look. "No Cully," she said, "That wasn't stealing. That was sharing and I'm very proud of you."

Dad stopped biting his lip. "Yeah," he said. "That's right. I'm glad you did it but don't you ever do it again without telling us. Besides there's plenty of dark meat left on the thigh."

Whew!

But the best part was yet to come. At exactly seven o'clock of the second morning after Thanksgiving my father left the kitchen to go out on the back steps to blow his nose mightily and greet the new day as was his custom (it was said in the village that some of our people set their watches when they heard that mighty blast.) But hardly had he opened the door when he returned. "Edyth," he yelled excitedly. "Come see!" Someone has left a whole hindquarter of deer in the entry. Now we can have venison mincemeat pie again." Mother didn't move from her chair. She just sighed, a long sigh that sounded like the suds going down our kitchen sink.

"I wonder who brought it," Dad mused. "Probably someone who hasn't been able to pay me what he owes. Lord knows there are plenty of them. Wonder who it was."

I knew!

Save The Last Dance For Me

In the old days about the beginning of this century Tioga wasn't the sleepy little forest village it is today. It was mainly a mining town, almost a little city, with more than a thousand men working in double shifts. It boasted three stores, five churches and a ten-bed whorehouse. Located at the junction of a north-south and an east-west railroad, the roar and whistles of locomotives hauling passengers, freight and ore filled the air day and night. There were two post offices, one at the bottom of our hill street and the other on top near the Big Mine, so called because it was the biggest and deepest of the five working mines in the area. Why, at one time, it was the deepest iron mine in the world, over a mile deep and at its lower levels so warm the men worked naked to the waist.

William Trelawney was Captain of the Big Mine. In his prime at forty-five, he ran the operation with an iron hand. A rough, tough man, the men called him, but fair. He could sure put out the ore. Unlike some of the other mining captains, Cap'n Bill didn't just sit in his office and give orders; he seemed to be everywhere, on surface and underground too. Slow to hire and quick to fire, he dominated the workings. "Cap'n coming! Cap'n coming!" When that news came over the mysterious information grapevine down the shaft, the trammers hurried, the carpenters hammered fast on the cribbing, and the drillers swung their sledges harder. Cap'n Bill tolerated no shirkers. "A driver-man" the miners called him.

Even the shift bosses feared him. One of them, Erick Salmonen, still with a hangover from a weekend drunk, was discovered sitting on an empty powder keg in one of the raises in level-nine just ten minutes before the half-hour noon break. Cap'n Bill knocked him senseless, dragged him to the cage and signalled the hoist engineer to pull up. "You'll never work in my mine again," he roared. "You're fired!" But the word went around that Cap'n Bill made arrangements for one of the other mining captains to hire Erick. After all, Erick had eleven kids and was usually a good worker.

The men thought that was fair enough. Moreover, they knew that Cap'n Bill cared for them. When, as happened three or four times each year, a man was killed, he always made sure the widow got a good pension and permission to live in the company house as long as she wanted. When one of the miners got hurt and had to go to my father's hospital, Cap'n Bill always went to see him there on the cot. Also, the men appreciated it when Cap'n Bill persuaded the mine superintendent, Henry Thompson, to put electric arc lights all along our hill street so they wouldn't have to walk in the dark to and from work in the winter months, and to put a pool table and bowling alley in the clubhouse that they could use if they had the money. "Ay, he's a hard man," our people said, "but he's got a soft side."

Captain Bill didn't look hard, except for a jutting lower jaw. Powerfully built but short in stature, he looked like Santa Claus without the beard or belly. Laugh lines crinkled out from his eyes onto a very rosy face and off the job the eyes were always twinkling. He liked little kids and they liked him, perhaps because he always carried in his pocket a handful of jelly beans to give them, or perhaps because he and his wife had no children of their own.

But I must tell you something about Eleanore, his wife. Certainly the most beautiful woman in Tioga, she was also among the gayest. My mother loved her visits to our house because she always made everyone feel happy. Some people are just that way. More educated than her husband who adored her, she had a gift for the right phrase that always put one at ease immediately. Eleanore was also a caring person, doing one good deed after another. If someone became ill, Eleanore was soon there to bring a meal or offer comfort. The high school girls confided in her more than to their own mothers, scrutinized the fashionable clothing she wore, and tried to walk as gracefully as she did. No one, not even Aunt Lizzie, ever had said a bad thing about her. They couldn't!

The Trelawney's yard in summer was one of the show places in our village. From spring to fall it was a riot of flowers almost as colorful as the dresses Eleanore always wore. Back then, most of our women wore long black or brown dresses that they had to lift slightly whenever they encountered a cow pasty on the wooden sidewalks. Not Eleanore! Hers were yellow, red or blue and barely touched the top of her shapely ankles. Soon the French Canadian girls downtown were emulating her. Not the Finns, though. Following three steps behind their husbands on the way to church in their long dark skirts, they kept to the old ways while secretly wishing they had the nerve to wear clothes like Eleanore Trelawney's.

Even after the snow came, the Trelawney house was full of flowers because they had turned a south-facing bay window into a little conservatory full of ferns, coleus, African violets and the blooming bulbs that Eleanore had forced. A few of the houses in our town had a single pork and bean can with a red geranium on the window sill to counteract the black and white of winter but every window in the Trelawney house had three or four pots of them–even the windows upstairs.

I was in that house only once, but I remember those flowers and the lighted candles on the table and especially the little reed organ in the corner. Both Cap'n Bill and Eleanore loved to sing in harmony, he with a deep bass and she in a contralto. Sometimes in the summer months we kids would go to their fence to hear their duets at eventide. They also occasionally sang them at a church service too because both were good Methodists and participated in all the church activities. That helped to counteract Aunt Lizzie's torturing of the high notes when the choir sang.

The Trelawneys also loved to dance, mainly the waltz and two step, and they belonged to the dance club in Ishpeming that my folks did. With the Gages and the Thompsons and a mining engineer and his wife, once a month they'd take the train to Ishpeming, stay overnight at the Mather Inn, have dinner, and go to a cotillion sponsored by the Ishpeming couples in the club. I remember how beautiful my mother looked in a new blue and white dancing gown and how handsome my father was as they left for the railroad station, leaving us kids in the stern care of Fannie Hedetniemi. I knew that Dad would rather be hunting or fishing but he knew how important it was for mother to dress up and be glamorous again.

The four couples were very close friends and once a month they held parties in their homes where they played whist. When they came to our house mother spent a week in preparation for the event. We, of course, were banished to our rooms upstairs but we'd listen through the register to their gaiety until we couldn't keep our eyes open any longer. Yes, before the big cave-in happened and the mine closed, the winters weren't too bad in Tioga, Mother always said.

But even before the cave-in things changed. Two feet of snow came down in a single night late in October, and it never left until the next May. Shoveling out, Cap'n Bill Trelawney suddenly died. Cardiac arrest was what my father wrote on the death certificate after he'd been called and had failed to resuscitate him. "I should have suspected it," he told my shocked and weeping mother. "Bill's ruddy complexion should have alerted me to the possibility of high blood pressure, but he always seemed so healthy and hearty I just missed it. You'd better pull yourself together and go up to see Eleanore. She's in a bad way and has no family to comfort her. Stay as long as you need to. I'll call Stenrud, the undertaker, and make the necessary arrangements. I've also told Henry Thompson so he and his wife may be there."

Mother was gone all day, and when she returned at five to get our supper, I thought for the first time that she looked as though she were getting old. "Oh, John," she said to my father. "It was terrible. Eleanore can't cry and can hardly talk. Just sits there with a frozen face staring, staring. When I tried to hold her hand she pulled it away. I don't think she heard anything Eva Thompson and I said when we tried to console her. About the only time she talked at all was when she asked us to keep anyone from coming in and there were a lot of them bringing food. When the pastor insisted on entering about three o'clock despite her wishes, she just shut her eyes and probably her ears too. Just sat there stiffly and acted as though he weren't there. Oh John, if only she could cry!"

"She's in shock," my father said. "I've seen it before. Only time will help her overcome it, time and sleep. I'll go up there this evening and give her a strong sleeping pill or shot. She'd better not stay alone though."

"No," replied mother. Eva's with her now and I'll go up again right after supper and Mick's wife will be there from midnight on, but oh if we could only help her to weep."

The next morning at six o'clock I was awakened by two sounds, by that of the mine whistle blowing not the usual two times but eleven times, and by that of my Mother treading the pedal of her sewing machine in the sewing room next to my bedroom.

"Do you think it looks all right, John?" she asked my father holding up the black dress on which she'd been working. "After you left last night Eleanore did fall asleep in her chair so we put her to bed, then looked in her closet to see if she had anything black or dark to wear for the mourning and funeral. John, there wasn't a thing there except bright dresses and dancing gowns, not a single suitable thing she could wear. So I thought of this dark dress of mine and that I could take off the colored collar and sash. She's just my size, you know, and I'm sure it would fit if she would wear it. Oh, I hope she's got herself together for the hard time ahead."

At this time Tioga had no funeral home. Mr. Stenrud, the undertaker, kept his coffins and did his dirty work in the back room of Callahan's store. Then the body was taken to the church in Mr. Marchand's horse-drawn hearse. I remember that hearse very clearly. It was a glassed-in box that could be fitted on a wagon in the summer and on a sleigh in winter. From the roof black tassels hung, almost like the fringe of our surrey and inside it were candelabra with candles lighting the coffin inside. Mr Marchand and usually one of the mourners rode on a spring seat in front. In our Methodist church, the open coffin lay in state in the Epworth League room for the viewing and paying of last respects. A small room, the mourners often had a hard time squeezing between the coffin and the coal stove and the many urns of flowers sent up on the train from Ishpeming. The fire was kept going day and night in winter time because some family members of the deceased were expected to stay there to keep the corpse company and the candles lit. A cold long vigil!

But there were no family members. Cap'n Bill still had a brother and sisters and some nephews but they were in Cornwall, England, from which he had emigrated when in his late teens, while Eleanore, an only child, had lost her parents only a few years before. Since my folks and the Thompsons and the Hadleys, her closest friends, were taking turns staying with Eleanore, others had to be found to be with the casket. There were many volunteers. We took care of each other in the U.P. back then.

When Mother came back at noon to get our dinner, Dad, who'd been making house calls all morning, asked her how Eleanore was doing.

"Much better, John." she replied. "That long sleep you gave her really helped. She even drank some coffee and nibbled at a piece of toast, and watered her flowers. Also she could talk a little but not about Bill. When the Pastor came, she anwered his questions. I hoped that when he gave a little prayer she might weep but she didn't. I think she's just denying the whole thing, pretending that nothing's happened. She appreciated the black dress I gave her but put a red rose on it, one of those you ordered to be sent up on the train from Ishpeming. And, John, she absolutely refuses to go with any of us to see Bill in the coffin at church. We told her we could arrange it so no one else would be there so she could be alone with him, but she was stubborn. "No," she said, "No, no, no!" and she made us promise that there would be no wake. I hope we can get her to go to the funeral tomorrow morning. She's much better, really. Now if only she could cry!"

The next morning Mother and Dad had a little argument about whether I should go to the funeral service. "No, he isn't too young," my father said. "It's time he had the experience. Who knows? Death could come to us too and he'd better be prepared." So Mother took me with her to the church though she left me in a rear pew so she could join Dad and the Thompsons and Hadleys when they came with Eleanore to sit down front.

The church was full of people but it was totally quiet except for the soft moaning of the organ that Annie played. The coffin, covered with flowers, had been placed before the altar. Everyone kept their coats and boots on because it was chilly in there despite the fact that the two potbellied stoves had been kept going all night. There was no singing of hymns, just silence. When the preacher read something from the *Bible* and asked all of us to pray for the dear departed and began to talk about Cap'n Bill, suddenly Eleanore broke away and fled from the church.

Everything stopped. People looked at each other. Mother and Mrs. Thompson ran up the aisle in pursuit, with Dad and the other two men after them but not until Henry Thompson, our mine superintendent, gave the order to continue the service and "to bury him." Huddled there in the back pew I didn't know what to do, so I just sat there. Finally, the preacher asked all of us to pray for Eleanore, Annie played some more on the organ, and the pallbearers came to take the coffin away. I went home to find Dad hunting for a pry bar. "She's locked her door," he said. Finding it, he left the house but not until he'd ordered me to go to the graveyard. "Better see the rest of it," Dad said.

I got to the cemetery just as the pallbearers were unloading the heavy mahogany coffin from the hearse. A large deep hole, perhaps eight by four feet, had been freshly dug in the ground with the dirt heaped up at both ends. The snow had been shoveled out around it and perhaps twenty men, mostly miners of the night shift, were standing in the little clearing talking quietly. I heard one of them say, "Well, it's a good thing the ground wasn't frozen yet. Poor Cap'n Bill would have to wait in the crypt till spring breakup." He nodded to an ugly wooden log cabin without windows and a padlocked door behind them. "Yep," said his listener. "Better to be in the ground."

The pallbearers grunted as they stooped, then kneeled to lower the coffin into the grave. Then the preacher came over, read something from a black book that I couldn't hear, and asked the men if anyone had anything to say about the deceased. They shuffled uneasily, holding their caps in their hands, until one of them said, "Cap'n Bill was a good boss. Hard but good." A murmur of agreement occurred. Then another man said, "Tough to die so young. In his prime, too." When no one else said anything, the preacher said a short prayer, and motioned the grave diggers to start shoveling. It seemed a shame to see that dirt going on top of the coffin. That was all. Everybody went home.

Mother wasn't home much the next few days except to prepare our meals and to put us kids in bed. She sure looked awfully tired. "John," she said to my father one morning, "I don't know how much longer things can go on like this. Your sleeping pills let Eleanore sleep but she's not eating anything, though there's enough food in the house for a month with all the dishes people have brought her. And she won't talk at all now. Just sits and stares again, hour after hour, wearing that black dress I gave her but without the flower. And she doesn't even water her own flowers now and we have to do it. Today I tried to help her weep at last by telling about all the good times she and Bill had with us, the picnics and dancing and such, but she just sat there. I'm all worn out, John."

"Yeah," said Dad, "It's been long enough. We can't let her spoil our lives too. She has to face up to it. Bill is in his grave and that's that! I've a mind to go up there and tell her so." Mother asked him to be gentle.

When Dad returned I could tell he was upset. "Well, I told her," he said. "Just laid it on the table. Said that though Bill was dead and buried she still had close friends who cared for her but that they couldn't be with her all the time, that she just had to start living again, that you and Eva and Mick's wife would come up for a short time each day to see if there was anything to do but that was all."

"How did she respond?" my mother asked.

"She didn't say a word. Just stared at me."

So it went on, day after day, for many weeks. Then one morning my father found Eleanore Trelawney dead on the couch in the living room, dressed in a beautiful red and white dancing gown and with scarlet dancing slippers on her feet.

As my father said when he filled out the death certificate to read 'cardiac arrest', "people do die of broken hearts." He did not mention the crumpled note he had found in Eleanore's clutched hand:

"Bill, save the last dance for me."

Yarn For Deer Camp

It was breakup time, the train from Milwaukee was many hours late, and a salesman who'd come up on the South Shore and Atlantic from Marquette was restless. Going up to the ticket window, he asked the stationmaster how much longer he'd have to wait. "God knows," replied that worthy. "Latest we've heard they've just pulled out of Pembine, Wisconsin. Got to go slow this time of year, you know, because of soft track. Why don't you go over to Higley's Saloon for two or three hours to pass the time? Just a block away west of here. False front building. You'll see the lights."

Lugging his two square bags, the salesman found his way and when he entered and bellied up to the bar he felt better. Lots of noise and laughter and people telling tales. All the regulars were there: Pete Half-Shoes in the corner of his booth, Pete Ramos already half snockered, Laf Bodine and Dinny Callahan playing cards at one of the tables, and ten or twelve other men nursing their beers. "What'll you have, stranger?" asked Higley, twirling the ends of his black mustache, "beer or whiskey?" The salesman looked over the array of fancy bottles behind Higley. "How about a shot of that Old Age Bourbon?" he suggested. "Naw," said Higley, "Them bottles got nothing in them but water. Just for show. You want whiskey, I got whiskey. Good rotgut right from the barrel." The salesman settled for a beer.

Two of the men beside him were talking about mosquitoes and mosquito dope. "They're going to be bad this year," one of them said. "Too much rain." "Can't be any worse than last year," said another. "Got so bad in June the cows quit giving milk because they had to keep their eyes shut and couldn't find grass to eat."

"Yeah," said a third man. "Never seen such big skeeters as last year. Over by Splatterdock Lake I had one chawing me that was an inch tall on my wrist. Left a hole as big as a deer fly."

"Oh hell, that's nothing," said a fourth, "Why up there by the Hayshed dam I..."

The stranger interrupted. "Yeah, that's nothing. Down in Wisconsin where I come from we got mosquitoes two, three inches tall in their stocking feet. We use them for muskie bait."

Our men grinned appreciatively. The lying had begun again; it would be a good evening. "What kind of dope do you use for them big Wisconsin mosquitoes?" a man asked, "Citronella or oil of pennyroyal?"

"Neither," said the salesman taking a big swallow from his mug. "Hell, those big Wisconsin mosquitoes drink citronella like soup. In June month to get any sleep at all we have to pull the covers over our heads and almost suffocate. Once I put a dish of citronella by my bed and right away a swarm of 'em come and drank the whole thing in five minutes."

"Sure must be bad, them Wisconsin skeeters," the man beside him said. "What do you do when you're out in the bush?"

"Well," said the salesman, "some wear helmets of fine screening over their heads and tucked in their shirts, and gauntlets of the same over their hands and wrists but the damned skeeters get stuck in 'em and then you can't see too good. Kerosene is the only thing that really works."

"Kerosene?" asked his listener. "That'd burn your hide off you put it on yer skin. Worse than the mosquitoes."

"Naw, we don't put it on our skin," the salesman answered. "We put it on their tails and set fire to 'em." What a roar of laughter went up from the bar. This guy was good. "Yessiree," he concluded, "we've got the biggest damned skeeters in the whole country there in Wisconsin. Yeah, and the biggest liars too." The salesman grinned.

The men at the bar hadn't noticed that Slimber Vester, Tioga's best liar, had entered the saloon and heard the last of the salesman's tale but when they saw him they let out a yell. "Hey Slimber, this bird sez that they got the biggest liars in the world in Wisconsin. Tell him about the time you crossed the blue heron with a duck."

"Yeah," said another, "Tell 'im about that horse you taught to point partridge or how you showed that there bullfrog to jump. Mister, see that big trout Mustamaya on the wall? Well, Slimber here caught that monster with a post-hole digger, he did, or so he sez. And how about Old Lunker that the bear swiped off you?"

"Now, boys, you know old Slimber allus tells the truth, the whole truth and nothing but the truth swelpme God." The old bugger's face assumed a modest expression. "Now I like listening to a good lie like them my friend here has been a-telling and bedamn he told 'em well. Yessiree! I just wish I had the gift he has but my mama, bless her, she's been dead fifty year now, made me swear I'd tell only the truth. Oh, mebbe I've stretched it a bit sometimes but I've kept my promise, swelpme. Trouble is these here bar bums don't know the truth when they hear it." A saintly look spread over old Slimber's rosy cheeks and what with his white hair and beard and all, he looked virtuous as hell.

The men waited and waited. What was wrong with the old coot? Didn't he see the challenge? Why the honor of Tioga and the whole U.P. was at stake. OK, buy him another beer.

Under the lubrication old Slimber finally spoke. "Mister," he said to the salesman, "I come in late and my hearing's not so good but how big were them there Wisconsin skeeters of yours?"

The stranger grinned. "Oh, two or three inches high," he said. "Maybe you got bigger ones around here?"

"Nope," answered Slimber. "We ot lots of them especially over by my cabin at Mud Lake but I never seen one taller than an inch at most. But when I was in Alaska..." He stopped to fill his corncob pipe and light it as the onlookers nudged each other and grinned. "Here it comes," one whispered, "God help Wisconsin!" They knew Slimber had never been further from Tioga than Marquette.

Slimber continued. "Well, as I was a'saying, when I was up in Alaska I seen some considerable bigger. Everything in Alaska is bigger, bigger fish, bigger bear, even bigger cabbage."

"That's the truth," a man said. "I've been there and they got cabbages big around as a barrel, weigh maybe thirty pound."

"How did you happen to be in Alaska?" the salesman asked.

Slimber tamped his pipe with a tobacco-stained forefinger. "Spent two year up there a-hunting for gold," he answered. "Rough country that. Took me a year before I finds paydirt. No, not dirt, rock it was. Found me a good quartz seam next to greenstone that was full of little gold threads so I stake a claim, build me a cabin and make a sluice box on a creek entering a good-sized lake. Ever see a sluice box, Mister?"

"No, can't say I ever have," replied the salesman, "we've got big mosquitoes in Wisconsin but no gold. I hear there used to be some gold mines in the U.P. That so?"

"Yep," said Slimber. He went into a long dissertation on how in Alaska you got to blast out the rock, then sledge or grind it down fine, then put it in the sluice box where the running water washes out the impurities and lets the gold dust and nuggest collect in the grooves.

"But how about those Alaskan mosquitoes?" The salesman sounded a bit impatient.

"I'm a-comin' to that, Mister. Don't hurry an honest old man," he said, taking another big swallow of beer. "As I was saying, I'd just finished that sluice box and was beginning to put the crushed rock in it one afternoon when I hear a big zoom comin' out the west and another even bigger one comin' from the north and then they joined, they did, and made a noise like the ore train coming around the Wabik curve and down the hill. Awful quiet up there back in the bush and that there sound almost filled me my pants. Then I seen them circling, bigger than eagles, above me and when they landed about thirty feet away I made me a dive for the cabin."

The salesman's mouth fell open. "Not mosquitoes?" he asked, trembling a bit.

"The hell they weren't," said Slimber. "They was two of 'em, mebbe six or seven feet tall and with eyes big as dinner plates and red beaks three feet long. And they was looking at me hungry-like even when they was a comin' down. As I say, I made a dive for the cabin to slam the door but one of 'em stuck a big foot in so I couldn't close it." Slimber, always a master of suspense, refilled his corncob pipe and blew a smoke ring. He knew he had his listeners hooked.

"What happened then, you old bastard?" one of the men yelled angrily.

"What I do then? I rolled myself under the table hopin' they couldn't bend their knees to get at me. Didn't know then that them Alaskan mosquitoes have knees. Well, both of them come in the cabin and looked me over and they was so tall they had to come in through the door on their knees, they did. Dadamighty I was scared. Then I heard then a-talking' to each other, arguing-like. 'Let's eat him here!' the bigger one said but the other one was all for lugging me outside. 'No!' said the big one, 'If we haul him outside, the blackflies will get 'im.' Well I seen I had to do something fast, so while they were jawing at each other I rolled over to the cellar trap door, dropped in and pulled it shut over me. Phew! Close call, that!"

The salesman was swallowing hard. "Gimme a double shot of that rotgut," he ordered and Higley obliged, downing a shot for himself.

"Well, there I was," Slimber continued. "I could see some 'cause of light that come from under the bottom log and I had the spare axe I always keep in the cellar in case my good one gets stole or lost. Thought come to me that mebbe I could use it to widen the hole, crawl out and then slam the door on the critters but no, the axe just bounced off, the ground being so froze."

"That's right!" said the man who'd been in Alaska. "Two feet down the dirt never thaws. Damned if he ain't telling the truth! They calls it permfrost."

Slimber didn't bat an eye. "Well boys, I was a-hoping they might leave. That trap door set pretty flush and I was hanging onto it hard when they tried prying. You ought to heerd them a buzzing and cussing on the floor above me. 'I told you we shoulda hauled him outside,' one said. 'Aw, all we gotta do is drill down and then lift off the cover,' the other growled, and then I hear a terrible whine noise like when the big mine generator starts up, and then a red beak tip starts comin' through the wood. And then another..." Slimber relit his corncob.

"C'mon! C'mon, you old fart," Laf roared. "What happened?"

"Man's got to keep his head when he's in such a per, perdika, in such a fix," said Slimber. "And I did, that I did. I took the flat of the axe and bent them red beaks of theirs over into the wood and clinched them tight. Ever hear a mosquito holler, Mister? Them big devils yelped so loud they almost lifted the roof and they yanked and pulled. Up goes the door over my head. Sure felt naked, I did but I was safe. They couldn't get their beaks out of the wood and squawking something terrible they backed out of the cabin door dragging it after them. Pulled that there trap door right off the hinges, they did. So I got my shotgun and let them have it. Pow! Pow! Blew their damned heads off."

A big sigh swept down the bar. The men hated to have the lie end. But there was more to come.

"Sure was a-shaking once it was over," Slimber said. "Had to sit a spell on the chopping block before I started cleaning them. Did the smaller one first, the cock. Just like dressing out a deer. Had me a mind to get some roasts outa the breast 'cause they had no drumsticks to speak of–just skinny legs full of scales. Well, that done, I started on the hen, the bigger one, seven feet long she was, and fat..."

Slimber tapped the ashes from his pipe and the men groaned. "Yeah, when I slit her belly, damned if nin blue-black eggs popped out and started rolling down the slope to the lake. Tried to stomp them cause I could see they wuz about ready to hatch, the shells being cracked and little beaks coming out, but I only got six of them, the other three getting into the lake before I could catch 'em. Sure hated seeing that, Mister. You know how skeeters breed in water."

There was a long silence finally interrupted by one of the men at the bar. "How about the gold, Slimber? How about the gold?"

"I dunno," he replied. "I got my gear and hightailed it out of there fast. Wasn't going to hang around till them three hatched!"

The salesman put a ten dollar bill on the bar. "Drinks for everyone," he told Higley and then turned to Slimber as he picked up his bags. "Sir," he said respectfully. "I'm a-going back to Wisconsin where the skeeters are puny and the liars are too."

The honor of Tioga and the U.P. had been upheld.

The Reclamation Of Scotty McGee

It had been a long rainy Sunday late in June and I'd been trying to read Dicken's *Martin Chuzzlewit* all afternoon. Lord, it was slow and tedious going. I would have quit but it was the only book in our house I hadn't read and besides with the mosquitoes and rain there was nothing to do outside. It wasn't bedtime yet. Dad had eaten his Sunday supper of a bowl of bread and milk, read all the *Chicago Tribune,* and smoked his fat cigar, so perhaps he might be in his storytelling mood. I sure hoped so. Much better than *Martin Chuzzlewit,* his tales about his patients were dandies. It was understood, of course, that no one in the family would ever dare tell them to another living soul. Even now I feel a little uneasy recounting them, but here are two that I remember.

"Old man Chivaud couldn't hold his liquor very well and one winter's night came staggering out of Higley's saloon, missed the road, and came down instead on the railroad tracks that parallel it. And got hit by the cowcatcher of the train coming down from the Copper Country! Good thing it was slowing down for the station, but even so it threw him twenty feet into a snowbank by the freight depot. People saw it happen and when they ran over to see if he were dead they found Chivaud all crumpled up and moaning, so they got the stretcher from the baggage room and lugged him up the hill to the hospital and laid him on the table in the emergency room.

When I got there Chivaud was still alive and breathing though his eyes were closed. Pulse was all right, so we began to undress him to see the injuries. You know how these French Canadians dress for winter with one layer of clothes over the other. Well, we peeled off his bearskin overcoat, then two sweaters, a flannel shirt, two pairs of pants and his long filthy underwear. There wasn't a bruise on the old bugger, nothing wrong at all. When I told him so, old Chivaud rose up and grinned. "Oui, I know," he said, "but, Doctaire, me, I have a fine ride."

The other tale was Dad's maggot story. Sometimes, to tease my Mother he'd begin to tell it when we had a dinner guest, perhaps one of the lady school teachers, "John," she would say, "Don't tell that awful story or I'll leave the table." Here it is.

"On a hot summer day they brought in a lumberjack who'd cut a big gash in his leg with an axe. His dirty long underwear was so crusted with blood I just cut off the lower part of it and found one of the nastiest wounds I've ever seen. They'd wrapped the leg with a dirty dishtowel too and smeared the but with axle grease and Lord knows what else. How many times have I told them not to put anything on such a wound but they just don't listen.

Must have been many hours since he cut it because a lot of infection had already set in. What a mess! Bloody pus and dirt and inflammation had appeared,–even streaks of red radiating from the cut. We put the jack on the operating table and I had the men hold him still while I poured peroxide and tried to scrape and swab the junk out. Took a long time and he was screaming before I was through. Couldn't blame him! Finally I put on a wet dressing, bandaged it, and told him to come back the next day to have it dressed again.

"Well, the lumberjack didn't show up then or the day after that either, so I sent some men to look for him. Knowing that I hadn't been able to get all the stuff out of the cut I was worried that the infection would be roaring again. Well, they found the coot back of our slaughter house, still half drunk, and I was thinking amputation when they brought him in. But you know what? Although he'd torn off the bandages and dressing, the leg looked pretty good overall. I found out why when I squeezed it and out came one maggot right after another. Must have been eight or nine of them and that wound was clean as a whistle. No pus, no pround flesh, no inflammation at all. Those maggots had eaten all the crap and cleaned it perfectly after the blowflies' eggs had hatched when he lay there in the hot sun. Thought I might write it up for a medical journal but never did. Later I read once that others had discovered the same thing, that during World War I they'd even raised sterile maggots to put in gunshot wounds."

It was stories like those that I was hoping to hear as I made myself inconspicuous as possible on the couch behind him pretending to be reading *Martin Chuzzelwit*. Yawning, he asked my Mother casually how the morning sermon had gone.

"It was awful, John," she replied. "We had another traveling evangelist who accused us of all the sins in the book, begged us to repent right then and there, and painted the whole church with fire and brimstone."

"Oh, oh," Dad exclaimed. "That means I'll be seeing old Scotty McGee tomorrow at office hours."

"Why do you say that?" my Mother asked.

"McGee has a classic case of cardiac neurosis," Dad explained. "He's certain that he's going to die at any time of heart trouble, and convinced that when he does he'll go to hell."

"Oh no," my Mother protested. "He's such a nice old man. No one goes to church more regularly. I did think he seemed very thin and sickly yesterday. Of course he must be in his late seventies…"

"He's seventy-eight," Dad interjected, "and in remarkably good shape for a man his age. I've examined him thoroughly several times in the last several years when he's come up complaining of heart trouble–usually after one of your preachers has scared him–but the pulse has always been strong and I couldn't find the slightest thing wrong when I listened to his heart. One time, thinking I might be missing something, I gave him some nitroglycerin to take if he had any pain and he said it just made him worse. It always does make the heart thump slower and stronger for a few moments but it always relieves any anginal pain. Moreover, Scotty says the pain was sharp like a toothache and when I asked where it was located he pointed to his left breast, not at the midline where it should be. McGee tells me it's worse at night rather than after hard effort which doesn't make sense either. Hypochondia, that's what it is. All in his head."

"But he's so thin, John, and now he walks with a stoop rather than erectly as he always did."

"He should," Dad said impatiently. "Lives on hardtack, bologna, coffee and a bit of whiskey now and then. I hear too that this year he's not planted a garden nor begun to put up any wood for next winter. Like all of us he used to do a lot of fishing and hunting, but for some time now he hasn't. Just stays in his cabin reading the *Bible* and talking to himself. Hypochondriacal depression, that's what he's got and he'll probably manage to make his fears of dying come true if he doesn't watch out. But I say again, he's healthy as a horse physically. Probably in better shape than I am."

Dad's prediction was incorrect. Mr. McGee didn't show up at office-hour time. Instead he was sitting on his front stoop talking to himself. "No point bothering Doctor, McGee. He can't help you. Pretty soon you're a-going to die and you know it. You've had your time, yeah seventy-eight years of it, and tha's long enough for an old crock like you. Got no wife, got no kids to mourn you either. You don't owe nobody nothing…"

He was interrupted by a yelping and yapping coming down the street as a dog with a bunch of cans tied to its tail tore down and the cans got stuck in a hole in McGee's picket fence. McGee hurried over to it. "Why it's just a pup!" he exclaimed. "Poor little fella. Damn kids to do a stunt like that. Ought to be a law agin it." Taking out his jackknife and talking soothingly he cut off the cans and the dog turned over on its back in supplication and fatigue. "That's all right' that's all right now, dog," he said, picking it up in his old arms and carrying it to the stoop where finally it stopped whimpering and began to like his hand.

McGee looked it over. Not much of a dog, really and not much more than half grown. "Mixed stuff!" commented the old man, using the U.P. term for unknown ancestry. "Got the bow legs of a hound, the fur and tail of a spaniel, but damn if the head ain't that of a terrier. A Scotch terrier if I ever seen one." Why it looked like the head of Tam O'Shanter, the dog he'd had as a boy in Scotland a million years ago. For a moment he was tempted just to keep it. Might be company to have a dog around the house. Something to talk to. But no, it belonged to somebody else up the street and a sick old man had no right to have a dog depend on him. Why he might be dead come morning! So Scotty McGee led the mutt outside the fence, shut the gate, then went into the house to read his *Bible*.

An hour later the dog was still there whimpering and because it had begun to sprinkle McGee brought it into the house, getting a face licking in the process. "Pore little critter's still scared," McGee said. "Guess I'll have to keep him overnight and take him uptown tomorrow to find where he lives."

It rained for three days and when it ended Old Man McGee was just about hooked. No Name, that was what he called the dog, had utterly delighted him, chasing its silly little tail in circles, offering to shake hands with uplifted paw, putting his head against the old man's leg and looking soulfully up into his eyes. Although McGee had made a bed for him out of an old Mackinaw, before morning the pup was beside him on the blankets. For a change he'd slept all night and hadn't had his usual three daily naps because it was just too interesting watching the little devil. How he liked to be stroked from the tail upward and rubbed around the ears. How he liked to be tickled on the belly just in front of a hind leg so the whole leg would start vibrating! How his silly tail waggled when McGee tossed an old sock and he brought it back for praising!

No Name was housebroken too, whining at the door to be let out, and whining again to be let in so the old man could wrap a towel around him and make him dry again. Feeding was a problem though. When McGee gave him a piece of the hardtack he'd broken off the black wheel the dog nosed it, dropped it on the floor, picked it up then dropped it again at his feet. "Guess yer teeth aren't hard enough yet," McGee said to the dog. "Mine aren't so good either being old as I am. Mebbe you want it soaked in coffee too?" But the pup wouldn't try to eat it–just looked at the old man with sad eyes. "Gotta get ye a bone, No Name; Gotta get ye a bone!" he said but all he had in the house was bologna and some korpua so the dog got those and wolfed them down. That made it so thirsty it drank from the water pail. "Smart dog!" McGee said admiringly. He said it again that evening when he read aloud as usual from the dog-eared *Bible* and the pup cocked its head first to the right and then to the left, listening. "Damned if he don't know what I'm a-reading," McGee exclaimed.

When the rain stopped and the sun shone brightly, the old man sure hated the thought of trying to find No Name's owner. He hadn't been so happy in a long time. Why, he'd even laughed aloud at the pup's antics several times. Maybe he ought to keep him. "Nope, McGee," he said aloud. "Nope. 'Twouldn't be honest and besides 'twouldn't be fair if I keeps him and then go off an die on the little bugger." He realized with a start that he hadn't been thinking much about dying for some time and had been feeling really good. Moreover, his arthritic hand hadn't even hurt a bit doing all that scratching of No Name's hide.

Should he take the dog along with him? McGee didn't want to. Dreaded the long walk back alone if he did find where the pup belonged. But they had to see to recognize him, so in the afternoon, with No Name following at his heels, the old man went up our long hill street peerng in every yard to see if there were any dogs resembling the puppy and stopping people to ask if anyone had lost a dog. No, they told him. Probably just another stray. Tioga had more dogs than people in those days, more dogs than they really could afford to feed.

McGee made one more try. At the post office he went in and asked Annie if she knew anyone who'd lost a dog. Annie knew everything that went on in town but no, she hadn't.

Going home, McGee stopped at my father's hospital knowing it was office-hour time. No one was in the anteroom waiting, so he went in. "Doctor," he said, "I gotta ask you something. How long you think I got before I croak? How much time kin you save me? Six months, one year or what days?" He explained about the dog and his concern for it in the event of his death. Dad examined him carefully, listened to his heart, and gave him some purple pills.

That night after supper I heard Dad telling Mother about it. "As I just said, Scotty wasn't worrying about himself so much as he was about the dog. Just wanted to be sure he'd live long enough to take care of it. I knew that dog right awa. Belongs to the Pelkies. Saw it last week when I was up there looking at Mrs. Pelkie's hernia. They've got some mean kids and when I came out of the house they had the puppy cornered between the barn and the woodshed and were throwing big stones at it. I gave them hell and stopped it."

"I hope you didn't tell Mr. McGee who owned it, John."

"Of course not," Dad replied. "The old man's bound to give it a better home than its got now."

"How long did you tell him he had yet to live?" asked Mother.

Dad grinned. "I thought I'd use a little psychology on him to try to get the thought of dying out of his head. So first of all I gave him a thorough examination using the stethoscope to listen to his heart, thumping his back good, and checking his reflexes. Then I took down one of my big medical books and pretended to read it. 'Yes,' I said, 'that's it!' Then I told McGee he had a rare disease called cardiac hypochondria which was always fatal. 'I knew it,' said McGee, 'but how long, Doctor, how long have I left?' I looked in the medical book again. 'Mr. McGee, it says here that there's a powerful new medicine that can hold off death for three or perhaps even more years providing the patient cooperates by taking it everyday. Fortunately, I have some of that medication, Mr. McGee,' and I gave him a bottle of those big purple pills I rolled and dried on the cookie sheet on your kitchen range last week."

"Oh John, you didn't! Those huge horrible looking pills? You told me they were just aspirin."

"Yep," said Dad grinning. "Just aspirin–salycilic paste colored a bilious purple with potassium permanganate and tincture of gentian and big as a marble. Horse pills! The placebo or placebos! The few people I've tried them on swear by them. Doesn't hurt them and the aspirin may relieve a bit of pain, but it's the placebo effect that counts especially on hypochondriacs like McGee."

"To make sure," Dad continued, "I told McGee that these were very powerful pills. Under no circumstances was he to take more than one each morning. "With milk," I added. He'd told me he'd been living on hardtack, korpua and bologna with an occasional can of beans. Sure looked it too. With his shirt off, his ribs showed. For that matter, the dog was starved too."

"Oh what a shame!" exclaimed Mother. "Is he that poor, John?"

"I don't know, Edyth. I understand he has a small pension from the mining company but he's a Scot and I'd bet he has a little cash stacked away somewhere. Enough for milk anyway. He sure winced when I told him the pills were terribly expensive, a dollar a pill."

"Oh John! You didn't say that!" My Mother was shocked.

"Yes I did. Had to impress upon him the value of those pills, but I also told him I'd give them free if he'd come up and sweep out the dispensary and office and waiting room each week. That will get him out of the house and give him some exercise. I did something else too. Having heard that he hadn't planted a garden, I told him to go help Widow Johnson with hers. Went by there the other day and saw that she'd overplanted her potatoes and beans but hadn't tended them. Just a mess of parsley and quackgrass. I told McGee to offer to weed and take care of them in exchange for half the crop. Plenty there for both of them."

McGee walked down the hill street feeling better than he had for a long time. "Three, four years, mebbe more," he said aloud half to himself and half to No Name. "That's a-plenty. You're a-going to stay with McGee and he'll take care of you good, he will. "But McGee, you got to get milk right away so you kin take them big pills."

When he reached his house, the old man went directly to the cellar and the two lard cans that were hidden behind the boards. The bigger one was the savings one, the other the spending can. McGee had never take a single bill out of the savings can. Never! Even before he'd retired from the mine he'd religiously put money in it from every pay check he received and only opened it thereafter to toss in at least one dollar bill from each month's pension. There had been many times when he'd been tempted, such as when the coffee ran out, but he'd never given in. No sir! "Lord, McGee, you've got a lot of money here," he said. "Damn near rich, ye are. What you saving for anyway? Got no heirs. Lots more than you need for burying money. Take a chunk of it, McGee, and buy milk and bones for yer dog!"

So he did. With No Name trotting by his side, the old man went to Flynn's store and bought some bread, two quart bottles of milk, two pounds of ground beef, a slab of bacon, a big bone and a pail of coffee. Feeling hungry for the first time in months, he fried up half of the ground beef, gave half to the dog and ate it with store bread and butter. And with milk. "Ye haven't tasted milk in a long time McGee," he said. "Better than java or even whiskey, it is." The puppy had wolfed down his meat in a hurry and was begging for more. "No, dog, that's enough," McGee said, "but mebbe ye'd like some milk too?" No Name wagged his tail and when the old man set a saucerful out for him he lapped it up quickly. "Pore little critter, he's starved," McGee said and gave him the rest of the bologna. "We'll both be eating better from now on," he said.

Well that was the beginning of some wonderful years for McGee and Tam O'Shanter. Yes, that was the dog's name now. Once the old man was certain that the purple pills were doing him some real good and when he was sure no one would be claiming the pup, McGee one evening performed the naming ceremony. Sitting in the rocking chair by the box stove and spreading his legs he called the dog to him. "Time you had a proper Christian name, pup," he said. "Old McGee's been thinking on it 'cause we both got Scot blood in us. Had a dog in the old country when I was a boy look like you and his name was Tam, Tam O'Shanter. Name come from one of Robbie Burns' poems we used to recite in school. How did it go, McGee?" The old man screwed up one eye and thought hard. All I kin remember is bits. Lessee now…"

Tam looked up soulfully as McGee scratched both their heads. "Och! Ye know the poem McGee. The one about how Tam O'Shanter rode his horse Maggie to the tavern against the wishes of his wife. Kate her name was. Ah yes.

> 'She told thee well thou was a blellum,
> a blethering, blustering, drunken blellum,
> that from November till October
> on market day thou was not sober!'
> "Ay, that's how it went.
> 'Gathering her brows like gathering storm
> Nursing her wrath to keep it warm…'

"Oh, I forgit when else except that Tam met a mess of devils and witches who chased him home and pulled Maggie's tail off at the bridge. Doesn't matter, I reckon, but from now on yer name is Tam. Understand?" Tam thumped his tail on the floor and raised a paw. They shook hands. No more No Name.

The two became inseparable and provided a common sight on our hill street as McGee with the dog at his heels made their daily journey to my Dad's hospital or the store. Oh there were times when McGee had to shut Tam in the house to go to church or such. Once he'd tried to smuggle Tam there under his overcoat, but Charley Olafson saw the bulge and shooed them out. In summer months they often could be seen on Lake Tioga too after Alphone DeCaire, who'd caught a basket of brook trout and his wife refused to cook them because they'd been having too many, brought them to McGee. Tam liked fish and the old man tried to take him with him after trout but that didn't work out because of the splashings. In a boat, though, Tam was fine, sitting silently in the stern like a Captain of the Fleet, while McGee rowed and trolled for pike. Didn't move a muscle until a big fish was thrashing in the bottom but then he barked like hell in celebration.

Hating to spend the money for milk, McGee thought of getting a cow but then heard that Mr. Salmi was in such bad shape he couldn't make hay so McGee did it for him and for milk and butter. Good excercise That! Tam liked eggs too and the old man thought of getting some chickens. He had the coop for them and some years before had all the eggs he needed, but Mrs. Johnson whose garden he now kept in fine shape often gave him a half dozen eggs when the hens were laying, also potatoes and rutabagas when the frosts came.

Tam had to stay in the house too when McGee got out his old rifle to hunt deer, though he got rewarded by having lots of bones to chew and venison to eat as well as a lot of extra petting. McGee was happier than he'd ever been. He had company to talk to, to bed with, to share his meals with. Religiously he swallowed one of those monster purple pills each day and had no fear of dying.

One afternoon next spring Dad called Mother's attention to the old man as he and Tam were walking up the street to the store. "Look at the old coot, Edyth," he commanded. "Look at him gallop! Why, he'd walking as fast as any young kid. And see how he's filled out, the dog too. Lots of excercise and better food and my purple pills have made him a new man. That psychology is good stuff."

Seven years later when I had to leave Tioga to go to college the two of them were still in fine shape, still going strong, and still inseparable.

Was it the dog or the purple pills?

The U.P. Dialect

Dad had just finished his breakfast when the box phone (the kind you had to crank to call Genevieve at Central), rang. He groaned. Dad always groaned when he heard the phone ring. "Wonder what wart thinks he's sick now?" he said, picking up the receiver. "Yes, yes. Where did you say your farm was? All right. I'll be there when I get there–sometime this morning, I hope." Turning to Mother, he said, "emergency call from a man who has a homestead near Black River; thinks his wife's dying. Two hours each way, I suppose, so don't expect me for dinner. I'd appreciate having a sandwich." Then to me he said, "Cully, you hitch up the horse to the buckboard and put some hay and oats in back. And then you get the mail. It won't be here until after nine but I want it when I get home."

Not much mail. Oh the *Chicago Tribune*, of course, and M.C. Flynn's monthly bill for groceries, and a long envelope from the University of Michigan.

When he returned early that afternoon, Dad had some milk and a piece of pie, then opened the long envelope first. He silently read the letter for a long time, then read it aloud to Mother. "Dear Dr. Gage: May I introduce myself? I am James R. Johnson, Ph.D., professor of linguistics at your alma mater, the University of Michigan. Planning on retirement next year, I am desirous of doing one last research, a definitive study of the U.P. dialect. To my knowledge, no other scholar has investigated this subject although many have mentioned that it exists because of the melting-pot effect produced by nationals of many lands who with their children emigrated to your land to work in the mines and forests. Seeking a site that might fit the purposes of my investigation, I found that Tioga, located in the center of the Upper Peninsula, with its iron mines and extensive lumbering operations, might well be the place where I could begin my linguistic analysis. I secured your name from our alumni association as a possible initial contact and I wonder, sir, if you could provide me with the name of a hotel or rooming house in your village so I can make the necessary arrangements. I plan to stay at least a week and am prepared to spend much longer if the opportunities to do this research are promising. I include a reprint of a similar study I did on the Creole dialect of Southern Louisiana. Help me if you can. Sincerely yours, James R. Johnson, Ph. D., Professor of Linguistics, the University of Michigan."

"You're going to answer him, aren't you John?" Mother asked.

"Of course I will," Dad replied. "If it weren't for the U. of M. I'd never become a doctor. I owe them a lot but I don't know what to say. There's no hotel in Tioga since the mine closed and the Beacon House shut down. No rooming house either."

Phonetic Symbol	Key Words English	Phonetics	Phonetic Symbol	Key Words English	Phonetics

Consonants

Phonetic Symbol	English	Phonetics	Phonetic Symbol	English	Phonetics
b	beg, tub	bɛg tʌb	p	paper, damper	pepɚ dæmpɚ
d	do, and	du ænd	r	run, far	rʌn fɑr
f	fan, scarf	fæn skɑrf	s	send, us	sɛnd ʌs
g	grow, bag	gro bæg	t	toe, ant	to ænt
dʒ	judge, enjoy	dʒʌdʒ ɪndʒɔɪ	ʃ	shed, ash	ʃɛd æʃ
h	hem, inhale	hɛm ɪnhel	tʃ	cheap, each	tʃip itʃ
k	kick, uncle	kɪk ʌŋkl	θ	thin, tooth	θɪn tuθ
l	let, pal	lɛt pæl	ð	then, breathe	ðɛn brið
l̩	apple, turtle	æpl̩ tɝtl̩	v	vow, have	vaʊ hæv
m	men, arm	mɛn ɑrm	w	wet, twin	wɛt twɪn
m̩	autumn, wisdom	otm̩ wɪzdm̩	hw	when, white	hwɛn hwaɪt
n	nose, gain	noz gen	j	you, yet	ju jɛt
n̩	sudden, curtain	sʌdn̩ kɝtn̩	ʒ	pleasure, vision	plɛʒɚ vɪʒən
ŋ	wrong, anger	rɔŋ æŋgɚ	z	zoo, ooze	zu uz

Vowels

Phonetic Symbol	English	Phonetics	Phonetic Symbol	English	Phonetics
a*	ask, rather	æsk raðɚ	ɒ*	log, toss	lɒg tɒs
ɑ	father, odd	fɑðɚ ad	ɝ	earn, fur	ɝn fɝ
e	make, eight	mek et	ɜ*	earn, fur	ɜn fɜ
æ	sat, act	sæt ækt	ɚ	never, percale	nɛvɚ pɚkel
i	fatigue, east	fətig ist	u	truth, blue	truθ blu
ɛ	red, end	rɛd ɛnd	ʊ	put, nook	pʊt nʊk
ɪ	it, since	ɪt sɪns	ʌ	under, love	ʌndɚ lʌv
o	hope, old	hop old	ə	about, second	əbaʊt sɛkənd
ɔ	sauce, off	sɔs ɔf			

Diphthongs

[aɪ]	sigh, aisle	[saɪ aɪl]	[ɔɪ]	coy, oil	[kɔɪ ɔɪl]
[aʊ]	now, owl	[naʊ aʊl]			

*These sounds are only rarely used in General American speech, but are common in the East and South. General American speech uses [æ] for [a], [ɔ] for [ɒ], and [ʃ] for [ɜ].

Reprinted with permission from An Introduction to General American Phonetics by Charles Van Riper. Harper and Row, New York.

"Aunt Lizzie sometimes takes boarders," Mother replied, her blue eyes twinkling. She knew how he'd respond.

"No, no, no, no!" Dad roared. "I wouldn't wish that on my worst enemy. Aunt Lizzie would clack him to death, the old hag." My father, to put it mildly, did not like Aunt Lizzie, our town gossip and troublemaker. Couldn't stand the old buzzard!

"Well, why don't you invite him to stay with us for a short time. I think he said he planned initially to spend a week exploring the possibilities of his research, and perhaps by then we could find someone to take him in or he could go to an Ishpeming hotel and do his research around there. He could have Grandma Van's room and one more mouth to feed for a week wouldn't be any problem. But what's linguistics, John?"

"Don't really know," Dad answered. "The study of languages and their grammar and pronunciation maybe. I may know more about it when I read that reprint of his, but that's a good idea. I'll tell him he can stay with us for a short time."

Mother was delighted. "Oh, it will be good, John, to have some civilized conversation again. Not that these aren't fine people in Tioga. They are! But do you realize that you, Mr. Donegal, and Father Hassel are the only men in town with a university degree? Even the school teachers have had only two years of normal school and whenever one of our own children, I mean those of other parents, gets through high school they leave immediately to get jobs Down Below. Yes, there are times when I hunger to talk with a person of some education. Imagine having a real University professor at our dinner table!"

Arriving on the morning train, Professor Johnson got a ride up our long hill street with Mr. Marchand, our mail carrier. He told us later that he and Marchand had talked French all the way up to our house. He was fascinated by the differences in pronunciation, he said. "M'sieur Marchand speaks a patois that is the French of three hundred years ago. That would make a good study all by itself."

Dad was making house calls but mother made him welcome with coffee, toast and wild strawberry jam. I almost laughed when I saw him with his hat off. A little old man with a forehead that ran up over and behind his head and with a little pointed white beard, he looked more like a merry old elf than a scholar. When Mother took him upstairs I tried to bring up his suitcase but he took it away from me. "It's too heavy," he said. "I have a lot of books init, mainly books about Finland and the Finnish language about which I know little. I understand, Mrs. Gage, that there is a substantial population of Finns and their offspring in this locality?"

"Yes," Mother replied. "More than half of us are Finns; perhaps a quarter are French Canadians and the rest are Cousin Jacks, Scandinavians, Indians and other assorted nationalities."

"Cousin Jacks?" he inquired.

"Oh, that's what we call the people who worked the tin mines in Cornwall, England, and emigrated to the U.P." Then Mother showed him Grandma's room. "This black walnut furniture was my mother-in-law's," she said. "She lived with us until she died. It's very old and very old fashioned. See the marble tops on the dresser and table and the carvings."

"It's beautiful," the Professor commented, running his hands over the gleaming wood. "And look at this escritoire desk with the built-in book shelves. A fine place to do my transcribing." He took down one of the volumes from the shelves, *The Memoirs of Ulysses S. Grant*.

"Yes," Mother said. "Most of those books are about the Civil War. My father-in-law, Grampa Van, fought in the Battle of Shiloh and was taken prisoner. Grandma Van had a pension."

"I'm a fortunate man, Mrs. Gage. I can't tell you how much I appreciate your hospitality. What a lovely room!"

"I'll leave you now to get organized," Mother said. "My husband will be back for dinner in about an hour, so come down whenever you're ready."

I don't remember too much about the conversation that noon and a lot of it I didn't understand, but the Professor described the work of a linguistic scholar and how he practiced it. "We dissect languages just as you dissected your cadavers, Doctor," he said. "We identify the surface features such as pronunciation and also the deep structures such as grammar–first the skin of the language and then the bones and muscles. We analyze how they fit together, determine their functions." There was more but I got thinking about how Mullu or Fisheye and I would be going fishing that afternoon when what he was saying got my attention.

"First I have to get a corpus, a representative collection of utterances spoken by the native speakers."

"You'd better not call them natives," Dad interjected. "They'll resent it."

"Yes, yes, I know. And then I transcribe those utterances into the International Phonetic Alphabet. I've trained myself to do what we call shadowing–covertly saying to myself the words the other person is speaking. If he says 'Don't (don't) tell (tell), your (your) mother. Then I try to echo the whole utterance to myself exactly as spoken, and finally I write it down in this new alphabet. Would you like to see it, Doctor? I have it upstairs."

He brought down two copies, one for each of my parents, and I looked at it over my Mother's shoulder as the professor explained. "English is a very unphonetic language," he said, "and the letters used in spelling it often do not represent the actual sounds. For example, we use the *t* and the *h* to spell the work "think" but the sound has neither a *t* nor an *h* in it. Therefore, to accurately transcribe the actual sound we use the symbol 0- . You'll observe that many of the symbols in this alphabet are like those of our ordinary alphabet but there are new ones we've had to invent. Let me transcribe what I've just said so you can understand." He did so.

"That's very interesting," Mother commented, "but I've noticed that a lot of our people also omit a lot of the words as in saying "You go store and buy meat, eh?"

"That's interesting too," replied the Professor. "So they omit prepositions and articles and end the sentence with a rising inflection? The latter suggests some Swedish influence or perhaps Finnish. Oh, I can hardly wait to get started collecting. I feel like a puppy with a new bone." His little goatee waggled with enthusiasm. "Have you any suggestions, Doctor, about where I could begin to get my specimens?"

Dad gave it some thought. "Well, you can't just go up to a door and ask for conversation," he said, "and if you try to explain what you're trying to do, they'll be offended or think you're crazy. They think they talk all right, and besides most of them are suspicious of strangers. No, you'll have to eavesdrop at first until you can establish some contacts. Let's see..."

After a pause to fill his pipe Dad continued. "I guess the best spots to do your collecting of specimens would be at Higley's saloon, the railroad depot, the post office, the barber shop and Flynn's store. I'll have Cully show you where they are and he can tell you about our village at the same time." My face fell. There went my afternoon's fishing!

The only person we met on our way uptown was Reino Okanen. "Hey, Cully," he said. "I yust seen Mullu. He look for you, I tink. Say you going fis-sing, mebbe so, eh?"

As we passed on, I heard the Professor say just what Reino had said and it was uncanny. He had the same voice and words and tones. He stopped right there on the sidewalk, pulled out a notebook and fountain pen, and began scribbling and muttering to himself as he did so. "Yust" for "just"; "seen" for "saw"; omitted "is"; substituted t for th in think; omitted pronoun "he"; used "say" for "said"; omitted "plan to"; substituted s for sh in fishing and split the syllables (fiss-sing); oh yes, and again the Scandinavian upward inflection at the end of the utterance." Lord, the old professor was sure excited. "Cully," he exclaimed. "Marvellous, marvellous! A genuine dialect for sure. But do other talk like that young man?"

I grinned, "Ya, I tink so," I said. "Ve all got goot U.P. brogue for talk ourself–but not for home or school, no."

When we reached Flynn's store, I told him it would usually be a good place to collect samples, that people liked to wander around looking for stuff and to talk to each other, but when we entered we were the only ones inside. "Maybe you'd like to buy me a little bag of candy" I suggested. "Olga, who'll wait on us, talks U.P. good." If I couldn't go fishing I could salvage something from the lost afternoon.

Olga did wait on us. "Vat kine candy you vant?" she asked the professor. He turned to me. "What kind would you like, Cully?" he asked.

Olga horned in. "Ve got gudt socolates wit tzerries in dem. Or dis box taffy, maybe so?" I said I'd just like some of the big round jawbreakers because they lasted so long. Olga was disappointed but she said tanks anyway. When we were leaving I noticed that old lady Terrance was in the meat market, so I nudged the professor to go in there with me. "I'll be 'aving some of they cheese, Mr. Ryan," she said to the butcher. "But if ye don't mind would ye cut me an 'alf (half) pound with they 'am knife. I dearly love they taste of 'am (ham)."

"Let's sit a bit on the fence railing, Cully," the professor said after we left the store. Again he mimicked both Olga and the old Cornish woman as he wrote in his notebook. "Incredible!" he said. "The melting pot indeed. I've found the mother lode in Tioga." I told him about the Cornish and their pasties and saffron bread and how they always said "they" for "the", and dropped their h's on some words while inserting them in others where they didn't belong. He complimented me for my keen observation and said perhaps I'd become a linguist too when I grew up. "No!" I answered. "I'm going to be a lumberjack."

Dad had suggested the barber shop and post office. We didn't enter the former. "There's no point going in there now." I told the professor. "Wait until evening when the men go there after work to play pool. Buy some soda pop and peanuts and just sit there listening. You'll hear plenty. Then I told him about Annie, our postmistress. Her folks had come from Sweden but though she'd been born in this country and gone to school in Tioga, her speech still had a lot of the flavor of the language her family had always spoken at home. I imitated how the last words of her sentences always rose in pitch. "Just introduce yourself, say you're staying with us and may be expecting some mail," I told him. "Annie knows almost everything that goes on in town," I said, "almost as much as Aunt Lizzie. She'll be asking you a lot of questions, so be prepared. But don't tell her why you're here or everyone in town will know and then they might not talk to you. Just ask her what sights you ought to see." Annie sure told him, a half hour's worth, and the professor was mopping his brow when we left.

"I think I'd better go back to your home now, Cully. My brain is reeling and I've got to get my transcription done right away." I asked him if he didn't want to go downtown to the saloon and railroad station as Dad had suggested and he said yes but that he'd like to have an hour at home first to rest and think.

Mother gave the professor some tea and cookies when he came downstairs and then he was ready to go again. Down the hill we went, past Old Blue Ball's house and the school and the three churches, and I'd just pointed out Callahan's store as a good place to collect samples when we met Fisheye, one of my two best friends. "Me, I was just coming up see you, Cully," he said after I'd introduced them to each other. "Eef I stay 'ome my mudder fine me work for to do." Out of the corner of my eye I could see the professor's lips moving silently. For the first time I noticed Fisheye's accent and speech. I'd never been aware that it was any different from my own.

"Come along with us, Fisheye", I suggested. "The professor wants to know where the depot and the saloon are. He's staying at our house and I'm to show him the town, what there is of it."

After seeing the depot and the saloon, Fisheye said, "I tink your fren like to see old fur-nace (he accented the second syllable) and ze waterfall, yes? My granpere, he haul ze stone for eet long time 'go. Ze waterfall, she is tirty feet high. Dey use zee wa-ter (again accenting the second syllable) for to cool peeg iron zat zey smelt dere in fur-nace. Yes." The professor admired the cascading water and the ruins of the old furnace but when he took out his notebook and began writing in it, Fisheye was curious. The professor turned over a page and rapidly drew a sketch of the furnace with the water flowing over the cliff behind it. "I like to remember and these notes and sketches help me," he said. He showed us the picture and it was very good. "Me, I nevair see artiste before," Fisheye exclaimed.

Just before we dropped off Fisheye, Dr. Johnson asked about the blacksmith's shop and why there was a huge iron triangle hanging from the roof peak. "Oh, dat's Paddy feeny's gong," Fisheye said. "Paddy, he bang dat for Saint Patrick's day ever year, yes. He Irish." I thought of going in so the professor could hear him talk but Paddy was busy. Paddy had a fine brogue, I told Mr. Johnson, and there were several other Irish families in town. Katy Flanagan's kids talked just like Paddy did.

That evening after supper the professor summarized his findings of the day to my interested parents. "Cully was a great help," he said. "I know where to collect my corpus of samples and have already got enough to convince me that there is indeed a U.P. dialect. It seems mainly to reflect two languages, French and Finnish, but other languages too have had their influence. Perhaps the most prevalent phonetic feature is the use of *t* and *d* for our two *th* sounds. They say 'dese, dose, and dem' for 'these, those and them', and they say 'tink' for 'think', 'tirsty' for 'thirsty'. That makes sense because neither Finnish nor French has a *th* sound."

"Yes," Mother interrupted. "I've had to get after Cully for saying 'duh' for 'the' and 'dat' for 'that'. He knows better but that's what he hears all the time."

"The people with whom I talked also seem to use the *s* for the *sh* fairly consistently," the professor continued. "That must be the Finnish influence because the French have a lot of *sh* words such as 'cherie' and 'chef'." He looked in his notebook. "Yes," he said, "I've heard 'wassing' for 'washing' and Annie, your postmistress, told Cully to be sure to 'sut the door'."

"I'll watch for that in Cully's speech," Mother interjected.

"Similarly, your people seem to substitute the 'y' for the voiced affricate 'j'. They say 'yump' for 'jump' and 'Yanuary' for 'January'. They use *v* for the *w* and *wh* sounds: 'vant' for 'want' and 'Vere you going, Cully?' for 'Where are you going?'"

Again he referred to his notebook. "Oh yes, many voiced sounds are unvoiced. They say 'poy' for 'boy' and 'iss' for 'is'. Oh, I've just begun to scratch the surface."

"You really can dissect the language," Dad said, admiringly.

"And then there are the vowel differences too. Cully's friend Fisheye nasalized a lot of them as the French do, but very frequently all of the speakers tended to use the short vowel 'eh' for the 'a' as in 'sat' or 'catch'. They say 'set' and 'ketch'! And then there's curious prolonging of vowels that may have a Finnish origin."

"Yes," said my father. "You'll hear them say 'Saatana' for Satan and 'puuko' for knife." There was more of the same but I went to bed early.

The next day Professor Johnson was bubbling with enthusiasm when we assembled for dinner. "I started at the post office as the mail was being distributed. 'Disturbed', they call it. As we waited, one woman approached me. 'You stay Doctor's house, eh? He fine man. You go fis-sing, maybe so? Doctor, he goodt fisserman.' I told her I hoped to although I've never fished in my whole life. But we had quite a conversation."

"Yes," Mother said, "the whole town knows you're here and are curious. Did you tell her of your project?"

"No, I was afraid it might stop her from talking."

"If it was Mrs. Erickson as I suspect, you didn't need to worry" said Mother, "but did you make any new discoveries?"

"Oh yes, indeed," replied the professor. "I'm coming to believe that a dominant feature of this dialect is the way the people handle the language itself. They omit many words, the articles and prepositions, mainly. They say, 'Go store?' for 'Are you going to the store?' Yes, and they often omit such auxiliary verbs as 'is' and 'are'. And oh, the double negatives that I hear everywhere! I was down in Callahan's store listening to two old codgers talking about 'deer hun-ting' and one said, 'Duh secon' veek in deer camp vee nevair soot no deer.', that sort of thing."

He turned to Dad. "Doctor," he said, "One of the problems I'm facing is determining the consistency of their utterances. Hearing snatches of conversation isn't enough. I need to have an opportunity to analyze the speech of just one person over a longer period of time. Have you any suggestions?"

Dad thought for a moment. "Yes," he said. "I think I could arrange to have Arvid Makela take you fishing, trolling for nothern pike in our big lake. That way you'd be with him for an extended time for sample collecting, and besides you should see our lovely Lake Tioga with its islands. If you'd pay him five dollars for being your guide, he'll be your friend forever. I understand he's out of work now and he has a boat down there."

The professor responded enthusiastically. "Wonderful!" he said. "I've wanted to go fishing all my life and never had a chance to do so. That sounds perfect. But is Mr. Makela a second generation Finn? I can't have my data corrupted by having samples from those who have just immigrated."

"Yes," Dad replied. "It was Arvid's grandfather who came over from the old country. I don't think the Makelas even speak Finnish in their home now, though he sure has a pronounced accent. How about tomorrow afternoon and evening? Edyth will fix you a snack if you miss supper. The fish bite better along toward sundown." The professor greeted the suggestion eagerly.

At suppertime Mr. Johnson told us of a new discovery. "Over and over again I've heard a language usage that come directly from the French," he said. "Your people often insert a pronoun after a subject noun. Here are some samples." He pulled out his notebook. "'Me, *I* go store now,' 'That old fart Slimber, *he* best liar in town,' 'My cow, *she* no give much milk now.' And there's another feature too that is common in French and your U.P. dialect: the final sounds are omitted or formed in the mouth but not spoken. 'Ole (old) man Viirta;' 'You get da verm (worms);' 'He dohn (don't) do nuttin but sit on ass alla time.' Oh, there were many other specimens of the same kind. I'm just fascinated." He spent the morning wandering around town and the early part of the afternoon upstairs working on his notes, but had tea with Mother about three o'clock. "Mrs. Gage," he said, after eating one of her big sugar cookies, "Have you noticed that the people up here often accent the wrong syllable? Not that it's wrong–just different."

"What do you mean?" asked Mother. "Can you give me an example?"

Well, they say'DEE-troit', not Detroit, and I've heard such locutions as 'ba-CON, om-LET, on-YAN' for 'onion' and 'pota-TOES'."

"Oh, that's how the French Canadians talk," said Mother. Changing the subject, she asked him a few personal questions. Was he married? He told her no, that being a scholar was a lonely life, that, except for his travels, he'd spent most of it in books and classrooms and his study. "Now that I'm almost sixty-five, Mrs. Gage, I know how much I've missed, but I guess it's too late to do anything about it now."

I overslept next morning and just got in on the tail end of the professor's report of his experiences in the barber shop and saloon. "The young man and I had a pleasant little conversation about the weather in winter. "Many times it go tirty peeloh and more. Lotsa snow. Vee go ski and snowshoe over drift up to ear, yah.' That sounded as though he were Finnish ancestry so I asked him from whence his forebears had come. For some reason that seemed to irritate the man 'Vatcha mean? I no got four bears, no got one even. You talk funny, Mister. Vere you from? You salesman, eh?" When I told him I was from Ann Arbor, he said, 'Oh, you be anudder bastard from Down Pelow.' and that was the end of the conversation."

"You can't use academic language like that," Dad commented. "You're lucky you didn't get a punch in the nose. We're proud people up here. Oh by the way, I've made the arrangements and Arvid Makela will come by about three o'clock to take you fishing. Don't forget to pay him. And don't overpay him either if you want to preserve your nose."

Just before I went to bed the professor came to the back door lugging a huge pike, perhaps ten pounds or more. His face was beaming. "I've never had so much fun in my life, Doctor," he said. "Arvid caught three and I caught this one. He cleaned and scaled it too. Would it be possible that Mrs. Gage might cook it tomorrow?"

"Of course, I will," said Mother. "My husband doesn't particularly care for pike because of the forked bones but he'll eat it and I'd welcome a change from the brook trout he's always bringing home."

"What a lovely lake you have. All those islands. And crystal clear water and the trees, birch, huge maples and pines. I've never seen such a beautiful place. Indeed, I almost forgot my mission but I've got a notebook full or Arvid's talk. Good talk too. He's quite a man! Oh, I'm so tired and happy, Mrs. Gage, I think I'll skip having anything to eat and just go to bed."

The rest of the week went by swiftly. Fisheye took him trout fishing twice. Mullu took him to Fish Lake and the cave-in at the old mine. The professor spent one whole day riding in a buckboard with Slimber Vester as old Maude, Mr. Marchand's horse, pulled them up the river road to the old Haysheds logging dam. Of course by that time the whole village knew why he was in Tioga. He was there to study how they talked. He was a professor from some big university Down Below and they felt flattered by his interest. So they made him welcome and talked to him every time they could manage it. If he was Dr. Gage's house guest he must be all right. Completely unconscious of their own speech, they were fascinated by his two pound words, as they called them. They also thought he was a bit crazy but that was OK in Tioga. We had always had our share of nuts and always enjoyed them and their doings. Something to talk about!

Before Professor Johnson left for Ann Arbor he took the train to Ishpeming, returning with a dozen yellow roses for Mother and a big box of El Perfecto cigars for Dad, the best they had in Toutloff's Drug Store.

"I just can't tell you how much I've appreciated being in your home and village," he said to my parents. "I've never, never know such wonderful people or had such a fine time. While I've only got a nucleus of the data I need on the U.P. dialect, I've made a good start and plan to return soon for a more extended stay. Moreover, I've persuaded the Widow Johnson to take me on as a boarder and roomer so I won't have to impose on your incredibly gracious hospitality. Who knows? Perhaps I'll stay here the rest of my life, collecting linguistic samples for a book. And experiencing all the things I've missed."

To know what happened, thereafter, you'll have to translate.

ðə profesɚ dɪd kʌm bæk tu tɑɹogə hwer hi
mɛrɪd hɪz lændledɪ ðə wɪdo ænd et hɪʒ
pæstiz ænd ðə frʃ hi kɔt ænd ðə dɪr hi
ʃɔt ænd brkɔz hi hæd pʊt so mʌtʃ əv arr
spɪtʃ ɪn hɪz mauθ kəlɛktɪŋ sæmplz hi
ɛndɪd ʌp wɪð ə faɪn ju pi æksɛnt tu

The Peaceful Little Village Of Tioga

In these Northwoods Readers I have tried to describe and perhaps preserve the culture of Tioga and the U.P. as it was in the early days of this century. Culture hell! We weren't cultured; we were tough and rough and rude and crude. We almost had to be to survive! Our men lived in danger most of their lives getting the iron ore out of the bowels of the earth, felling the great white pines and riding the logs down turbulent, roaring streams at breakup. Our women grew old and bent before their time, washing, ironing, canning without any of today's conveniences and also raising huge hordes of children. The harsh climate with its nine months of bitter winter and three months of poor sledding demanded of all of us the courageous endurance that the Finns called *sisu*. Isolated in the ever encroaching dark forest, we made the best of it and despite everything lived surprisingly happy lives.

From the very beginning we kids in Tioga were taught by precept and example to be tough, to endure pain, punishment, and drudgery. At three, the Finn boys were getting boiled and roasted (broasted) in the sauna once or twice a week. At four, the French Canadian children were hoeing and weeding the potato patch. At five, when I slipped on some rocks and badly bruised and scraped my leg from stem to stern, my father looked it over. "Nothing's broken. Stop your bawling!" he said contemptuously. No matter what happened we weren't supposed to cry. "Crybaby! Crybaby!" That taunt soon taught us not to.

We also taught ourselves to be tough. Pulling our heavy sleds up the mile-long, very steep hill street was very hard when you were only half-past six and your feet and hands seemed frozen but you didn't dare stop to rest lest some other kid came along to yell

"Kindergarten Baby, Slopped in the gravy!" In June we'd bare our wrists and let a big mosquito gorge on it until it was finally full enough to swat. The boy with the biggest blood spot was the winner. In April or May when the crows had come back but there was only a ring of black water around the giant ice cake in the middle of Fish Lake, we had to jump into the icy fire and see how long we could bear it. Barefoot in July we'd climb the big cinder pile at the mine until our soles were bleeding and burning in the hot sun. At ten, playing Nosey Poker in the haymow, we did our utmost to restrain our tears when we lost. I should explain that the person with the lowest draw poker hand got ten swats across the tip of the nose with the cards held by each of the other players. We had no money to play with so we didn't bet, but that penalty kept the game interesting if hazardous to the health. Mullu found a magneto from an old Model-T Ford and rigged up a crank so it would give a good shock if you held the terminal wires. The faster you cranked the contraption, the worse the shock. It was murder but we had to see who could endure it the longest. Kids had to be tough in Tioga!

The ability to bear pain without crying, however, sometimes presented a problem. I soon learned that when my father was spanking me (Dad called it "thrashing", a more accurate description), that if I bore the beating stoically his walloping would be harder and last longer. I pondered the dilemma and came up with a more or less satisfactory solution. I wouldn't cry but just groan "Oh, oh, oh" piteously and make sure I got the timing right. One day coming home early from his house calls, Dad found me playing cowboy by riding Rosie, our Jersey milk cow, around the barnyard. I knew it wasn't particularly good for the milk production but I liked the way she galloped and bellowed. Well, Dad caught me by the scruff of the neck, opened the back gate of the buckboard, put me in it prone, and started whaling me good. The pitiful oh-oh-ooh groanings worked fine. Not too bad! Not as bad as when Old Blue Balls, our school superintendent, hit me when we got caught playing hooky at Fish Lake.

This training in the inhibition of emotion had its drawbacks. For example, the outward expression of affection was frowned upon too in Tioga. Although I'm sure that my mother and father loved each other dearly, never once in all those years did I ever see them hug or kiss each other, or even touch each other fondly. That was for the bedroom behind closed door, I guess. Any display of tenderness in public was never seen in Tioga, except perhaps a few of the French Canadians when they'd had too much chokecherry wine. It was unmanly, a sign of weakness. In a rough land we had to be tough!

We also had to be fearless. This dubious virtue was instilled in us very early, at least by the time we entered school. To be called a sissy was bad enough; to geel that you were a coward was infinitely worse! Our fathers faced danger everyday of their lives in the mines, cutting down those giant trees, or on their traplines. Every week some of them came wounded to our door or were carried into my father's hospital on a stretcher. Scared by a bear raiding our garbage piles, there were occasionally runaways going down our street, the carriages careening wildly from one side to another behind horses mad with terror. At night in the grove behind my father's hospital we heard wolves chasing deer. There were train wrecks. There were explosions in the fields as farmers dynamited the stumps that thwarted their plows. There were gunshot wounds or deaths. Danger was everywhere back then in Tioga but we coped with it. No big deal! Just had to make it through the winter.

It's a wonder any of us kids ever made it to maturity, the risks we took to prove our bravery. We ran along the rails of sharp picket fences; we made our way precariously down the steep slopes of old ore pits; we scaled the sheer faces of granite cliffs. Last summer I visited the locale of a ski run we made in the hilly woods below the west edge of Company Field. Very steep, the trail wove narrowly through the maples, then angled sharply left to avoid a jumbled mess of huge craggy boulders. To make the sudden turn we had to grap a sapling, swing our skis around, and at the precise second let go to continue the descent. If we didn't do it just right, into that mass of sharp rocks we'd go. Insane! Yet we barreled down that trail day after day and no one got hurt.

We were always daring each other. "Bet you're scared to knock down that wasp's nest!" "Bet you ain't got the guts to taste that jack-in-the-pulpit root!" (Unboiled, it tasted like fire as we all knew). "Let's run across the field!" (The field in which Mr. Salo's vicious bull pawed the ground and bellowed.) "Let's go steal some of Chervais' green apples. He just got rock salt in his shotgun."

We rigged up an old cable from the closed mine between two trees and descended down it hand over hand, over a deep gully. We threw rocks at discarded dynamite caps almost hoping they wouldn't go off though some of them did. We'd climb birch or maple saplings to their tops, then kick our legs outward to make them bend to the forest floor. Some of them only bent part way and then we'd have a long drop to the hard ground. After eating a swiped can of pork and beans in our shack in the woods, we'd take a match and set fire to the farts that resulted. Made a clear blue flame! We hunted snakes and snapped their heads off; we trapped skunks; and we played tricks in school that risked Old Blue Balls' ruler, hand or strap. It was the delicious smell of danger that we wanted in our nostrils as we played our versions of Russian Roulette. We weren't cowards. Nosirrie! Sulu wasn't afraid to eat worms; Fisheye would tuck a big bloodsucker between his thumb and firefinger to watch it swell and change color; Mullu would hand from his legs on the high limb of a tree and swing back and forth; and I, well, I did a lot of damfool things too.

We needed all the courage we could develop back then in Tioga because of all the fighting that went on. It was a way of life, almost a cultural mandate. Was it because civilization, a term that hardly fits, had come to the U.P. and our town only thirty years before, when the first iron mines had opened and the pines were logged? Frontiersmen have always had ready fists everywhere. All I know is that I had to fight my way to and from school far too often and most of my classmates had to do the same. At recess there was always a ring of onlookers reveling in watching two kids battling within it, and when one got licked, another ring would soon be formed with another two boys slugging each other. Our daily entertainment!

There were dog fights, cat fights, impromptu rooster fights. We'd put a handful of red pissants on an anthill of black ants to see them battling to the death. In rutting season the bucks clashed antlers in the nearby forest. Growling cub bears cuffed each other in their play. Chipmunks wrestled and bit each other. Often we'd go up to the old mining pit behind Flynn's store that was used as our town's garbage dump, so we could watch the rats committing mayhem on each other.

Our men fought too, though not as often as we kids did. My father, the doctor, always dreaded Saturday night because he knew he'd have to sew up the slashes made by the Finn's long puuko knives. Finns never stabbed when they fought, just sliced enough to leave a reminder. Most of our young men just used their huge fists, grunting and swinging roundhouse blows until the opponent went down cursing his luck. Outside Higley's saloon, or on the platform of the depot, such fights were a common sight. No one ever interfered. They knew that if they did they'd get clobbered by both of the battlers. Once by the depot I saw two tottering old men hitting each other with their canes and when a brakeman tried to intercede they both began beating him.

Girls and women fought too, though more rarely. Compared to the fights between males, however, their battles were much more vicious. They pulled each other's hair and used their fingernails to scratch faces into bloody messes. As they fought, they cried and wept and screamed, whereas most of the battles between men or boys were pretty silent except when a good blow produced an involuntary ow! Moreover, after the scrap, girls and women held a grudge for a long time, whereas we did not.

There were only two uspoken Marquis of Queensberry rules that seemed to govern our schoolyard battles: No fair hitting your opponent when he was on the ground or not looking, and no fair kicking him in the crotch. The first of these was important because when you knew you were licked you could fall to the ground and escape any further punishment.

Neither of these rules held for men. Many of our old lumberjacks had faces full of scars from the boot caulks of ancient enemies who had not only knocked them down but stomped them. As a boy I never witnessed any fights like that but I sure heard a lot of tales of chokings, ear biting, eye gouging, and the like that had occurred when the lumberjacks came out of the woods in the spring to get drunk and tear up the town. Indeed, I once went fishing overnight up at the headwaters of the Tioga River with Nick Maloney who had spent ten years in prison for killing a man with his fists and then stomping him. He sure had some hair-raising tales of fighting there by the night fire but I liked him and he sure knew how to catch brook trout.

Our schoolyard fights were never as brutal nor did they last as long. We tried only to give the other kid a black eye or bloody nose or to make him bawl and cry uncle.

Why did we kids fight? A part from the tradition, we probably battled because of the frustration we encountered in school, the tough discipline, the feeling of being cooped up. We fought too in the effort to achieve dominance, to move up in the peck order. "I kin lick you!" was a challenge that started many of our altercations. No anger was involved. We just had to be sure we were the better one when it came to fisticuffs. When someone put a chip on his shoulder or spit on your shoes, you had to accept the dare or be dispised. Many of our fights, certainly my own, began with being teased unmercifully. "Cully's a stutter-cat; Cully's a stutter-cat; K-K-K-Katy (from the old song) K-K-K-K-Katy." That's all that was needed to set me swinging for blood. Even after I got so I could lick all the kids in my grade and below, the bigger ones would call me those names knowing that I would fight and that they could give me a trimming. Dear old golden school days? Nuts! Dear old bloody school days, they were. I had more black eyes and bloody noses than anyone in our school.

Until Grampa Gage gave me some lessons! Distressed to see my bruises and battle wounds, he bought a pair of boxing gloves and everyday we'd go a few rounds. I learned to hit straight, not in semicircles; I learned how to jab repeatedly with my left hand, then use the right to cream my opponent. Best of all, he taught me to duck my head to the side, ward off a blow with my elbow, and to take a hard blow yet continue fighting even harder. That training sure paid off and most of the teasing stopped.

But I should also mention the gang fighting that characterized those early years in Tioga. Gang is the wrong word. We had no gangs in the modern sense of the word but there had always been a keen rivalry between the Up-towners and the Down-towners, between the French-Canadian and Indian kids who lived in the valley and the Finns, English, Swede and other kinds who lived on top of the hill.

Those battles were fun fights really, not like the one-on-one scraps in the schoolyard. From ten to twenty kids would assemble, make their plans, gather their ammunition and then send word to the other side that at such an hour we'd be ready for them at a certain place. Rarely was the challenge refused. Depending on the season, we'd fight with slingshots, using pebbles or hazelnuts for bullets, or spears made of cattails, or wild cucumbers (those spiny oblong fruits that sure sting when you get one on the neck), or snowballs, or the frozen horse turds which hurt the most.

We'd line up our forces at each end of the little side street just beyond the Methodist Church by Old Blue Balls' house, advance on each other and try to break each others lines into disarray and flight. Each side had a general, tactics and reinforcements but no prisoners were taken. Unlike our solitary fights which were usually silently carried out, these were full of yelling and shouting as we clashed, so much so that sometimes they called Charles Olafson, our town constable, to restore some calm. These were fun fights because we never used our fists and rarely did anyone get seriously hurt. The last and the best of these battles I have described in my tale "Old Blue Balls" in my first Northwoods Reader so I won't repeat it here, except to say that the cowpasties flew fast and furious and we joined together to chase him back into his house.

So that's the way it was in the peaceful little forest village of Tioga in the early 1900s.

One afterthought: Grampa Gage told me a tale which I've heard several times since and which you may have heard too. A man was going around the corner to great granite hill when suddenly he saw a huge bear coming right toward him. He got out his jackknife and prayed. "Dear Lord," he said. "If you're on the bear's side, make it quick! And if you're on my side, make it quick! But if you're neutral, Lord, you're going to watch the damndest fight you ever did see."

God was always neutral in Tioga.

Killing Three Birds
With One Cheese

It really was my father's fault. If he hadn't told us why he'd been kicked out of his rooming house when he was in medical school, I never would have thought of the idea.

But I'd better start at the beginning, which was when Dad pushed aside the big wedge of yellow store cheese and roared that he was sick of it. "Edyth," he said to my mother, "How many times have I told you not to buy this miserable stuff? Where's that stinky cheese, the white brick cheese, we used to have?"

"Mr. Flynn doesn't keep it any more," she replied calmly. "I know you like your cheese ripe and strong but I just can't get it in town. Perhaps the next time you go to Ishpeming…"

"No!" Dad interrupted. "I'll stop in this afternoon and tell Flynn I want some better cheese even if he has to go to Wisconsing to get it. Lord, we're the best customer he has and he knows it. It's not right to spoil one of your fine pies with this junk!"

That evening Mother asked him if he'd seen Mr. Flynn and he said yes, he had, that Flynn had told him his supplier didn't make the stinky brick cheese any more, and that no one except the Gages bought it anyway. He did give Dad the address of a firm that made limburger and my father had already ordered five pounds of it by mail.

"Oh no!" my Mother wailed. "Not Limburger. That'll smell up the whole house. It's putrid! I've never tasted it and I don't want to. My father brought some home once when I was a little girl and I still remember that horrid odor."

Dad grinned. "Yes, it's pretty strong, I'll admit. When I was in Medical School in Ann

Arbor, all of us students used to eat some on crackers to get the stink of the cadavers we were dissecting out of our nostrils. Not much refrigeration back then and the formaldehyde they used didn't help much either. Sometimes we'd toast a chunk of Limburger over one of the laboratory lamps to cancel the smell of the stiffs when they were hauled out of the cold room. Boy, did that really clear the air–or pollute it even more!"

I was all ears. I liked the tales Dad told of his days in medical school–like the one where he used a human finger for a book mark. That always drove Mother from the table.

"We were always hungry back then," Dad continued, "and often we'd bring back some of the crackers and Limburger to eat at night when we were studying in the rooming house. Not bad, not bad at all, though you couldn't eat much at a time. I admit it did stink up the place and when our landlady came up one night and found us toasting a bit of it over our kerosene lamp, she raised the roof and insisted we leave the next day."

"Don't blame her a bit!" said Mother. "I'll probably chase you out too when that Limburger cheese comes."

It came! When Annie the postmistress handed me the box as I collected our mail she told me to hurry home, that there must be something very dead inside. Yes, It sure stank even through the cardboard. Mother made me put it, not in the pantry, but in the woodshed, and made Dad open the box and cut the slice he wanted for his pie. I had to taste it too, of course, and if I held my nose it wasn't really too bad. Sorta lingered in your mouth and on your hands for hours though.

Well, Dad had his Limburger cheese with his daily pie for a week or two, but I noticed the slices he cut were getting smaller and then the day came when he said, "Well, that's enough Limburger. From now on let's go back to cheddar." He told me to bury the rest of the box in the manure pile.

That happened about the end of October and now it was the end of February, that bad time of the U.P. year–the dog days of winter when everyone had sickened of snow and spring was a million weeks away. It was even bad for us kids, too. Way below zero for a month, it wasn't much fun playing outside and in school it was worse. We were in P.P. Polson's room for the second year she'd taught us, or rather tyrannized us. Rules, rules, rules! So many of them it wasn't even fun trying to outwit them. Besides Miss Polson always won. And she drove us and drilled us and disciplined us! Who cared about the capital of Patagonia or distinguishing participles from verbs! Who gave a damn if the push-pulls weren't slanted correctly in the ovals of the Palmer writing? None of us did. I didn't! I was bored silly. I'd read all the textbooks three times, had mastered fractions, memorized all the junk I had to and was sick, sick, sick of school. Sometimes in the morning I'd lie a bit longer in bed trying to decde if I'd play sick that day so I could stay home, even though I knew it meant calomel and castor oil. Washington's Birthday, Birthington's Washday, Bleah!

I was also afraid to go to school because of Toivo Maki, the school bully, who I knew would hurt or humiliate me. A big Finn kid, he was, and mean! A really good fighter too, he had even licked some of the high-school boys as well as all of us in the seventh grade. Once, when he was beating on me and Fisheye and Mullu came to my defense, he trimmed the three of us but good. Everyday I knew he'd be waiting for me in the morning. "Kiss my ass!" he'd demand and when I wouldn't he'd slug me till I cried. I'd often try to make an excuse so I wouldn't have to go out for recess but that didn't always work, so he'd get me again. At noon it wasn't so bad because I was one of those who went home for lunch and Toivo didn't. He carried his dinner pail, ate in the basement and tortured other kids till the bell rang and he had to go to class. But when school let out Toivo would be ready for me again.

Perhaps nowdays a kid in the same predicament might tell his parents or teachers about a similar situation, but that would have been unthinkable back then in the Tioga of the early nineteen hundreds. My father would have told me to fight my own battles and to take my lickings if I had to, that it was character building. As for telling P.P. Polson, why I would have been ostracized by the other kids from then on! So instead, up there in bed each morning I fantasized. I'd put that Toivo in a cage with some big rats and let them eat him as I gloated. That sort of thing. But one morning in bed I had and idea about revenge that shocked me, it was so perfect. Why I could kill three birds with one stone: get even with Toivo, play a good trick on P.P. Polson, and maybe even succeed in getting school dismissed! The enormity of it made me shiver. But did I have the guts to carry it out?

No, I decided, but Fisheye might. Fisheye wasn't afraid of anything, and if his folks found out they wouldn't give a damn. Fisheye was the oldest of nine children and slept in the cowbarn at night because there was no room for him in the house. Yes, he'd go for it. If he got caught and Old Blue Balls gave him The Strap, well, he'd had it before and survived. My friend had known beatings both at school and at home all his life so the prospect of one more wouldn't faze him.

Like Toivo, Fisheye didn't go home for lunch because he lived way down in the valley and there had been many times when he came to school with no lunch at all. When I told my mother about it, she told me that when that happened I was always to bring him home to eat with us, and he had often done so.

That morning I had a hard time concentrating in school and had my ears pulled and felt Miss Polson's ruler twice, so intent I was in the planning. I'd bring Fisheye home at noon and after we'd eaten we'd get that Limburger cheese out of the manure pile, take it to the classroom and he'd sneak in and put it on the steam radiator and...and...and...And all hell would break loose!

Coming home with Fisheye that noon, I explained my plan and he was entranced. "That's a good one," he said. "That's a dandy!" We ate hurriedly, then went to the barn where I got a pitchfork to unearth the Limburger box. It took some work because the manure pile was pretty frozen but that was good because when we found it the cheese had frozen too and stank more of manure than anything else, but I knew that when it thawed under the steam radiator it would smell plenty. Indeed it was so frozen I had to chop it with an axe to break off a big piece and a little one and put them in a brown store bag I'd already hidden in the barn. "Just tuck it behind and under the radiator, bag and all," I told Fisheye. "There's lots of bags like that and nobody will know where it came from. A lot of kids bring their lunches in them."

We hurried back to school, getting there about twenty minutes before the bell was to ring. I should explain that at noon all the classrooms were empty and no pupil was to go back to his room until the bell rang. We either had to play outside or, in the winter months, play in the basement gym where the kids ate their lunches under the supervision of one of the teachers. We knew that P.P. Polson, had that supervising duty that month so she wouldn't be in our classroom. Nevertheless, we were plenty scared as Fisheye did his dirty work while I watched outside the door in case someone did come by.

It didn't take long, so Fisheye and I went down to the basement to join the other kids until the bell rang. Toivo was there, of course, hogging the basketball so others couldn't have a turn shooting it. I winked at Fisheye and whispered, "He's got a surprise coming!"

Finally the bell rang and all of us ascended the stairs to our classrooms. "Quiet, children," P.P. said, "Quiet! We will have five minutes of quiet before we begin!" Fisheye and I looked across at each other. We couldn't smell a damned thing.

The wall clock said one-thirty before we got the first whiff of the thawing Limburger, but by one-forty-five it was coming on loud and clear. Eva Thompson raised her hand. "Miss Polson, please, Howard smells awful bad." Howard (Mule) Cardinal's seat was next to the radiator. "Aw, shut up," he said. "Every fox smells his own hole first." Miss Polson came down and sniffed. "You're right!" she said. "Howard, you go immediately to the bathroom and wash thoroughly and if your shoes smell of manure, wash them too." I didn't dare look at Fisheye.

Within minutes, however, it was certain that the smell wasn't coming from Howard and that it wasn't manure either. That cheese had sure ripened in that manure pile those four months. Wow! What a stink of stinks! The kids first began holding their noses, then began choking. Some of the girls began to cry. Even Miss Polson couldn't stand it. "Children," she screamed over the tumult. "Leave the room. Go to the hall outside and stay there until I get Mr. Donegal and find out what's wrong. And be quiet!"

Down came Old Blue Balls taking two steps at a time, with P.P. following to enter the room. Quiet? You could have heard a pin drop there in the hall. Finally, out he came with the brown paper bag and a sticky mess in his hands. Oh how he glared at us. "I'll find out who did this dirty trick if it takes me a month, and I'll tan his hide so he won't be able to sit down for two!" he roared. Wow, was he mad! Fisheye rolled his eyeballs up into his head and I almost filled my pants. "You children stay right here in the hall until I get rid of this and come back, and Miss Polson, you open all the windows wide," he ordered.

The putrid smell of that Limburger had begun to seep into the hall when Old Blue Balls returned. "Line up along the wall and hold out your hands," he commanded. "There's no danger, but one of you put some Limburger cheese on the steam radiator and I'm going to find out who it was. Then he went down the line, sniffing the hands of everyone of us. Lord, how I hoped my own hands didn't smell though I couldn't see how they could, the cheese having been frozen so hard. It was difficult to keep them from trembling but I did, and he passed on. He seemed to linger a bit longer when he came to Howard, perhaps because he'd been closest to it, and did so again when he came to Fisheye, perhaps because he always had a barn smell, sleeping there with the cow as he always had to, but finally he passed on and it was obvious that he hadn't found his quarry.

Old Blue Balls then turned to P.P. "Miss Polson, which of these pupils had been to the bathroom to wash their hands?" he demanded. She told him she didn't know of any. "Well, then, I'll have to examine their coats and mittens," he said. "Whoever carried that damned cheese in here must have left some smells somewhere." He disappeared into the cloakroom. Fisheye and I raised our eyebrows at each other. Then we heard a terrible roar and out Blue

Balls stormed, waving a jacket. "Whose coat is this?" he yelled. "It's Toivo's," several kids shouted. "It's Toivo's." Old Blue Balls didn't waste a minute. He grabbed Toivo by the hair and dragged him screaming up the stairs to his office. Pow! Pow! Pow! Oh, how Toivo yelled as The Hand and The Strap walloped him. You could hear him hollering all over the school. "We'll dismiss the class for the rest of the day, children," Miss Polson said. "I trust you have learned that it is unwise to play such an abominable trick. It wasn't funny at all."

Three birds with one stone! I went home pretty happy for once and glad that I had told Fisheye to put the small hunk of the Limburger in Toivo's jacket.

Smoke Rings

Occasionally there were times when I begged my Grampa Gage to tell me another story and he would say, "No, Mr. McGillicuddy. I'm not in the mood." He'd talk about other things but no amount of coaxing could sway him. I didn't understand that then but I do now for, as of this moment, I'm not in the mood either. No more tales of the U.P. tonight, my friends!

So let me ramble instead about pipe smoking, a messy habit that I have loved for most of my many years. The first pipe I smoked was an ancient black corncob owned by an old French Canadian named Dick DeGon. He'd seen my friend Rudy and me trying to roll dead leaves into cigars when we were only six years old. "Non, non! mes amis," he said. "Zat no good for to smoke. I geeve you good smoke, oui!" He filled his black corncob with Peerless tobacco, lit it, and handed it to us. It was awful but we kept taking turns, pretending to be tough big men, until nausea overwhelmed us. How the old Frenchman laughed when we dizzily staggered away. "Me, I teach you good lesson, I tink," he said.

That lesson lasted until I was about eleven or twelve when Mullu had swiped some cigarette papers and tobacco from his father and we smoked them down at our shack in Beaverdam swamp. We didn't get sick that time for some reason but the experience was not a pleasant one. About that same year Fisheye and I made little pipes from acorns by removing their caps, taking out the kernel, and boring a hole at the base into which we inserted straws. They weren't too satisfactory because the straws usually collapsed after two or three puffs and Dad's Granger tobacco was terribly strong.

In high school most of us tried to chew snuff or Redman plug tobacco, but I could never manage them. They tasted awful and the taste lingered for hours in my mouth. I also swallowed some juice once and that was the end of that. Once I tried a cigarette, a "coffin nail", as we called them back then, but I didn't like it either. Indeed, I've never smoked cigarettes in all my life and that perhaps is probably why I've lived so long. In college, in an effort to appear sophisticated, during my freshman year, I did smoke cigars for a short time, mainly long black stogies, but there's nothing so foul as a dead cigar butt, so I quit.

It was in my senior year at the University of Michigan that I really began to smoke a pipe, and I probably never would have done so had I not finished an unfinished song in one of Chaucer's works. Professor Sanford, a world-famous scholar who had written many books on Chaucer and the old English ballads and Keats, taught one class a semester in Chaucer and somehow I managed to get into it. One of the best teachers I have ever known, he made the subject so fascinating I looked forward to each class with great excitement. One day he read to us, using the old English pronunciation, two songs of Chaucer that had been left unfinished in the text, and expressed great regret that the remaining lines had been lost forever. So that evening I finished the songs as I thought they might have ended using all the quaint words and spellings current at Chaucer's time. It was a tricky business getting the verses to rhyme so I worked all night on the task, then early the next morning slipped the completed songs under the professor's office door. I did not sign my name.

Well, when I came to his class that afternoon, I found that Dr. Sanford had written the two songs on the blackboard along with my additional verses. He said he was utterly delighted, that there were only a few mistakes which he pointed out, and then asked the student who had written them to see him after class. Too shy, and fearing that my stuttering would make the situation uncomfortable for both of us, I did not accept the invitation, hating myself for not doing so. He was not to be deterred, however, and by having us write something in class so he could identify the handwriting, he insisted that I come with him to his office for afternoon tea and so he could know me better.

That was the beginning of a wonderful treasured experience. Professor Sandford took me under his wing, made me his assistant, shared with me his great learning and wisdom, and became my friend and model. He read all the stuff I'd been writing and encouraged me to write more. With his considerable influence he opened many doors that had been closed to me, arranging to let me have access to the library's stacks and rare book room, and gave me tickets to symphonic concerts, plays, and art exhibitions. Through him I met many of the famous poets and writers of the time. He was my mentor and I was his protege.

I was also his errand boy, getting the books he wanted, abstracting articles, occasionally correcting student papers, and even buying him shoestrings and tobacco. Not any old kind of tobacco either; it had to be Serene Mixture. The professor was a pipe smoker. In his office, lined with books from ceiling to floor, a halo of pipe smoke always hung over his head. On his desk was a large pipe rack, the holes holding at least ten or eleven briar pipes of various sizes and shapes. Each one of them had a name but I can only recall Aristophanes and Marcus Aurelius, his favorites. Never did he smoke the same pipe again on a single day. "That's the only way to keep them sweet, Cully," he told me. "Any fool who keeps smoking the same pipe all day will have a raw tongue and a bad pipe too." Nor did he ever return one to its rack without running a pipe cleaner through it.

One day, after I'd deposited a royalty check for him at the bank, he gave me a twenty dollar bill which back then had the same purchasing power as a hundred dollar bill would now. "I want you to go to the tobacconist and buy a pipe for me, please," he said. When I protested that I wouldn't know a good one from a bad one, he grinned and said, "Well, I'll tell you. Buy one that looks a bit like Marcus Aurelius here: straight stem but slightly curved at the mouthpiece, not too long, and be sure the rim of the bowl is about a quarter of an inch wide. Thin bowls never get a good cake. Try to get one with briar that is straight-grained and with no signs of knots or flaws. See if it fits lovingly between the thumb and forefingers and shake it by the tip to be sure it isn't top heavy."

I sure didn't relish the assignment and when I returned I was very apprehensive as I handed him the case and his change. Dr. Sanford opened it, took out the pipe and examined it for a long time before he spoke. "A good one," he said. "I couldn't have selected a better one myself. With the proper breaking in, It will be a comfort to you all your life." Noticing my incredulous expression, the old man smiled. "Yes, Cully, this pipe is yours. Please accept it as a token of my appreciation for all the help you've given me–and for your companionship too." I was so overcome by the gift I incoherently stammered my thanks and fled from his office.

The next afternoon when I stopped by to see if he had anything he wanted me to do, I found Professor Sanford and another man playing guitars and singing, having a high old time. "This is Carl Sandburg, Cully," he said, "and we're comparing his Appalachian collections of old English songs with those I've unearthed from Elizabethan times. If you want to, just sit in the corner and listen." I did so and it was one of the best afternoons in my life. Carl Sandburg was one of the most prominent poets in America at that time. You probably know his poem about Chicago or the line about how the fog came in on little cat feet. Anyway, they ignored me from that time on and had a ball, but I've never forgotten it.

Dr. Sandford (a lonely man, whose wife had died a few years before,) always was in his office until midnight so, the evening I dropped in again to see him and to express my appreciation. "I'm glad you came, Cully," he said. "Do you have your pipe with you? I want to show you how to break it in."

I had purchased a pouch of Sir Walter Raleigh smoking tobacco but had not yet tried the pipe. The Professor approved of my choice. "It's a very mild tobacco," he said, "a fine one to use at first. You may want to have a stronger kind later."

Then he showed me how to fill it just one small layer at a time and each one lovingly tamped down before the next layer was added. "Tuck it down around the edges with your forefinger so it's firm but not hard," he said. "For the first month or so, never fill it more than half way to the rim and smoke all of it before refilling. That way you'll establish a fine-grained cake all around the inside of the bowl. Some benighted souls smear the inside of the bowl first with honey because it makes a cake swiftly, but I never do. Honey makes for a coarse cake, one that will not absorb the tobacco tars as well." He handed me a bunch of kitchen matches. "These work best," he said. "They hold a flame longer. Just don't scratch them on your pants or they'll leave a mark." He showed me how to twirl the match just after lighting it so the flame would be a steady one and to hold it just above the tobacco until all the surface was ignited. "Take little short puffs," he insisted, "but slow, not fast ones. Never inhale or blow smoke out of your nostrils. Just hold it in your mouth and then let it come out slowly and gracefully. Most of the pleasure of pipe smoking is visual, as you'll find if you try to smoke in the dark." Oh there was a lot more, but I've forgotten.

That happened sixty-three years ago and I've been a pipe smoker ever since. Lord, the pipes I've had and lost and broken and discarded in that time. People keep giving me more of them each year so I always have a-plenty. I've had curved ones, pipes with twelve-inch stems, one made from a calabash gourd, several made of clay. One of the latter that I purchased in Ireland turned out to be an excellent pipe and as it aged it took on a beautiful brown color. A stutterer from Iran named Abdullah sent me a water pipe (a hookah) in appreciation for my successful therapy with him. That hookah was fun to smoke at first. The tobacco bowl sat on a vase of water which in turn sat on the floor at my feet and when I puffed, delightful volleys of filtering bubbles occurred in the vase. Unfortunately, the six-foot pliable rubber stem to my mouth was impossible to clean and soon I could not bear to smoke it.

I also have some meerschaum pipes from Turkey that are still virgin, because once when I was a young man I went to a famous pipe shop in Chicago and asked to buy a good meerschaum. The proprietor refused to sell me one. "Nein, nein!" he said, "You are too young. Save something for your old age," and sold me a briar pipe instead. Perhaps in a few more years I'll be old enough to smoke a meerschaum.

I've experimented with many kinds of pipe tobacco too. The aromatic ones smell fine when you open the pouch, but they're too strong for me and I found they soon spoil a good pipe. Once I bought a large set of many different kinds of tobacco from many lands and attempted to design a perfect mixture of my own, only to discover that I couldn't. So I've been smoking Sir Walter Raleigh, the kind I started with, ever since.

Have I become addicted? Oddly, I do not believe so. Certainly not in the physiological sense of an addiction to the nicotine. I never inhale the smoke, just let it linger in the mouth for a bit before slowly blowing it out. For forty years, to make sure, I quit pipe smoking for a month every single year and found it very easy, with no withdrawal symptoms. I just missed the pleasure of the whole process from scratching the match to tapping out the final ashes, but I didn't miss it very much. These last years, however, I've quit trying to build character and so enjoy my pipes all year long.

A psychiatrist told me once that I was a pipe smoker because of an oral fixation on my mother's breast, that I was still an infantile suckling. I didn't tell him that I had been a bottle baby from the beginning because I knew he'd say of course, that I was still trying to make up for my deprivation. If so, so be it! All I know is that it's very comforting to suck sweet lazy smoke from a good pipe.

And my pipes are good ones. I have two sets of them, each with ten pipes in their racks, and not one of them bites. I smoke each set for two weeks, using a different pipe each time and no more than six or seven different ones on a given day. I clean each one with a pipe cleaner after smoking it, and after the two weeks on one set I burn out their stems with a straightened coat hanger heated cherry red before turning to the other set. Many modern pipes have a place in the stem for a filter but I used a twisted pipe cleaner instead which works much better. Sometimes I use my jackknife to scrape an excessive cake from the bowl.

Where and when do I smoke these pipes of mine? When I'm not at my beloved cabins in the U.P. I live in a 130-year-old brick farmhouse on an eighty-acre farm, now surrounded by the city of Portage. Just behind the barns is a four-acre plot that my wife and I long ago turned into a park planted with pines and birch and maple, my miniature U.P. The trees, now forty feet tall, hold a little pool and that is where I have my early morning pipe as I watch the birds and animals coming to drink. We've even had deer.

Behind the garage I have my Secret Garden, so hidden by bushes and tall flowers you wouldn't suspect it was there. A mass of flowers circles a crab apple tree, and in one corner opposite the arbor where I sit is a fountain dancing in a huge cast iron hog-scalding kettle. Overhead are the great branches of burr oak trees, trees that were saplings when the house was built before the Civil War. It's a quiet, lovely spot and there I smoke another pipe midmorning.

After lunch I enjoy still another and different pipe either on the front porch of the old house watching the cars go by the mailbox at the end of the long lawn, or when sitting on the shaded circular bench built around the largest of our great oaks. Then, after a mandatory nap which I still resent, I usually smoke another one in my big chair as I mull over the stuff that should go into a story I'm about to write, but I never smoke while writing or chopping wood or working in my gardens. I save my best pipe for Happy Hour at five and have another one just before I go to bed.

So in a few minutes I will be sitting by a fine black walnut fire blazing in the big fireplace, a very old man in a very old house contentedly smoking a very old pipe named Professor Sanford. I'll blow a smoke ring for you, my friend.

The Sad Side

In my endeavor to portray the life we led in the U.P. during the early part of this century I fear that I may have painted too rosy a picture. Old men seem to remember the funny, happy experiences of their past lives more than the unhappy ones. Tioga had its share of both and so I'm going to try to recall a bit of its sad side.

I. *Mullu*

Some tragedies are major; others are played in a minor key. Let me begin with one of the latter, the tale of how my friend Mullu got his heart broken. As you may recall, he, Fisheye and I were very close friends–the Unholy Trio of Tioga–always getting into one trouble after another, always enjoying each other's company. Unfortunately that relationship began to change when we entered high school, mainly because Mullu had fallen in love. Yes, he had it bad! Why, rather than go swimming with us after school, he'd walk Amy Erickson home carrying her books. Also, on weekends, he was always cutting pulp on his father's forty at five cents a stick. ("A Stick?" A stick was eight feet long and varied in diameter from six inches to a foot. Besides you had to take off the limbs from that spruce or balsam to get that nickle.) Mullu didn't really have to cut the pulp, but he needed

money to spend on Amy and to save so he could buy a new suit and shoes. And he was always combing his hair, for Gosh sakes!

Most of our boys had a crush on Amy Erickson–except Fisheye and me. Oh, I'd had one too earlier as my Valentine tale revealed, but, since it got me nowhere I forgot her blonde hair, brown eyes and that crazy giggle. She was pretty, all right, but not as beautiful as a brook trout. Occasionally when she flirted with me as she did with every other boy, I felt good but

159

even better when I could spurn her. As for Fisheye, well he didn't like girls either. Both of us felt badly to see poor Mullu caught in her net.

Things came to a head when the end of May brought the Senior Prom. It wasn't much of a shindig compared to the ones they have now, but it was "big doings" back then. For weeks the girls made their plans. They would put streamers overhead in the gymnasium and have a bower made of fir brances for the Queen. The music would be provided by our little High School makeshift dance band. Not much of a band! I played the saxophone; Mule Cardinal, the trumpet; Fisheye, the school drums, and I forget who had the clarinet and accordion. All of us played by ear and if I recall aright, our repertoire consisted of three different waltzes, two foxtrots, and one polka. That was it! When we played them all we just played them again. Unfortunately when the prom committee heard us rehearse one night after school, they decided not to have us if they could help it. So they made a lot of Prom programs out of flowered wallpaper and sold them for a quarter apiece until they had enough raha to hire a three-piece accordion band from Michigamme.

By this time Mullu had earned enough money to get his new suit and shoes from Sears Roebuck, though his mother had to spend half the night lengthening the sleeves and legs. He also had enough left to buy his program and to persuade Amy to put him down for six of the ten dances. No, he did not ask any other girl to fill in the blank spaces. Holding that brown-eyed blonde in his arms six times would be enough!

Back then no boy ever took his girl to such a dance, though he'd take her home if willing. All the boys went together and stood together in a corner of the hall and the girls did too. Then when the music started and if the boy had the girl's name on his program, he'd go over to her and away they'd go. This system worked well because if, by chance a girl's program was not entirely filled, you could see who was available. Even the plainer ones got picked up.

Mullu's tragedy, as I said, was a minor one–but not to Mullu. Indeed, I don't think he ever got over it. What happened was this. A week before the prom, he noticed a couple of little sores on his left cheek and the next day there were six of them. Then they appeared on his right cheek. Acne! Someone told him to daub carbolic acid salve on them but when he did, they got worse. When he went to school the day before the big night, Amy asked for his program and scratched out her name six times. "You're repulsive, Mullu," she said brutally. "I don't want you near me. Stay home or dance by yourself in the outhouse." A minor tragedy, I suppose, but Mullu never did get married, not to Amy nor to anyone else.

II. *Mrs. Beatty*

Mrs. Beatty lived in a little white house about four doors from us. When I was a young boy she was very, very old, just waiting to die, our people said, but they took good care of her. Tioga always took care of its own. The neighbors kept her woodbox filled and brought her berries, apples, and garden produce when they checked up on her. My father, the doctor, paid her a visit each week to listen to her arthritic aches and pains without charging her his usual fee of three dollars for a home call. My mother often dropped in for afternoon tea, though she usually had to make it and pour it because Mrs. Beatty's hands shook so hard. Over and over again she heard the old lady's accounts of her son George's boyhood, the foods he liked, the way she always had to keep his hair combed, the time he found a dozen rotten eggs hidden by a roving hen, his minor escapades. "Jarge is in California now," she'd say, "but I hear from him every Christmas, I do, and sometime he'll be coming home, he will. He's a good boy, Jarge is." Mrs. Beatty lived entirely in the past, and was confused by the present. Often, when I'd go to Flynn's store for her, she'd call me "Jargie-Boy" and give me a brown tart with cinnamon on it as a reward.

One Christmas Mrs. Beatty got a present from her son in California, a large box containing a gramaphone. You may have seen pictures of these early phonographs showing the fluted wooden horn with a white dog listening to scratchy music coming from the wax cylinders on the box below it. Using the pamphlet of instructions, my father finally managed to assemble it and I was there when he put the needle against the revolving cylinder. Suddenly, we heard Sir Harry Lauder singing:

> "Oh, a-roaming in the gloaming
> On the bonny banks of Clyde,
> Oh, a roaming in the gloaming
> With my Bonnie by my side,
> When the sun has gone to rest
> That's the time that I love best,
> Oh it's lovely roaming in the gloaming."

What a thrill! What a miracle! We'd read about Thomas Edison's marvellous invention but now we were hearing it for the first time. Dad taught me how to run it because Mrs. Beatty just couldn't handle the machine herself, her hands shaking as they did. So whenever I'd go up there to do her errands, I'd play one of the ten cylinders that had come in the box. Sure made me feel proud to operate it when many townspeople came to hear real music coming out of that big horn.

A lot of boys came too and their favorite was the cylinder called "A Man and His Dog." To hear a real dog barking out of that machine was entrancing. To all her visitors Mrs. Beatty would say over and over again, "My Jargie-Boy sent that to me. He'll be coming home to see his mother some day." About once a month to my mother she'd dictate a letter to him, her eyesight being so poor and her hands so crippled. She never got a letter until one day just before Christmas she received one saying that he had taken a week's vacation and would be arriving to spend the holiday with her. When my mother read it to Mrs. Beatty she said the old lady was so joyful she couldn't stop crying and didn't even take a sip of her tea.

When her son did arrive, Mrs. Beatty was so happy her eyes were wet all day. She'd cooked up a storm, making all his favorite foods, even saffron buns (with currant jam to go with them) and a Yorkshire pudding. At dinner she even tried to feed him a spoonful of it.

A short day for his mother, it was a very long one for the son. When he tried to describe California or talked about his jobs and experiences she would interrupt with some memory of his childhood. She talked and wept constantly. Somehow the hours went by, but after supper George had to escape so, despite her entreaties, he walked down the hill to Higley's saloon and had a couple of beers. When he returned, she wept again so he went to bed. She insisted on tucking him in.

About midnight Mrs. Beatty, as she had done many times when he was a child, took a kerosene lamp and went to the bedroom to make sure her Jargie-boy was all right.

Unfortunately, her hands shook so much, the hot lamp chimney fell off on his sleeping face.

The next morning, George Beatty took the train for California. He never came back again.

III. *Antoine*

Big families were very common in the U.P. during the first decades of this century. In Tioga back then it was not unusual for a woman to bear eight or nine children. Some had many more. Andre Toulec down in the valley sired twenty-three but of course he had two wives, one after another I must say. No, I don't think it was the clean U.P. air or water that accounted for the fertility. Perhaps it was the weather. Most of my father's baby cases came during the months from September through December, which meant that the babies were conceived during the dog days of winter when a man couldn't go hunting or fishing. Short days and long nights! If, as someone has remarked, sex is the poetry of the poor, then there were sure a lot of poets in our little forest village.

But there were economic as well as recreational reasons for having a lot of children. Everyone of them, sons and daughters alike, had to earn their keep. The boys at the age of four were keeping the woodbox full and emptying the ashes and gathering the eggs; at seven they were chopping that wood; at ten they were out trimming the limbs off the spruce their fathers were cutting for pulp. Potatoes had to be hoed; hay had to be raked; the cow and horse barns had to be cleaned. I've just hinted at the chores that were our daily lot. There were no child labor laws in Tioga.

The girls also labored mightily, sewing, washing, cooking, milking, churning butter or taking care of the younger ones. In berry time, boys and girls alike carried large pails that had to be filled before they could come home. When potato digging time arrived, children were invaluable. What I'm trying to say is that people had a lot of children because of the help they provided.

But there was another reason too. It was the fear of old age, the fear that they might have to end their days in the County Poorhouse. It was a real fear back then. There was no Social Security. There were no nursing homes for the aged. Few of our people were ever able to store away any savings except for a few bills or coins in the sugar bowl above the stove. They lived, surviving from day to day and just hoping they'd be able to make it through the next winter. Because of their hard labor most were very old at sixty, and when they hit fifty they began to worry about what would happen to them when they could work no more. Couples with many children worried the least. Surely one of their kids would take them in or stay with them. Ugly daughters were especially prized for this reason. If they didn't get married, they would have to stay home to care for the old folks.

I began to understand that fear when once my father, who served on the Health Committee of the Marquette County Board of Supervisors, took me with him as he inspected the Morgan Heights Tuberculosis Sanitorium and the County Poorhouse. The latter was an old red brick building with two wings, one for women and the other for men. It sat on the outskirts of the little city surrounded by carefully tended lawns, and apple orchard and vegetable gardens. It really looked pretty good from the outside. When we climbed the wide steps to the porch that ran alongside the front of the building, two men were sitting in chairs far apart from each other smoking pipes, but when Dad spoke to them, neither answered.

Entering the wide doorway we came into a large room with many rocking chairs along the wall, a few card tables, some bookshelves, cuspidors, and two big potbellied stoves. It was very clean but very bare. Five or six old men and three old women sat in those chairs, not speaking to each other, just rocking aimlessly. They too didn't respond to Dad's greetings. Beyond this big room was a dining hall with two long tables, and beyond that a spotless kitchen in which two cooks were busy preparing a meal. Next Dad inspected the dormitory sleeping rooms in the wings. In the women's ward all the beds were neatly made up, but in one of them was a very old lady, Mrs. Toussaint from Tioga. When she saw my father she began to cry. "Oh, Doctor," she said. "Get me out of here. Please! Please!" Dad did what he could to comfort her but made no promises. In the men's dormitory, four men, fully clothed, were lying on their cots. Dad went to each of them asking if they had any complaints. None of them answered; just stared at him with vacant eyes.

Going into the office of the superintendent of the Poorhouse, Dad complimented him on the cleanliness of the building but begged him to find some way of enriching the lives of those poor old people. "Can't be done, Doctor," the man replied. "We've tried but they're just waiting to die. You've seen the worst of them, those who've given up. The better ones are outside working in the gardens and orchard or cowbarns." When we left, I could tell that Dad was depressed. "Be sure to save your money, Cully, so you won't have to end up in a place like this," was all he said to me.

Antoine Saintonge wasn't thinking of the Poorhouse on that twentieth of June when he had his seventieth birthday. A bon jour, it was. A perfect U.P. day, warm sun, blue skies and a few lazy clouds drifting by. As he took a pail of oats down the lane to Pitou, his horse, he felt very wealthy. He had a good farm there on the old flood plain of the Tioga River, eighty acres all told. The rich soil, clay loam on top and gravel underneath, produced all the hay and oats and pasture his cow and horse required. A little stream coming from the granite hills ran inside and along the northern fence. Antoine had divided the tract into four ten-acre fields so he could rotate them every two years, one for pasture, one for clover, one for oats, one for timothy hay. Each had its own tightly strung barbed wire fence but only the pasture had a swinging gate. Antoine had never been able to save up enough money to buy the other three gates so he just moved it every two years to the field that would be the pasture.

Pitou, his horse, was drinking from the stream but when Antoine called he galloped over to get the oats. Antoine sure loved that horse. Twelve years old, it was in its prime. A good worker, very strong, Pitou could plow all day and still have enough left to pull a buggy smartly to Tioga, two miles away, then home again.

As Pitou munched the oats in the pail Antoine looked over the other three fields. The timothy stood tall and thick. No bare spots. Oui, he'd done a good job of sowing. In a few days he and Pitou would have to cut it with the mowing machine. The oats too were fine, almost heading out. Antoine loved the way the wind blew waves of bluish green across that field. After the haying was done, he and Pitou would cut that field. Antoine had already arranged with Toussaint Bergeron to have him thresh the oats in exchange for five cords of maple from the woodlot beyond the creek. Had to deliver it, of course, but with Pitou to haul the lumber wagon, that was no problem. And the clover! Never had Antoine seen a better crop. Every plant was so full of the first pink blossoms the field looked like a flower garden. Cutting that would come last but there would be more than enough for his cow all next winter. Oui, he'd even have clover hay and oats to sell for biting money. Yes, Pitou and he would make it through another winter. Antoine stroked the horse's mane. So long as he had Pitou, all was well.

When the horse had finished it went to the creek to have a drink and Antoine limped back to the house. That knee of his had been hurting badly lately. A good thing he had Pitou or he'd never be able to make it to town or, for that matter, even to take care of his big garden. It was looking good too. Widely spaced rows of potatoes, turnips, and beans would have to be cultivated soon but with the horse that was easy. Perhaps he'd have extra potatoes to sell next fall.

"Oh, mais non!" Antoine said aloud to himself. He'd forgotten to bring back the oat pail from the pasture, so he retraced his steps to get it. He'd noticed that lately he'd been becoming more forgetful. Sometimes he even fed the chickens twice. Sometimes he even forgot whether he himself had eaten. Well, what would you expect of a man seventy years old!

Hurting hard by the time he reached the house, he sat a spell on its back porch thinking about old age. Except for the bum knee he was physically in good shape. Not as strong as when he was a young buck, par certainement, but strong enough for what he had to do. He could see and hear well and had almost all his teeth. Yes, he was lonely now that his wife had died but at least he had Pitou, the horse. Too bad he and his wife had not been able to have children for his old age. It had been a great sorrow between them. No kinfolk either that he knew of. Yes, he was alone but so long as he had Pitou and the farm he didn't have to worry about going to the Poorhouse.

For a moment the old man thought about doing a washing. A good day to hang out clothes. With that breeze and sunshine they would dry in a hurry. Again he missed Maxine. She had been a good woman, good company too. That big pile of winter underwear and towels and shirts would have been long gone had she still been around. He missed her cooking and baking too. Somehow he'd never been able to bake bread like hers with the brown crust. Never! No, he'd do no washing today. Perhaps tomorrow or sometime.

Suddenly feeling very hungry, Antoine entered the kitchen. Had he eaten breakfast? The coffee pot, still warm on the range, was almost full. The dishpan full of unwashed dishes held a coffee cup on top that had a bit of coffee still in it. Oh well, it didn't matter; he was hungry, so Antoine got a cup of coffee and some korpua and took them with him out to the backsteps and the June sunshine. Then he lit his old corncob pipe. All was well, tres bien!

But it wasn't! The next morning when Antoine took the pail of oats out to the pasture Pitou wasn't there! He'd forgotten to close the gate yesterday. Where was the horse? Antoine found Pitou by the creek at the far corner of the clover field. Dead! Bloated, the horse lay on its side with its belly horrible distended and with foam around its mouth. Gorging on the fresh clover had killed Pitou.

Two years later when my father made his annual inspection of the County Poorhouse he saw a man sitting in a rocker on the far side of the long porch facing the blank brick wall. It was Antoine Saintonge. Dad went over to him. "Hello, Antoine," he said. "How are things going?" Antoine didn't answer.

Laughing Our Way
Through Winter

In the early years of this century from November until May the board sidewalk that lines one side of Tioga's steep hill street was completely deserted. Too much snow! We walked in the roadway when we wanted to get to the stores, school, churches or to the depot or saloon because the road was usually plowed two sleigh widths wide so one team could pass another. When the winter storms roaring down from Lake Superior deposited four feet of the white stuff it was all we could do to keep paths shoveled out to that road or to the barn and outhouse. These paths were always kept open because we had to make it through the winter by visiting each other to share a cup of coffee or a laugh.

All of us knew the dangers of cabin fever when the snows grew as deep as the depression that threatened to overwhelm us. With no radio or TV and only a few newspaper in town, with the two-rut wagon roads closed from one village to another, with spring a thousands days away, we coped by laughing at each other's jokes and stories. In this tale I'm going to try to recall some of them.

I do so with some uneasiness because I know that you may have heard some of them before and a twice-told joke is often as flat as a cold pancake. On the other hand, since I heard them more than seventy years ago, perhaps they may still have some freshness. Here's one that started in Higley's saloon and climbed our hill from house to house in 1913:

Matti Makela, a farmer by Clowry, bought a bull, the biggest bull in the U.P. A whopper! So many people came to see it Matti thought he'd charge admissiom so he put up a sign in front of his house saying:

For Looking da Bull 10¢

Not many people came after news of the sign went around, but one day Erkki Salo brought his wife and thirteen kids. When he saw the sign Erkki protested. "Too much raha," he said. "I no pay dollar fifty for see your bull, no! You give discount, mebbe, eh?" Matti counted the children. "All dose kids yours, Erkki?" he asked. "yah, dey mine." "Well," said Matti, "I pay you dollar fifty for having mine bull look at you."

Many of these stories were told using a heavy foreign accent, because most of our people were immigrants from the old countries overseas and their speech reflected their origins. Consequently, since the jokes lose some of their flavor when put on a printed page, I shall just hint at their dialects. Here's one involving the Swedish foreign accent that uses y for the j sound as in "My name is Yonny Yohnson and I come from Wisconsin."

Eino Ysitalo came home yearly one afternoon from cutting pulp to find his wife, Lena, coming out of the barn with her face flushed and with hay in her hair. "I been cleaning barn for you, Eino" she explained. But Eino had noticed that a man's footprints in the snow had led to the barn along with hers. "Mebbe so, mebbe so, but I tink mebbe you been having some nooky wit dat Swede fellow been hanging round. You come wit me!"

Going to the barn, Eino looked all over but didn't find anything except that there was a big pile of stuff in the corner. "What dis?" he asked.

"Oh dat just pile junk for haul away in spring. I told you I clean barn. Just old boards, harness, horse blankets, jingle bells for sleigh. Old stuff, no good."

Eino gave the heap a good kick. "Yingle, yingle," said the pile.

Because Tioga was a melting pot of many nationalities there were hundreds of jokes in which they poked fun at each other. Often the same joke about the dumb Swede would be told about the dumb Norwegian if a person of Swedish descent were telling it. For example:

Leif Backe and Alf Preus, two old Norwegian lumberjacks decided to go ice fishing, though neither of them had ever done so nor knew anything about it. They fished for two hours and never had a bite, although they noticed that a man further out on the ice kept catching one fish after another. So when the man left they decided to go where he had been and fish there. When they did, Leif said, "Hey Alf, look! He make hole in ice."

Some of the things that were passed from house to house were not jokes at all. They were "sayings." "Two can live as cheaply as one if they are a flea and his dog." "Every minnow wants to be a pike." "Never look down the outhouse hole." "The only thing stinks worse than a dead horse is a Frenchman in the sauna."

One of those sayings always puzzled me as a kid. It was "Lots of water in the swamp for you" and was used as a statement of rejection, as the equivalent of "No!" Then one day an old Finn told me its origin. An Irishman on one of the few hot days of a U.P. summer had gone up to the door of Mrs. Koski's farmhouse and asked for a drink of water. "What national are you?" "I'm Irish," he said. "There's lotsa water in the swamp for you, you Catholic!" she yelled and slammed the door.

In those early days there was much enmity between nationalities, partly because of religion and partly because of old prejudices brought to Tioga from the old country. The Protestants hated the Catholics; the Swedes the Norwegians, the French the Finns, and so on. Now they're all intermarried and the old antagonisms are gone, but back then they were hot indeed. One example:

A Swede lumberjack named Sven Anderson came out of the woods at breakup time for his annual spree, spent a lot of his money setting up drinks at Higley's saloon and was so drunk when he arrived at our whorehouse they wouldn't let him in. Sven staggered around outside for a bit in the cold, then crawled in Alphonse Verlaine's pig house to sleep it off. Finally next morning, when he began to come to he felt a warm body beside him. Still with his eyes shut, he put his arms around the warm body and murmured affectionately, "Ar du Svensk?" (Are you Swedish?) "Norsk, Norsk," said the pig and Sven tore out of the pigpen yelling "I vant mine money back!" (Norsk means Norwegian).

And there was the tale about old man Joe LaCosse who ran a tavern up at Big Bay. It seems that a Finn riverman had been killed in a log jam on the Yellow Dog River, and some of his friends were soliciting funds to give him a decent funeral. Although they knew that Joe hated Finns, they asked him for a dollar to help do it. "Zat man who die, he Frenchman, oui?" Joe asked. "No, he's Finn," they replied. Joe pulls out his wallet and gives them four dollars. "Bury four of dem," he said.

Lon Boland, a young Cornish miner, married Jenny but she was lazy as well as pretty. Didn't know how to bake a pasty or pudding or saffron bread. Didn't clean the house well. Didn't fill his dinner pail even though he worked the night shift at the mine. Lon stood it for a long time, but one morning coming home from work he noticed that there was smoke coming out of the chimney of every house in Tioga but his. As he had expected, his lazy wife was still sleeping and the house was cold. So Lon lowered a twelve-quart pail into the well, pulled it up, then threw it onto Jenny's face, yelling, "Fire! Fire! Fire!" Jenny jumps out of bed. "Where? Where the fire?" "In every bloody house in town but ours!"

Another Cousin Jack story: When telephones first came to Tioga they could be found in only four places; in the mining office, in the company store, in the doctor's house and in the mining captain's home. Though many of our people were curious, and some believed that it was impossible to talk through wires, most of them feared using them. Next to the mining captain's house lived a hard-rock Cornish miner named Johnny Lowe who worked nights but slept days. One day his wife, Thirsa, a big powerful woman who regularly beat up her husband, hung up the clothes to dry then went to Ishpeming to see her daughter, but when it started to rain and thunder she said she had to take the train back home. "Your feyther will never ha' the sense to bring in the wash," she said. Her daughter had a better idea. "Mither, why don't 'ee use my new telyphone and call up Cap'n Campon and ask him to go over and get feyther to talk to you and then you can tell him what to do?" So they did and Cap'n Campton goes over to Johnny Rowe's house and said, "Johnny, your missus wants to talk to ye on my telyphone so come over and I'll show ye what to do." The phone, of course, was one of the old fashioned box kind hung on the wall. "Now Johnny," said the Captain, "You stand up against that h'instrument, put yer mouth against that pipe and hold that horn agin yer ear. Then say 'Ello' and the missus will be talking to 'ee." Johnny did as he was told but just as he said 'ello' a bolt of lightning hit the line and knocked him down. Picking himself up, he looked at the Captain and said, "Aye, that's my bloody old lady, for sure."

Another, still another: A Cousin Jack miner came to work one morning and told his partner on the drilling crew, "Well, Jimmy, great thing come to my house last night." "And what was that?" "We 'ad driblets come, we did." "Driblets? What's driblets, never hear of driblets?" asked Jimmy. His friend told him his wife had just given birth to three babies all at once. "Can't believe it," said Jimmy, "Taint possible." "We finish this shift and you come to my 'ouse and I show 'ee." So they did and when Jimmy saw the three fine babies, he exclaimed, "Ah, but they be grand indeed. Never seen nawthing like it in my life." Then, pointing to the middle one, he said "Damn, pardner, if it were me, I'd keep this one."

The Finns had quite a sense of humor too. Arne Sippola amused himself and others of us by painting signs and then placing them way back in the woods. Half way to Republic in the middle of a cedar swamp I once saw one of those signs saying, "You are Here!"

Seppo Keski was an old Finlander who spent all his free time fishing for pike on Lake Tioga, at least all of it that wasn't spent down at Higley's saloon singing lugubrious Finnish songs when he got lubricated right. He never went to church and only once a year to the sauna but he had a gay spirit. Yes, everyone liked that dissolute old character, at least everyone except the Finnish pastor who thoroughly disapproved of the old scoundrel. Meeting Seppo on the street one day, the pastor gave him the devil for his evil ways. "You going to hell, Seppo. You getting old, not much more time for being save." And then the preacher painted a word picture of Seppo's destination, the devils with pitchforks, the glowing coals, the lake of fire. Seppo interrupted. "You say hell got lake of fire?" "Yah," said the preacher. "Good," said Seppo. "Den I fish forever and when I catch fish dey already cooked."

We also enjoyed what we called happenings, true stories of incidents that had occurred in Tioga. Here's one: "We had a flock of laying chickens on our farm by Half Way and one summer some varmint began killing one or two every night. Well, my father got fed up with that and staked out one of his hunting dogs to a tree beside the chicken coop, knowing that the dog would start yelping when the varmint come around. Now as I said, this was summer so Dad was wearing a short nightshirt to bed instead of the long underwear he used in winter time. Well, he loaded up his double-barreled shotgun and was sleeping when he heard the dog howling, so he gets up and sneaks out to the chicken coop but untied the hound first so if he couldn't see to shoot, it being so dark, the dog might get the critter. Once he opened the door, Dad first couldn't see anything it being so black in there, but then he saw something moving on the floor, raised up to aim and just then that old hound dog, he poked his cold nose under my father's nightshirt. Pow! When the feathers settled we had seven chickens to clean but never saw that varmint at all." That story had Tioga laughing for a week even though it snowed everyday.

The Old Logging Days

I was born too late, in 1905, to have known the great white pine forest that covered the Upper Peninsula of Michigan. The last log drive down one of Tioga River's tributaries, Wabeek Creek, occurred when I was seven years old, but throughout my childhood I was entranced by the tales of the old lumberjacks who had logged off that great forest. Actually they weren't very old, perhaps in their late forties or fifties, young enough to recall fondly the heroic or dirty deeds of their own rambunctious youth. Pete Ramos was one of them. Physically broken by terribly hard labor in the woods and by alcohol, it wasn't hard to get him started if he were only half drunk, and I'd brought him on of my father's cigars.

"Tell me how they logged off the Tioga in the old days?" I'd beg. "What happened first?"

"First?" Pete looked puzzled. "Well, I guess Silverthorne and Company bought them a big chunk of land, maybe seventy, eighty sections on both sides of the river. That's over three hundred forties. Got it from the government for about a dollar an acre, they did. Damned steal, it was. And after they logged the lower part of the river they bought a lot more upstream. That was when I started working for 'em up at Camp 10 by the Haysheds dam. I helped build that dam and was lucky. Two men got killed doing it."

Pete told me that the big logging company hired timber cruisers (landlookers) to explore the area first, estimating the amound of board feet of prime pine in each forty acres, locating the camp site and figuring out where the logging dams should be built so that a sufficient head of water could be stored to float the logs down the river to Lake Tioga where the sawmill was.

"Them cruisers had to be damned good," Pete said. "Had to find the corner posts of the sections so they'd know where one forty left off and another begin. Had to lay out where the roads would run level enough for icing. Had to size up a big pine and say it'd make maybe nine sawlogs and go maybe 8,000 board feet. I was thinking to be a cruiser myself but I went in the bush with one once and knows I never had the brains for it. Naw, just a lumberjack and riverman, that was all I could be and all I ever wuz."

"You mentioned that you helped build the Haysheds dam. Did you do that before the lumber camps were built?" I asked.

"Yes and no," Pete replied. "I was on a crew of maybe thirty men, but we had to repair the other dams lower on the river while the camps were built: Rock Dam, Plank Dam, and Brown's Dam, oh yeah, and the Wabeek Dam too. Lived in tents and the bugs were awful. When we got done with that job and started on the Haysheds they had the bunkhouse roof on but no windows or bunks, so we slept on the floor."

"I've been up to that dam with my father," I said. "It sure was a good place to put it."

"Yeah, the only notch in them big granite hills. When it was full there was a lake two mile long behind it. Had a big waterfall there before we cribbed it."

"What's cribbing?" I inquired.

"You don't know what cribbing is?" Pete was incredulous. "It's big boxes made of big logs spiked together on the corners. Some of them spikes were two feet long or more. Made you grunt sledging them. Then we filled 'em with rocks and dirt and put one crib on top another till they was high enough."

"But what did you do with the water, the river I mean?"

"Dammed off one side at a time. Trick come when we had to join the cribs in the middle. That's when Pat Leahy got kilt. Had a big log beam fall on him when he wuz putting up the underpinning for the sluice gate. Never knowed what happened to him, it come so sudden."

"Did they bring him to town to bury him?"

"Hell no," said Pete. "Just dug a hole and put 'im in it back in the bush with rocks on top to keep out the wolves. We did nail one of his boots to a tree along the river. One time I counted eight boots like that along the bank trail. Lot of men got killed in the woods back then, but me, I got my boots on even now." Dad's cigar had been finished and the old man left for Higley's saloon. I was a bit shaken remembering that once I'd seen the remnants of such an old boot on the bank of the river.

I was also sorry he had left before I could learn more about the lumber camps and the lumberjacks, but I soon had an even better informant. It happened like this. One afternoon I rode my old white horse, Billy, down the big hill behind Delongchamp's farm to the west branch of the Escanaba to do some wet fly fishing for trout. They bit very slowly and I suddenly realized it was getting late so I headed back, meeting my father in his 1914 Ford coming to find me. "It's suppertime," he said crossly, "your mother is worried. She said you told her you'd be back by five. So get going!"

While he turned his car around on the Furnace road, I got Billy into a good gallop and foolishly galloped him across the railroad tracks by the depot. Catching his horseshoe in the crossing boards he fell heavily upon me, breaking my right leg in two places, above and below the knee. Well, Dad was right there so he took me home and soon had me in a heavy plaster cast from hip to toe. The next month I spent up in Grandma Van's room regretting my folly. However, some good came out of the accident. Dad hired Anders Lundberg, an old Swede carpenter, to put new sashes in the windows of that room so they could be opened easily, and I soon discovered that Anders had been the boss carpenter when they built Camp 10 at the Haysheds. Moreover, once the windows had been fixed, Dad hired him to teach me to play the guitar, probably because he couldn't bear hearing me pick out tunes on a primitive instrument I'd made out of a cigar box and strung with one of the catgut sutures he used for sewing up wounds. So I had a fine opportunity to learn a lot about the old logging days from Anders too.

"We started building the camps in May month," the old man said, "and had them all done by October. A helluva big job it was. We turned that beaver meadow into a small town. They hired four log butchers to help me and a crew of about twenty jacks, and two team of horses. The big boss, Mike Terson, told me to build his cabin first, then the cook and bunk shacks, then the ox and horse barn with a blacksmith shop joined to the barn. He said the cabin for the clerk and scaler could come later. There would be a crew of a hundred men working there for two or three years. I still don't know how we got it done in time for the fall cutting."

"How big were the buildings?" I asked.

"Lemme see. The bunkhouse was 80 by 40 feet. That was the biggest one. Had to be because on each side we built 25 double bunks to hold four men each, with deacon seats running in front of them."

"What's a deacon seat, Anders?"

"That's a long bench where the men sat. No chairs in camp. On Sundays when the jacks played cards or filed their saws and axes they sat on nail kegs."

"I suppose they heated it with those long stoves I've seen pictures of," I said.

"Yah," he replied. "Long square ones, two of them, that could take five-foot logs and burn all night. Above them they had wood racks and haywire to hang their clothes for drying, and beside them the hot water barrel fed by copper pipe from a coil of it inside the stove. It was so warm in there even when it was twenty below what with the body heat and all that later we had to put two skylights into the roof that could be opened to let out the stink. Only four windows, so it was dark in there even in daylight, and the coal oil lanterns were always burning until lights out at 9 o'clock."

"Did the men eat in the bunkhouse?" I asked.

"Oh no," said Anders. "We built another shack for eating but I misremember exactly how big. Must have been over fifty feet long and thirty feet across because the two tables in them were forty feet long. Even then the men had to eat in two shifts, half an hour apart. Camp 10 had two cookees, young kids who hauled in the food and cleared the tables for the next batch of eaters. They also tended the fires and swept and did all the dirty jobs around the kitchen and cook shack. Tough job in camp being a cookee."

"Anders, I've heard that nobody was supposed to talk at mealtime. Is that right?"

You damned tooting!" he replied. "Oh you could ask for someone to pass the potatoes or stew but nothing else. No conversation. If there was, the bull cook would come in with his cleaver. No, we ate silent. Every logging camp had that rule."

"Feeding a hundred men must have been a real job," I said. "How many cookstoves did they have?"

"Three big kitchen ranges at Camp 10," Anders answered. "They were in the cook shack, a different building but joined to the dining shack by a door. The cook and chore boys slept there at one end, not in the bunkhouse, having to get up at two, three in the morning to start breakfast."

"I hear they fed them good," I said.

"Yah, Silverthorne's camps anyway did. Breakfast at six o'clock still dark had pancakes and molasses, sowbelly, oatmeal, bread and coffee, all you could eat. They brung it in big dishpans for the table. Supper the biggest meal. Big pots of stew, venison or beef or pork. Always potatoes, beans (we called 'em firecrackers) and fresh bread. Pies too. Some camps didn't have it so good but Silverthorne's always. That's how they kept the best jacks."

"What about lunch?" I asked. "Did they come back for that?"

"Naw! Teamsters hauled dishpans full of sandwiches, ham often, out to the cuttings, along with ten gallon kettles of hot tea wrapped in blankets to keep them warm. Can of sugar lumps too. Men had only half an hour to eat it, then back to work until too dark to see. Long hours, them."

"Tell me about the horse barns," I begged.

Anders thought for a moment. "They had two of them up at Camp 10, fifty feet long and thirty wide. Ox stalls on north end and horse stalls along sides. No stoves. Didn't need 'em. Next to it we built the blacksmith shop, thirty by twenty feet. Had two forges and the blacksmith slept there. Blacksmith always important man in lumbercamp. Made sleds, jammers, runners, chains, wagon wheels, hinges, anything, and shoed horses of course. I helped on sleds and wheels."

"What's a jammer?" I inquired.

"An outfit, like a derrick, for lifting logs. Them big pine logs sure were heavy. Most of the time though, the loaders could put twenty, thirty, sixteen-foot logs on the sleighs just using canthooks and rolling them up on stringers before chaining them tight. I hear tell that up at Ontonagon in the late 1800s they hauled fifty logs on one sleigh. Took a ton of half-inch chain to hold them and only two horses pulled that load. Of course the roads were iced with ruts carved in them so the sleighs wouldn't slip sidewise."

"You said something about having to build a clerk and scaler's shack. What did they do and why did they have their own buildings?"

Anders lit his pipe. "Most camps had just one man for both jobs but Camp 10 had two. The scaler, he measured butts of all logs when they was on the sleighs and make estimate of how many board feet for each one. Put it down in notebook and put blue chalk mark to show he'd done it. Sometimes he'd use sledge with Silverthorne marker *ST* so when logs get to sawmill they know whose it was. They did that when different companies were logging same rivershed. The clerk, he was company man. He keep accounts of how much wood was cut and also he keep store. The jacks could buy blankets, tobacco, files, axes, shirts, things like that in the store and charge them against their wages."

"Did they pay them off only in the spring?" I asked.

"Yah, but he just give piece of paper showing how much, maybe four, five hundred dollars, but then the jack had to walk maybe twenty miles to Tioga or to headquarters camp to get cash; often in gold."

"And then they blew it," I said.

"Not all of them. Some family men, they didn't but most hit for the saloons right away. Had to have bit spree after being up there in the bush so long."

I'd hoped that Anders could tell me more about the actual cutting and hauling, but he really didn't know much about it. He wanted to tell me about how the lumber camps were built.

"When we first got to the beaver meadow there was a thick stand of white pine, all 150 feet tall, just beyond the creek, and we used them for the logs. Used the biggest ones for the foundation. Put on the next log with the butt on the other end and so on. Had to square off the top and bottom of each of 'em so they'd fit tight when notched at the ends. Used a broadaxe for that."

"What's a broadaxe?" I asked.

"A big axe with a blade three times as big as ordinary one. Would weigh maybe sixteen pounds. One of the log butchers on my crew, Axel Aronson, his name was, could slab a log better than anyone, better than I could, leaving the surface of that log so smooth it looked like it had been planed. And never went beyond the blue line either.

"What's the blue line, Anders?"

"Got to have one to keep the cut straight," he said. "To mark and score you chalk a line good with blue chalk, put one end of it on the butt of a log, then stretch it tight all along the length, fastening it tight on the other end. Then you hold about three feet of the line out from one end, pull it up, and then snap it down hard. That'll leave a straight blue mark on the log. Then you move on and do it again and again. I'll show you how on the guitar." He illustrated.

There was much more that I've forgotten, but it was certain that old Anders knew his stuff about building if not logging. The latter information came to me from other older men whom I quizzed later after I could walk again.

In the early days, they told me, they had to fell the trees with double-bitted axes, but soon crosscut saws appeared and they were of course much more efficient. The cutters first made a deep horizontal cut across the base of the tree about waist-high, chopped out a triangular notch, then went to the other side of the tree and made another horizontal saw cut above it until the tree cracked, groaned and toppled. A good sawyer could drive a stake and then put that great pine right on top of it, driving it into the ground. Some real skill was involved in figuring out the effects of wind and the lay of the land, as well as in the sawing itself. One old man told me how he'd knocked the man on the opposite end of the saw on his ass when he hadn't done his fair share of the pulling and pushing. "If you gonna ride the saw den you might as well sit down," he said. It was very hard labor. A good lumberjack, and they prided themselves on being one, could cut, with his partner, perhaps four or five of those tall pines in a single day, one that lasted from daybreak to dark. Having seen stumps of those pines that measured seven feet across, I cannot understand how they could have done so much in a single day but they rarely rested. They couldn't even smoke their pipes because that would take too much time. Instead they chewed tobacco. "Every stump, it had a ring of brown tobacco juice around it," one man told me.

The lumberjacks who did the cutting were top dogs in the hierarchy, kings of the woods. Below them came the buckers, the men who sawed up the fallen logs into sixteen-foot lengths, trimming off the branches. Below these were the swampers and skidders who, with oxen or horses, "snaked" those logs to the nearest logging trail, a road that was made as level as possible, and then iced so the big lumber sleighs or sleds could haul them to the rollways or landings at the edge of the river. There they were stacked in huge piles to await the spring thaws and the torrents of water released from the logging dams that would float them down the Tioga River to the sawmills at Lake Tioga.

Teamsters were also among the elite, especially those who could handle the oxen. When the land was fairly level, horses could be used to "twitch" or skid the big logs down to the iced river road, but when they were down in a gully or up on a hill the oxen did a better job. Huge, castrated bulls of various breeds, and well-trained, they could snake out those big logs with their powerful steady pulling. Ox teamsters used no reins; they had twitches, long whips with which they touched the oxen's heads to steer them right or left on the skidding paths or to urge them to pull harder, with accompanying yells of "Gee!" (for right) or "Haw!" (for left). Many of the best teamsters were French Canadians.

All of the old men agreed that the worst job in camp was that of "bucket monkey". Since the river roads had to be kept paved with ice and the work was done at night when water froze best, the bucket monkey had to fill the large square tank of the sprinkler sleigh from the nearest pond or stream. Sometimes they filled it by hand, sometimes using a jammer with a bucket. always wet and half frozen, the men had to fill those tanks over and over again each night, so that the heavy log sleighs could glide easily over the iced pavement down to the banking area. Ruts were also made in the ice so the sleighs wouldn't slip sideways.

One of the most dangerous jobs involved the loading, unloading, and stacking of the logs, especially at the rollways by the river. There the logs were piled horizontally along a slanting bank so that in the spring break-up they could be rolled down into the stream after the bottom key log was loosened. Since some of those logs weighed almost a ton, many accidents occurred at the rollways. One old lumberjack told me a harrowing tale about one such mishap.

"Me, I tell ze woods boss, ze stack beeg enough," he said. "No more log or she let go, but he say put more on. Me an' Raoul we on top of her to make straight with canthook. Den Ow! She go like tonnaire (thunder). Me, I jump off side but Raoul, my fren'. Dey grind him to nuttin! Oui, dey make pea soup of him."

When the spring breakup came, most of the lumberjacks were discharged except for those who would participate in the drives, in floating the logs down river to Lake Tioga and its sawmills. After being in the woods for six or seven months, and with plenty of money in their pockets, it was time for the annual spree. How those old men liked to tell about it!

"We hadn't had a drink or seen a woman all winter," they told me. "We couldn't fight in camp but we sure made up for it when breakup come." Tioga's ten-bed whore house was busy day and night because they'd added six or seven more girls who came up on the train from Milwaukee. Higley's saloon was jumping too. But most of the jacks took the train for Ishpeming or Seney where service was better. Oh the fighting that went on! My father, the doctor, sewed on ears and noses that had been bitten off, and dressed the gouges and bruises if they were bad enough. Men fought until one went down and then the other stomped on his face, twisting the caulks of his boots so that he would always be remembered. They fought without reason as brutally as possible. "I kin lick any man in the house," one would yell, and there were always takers of his challenge. It was the code!

"Gad, we wuz horny when we come out the woods," one old bugger said. "Had to find a woman right away. I seen one jack at Seney kick in the window of a store with his boots to get at a whatyoucallit, statue like of a woman (manikin), and he screwed that statue up and down the street."

The lumberjacks though had a great respect for decent women and would take off their hats to them when meeting one on the street. Most of the hell-raising in Tioga took place downtown in the valley by the saloon and depot so they rarely came up the long hill street for their brawling. The few who did were so drunk they didn't know any better and Charley Olafson, our constable, put them to bed in the cages of our jail in the town hall until they sobered up. Higley's saloon, like most of those in the U.P. also had a holding tank, a back room where lumberjacks were stacked until they sobered up. No big deal!

Back at Silverthorne's camp, the men chosen to drive the logs downriver filed the corks (caulks) of their boots and sharpened their pike-poles. These rivermen were a select crew, agile and fearless, the best of the lot. They had to be! Breaking the huge stacks of logs on the rollways so they would cascade into the river or into the ponds above the logging dam, they had to shepherd those logs all the way downstream. This often called for running across the slippery logs floating crazily in the torrent of water released from the dam. They had to prevent them from crisscrossing and forming the dreaded log jams, those massive tangles of logs that could back up the water for miles. The river hogs, as they called themselves, were stationed at half-mile intervals along the stream and when one of them saw that a log jam might be forming he'd let out the alarm cry "Ah-eeee!". This would be echoed by the men above and below him, and soon enough rivermen would be assembled at the spot so they could try to pry or dynamite out the key log that held the jam tight. Once the logs started moving again, the men had to make their way precariously to shore, leaping from log to log. One misstep meant death. There were many casualties on those river drives, many boots to be nailed to the trees along the riverbank.

To keep the logs moving, one dam after another was opened in turn, first the Hayshed dam, then the Brown's dam, then the Plank dam. The rivermen slept in the snow beside the stream but were fed from the wanigan, a barge-like raft that carried the cookshack and tool shed. It was a rough life, a dangerous one!

Somehow they got the logs to Lake Tioga. There they were assembled into large rafts enclosed by boom logs and blown by the prevailing west wind to the sawmill at the east end of the lake. When the wind didn't blow hard enough and the rafts stalled, a procedure called kedging was used. At the head end of the log raft a platform was built, and on it was fastened a large vertical spool called a capstan, wound with heavy rope or cable. Then a large anchor was put in a rowboat and dropped off ahead of the raft. Its rope was then fastened to that of the capstan, and by great effort men could turn the capstan so the raft could be winched forward. They prayed for wind, those men on the double shift than manned the spokes of the huge spool. Somehow year after year, they got the logs to the mill.

And when they did, all hell broke loose in Tioga again. The terribly long winter and the constant dangers had stored up hungers for booze and women and mayhem that few of the riverhogs could resist. Again the holding tank at Higley's saloon had them stacked up like cordwood; Charley Olafson's jail overflowed and our red whorehouse needed more beds and girls. Then suddenly it was all over. Peace returned to Tioga as though nothing had happened. Only one memento was left: a pair of lumberjack boots nailed to the whorehouse door.

Teaching My Bride
To Fish

When my new wife and I stopped off at Tioga on our way to the Old Cabin for our honeymoon, I asked my father jokingly if he had any wise advice about how I could have a happy marriage. "Yes," he said. "Just one thing: don't ever teach your wife to hunt or fish!"

That didn't make any sense to me back then, though there have been a few times in the ensuing years when I felt he was right. Of course I'd teach Milove to fish. Brook trout fishing had been the best part of my existence since I caught that first speckled beauty at the age of six and became hooked forever. To think that I could not share all the delights of that lovely addiction with the woman I loved, well, that was unthinkable!

It's almost impossible to explain the fascination of trout fishing to anyone who had not enjoyed it. Why do we love to fish for *salmon fontinalis* (trout of springs)? Certainly it is not for the poundage. The biggest one I ever caught was just a shade under three pounds

and most were no longer than ten inches. Nor is it the battle they put up–though ounce for ounce, a brook trout will hold its own with any fish. I've caught bass, pike, salmon, steelhead, bonefish and salmon that put on spectacular fights that left me exhausted, but I'd rather catch an eight-inch trout in the U.P. than any of them. Nor is it their edibility, wonderful as that may be when trout are broiled or sizzled in a frying pan over a campfire just after being caught.

I believe that the reason lies in where trout are caught, how they are caught, and when. Brook trout are the children of the dawn and dusk; that is when they are most active. How often have I set the alarm, snatched a quick breakfast and then hiked up logging roads, watching the white mist over the river become pink with the first rays of the sun! Even in the old days when there were lots of trout, they usually stopped biting by nine o'clock and did not resume until the evening sun descended behind our huge hills in a burst of glorious sunset.

Perhaps I've loved brook trout fishing because they're more beautiful than any other fish, yes, even more beautiful than an arctic grayling. A freshly caught brook trout with its iridescent scarlet spots is breath-taking. I'm sure they get that way because they live out their lives in beautiful surroundings. Preferring the smaller, rocky streams, they seem to select the loveliest rapids, waterfalls, and pools as their habitat. Sometimes at night when I cannot sleep I drowsily let my mind wander up the Tioga River and its tributaries recalling where I had caught them. Invariably, every one of those spots is a beautiful one.

Much of the pleasure in trout fishing comes from the challenge it presents. It isn't easy fishing. You walk upstream a long way then slowly wade down, feeling the slippery rocks underfoot lest you use your nose for a cane. You never hurry! Splashing would disturb the trout below you and besides, you might miss seeing something on the riverbank. Constantly, you "read the stream," seeking to discover where the fish may lie. "Ah, there beside that sunken boulder should be a good place!" "There ought to be one under that white foam where that eddy comes out from under the bushes." "Will the trout be at the head of the pool in the fast water or down at the tail near that snag?" You become so completely engrossed in this constant evaluation of probabilities that all your little cares and worries disappear. The happy hours go by before you know it.

Then too, when you have located a spot where a trout might be, you must devise strategies for attracting and taking him. Often, when wading down the middle of a stream, you can cast your bait directly ahead of you, letting the current take it to the trout, and nudging the hook along the bottom. Never cast directly at the trout or he will bolt for cover. Often it's wiser to make your cast from the side of the pool or rapids, allowing the line to swing in an arc so it passes directly behind you, projecting your moving shadow onto the surface, you don't have a chance! Trout are very sensitive to fleeting shadows and also to vibrations, so you also have to walk very carefully even when you are on the riverbank.

Like all U.P. trout fishermen, I began by using worms for bait and although I graduated to using flies, thanks to my Grampa Gage, I never became a purist. Unto their tastes, has been my motto. There's almost as much skill involved in bait fishing as in fly casting if you do it right. For example, there are three kinds of worms, each of which under certain circumstances, will take trout when the others won't. On a warm, windless day when the surface of the pool mirrors white clouds lazily floating across a blue sky, five or six tiny redworms on a hook allowed to settle on the bottom for ten minutes will entice a wary trout. Leaf worms, so-called because that's where you find them, are bigger and not so wiggly, but if you string two of them on a hook below a little golden spinner you'll find them excellent in a roaring rapids. When you find a pool full of little trout or trout that you don't want to catch, and they are always the first to bite, a big glob of night crawler will do the job. My father never used anything but those crawlers and he usually caught bigger fish than I did, but not as many.

There's even an art to putting worms on hooks, as I learned one evening from Laf Bodine, Tioga's best poacher, who showed me fourteen different ways of doing so. There are sunny summer days when only a grasshopper thrashing on the surface will yield a strike. I've caught bigger trout on two-inch minnows, on a belly slice from a hapless perch, on white grubs, and some little ones on yellow kernels of canned sweet corn. But enough! Although I've barely scratched the surface of my topic and could write a whole book about trout fishing, I fear I'm in danger of losing a reader or two, so let me tell how I taught my new wife to fish.

We had spent a fine morning and early afternoon walking the trails around our big lake, climbing Porcupine Bluff to see the caves among its huge boulders, having a drink from the big spring, crossing the outlet on a beaver dam, and finally circling the north shore back to the old cabin. I let Milove lead the way, not only to intercept the cobwebs across the path but because half of the fun lies in following the blazes on the trees and recognizing them. Only once did she lose the trail. Yes, she would make me a fine wife.

We were tired and hungry after the long jaunt, so after eating two cookies we lay down in the upper bunk to rest in each other's arms. After about an hour I awakened to find her gone and to hear her messing with some pans. "What will you have, Milord?" she asked. "Canned corned beef with potatoes, or potatoes with corned beef?"

"Neither," I replied. "We're having brook trout for supper and you'll have to catch them." I climbed down from the upper bunk and put the coffee pail, frying pan, two cups, two forks, a thick slice of bacon, and some salt and flour into my packsack. Leaving the cabin, I also carried a small can of leaf worms, my tackle bag, and the new bamboo flyrod I'd purchased for her wedding present. I was anxious to see how it would work. Lord knows, It should cast well. A wisp of a rod, only seven feet, three inches long and weighing only four ounces, I had paid the Orvis Company much more for it than I should have afforded.

Soon we were at the big pool on Wabeek Creek just below the old logging dam. It's a lovely spot and often I'd dreamed that someday I might take a wife or lover there. A long pool and a wide one with a torrent of silvery water cascading into it from the apron of the dam's sluice gate, it always held some trout though often they did not bite. On the southern shore, a spring entered the pool from under some bushes and flowed into submerged boulders and sunken logs over which an eddy circled strings of foam. The north bank where we stood, however, had a little grassy clearing where ovals of dead embers showed that other fishermen had built coffee fires there. Yes, it was the right place and the right time too because the sun had just begun to descend behind the hills. A lovely place!

"I'll make our cooking fire here, Milove," I said, "but you'll have to catch our supper. If you don't it will be a sparse one, just coffee, korpua, and that one strip of bacon, so assemble the rod. Be sure to join the two pieces so that the guides are in line."

Noticing that she was having difficulty, I took the two pieces of the rod from her. "Observe, woman!" I said pontifically. "This silver place where they join is called a ferrule. The upper section ends in the male part of the ferule; the lower section ends in the hollow female part. You have to marry them. Here, I'll show you."

"Yes, sire," she replied. But I was having difficulty too. Brand new rods are like that at first before they're broken in. Explaining that some grease was needed and that the sebaceous glands along the side of the nose held just the right amount. I began to twirl the end of the upper section against it. Suddenly Milove began to giggle outrageously and when I asked her how come she said, "That's the first time I ever saw a man wiping his nose with his p- pe-." She couldn't say the word but went into another burst of giggling. Then, noticing that I was still having trouble getting the male end all the way in, she took it from me and soon had them joined tightly. "Cully," she said, still giggling, "This reminds me of our wedding night."

I had her then put on the reel, string the black braided line through the guides, and then tie on the seven-foot leader which I'd had soaking at the edge of the stream. "No," I said, "That's a poor knot. Do it like this, Woman."

"Don't call me woman!" she exclaimed, "or I'll start callig you Man. I'm your blushing bride, remember?"

Then came the baiting of the hook I'd attached. I did it first, threading one of the leaf worms up the shank and over the knot, then looping another one around the curve and barb so the tips of both ends could wiggle freely. Stripping off the worms, I handed her the bare hook for rebaiting. "Now you do it, wo...Milove," I said. "You're a fast learner, Mr. Gage," she replied. "And so are you Madam," I responded, admiring how well she'd strung on the wigglers. "Now try a few casts from here, stripping some line off the reel with your left hand first in loops, then flicking the rod forward until it's all gone." She caught on immediately.

I told her to go over to the big log beam at the base of the dam, cast the bait into the current, and let it go downstream until it came close to a gray snag that was sticking out of the water, then wait and do it again and again until you get a bite. "You may have to pull out more line from the reel to reach the spot." I suggested.

Nothing happened on that first cast so I told her to crank the line back on the reel and begin again, and not to point the rod at the bait but to keep the tip high, and that if she had a bite, to jerk the tip back slightly so she could hook the fish. She grinned and saluted mockingly, but when a fish grabbed the bait she let out a war whoop. "I've got one, Cully," she yelled. "I've got one. Now what do I do? Do I crank the spool?"

I told her to keep a taut line and to walk over beside me where I'd hand her the little green net to lift it out of the water, and not to say spool. It was a reel, not a spool. She had some trouble holding the rod with her left hand behind her as she scooped the fish into the net. "Oh, what a beauty!" she exclaimed. "I've caught my first trout ever."

"No, you haven't" I interrupted. "That's just a damned chub, an eight-inch chub, the ugliest fish in the river. A nuisance fish, soft and inedible. I'll show you how to take it off this time but never again, so watch. Hold it firmly around its sides with one hand, then pry out the hook with the other. See?" I threw the chub up into the bushes as I've always done. "Don't! Don't," she screamed, as she ran over to find it. "Poor little fishy in the bush, let me put you back where you belong," she said as she picked it up and let it swim away. "Well, anyway, she's not squeamish," I thought, "but she sure has a lot to learn."

After putting three leaf worms instead of two on the hook, she returned to the dam and cast again into the current. I saw the line jerk slightly and heard her yelp. "Cully, I've got another bite but it's different, harder. There's another."

"Let it have it," I shouted above the roar of the water coming over the dam. "Take up the slack till you feel the fish." I saw the line moving steadily sideways. "OK, strike it! Jerk the tip of your rod." The trout was hooked and on that little rod it put up a terrific fight all over the lower pool. Once it broke water and I could see that it was a good one. "Don't give it any slack," I yelled. "Keep the rod tip high!" Once when it headed right for the snag I said a little prayer and the big trout turned away just before the leader was wrapped around it. Back and forth the trout surged, but finally its struggles diminished enough so she could lead it to the bank where I stood and slide it up onto the sand and gravel. "Oh, I forgot about netting it," Milove exclaimed shakily as I pounced upon the fish and laid it on some moss far from the water's edge.

"Oh, you beautiful, beautiful thing," she said. "Cully, let's put it back before it dies."

"Like hell," I roared. "That's our supper and I'm hungry. Must be ten or eleven inches long, you lucky woman. Almost enough for both of us. Not quite, so you'd better go catch another. But not now! He raised such a commotion all the other trout in the pool will be hiding and won't bite again for half an hour. I looked at her, flushed, breathless, and excited beyond measure, her brown eyes dancing. I can see her still, even though that happened fifty years ago and forty-five before she died. Only once have I seen her more beautiful and that was when she held our first child Cathy, in her arms at the hospital.

While we waited for the fish to calm themselves, she watched me clean the big trout. "See, it's easy," I said. "Just slit it below the gills sidewise, then slit it up the middle like this, then take your thumb and forefingers and strip out all the entrails with a single motion. No need to scale trout but you do have to take your thumbnail and scrape out the black blood on the inside of the backbone like this. Now let's put it back on the moss until I've built the cooking fire and have some coals, and until you catch a bigger one. But for now, just sit down on that log and look at that glorious orange and red U.P. sunset." Shakily, she did so as I built a little fire of dry driftwood between two logs.

"Oh, Cully," she exclaimed. "Now I can understand your love for trout fishing. It's the most exciting thing I've ever done. You'll never fish alone again." I rolled my eyes, remembering my father's words of wisdom.

As the fire burned down and we sat on the log with our arms around each other watching the western skies, the half-hour passed swiftly and she was out on the dam again. And soon she had caught another trout not as large as the first one, but at least nine inches long. This she cleaned herself, with only a few suggestions from me. "Now it's my turn," I said. I want to try fly fishing with your rod and I've seen some trout rising over there where the spring comes in. Dry the fish with this toilet paper, sprinkle salt all along the insides, and roll them in the flour that's in this little bag, then lightly salt again on the outside. You can use this slab of birchbark for a table. Cook them slowly in the frying pan until they're a deep brown outside, then call me when they're ready. Oh yes, fry the bacon first."

Unstringing the rod, I substituted another reel from my pocket that held a fly line, put on a new leader and attached a number sixteen caddis dry fly to its end. Walking along the shore to the foot of the pool, I then waded back upstream along a hidden sand bar almost to the snag. Once there I took several false casts to get the feel of the little rod, then let one cast carry the fly to a patch of foam where the eddy began. The fly lit perfectly for once and without any drag, when suddenly a big trout leaped out of the water and hit it on the way down. It too put up quite a fight on that little rod, once almost taking the line into some bushes, but I turned him back into the pool and soon had him in the net. It was larger than the one Milove had caught so I took out the hook and carefully slid the fish back into the pool. What a good moment! To be there at sunset in a lovely pool of clear water with a beautiful new wife waiting for me on shore with trout in the frying pan; well, it's a picture I've never forgotten. Resisting a temptation to try for another, I joined Milove. Yes, she had seen the whole thing. "How big was your trout?" she asked.

"Oh, not as large as yours," I lied happily. I see you had to cut the heads off your so they'd fit in the pan. They'll be ready soon."

It was a memorable meal though I had to show her how to cut the skin lengthwise along the side, then flake off the pink meat, leaving the backbone intact. Even the korpua and coffee were very good, and before we left for camp I taught Milove how to do my Grampa Gage's Dance of the Wild Cucumber all along the bank.

One of the best days of my life!

The Lie

Besides the stories, jokes and sayings that kept the tongues of Tioga wagging throughout the winter, we also had rumors that swept the village all year round. "They say that the new English teacher, Miss Young, doesn't wear any panties under her skirts." "I hear that the Northwestern Railroad is going to pull up its tracks to Michigamme." "Did you know that Bessie Siemen is pregnant with her fourteenth kid? Hope that won't be feebleminded too." "Hear tell that Joe Paquette come back from Lake Tioga with a forty-five pound pike. Probably netted it." "Someone told me the Jensons are selling their homestead and going to move to Republic." Every year or two when I was growing up a same rumor appeared: the Oliver Iron Mining Company was going to reopen the Tioga mine. "Yah, Charlie Schwartz, the telegrapher down at the depot, heard that from the one in Marquette who heard it from a man high up in Cleveland Cliffs who got it from someone in Duluth."

Unlike jokes which demand a certain consistency in the retelling, our rumors changed as they went up the hill or around the valley with so many revisions and embellishments that finally they were completely unlike the original. When Eric Niemi came to town after breakup one spring he asked Annie, our post-mistress, if it was true that the Cleveland Cliffs had bought the Oliver Mining Company. Even if only one mouth had done the telling, the tale could change. Collecting tidbits of gossip on her daily rounds, Aunt Lizzie had heard from Mrs. Dusaine at the bottom of the hill that Andy Axelson had been seen making eyes at Marguerite, her daughter. By the time Aunt Lizzie visited Mrs. Christenson at the top of the hill she was saying that she'd heard that

Andy had raped Marguerite in the Bellaire's haymow. Not that it mattered too much. No one believed Aunt Lizzie anyway, but the rumor was repeated just the same. Something to talk about over coffee.

Since this is the story about the ugliest rumor ever to raise hell in Tioga, I must tell you something about the people involved.

Henri Bonet had been a very strange child compared to other kids in Tioga. He never fought at all. Why, he'd even let much smaller boys beat him up. They called him "Goody-goody" or "Angel-face." He did have the face and disposition of an angel and Henri was smart too, always getting 100s on his report card–even in deportment. Unlike the rest of the village boys, he never went fishing or hunting or swimming. Certainly, he never played hooky. Instead, he usually hung around the Catholic church where he served as an acolyte and altar boy to Father Hassel, the parish priest. Not only on Sundays, Henri was also there after school on weekdays doing what he could to make himself useful because, as he told Father Hassel once, he wanted to become a priest too some day. The first of his class to master the catechism, he soon began to pick up some of the Latin phrases used in the liturgy and constantly pored over his little black bible, often asking the priest the meanings of many of the verses. Impressed by the boy's devotion and piety, Father Hassel encouraged Henri, gave him religious books to read, and soon found himself playing the role of a real father as well as a pastoral one.

One day when he discovered that Henri had cleaned and polished all the candlesticks without being told to do so, Father Hassel patted Henri on the head and said, "Henri, you are a great comfort to an old man, my son. Yes, you are like a son to me." Henri began to weep. "But I'm not my own father's son," he said. "Mon pere, he don't like me at all. He spits on the floor when he sees me and makes a face. He doesn't want me to be a priest. He calls me a weak poulet (chicken), no son of his." The boy sobbed for a long time and then he told the priest how worried he was about his mother, that she had spells when she was very sick, when she could hardly breathe, when her face was covered with sweat and she would bang her heart place with her fist. "Has she been to see Dr. Gage?" the priest asked. "No," answered Henri. "Mon pere, he say no."

That afternoon Father Hassel came to our house to have his weekly chess game with my Dad and the usual glass of whiskey and one of the undertaker's good cigars. (Both my father and the priest got a box of those cigars from Mr. Stenrud every Christmas.) Occasionally, as they lifted their glasses, one would toast Mr. Stenrud: "First, the doctor; then the priest; then the undertaker." But that afternoon, things were more serious as Father Hassel told Dad about Mrs. Bonet and asked him to call on her. "I'll pay your fee, Doctor. Her son, Henri is a treasure to me and he's greatly concerned." Dad told him of course he'd be glad to go and that the fee would be a mass for his benighted agnostic soul after he died. They were very good friends and always enjoyed each other.

When my father returned from seeing Henri's mother, he phoned Father Hassel. "She's in a bad way, Father," Dad said. "She has ventricular tachycardia, a heart disease characterized by episodes of heartbeats that race completely out of control. Mrs. Bonet had a minor attack when I was there and the pulse was so fast I couldn't count it, let along feel it. She recovered but it's very probable that some time soon the heart muscle will go into fibrillation and that will be it. You'd better go down there and prepare them for her death. It could come any time. She'll be lucky to be alive a month from now."

Dad's prognosis was wrong for once. Henri's mother lived another year before the fibrillation took her. Henri was a sophomore in high school, taking his first course in Latin, when his world fell apart. His father gave him ten dollars and told him to get the hell out and make his own way in the world as he had done when he was fifteen. A married sister who lived in Tioga couldn't take him in so he could finish his schooling, so arrangements were made for him to live with an aunt in Marquette. In desperation Henri asked Father Hassel if he could live with him. "No, my son," the old priest said, "It is against the rules of the church." He wept as he said the words.

Not much was heard of Henri in the next years except that he changed from being an angel into a devil. In Marquette his aunt couldn't control him at all. He fought, got drunk, and even stole money from her until finally she showed him the door. Later, Annie said his sister had sent Henri a postal money order to a jail address in Milwaukee. Someone also said he'd gotten into trouble with the police in Detroit but didn't know the details. Henri finally did return to the U.P., however, because a little piece in the *Marquette Mining Journal* mentioned that a Henri Bonet, age 22, formerly of Tioga, had been arrested for aggravated assault and was being held in jail there awaiting trial.

When Father Hassel saw the item, he immediately took the train to Marquette to see what he could do to help. Entering the cell, he hardly recognized Henri at first and, when he tried to talk with him, Henri just turned his face to the wall. The priest conferred with the prosecuting attorney and the judge and hired a lawyer. In the end, Henri got off lightly because of the priest's efforts: one year in the county jail and a sentence of four more which would be suspended on condition that Father Hassel be held responsible for his good behavior. Henri had almost killed that man, they said, and would have done so if bystanders had not pulled his hands off the man's throat.

Every Friday for the fifty-two weeks of the sentence Father Hassel went to Marquette to see his wayward son, and although at first the visits were most unpleasant and frustrating, by the end of that year much of their old relationship had been reestablished. When the jail door finally opened, Father Hassel was there to welcome Henri to a new life. The ladies of the Order of the Eastern Star had cleaned the old house, vacant since his father had died two years before, and they had a hot supper ready for the two of them. The priest told Henri that he was to go to the section house at seven the next morning because he'd gotten him a job patrolling the railroad right-of-way by handcar. Joe Velain would be his partner and show him how to do the job. He said he hoped to see Henri at confession Saturday afternoon and at Mass on Sunday.

Well, everything turned out fine. Henri did well enough to be made foreman of another railroad maintenance crew. Remembering the terms of his probation, he never went to Higley's saloon nor did any fighting. After the second year, Henri married Fred Vachon's daughter, Michelle, and soon they had a son who was baptized by Father Hassel. Every week, Henri not only went to confession and mass but also visited the priest for conversation and to do odd chores for him. He loved the old man who had been so good to him and who had given him a new life.

That isn't the end of Henri's story, however. But first I must tell you about Sylvie Vautrin, certainly the ugliest woman in Tioga and perhaps the ugliest in the whole U.P. She was also Father Hassel's housekeeper and had been so for many years. Saying that Sylvie was ugly is an understatement. "Repulsive" might be a better word. Thin as a wagon spoke, when she walked she seemed to be crouching but it was her face that hit you hardest. The left side of it was colored by a huge red and purple birthmark that ran up into her straggly hair almost surrounding one eye. (Back then there was no cosmetic surgery and if you had a birthmark it stayed with you all your days.) The right half of Sylvie's face had no birthmark but there were several prominent moles, each with a tiny tuft of hair protruding from it. And she was hairy, hirsute beyond belief, with a visible brown mustache and arms covered with brown fuzz beyond her wrists to her knuckles. The word was that someone had seen her swimming naked once and that she even had hair on her breasts.

If these words seem cruel instead of factual (which they are), they simply reflect the cruelty of the God that formed her or perhaps the cruelty from others that she had known all her life. No one in Tioga ever looked at Sylvie when they met her on the street even if they politely said, "Bon Jour, Mamselle." When her parents went to church, they left Sylvie at home. When company came, she went to her bedroom. Her school years must have been terrible ones. I don't know; I was too young to have known her then. Although she was smart and did well in school, she quit after the fourth grade to escape the cruelty of her peers and to help her mother with the washing and ironing of the clothes brought to them by the trainmen. Thereafter Sylvie remained invisible, almost forgotten by the village.

At that time, this was not unusual. Several families in Tioga had "hiddens", as we called them: a demented aunt, a grossly mentally retarded son, a severely crippled daughter. There were few social services. Except for the insane asylum in Newberry, there was literally no place to put the severly impaired, so we kept them hidden at home.

Sylvie was eighteen when a series of circumstances freed her from isolation and drudgery. A very young priest who had probably been assigned to Tioga for testing, or perhaps as a punishment for his rebellious behavior at the seminary, almost wrecked the parish. He was arrogant, made few pastoral calls, missed confessionals, didn't do the mass very well, and gave terribly severe penances for small sins. There were Sundays when only a handful of the faithful showed up in church. Finally when one evening he took the train for Chicago along with his housekeeper, all the parish sighed with relief and said "Good riddance."

His replacement was Father Hassel, a man who had served brilliantly as the deputy of the archbishop in Chicago and was being considered as a possible bishop when an opening would occur. However, when one did appear, Father Hassel refused. "I am too old," he protested. "I am tired of administration. Find me a little parish in some isolated village where I can tend my flock and really be a priest in my old age."

When the news came from Marquette that Tioga was getting a new priest, the parishioners got busy in a hurry. The church was scrubbed from stem to stern; the altar cloths washed and ironed; the candlesticks polished; the parsonage spruced up and ready for him. But they couldn't find a housekeeper. They searched and threatened and begged, but to no avail. Finally some one thought of Sylvie. "Non! Non!" said Pierre DuPont. "He take wan look for her an' take next train out." Others disagreed. "Every priest should have an ugly housekeeper," one said. "Sylvie is smart; she can cook and clean; she will be grateful to get out of the closet and have her own money for once. If he is a holy man, he can bear how she looks." Nevertheless, they were greatly worried about how their new priest might react when he saw Sylvie, the horrible.

They needn't have been so concerned. Father Hassel accepted the situation easily. As he told my father once when Dad gently teased him about his ugly housekeeper, "I do not see faces, Doctor. I see souls."

Within two years Father Hassel changed his parish completely. Every Sunday the church was filled to capacity; so was the poor box. Father Hassel, unlike the other priests, never begged for money. He didn't need to. People gave all they could and then a bit more because they knew he cared for them not only when they were sick or dying, but even when they were well. A familiar sight on our hill street and back roads, he made his rounds daily. Even in the winter when the deep snows came and the wind blew cold, we would see Father Hassel plunging through the drifts, holding his cassock high above the boots an heavy wool pants he wore as he made his missions to the troubled of flesh or heart. Speaking to everyone he met in that deep calm voice, he made us all feel good. I remember feeling really blessed when once he stopped me, laid a big hand on my head, and held a brief conversation. Father Hassel loved little kids and often had an entourage of them as he went from house to house on his pastoral calls. French Canadians who hadn't been to confession or mass for years found their faith renewed when he sought them out in isolated cabins that had never seen a priest. Seeming to have no fear, my father sometimes would beg him not to enter a house that he had plastered with a quarantine sign bearing the big red letters of **"SCARLET FEVER"**. "No," said Father Hassel. "If you will enter to save their bodies, I will enter to save their souls." I have already told you how Henri adored the old priest. He was not alone.

One day during their chess game when Dad discovered that Father Hassel would soon be celebrating his 78th birthday, he organized a banquet of appreciation for his 18 years of services to the community. It would be held in the school gymnasium; there would be free food and speeches. Thanks not only to the Catholic ladies of the Order of the Eastern Star, but also to those of the Methodist and Swedish Lutheran Churches, it was a great success. Even Finns came, even some who would never eat the meat off the tail bone of a chicken because it was called "the pope's nose." Indeed, even the Finnish and Lutheran attended, and when the bishop from Marquette sang Father Hassel's praises, they applauded. Never had our little village felt so united.

That unity lasted only a few months. It was shattered when Sylvie became pregnant. Impossible! Oh, a few had noticed with approval that finally she had begun to put a little weight on that gaunt frame as she daily climbed and descended the hill street from the parsonage. Probably because she shared the good meals she cooked for the priest, they said. But when that weight seemed to get more concentrated, tongues began to wag. Then one day, when Sylvie was seen going to my father's hospital at office hour time, and then that night boarding the train to Green Bay where her sister lived, all hell broke loose.

Sylvie pregnant? What man, no matter how drunk, would touch her? Who was the father of that unborn child? Could it have been the priest? NO! That was incredible. And yet...

Oh, the ugly rumors! Oh, the vicious gossip! Father Hassel was too old. But was he? Old man Vattila had fathered a child by his second young wife at the age of 89. No, that didn't mean anything. Vattila just had good neighbors. But Father Hassel was a truly good man. He wouldn't do such hanky-panky. He was a wise man; he'd have too much sens. And yet? Who else might have done it? How about that feeble minded moron, Willie Martel? No, he'd been cookee in Silverthorne's logging camp all winter. Who else?

So far as Father Hassel was concerned, nothing seemed to have changed. Benevolently he cared for his people, his face calm and peaceful. Some of them wondered if he had ever heard any of the cruel gossip. Until a new housekeeper could be found, Mrs. Bussiere and other women took weekly turns cooking and cleaning for him up at the parsonage. Life went on very smoothly. The whole matter would soon be forgotten.

But that was only on the surface. Beneath it were doubt and evil thoughts. When Antoine Bizet remarked regarding Pere Hassel that "En la nuit toutes les chats sont gris" (At night all cats are gray), his neighbor threw an axe at him. An old Finnish saying swept the town: "Once you get them 'neath the blankets, all women are the same." When Aunt Lizzie who, for all her faults, feared God but no man, came to my father's office and asked him point blank if he'd found Sylvie pregnant and if the priest was the father, Dad grabbed her by the scruff of the neck and literally kicked her down the hospital steps. At supper he was still so furious I didn't even dare ask him to pass the butter.

Uptown, innuendos, slurs, and nasty little jokes about the Catholics were passed from one Finn house to another. For the older ones, the happening merely corroborated what they had always known about the Catholics and their priests. After school the Finn and French kids slugged it out. Even in the woods, the young men fought. Joe Pitou and Andy Avila, who had been friends for years, beat each other to a pulp when Andy, referring to Father Hassel, had spoken the word "father" with a certain intonation.

The worst of these fights occurred in the post office and involved Henri Bonet who should have remembered that he still had a year to go on his probation. Henri had come to mail his wife's letter to her sister in Hancock when, entering the door, he heard Untu Pekkari and a friend laughing, and Untu saying something about Father Hassel and reciting "The holy pole is in your hole so wiggle your ass to save your soul."

Of cours Henri jumped him, got him down on the floor and began choking Untu until his face was turning blue, just as he had done to that other man four years earlier. When they broke his throat grip, Henri began to weep, then straightened up and said very slowly "Father Hassel is a saint. He wasn't the one who knocked up Sylvie. It was me! I tell you it was me and if Sylvie comes back with child I will adopt it and make it my own. Say no more about my priest."

Within the hour the news of what Henri had said swept the valley and the furthest Finn houses uptown. It had even preceded him to his own house where he found Michelle rocking their little son and weeping bitterly. Henri could not talk; he just wept too.

It was three weeks before Henri could bring himself to go to confession and when he did, he said nothing about Sylvie. Father Hassel gently urged him to say more and then urged him again. "I have heard, my son, what you have told about my housekeeper. Surely you can tell me."

Henri was silent for a long time before he spoke. "Father," he said. "As you may or may not know, I lied."

Going Back To The U.P.

Tom Hedet's boyhood in Tioga had been a wonderful experience and he'd loved every moment of it. Roaming the forest, fishing the lakes and streams, yes, evening going to school had been good, but when he entered his senior year in high school the future didn't look so promising. It was 1931, the depth of the Great Depression. Banks had failed; mines were closed or closing; every freight train had a boxcar full of hopeless, homeless men searching for a place where some job might be available. Cars loaded with pulp sat on the railroad siding because there was no market for it. No one had biting money.

Tom saw that he, like many others, would have to leave Tioga and the U.P. Perhaps in the cities Down Below there would be an opportunity to make a living. He didn't want to go. He wanted to live in the U.P. all his life, to raise a family there so his children could have the joys he'd had.

Taking stock of himself, he tried to decide what kind of work he'd want to do the rest of his life, what his assets and liabilities were. Well, he'd always been especially good in mathematics. Maybe he'd become a mathematics teacher in some high school. But that didn't appeal to him. Teachers never made much money and they had to spend a lot of time disciplining. He didn't want to grow up to be like Old Blue Balls, no sir! What he'd really like would be a job in business or a business of his own so he could make a lot of money, retire early, and come back to spend the rest of his days in the U.P.

So Tom came up to our house to see my father for advice. "Work your way through college," said Dad. "I did, and you can too. I clerked for a year in a hotel doing bookkeeping, taught a year in a country school, worked in a bank as a teller and bookkeeper, oh a lot of things, but I got an education and became a doctor that way. Times are tough right now but they'll get better, so prepare yourself for them. Go to school. Go to the University of Michigan and become an accountant. If you want to have a business of your own you've got to learn how to keep books."

Dad also made arrangements with Mr. Flynn so that he would teach Tom how to keep the store's books, if he'd work without pay and just for the experience. Mr. Flynn told Dad later that Tom was a natural, that he was very good at figures, was well organized, and had been a lot of help once he'd learned the ropes.

The day following his high school graduation Tom spent in walking all the street of Tioga, swimming in Fish Lake off Big Rock, and catching a mess of trout up in the Escanaba. He was homesick already. But the next morning he started hitchhiking to Ann Arbor with fifty dollars in his pocket from the family sugar bowl. "It's a loan," his father told him, "and it comes hard, so pay it back as soon as you can." His mother made him some sandwiches and wiped some of her tears. Tom wiped some too.

The hitchhiking took three days and after paying the fare to cross on the ferry at the Straits, he arrived in Ann Arbor still with forty-two dollars and a bad case of homesickness. Then, armed with a "To Whom It May Concern" recommendation from Mr. Flynn, Tom made the rounds of all the businesses on State Street hunting for a job. Finally he found one at Wahr's bookstore. No, they didn't need a full-time bookkeeper but they were taking inventory now that the Univerisity was not in session, and if he did well they would pay him fifteen dollars a week for as long as the job lasted. Tom also soon got another job as a janitor, sweeping and cleaning one of the classroom buildings from six P.M. until two in the morning, which paid forty dollars a month. Then a nice old lady rented him an attic room with a cot and a chair and a table for twenty dollars a month. Food, however, seemed terribly expensive and all that first year Tom lived on day-old bakery bread, peanut butter and strawberry jam. Although he saved every penny, he found in the fall that he had only enough to pay for matriculation and two courses at the university, neither of which were in business. No matter! He was on his way. Someday he'd have his own business, make a lot of money, and get back to the U.P.

It took Tom six years instead of four to graduate from the U of M business school, six tough years of holding two and sometimes three jobs. Throughout that time he found himself constantly dreaming of the U.P. and Tioga. Someday he'd fish the headwaters beyond the Haysheds. Sometime he'd sit again under that waterfall on the east branch. Sometime he'd smell arbutus again. Often it was hard to study.

He almost got back there at the end of his third year. A student had an old Model-T Ford he wanted to sell for only thirty dollars. It was in bad shape inside and out but the owner said it ran fine, so Tom, against his good judgement, bought the thing. He had a week of vacation after classes had ended, not enough to get home hitchhiking, but enough if he drove all night. He got only as far as Clare where a garage mechanic told him the block was cracked and he needed a new motor, that it would cost at least one hundred and fifty dollars. Tom left it and his dreams there and made his way back to Ann Arbor.

Again, after he had graduated he planned to take a few weeks off before beginning the new job that he'd been offered. A good job. He'd be a junior accountant at the headquarter of the Atlantic and Pacific Tea Company in Detroit. Good pay and fine possibilities for advancement. Tom wrote his parents telling them the good news and saying he'd be with them the last week of June. For a week he pictured to himself all the things he'd do. Then he got a special delivery letter saying that they'd sold the house and were moving to Marinette, Wisconsin. They wouldn't be there in Tioga but would love to have him come see them in their new home. Instead Tom went to Detroit to find a place to live. Would he ever get back to Tioga? Where would he stay if he did?

For the first six months Tom found the new job fascinating as he mastered the various skills involved. Mr. Phillipson, the senior accountant, was a good boss, always willing to help or explain, and better yet, to forgive when Tom made the inevitable mistakes of a beginner. Oh, there were some things about the job that he didn't like. Sitting all day at a desk in a large room full of other desks, poring over papers, doing the same things over and over again. Moreover he hated the city. Too many people; too much noise; everyone in a hurry! Tom resented the morning and evening hassle of taking the streetcars to and from work. He'd found a good room in the suburbs but that meant a forty minute ride each way. On weekends he was often lonely and going to the zoo or a museum didn't help much. There were always crowds there too. Tioga had no crowds. Tom found himself doing a lot of daydreaming about the U.P.

After the holidays, the daydreaming increased. *Accounts payable:* A huge stack of them arrived every day on his desk for him to sort, organize and enter. (How deep would the snow be in Tioga now? Would the drifts cover the fence around the old school? Would the snow squeak under your footsteps?) *Accounts receivable:* (Remember how we made that ski jump in Company Field? Are the ravens still croaking as they soar over The Grove?) *Cash payments:* (They'll probably have a basketball game tonight in the Town Hall: the Michigamme versus Tioga town teams. There'll be some good fights and maybe a howl or two if some player brushes against the potbellied stove.) *Cash receipts:* (How good it was to have breakup time in the spring. Remember how we made snow dams across the hill street? Remember that first arbutus? The pink kind always smelled more fragrant than the white.) *Posting and vouchers:* (Fishing for trout in the rapids; cowslips and marsh marigolds in the swamps; eating the new shoots of wild raspberries with salt.) *Trial balances:* (Tapping the big maple trees and driving in the spigots made from hollowed-out elderberry branches; sap icicles; maple sugar wax on new snow.) *Inventory Checking:* (Swimming in Tioga Lake when the great ice cakes still floats in the middle of it; partridge drumming on a hollow log; sunsets and sunrises.) Yes, there were many times when Tom found it hard to concentrate on his work.

Nevertheless, after just two years he received a promotion to be a senior accountant with his own office and a secretary. Now he had to supervise several junior accountants and various clerks, prepare financial statements of profits and losses, balance sheets, and work out budgets. There were times when he was so busy he almost forgot there was an Upper Peninsula. Also he was studying hard to prepare for the C.P.A. examinations, because he knew that unless he became licensed as a certified public accountant, his career upward would be blocked. Having had to work so hard during his university days, his grades had only been Cs and Bs and there was much he had missed, but by studying hard evenings and weekends Tom finally passed all four parts of that tough examination. It paid off because soon he was promoted to be a chief accountant with a big boost in salary.

After three more years, Tom Hedet had a house, a new car, and a pregnant wife. He'd almost made it back to the U.P. for their honeymoon. The planning of that honeymoon had been fun. Having read a lot of books about the U.P., he'd sketched out the route. They'd spend the first night in St. Ignace, then drive to the Soo to watch the ships going through the canal. From there they'd visit the Tahquamenon Falls and spend the second night either in Grand Marais or Munising. The third night they'd be in a hotel in Marquette or Ishpeming and use that as a base from which they'd visit Tioga and all his old haunts. Then they'd go to L'Anse, the Keweenaw Peninsula, and over to Ironwood, and finally back to the Straits on US-2, along the shore of Lake Michigan, stopping in to see the great spring by Manistique. Oh, there was so much to see and do on that honeymoon!

But his new bride insisted on going to Niagara Falls instead.

In 1958 Tom Hedet was forty-five years old when they promoted him to be Comptroller of the company. Yes, his rise up the corporate ladder had been swift, almost meteoric, but Tom had paid the price. Now living in a big house in Bloomfield Hills, he had three children: Tom, Jr. aged 14; Jack 12 and Lisa 8. The trouble was that he hardly knew them. Oh, he gave them everything they wished including a new swimming pool, everything but his time. Each night he came home from the office with a brief case full of work he would have to do that night. Often his weekends meant a day back at work. He ate too much and too fast, his wife said. He was too heavy and wheezed now when he climbed the stairs up to the bedroom where he slept fitfully when he slept at all. Of late he'd been very irritable, his wife told him. Well, he'd change now that he'd been made Comptroller. He'd take it easier and start having some fun with his kids. Yes, if he did an extra good job, they would probably make him Vice President in charge of financial services, but it was time to quit sacrificing his family and begin enjoying life. Lord, he hadn't had a real vacation in twenty-eight years. It was about time–about time he went back to Tioga and its lovely lakes and streams and forests. Forty-five wasn't really old, but there were times when he felt he was.

So Tom Hedet asked for and received a month's vacation before assuming his new duties. Then he bought one of the new travel trailers with all the conveniences, big enough for the whole family and then some. They would take the honeymoon he'd never had, cover the U.P. from stem to stern, see all the sights, and camp at Lake Tioga (where he'd heard they now had a State Park) for as long as they wished. Perhaps he'd take the camper up the river road to the Haysheds and catch a trout or two in that lovely pool below the old logging dam. Or let the kids catch some and cook them over an open fire at twilight. Oh, it would be good going back and being a boy again. Of course his old house would be there with some other family in it and there would be other changes, but perhaps he could find a cottage on Lake Tioga to buy for a summer or retirement home. Just the same he was going back, day after tomorrow, finally going back. He'd have to make just one more trip to the office to arrange for the switchover to his new suite of offices.

But Tom Hedet never did go back to Tioga. They found him slumped over his desk, dead. A massive heart attack! Probably never knew what hit him, the doctor said.

I guess the moral is obvious. To you who live in the U.P., cherish our lovely land. To you who don't, what the hell are you waiting for?

Not Yet

It had been a hard night on the sleeping car from Chicago. Every time the train stopped, and it must have stopped a hundred times, Jim Heiken had almost fallen out of his narrow berth. Oh, he'd managed to sleep a bit at Green Bay when the clicking and jolting had stopped for a time, but by Pembine he was so wide awake he was shaved and dressed when daylight came. Putting up the window shade, he peered out to see nothing but trees and more trees going by. There were no houses, no farms, just forest or stumps where the forest had been. At Iron Mountain he parted the curtains, put on his freshly shined shoes, then staggered up the swaying aisle to give the porter a quarter tip and to ask when the dining car would start serving. "Oh no, boss," the porter said. "Dining car don't open until Michigamme at 7:30."

Jim consulted his timetable. Two more stops at Sagola and Republic and then Tioga at 6:30. Tioga! The name had a good ring to it. It was where he'd live until next summer as their new high school math and science teacher. His first job! Hoped he could handle it. Jim reread the letter he'd received from the superintendent. 'Dear Mr. Heiken: Although school will not open until Monday, September 3rd, you should be here at least by the Saturday before, so we can get acquainted and I can outline your duties. After some difficulty, I have been able to arrange room and board for you at Mrs. Lizzie Campton's house for which you will pay thirty dollars a month. I shall be either at home or at the school and I'm sure someone will be able to direct you there. Sincerely, E.K. Aronson, Superintendent of Schools.'

Finally the train pulled in at the Tioga Station. As Jim descended the steps, he looked around. Where was the town? The business district? All he could see was a road ascending a huge hill on his left lined sparsely with houses and big maple trees. Perhaps it was on the other side of the depot. No, again all he saw were dirt roads with some whitewashed log cabins along them and a larger frame building beside the tracks which bore the sign "Higley's Saloon" on its false front. He went to the ticket window and stood there for some time watching a man with a green head visor tapping and listening to a bank of telegraph keys. Finally the clattering stopped and the man came to the window.

"Could you tell me where I could find a restaurant, please?" Jim asked. "They weren't serving breakfast on the train from Chicago."

"Naw!" said the man. "You come seven years too late. That's when the mine closed and so did the cafe and the hotel and the boarding house. You the new science teacher for the high school?"

"Yes, my name's Jim Heiken. I'm to meet Mr. Aronson this morning to find out what I have to do. Can you tell me how I can find his house?"

"Why sure," said the telegrapher. "You just climb the hill street past the new school. His house is the big yellow and brown one just opposite the Methodist church. Let's see. It's Saturday. Eskil will be having his breakfast about eight o'clock, it not being a school day, so maybe you could get a cup of coffee there if you time it right. He and his wife are good people, the Aronsons are. Not like Old Blue Balls who used to be our super. Why don't you leave your bag here and look around the valley? We got a lot of French Canadians and Indians down here back of the station and uptown you'll find the Finns and Cousin Jacks and such. Why don't you go see the old iron smelter furnace and the waterfall? Cross the tracks and take the road to the left, but don't go up the hill."

Jim thanked him and did so. On his way a little girl said hello and a bit further two old men were leaning against a fence talking French. When he said good morning to them they smiled and said, "Bon Jour, Msieu," Then one said, "I think you be ze new high school teachair, oui? You like it here. We got fine new school now." Well, though Jim, the natives were sure friendly. Despite the gnawing in his stomach, he was beginning to feel good, and the old furnace and waterfall were sure picturesque. By the time he returned to the depot to pick up his bag it was a quarter to eight.

The hill street was even steeper than it looked and Jim's arm was almost ready to fall off from carrying his bag when he came upon the school on his left. It was impressive. A large brick two-story building set upon a knoll surrounded by a large schoolyard, it looked very new. Just beyond it at the steepest part of the hill he'd yet encountered, he also found the Methodist-Episcopal church and across from it the superintendent's house. He pulled out his watch, and since it read 8:15 Jim climbed the steps to the porch and knocked on the door.

The Aronsons, as the telegrapher had predicted, were having breakfast and insisted that he join them. Oatmeal with wild blueberries smothered with thick yellow cream, it was accompanied by a curious cold hard toast that they called korpua. When Mrs. Aronson poured Jim a cup of coffee and Jim refused, saying that he'd never learned to drink it yet, they both insisted that he do so. "You'll soon find that in Tioga they always offer you coffee the moment you step inside the door," Mrs. Aronson said. "Yes, that's right, Jim. You'll discover a lot of odd customs in this out-of-the-way place. Have you ever had a sauna?"

"No, what's a sauna?"

"A steam bath. All the Finns go sauna every Saturday night and sometimes even during the week. They're a very clean people. It will be an experience the first time. By the way, do you have enough money to pay Mrs. Campton in advance for your room and board? If you don't I'll lend you some till pay day." When Jim said that he had fifty dollars in his wallet, Mr. Aronson said that would be enough and that he'd walk with him up to her house.

As they did so, Mr. Aronson pointed out my Dad's hospital and the boarded-up Beacon House with its long veranda. "Until the mine suddenly closed after the cave-in, Tioga must have been quite a little city," the Superintendent said. "Had its own hotel, fire department, club house, and there's the boarding house where the miners without families lived. The building next to it is Flynn's store where you can still buy anything. By the way, I suggest you buy a felt hat or cap, Jim, as soon as you can. I know that Down Below and in Chicago all the men wear straw hats like yours, but up here they'll poke fun at you and think you're a sissy for wearing one and knock it off your head perhaps. Just look carefully inside the hat to make sure there aren't any lice. That big building across from the store is our Town Hall where town meetings are held. It's also our jail. We also have a little village library upstairs in it that is open on Thursday afternoons and evenings. Not many books in it though."

They met several tow-headed children whom Mr. Aronson greeted by name and an old lady with whom he stopped for a brief conversation after introducing the new teacher. "Always say hello to every person you meet," the superintendent advised, "and tell them who you are and how much you like our town even if you don't. It's a custom. Oh yes, and watch your feet when walking on this board sidewalk. The cows and horses roam up and down our street freely and you have to dodge their manure. Not like Chicago, is it?" He grinned.

Just before they came to Easy Street where Mrs. Campton lived, the superintendent told Jim a bit about her. "We call her Aunt Lizzie and she's quite a character, to put it mildly. She's the town gossip and not a nice one either. I really didn't want to have you board with her but I couldn't for the life of me find any other place. Perhaps we can later if you just can't stand her yakking, but she's a fine cook and will put some meat on those bones of yours." Jim was a bit surprised when they went to the back rather than the front door. "That's another of our customs," Mr. Aronson said. "Front doors are for funerals."

Mrs. Campton came to the door when they knocked. A tall, rawboned woman with a sharp nose and jaw, she was holding a tiny Pekinese dog who kept barking. "Hush now, Sweetie Pie," she said to it as Mr. Aronson introduced Jim. "I know you don't like nasty men but he's our new boarder so shush!" The Superintendent didn't stay long. "Drop in at the school after dinner, Jim, and I'll show you around and tell you your duties," he said as he departed.

Mrs. Campton sat Jim down at the kitchen table. "Well?" Her voice was as sharp as her nose. "You must pay in advance, young man. Do you have towels and soap?" Jim shook his head. "Well, I'll furnish them then and do your laundry for five dollars extra a month, so it will be thirty-five dollars right now. You'll have to iron your own shirts though."

When Jim paid her the money, Aunt Lizzie took him upstairs. Like the kitchen, the little bedroom was spotless–too spotless. It held only a large bed, a small table with a kerosene lamp, and two chairs, one a sagging stuffed purple monster. Also there was a commode with pitcher, basine and slop jar. That was all. Jim asked about the bathroom and when she led him to it all he saw was an empty claw-footed bathtub without faucets. No toilet! Aunt Lizzie saw his puzzlement. "I don't have running water," she explained. "If you want to take a bath, you'll have to bring up teakettles of hot water from the kitchen or have a sauna over at Mrs. Kutinen's house next door. They heat it every Saturday and only charge ten cents. As for the toilet, you'll use the outhouse out back by the barn or the slop jar. And mind you, you'll have to empty and clean it every time. I keep a clean house, Mr. Heiken. Leave your bag up here and come down to the kitchen for a cup of coffee and I'll tell you the rules."

There were a lot of them. No hanky-panky. No visitors, no women! He would have to make his bed before he left in the morning. Breakfast, dinner and supper were at seven, twelve and six on the dot. No tracking mud into the kitchen. No, he couldn't play the organ except when she asked him to. He could come downstairs and sit in the kitchen with her, but only if she gave permission. He had to be nice to Lulubelle. There were a lot more of those rules before Jim fled upstairs to unpack.

After doing so, he decided to wash up but found no water in the pitcher, and when he asked Aunt Lizzie for some, she told him to get a pailful from the well outside. Jim took the pail but when he got to the well beside the woodshed he didn't know what to do. There was a rope and windlass but when he lowered the pail it just floated and wouldn't fill. Aunt Lizzie who'd been watching him through the kitchen curtains finally came out and showed him how to gather up the rope loosely, then plunge the pail upside down into the water. "Lordamighty," she said contemptuously, "you city folks don't even know how to get a pail of water from the well. On your way back, bring in an armful of small wood to make up for that I've used to heat your teakettle." Jim sure felt intimidated.

The noon meal, however, was very good: swiss steak, mashed potatoes and a fine apple pie. As Mr. Aronson had told him, his landlady was an excellent cook. Jim devoured the food but only between his answers to constant questions and Lulubelle's niping at his ankles under the table. Finally he got away and en route to the school he bought a felt hat at Flynn's store. No lice!

The superintendent proudly showed him around the building. "It's as fine a school as you'll find in the U.P.," he said. "Although Tioga is a poor town, when the company suddenly closed the mine down and pulled up the railroad tracks, they forgot a large ore pile on the surface and the taxes on it are paying for the school. No, we're not hurting for money. We even provide free textbooks. Here, I'll get you copies of your texts. You'll teach algebra, geometry, trigonometry and physics and be in charge of the study hall when you aren't teaching. Later, look over your laboratories and see what other things you might need. We alternate physics and chemistry every other year and this year it's physics. I think we're well equipped." Mr. Aronson led the way to the teachers' room where he showed Jim his locker and then to the gymnasium downstairs. "I hope you know something about basketball because you'll have to coach our boy's team. It's our one sport and the town goes crazy if we can beat Michigamme or Republic. We'll pay you twenty dollars extra for each of the months you coach, from October to March." Jim told him he'd played the game in high school and would enjoy coaching. "But can you tell me something about the school policies concerning discipline," he asked. "This is my first teaching job and I'll need some guidance in a lot of things."

"Most of the discipline problems are in the lower grades," the superintendant replied. "Most of the troublemakers have quit school to work in the bush by the time they get to high school. There's one, Toivo Maki, who may give you a bad time because he wants to quit and his folks won't let him. All the students will have to test you, of course. Just start by being very tough and businesslike. You can always ease up later. Have them call you Mr. Heiken, never Jim, and learn their names as quickly as you can. Don't ever be sarcastic! Make your classes interesting and if you assign homework, make it brief. These kids all have a lot of chores to do when they get home from school. Let me see a lesson plan for one of your classes each day for about a month and expect me to visit your room to watch you teach occasionally. I won't be there the first couple of weeks, though. Come see me if you have any problems. Oh, by the way, you aren't ever to go to Higley's Saloon or to the poolroom. Have to be a model, you know. Well, I'll see you at seven-thirty Monday morning in the teachers' room for a brief meeting with the other teachers."

Supper at Mrs. Campton's was also good: baked hash with an egg on top and some of the leftover pie. When Jim hesitantly asked if he could have milk instead of coffee, Aunt Lizzie told him he could but would have to pay an extra dollar a week if he wanted it with his meals. Then she asked him if he planned to go to the sauna, it being Saturday night. Jim demurred. "I had a bath last night just before getting on the train," he said defensively. Then came a long interrogation about his religious beliefs and affiliation. "You have to go to church," she told him. "All teachers are supposed to go to church. You aren't Catholic, I hope." No, Jim told her, he'd been brought up to be a Presbyterian but hadn't gone to church much in his college years. "Well, I'll take you with me to my church," she said. "It's Methodist Episcopal, the one near the school. We have Finnish Lutheran, Swedish Lutheran, Catholic and Holy Jumper churches, but the Methodist comes closest to Presbyterian, I think." For a moment Jim thought of rebelling before finally he agreed to go with her. She sure was bossy!

Needing some exercise, that evening he walked up the road, there being no sidewalks, to the abandoned mine and spent a long time watching the swallows circling above the tall chimney, then plunging down into it. Some kids came to a fence to watch him walk by and a few lace curtains fluttered as he passed but he met no other person. How would he spend his waking hours when he wasn't in school? Suddenly he felt very much alone.

The next morning after breakfast Jim studied the textbooks he would have to use until it was time to go to church. When he came down from his room Aunt Lizzie looked him over critically. "You've got to shine your shoes," she said. "I don't have any shoe polish but I'll get you a cloth and some lard. School teachers always have to have their shoes polished." Jim complied and down the hill street they went. Aunt Lizzie talked all the way about all of the families who lived on the street. "The Hall sisters live there. They fight like cats and dogs, pulling hair and scratching till the blood comes. Old Mrs. Beatty lives there. She's batty with old age. In the brown house live the Hendersons. Four boys, no girls, but her father hung himself when Millie was born. Wanted a son and got six girls. Millie's made up for it. Has four boys. That's Dr. Gage's hospital and he lives in the house across from it. He doesn't like me and I don't know why. Has a boy Cully, who stammers. Probably be in one of your classes so don't ask him to recite." So it went until they got to the church where she wanted him to sit in the front pew but he insisted on sitting in the back, a decision he regretted when he found the parishioners turning around to look at him and whispering among themselves.

The sermon was long and dull but the congregation lustily sang many of the old hymns that he knew. Jim had a bit of a problem getting up and down because the varnish on the pews was a bit sticky, but all in all it was a bearable experience–except when Aunt Lizzie, who sang soprano in the choir, hit some of the high notes way off key. He noted with a bit of amusement that the organist tried to drown her out but the louder she played, the louder Aunt Lizzie screeched. After the service, among many introductions, he met the organist. "I'm Annie Anderson, the postmistress," she said. "I'll have a box ready for you, Jim, but the Chicago mail won't be disturbed until eight o'clock so you'll probably have to pick it up when you come home from school." How did she already know that he came from Chicago? Jim was soon to learn that in Tioga everyone knew everything about everybody.

The next morning the teachers' meeting was brief. Mr. Aronson walked into it with Jim and introduced him to the eleven teachers already there. "I see that you've already met Ruth Keski, our new seventh grade teacher," he said to them. "Her home is in the Soo and she has her life certificate from the Normal School in Marquette. This is Jim Heiken who will teach math and science for us. He hails from the University of Chicago. Both Ruth and Jim are first year teachers, so I hope you'll help them all you can over the first rough weeks. I'll pass out your class rolls now. If there are additions or deletions, please let me know and be sure to tell me when there are more than two consecutive unexcused absences. Just one other thing: students this year may not be in the classrooms until the first bell rings. You'll recall that we had some problems last year about that. Let's have a fine good year." That was all.

Before the teachers left for their classrooms, Jim looked them over. Except for Ruth they were all women in their forties or fifties, veterans of many years of coping with children. The new one, Ruth, seemed very young and not particularly attractive with her horn-rimmed glasses and blonde hair swept back into a tight bun. Probably Finnish. Jim wished that there had been at least one other male. Well, all of them seemed pleasant enough.

His classes went well enough except that he had a lot of trouble when calling the roll, soon learning from the pupils' laughter that Delongchamp was pronounced "Delosha" and Deroche was "Derushy." Ysitalo was not "Yess-o-tolo" but "Issatalo." They were otherwise well-behaved and seemed interested in his explanation of the course contents. He gave each of them a first assignment: to write a one-page summary of who they were and what their interests were so he could become acquainted. The day went swiftly but he found he was very tired when it ended. Although it was fascinating and fun, teaching was hard work too.

However, as the month of September passed, Jim found himself becoming more depressed and miserable than he'd ever been in his whole life. It wasn't the teaching. That was the best part with its constant challenges, but once school was out for the day he just didn't know what to do with his empty time. He'd walked all the streets of the village and taken the back road to Lake Tioga several times. Once he'd picked up rock specimens at the old mine and visited the little town library on Thursday evening when it was open, hoping to find a book on geology so he could identify the samples, but there was no such book. Afraid to venture into the deep woods, he felt imprisoned. Hungering for male companionship, he once introduced himself to some younger men at the post office intending to ask them who might rent him a boat so he could row out to the islands on the big lake. "I'm Jim Heiken," he said. "I'm the new math and science teacher, and…" That's as far as he got. They coldly looked him over and said, "Is that so?" and walked away. He even thought of asking Ruth, the new seventh grade teacher for a date, but where would they go? To see the evening train pull out of the depot? No movie, no dances, no nothing! There was absolutely nothing to do in Tioga.

Life at Aunt Lizzie's house became almost unbearable. She talked and questioned him until he couldn't stand it. She also exploited him, asking him to do this and that. One Saturday morning, she came in and begged him to lend her a hand in cleaning out the chicken coop. I'm a poor old widow woman," she'd said, "and I don't have my old strength any more," but as soon as she'd put the shovel in his hand she left for one of her gossip collecting trips down the street. "Will you chop some wood for me?" "Will you help me beat the carpets?" "Will you please fetch some more water from the well?" One day Him rebelled. "No!" he almost shouted. "I pay for my room and board. I'm not your choreboy!" It didn't do any good. Aunt Lizzie didn't bat an eye, and soon she was demanding he do other things for her. It was her voice, that rasping whine, that almost drove him up the wall. And that damned dog, Lulubelle, always nipping at his ankles or yipping constantly even when it was out in the yard. He could hear her even when he was up in his little room sitting in the sagging purple chair trying to perpare a lesson for the following day. There was nothing to do if he left the house and just plain misery when he was in it! When the high school classes were dismissed for two days because it was potato picking time, Jim almost went nuts. Weekends also were always bad because they meant having to go to church with Aunt Lizzie. Once he asked Ruth if he might attend the Finnish Lutheran church with her. "No," she answered. "That would mean that we were engaged to be married and I don't think either of us is quite ready for that yet. It would be like asking me to go sauna with you."

"Yet?" Hey, maybe behind those horned-rimmed glasses there might be somebody interesting. Oh nuts! To hell with her and to hell with Tioga! Why had he ever left Chicago?

Things kept getting worse and by the time he got his first paycheck on September 25th (schoolteachers always get that first check early because school boards know they're broke after the summer), Jim had decided to quit. The thought of paying Aunt Lizzie about a third of that check for another month's misery was unendurable, so he told Mr. Aronson he was resigning. The superintendent didn't seem surprised but he asked for a few days to see if he couldn't find another place for him to live. "You're a fine teacher, Jim, and I'd sure hate to lose you. All of us know Aunt Lizzie and having to live with her nastiness must be hard, so I don't blame you a bit. I really didn't want to put you up with her but could find no other place then. Now I'll try again. Just give me a few more days." Jim agreed.

Two days later the superintendent called Jim into his office. "I've a place for you that ought to be fine, Jim," he said. "Mrs. Salmi has agreed to give you room and board until the end of school next May. You know her son, John. He's a senior this year and will probably be captain of the basketball team. I think he's in your physics class, isn't he?" Jim nodded and Mr. Aronson continued, "You can move in this afternoon after school if you want to. Ask John to go with you when you get your bags from Aunt Lizzie's and he'll show you where his house is. You'll like it there. No better woman in town than Mrs. Salmi. Her husband is away. He's on the crew of a diamond drilling outfit that travels all over the world hunting for iron ore, and right now he's in South America somewhere. You'll be in a typical Finnish home and have to eat what they eat and do as they do, but I think you'll enjoy every moment of it. Anyway, give it a try."

Aunt Lizzie wasn't home when Jim and John Salmi went to get his bag so he left her a little note and a five dollar bill just in case she had thought of something else he owed. Lord, was he glad to get out of there! Restraining an urge to give the yapping Lulubelle a kick, he sat down at the forbidden organ to honk a farewell.

The Salmi's house was about a quarter mile up a side road in a cluster of houses that was called Finn Town. Each had a wide yard, a cowbarn, garden, outhouse and chicken coop. Some of the houses including the Salmi's also had a log sauna. When they entered the back door and John introduced Jim, Mrs. Salmi welcomed him warmly. A large smiling woman wearing a white apron, she'd just taken some loaves of bread from the oven. "This morning," she said, "I just have iksi poika (one boy); now I have koksi (two), Yonny and Yimmy." She held both his hands and pumped them vigorously. "Don't call me Mrs. Salmi. Call me aiti (mother) like Yonny does. Yonny, you show Yimmy where he sleep and I then give you new leipa (bread) when you come down." John led the way upstairs to the bedrooms. "I'll keep the lower bunk, Mr. Heiken, and you take the top one." The room was spotless.

"Around here, Johnny, don't call me Mr. Heiken" Jim told him. "Call me Jim, though of course in school you'll have to use the Mister." What a change! What a change! It sure had been tough living at Aunt Lizzie's. When they came down, Mrs. Salmi gave them thick slices of the new buttered bread powdered with sugar and cinnamon and mugs of milk. Jim got the crust. She was beaming.

That whole weekend was an utter delight. On Saturday morning after John had done his chores, they dug a few worms and walked the woods trail to Fish Lake, caught a few little perch for bait, then sat on Big Rock fishing for Northern Pike. Jim's big bobber went down once but he struck too soon and missed the fish. "You have to let them have it a long time," John told him. It didn't matter. It was just good to sit there on the shore of a lovely lake watching the last brown leaves swirling on the surface. John knew so many things about the woods that a whole new world was opened for Jim. On their way back, the scuffling of their feet in the fallen leaves jumped a deer and flushed a partridge. "I'll ask Ma if I can use my Dad's Winchester pump gun and you can use my singleshot and we'll go hunting next weekend," John said. "Look, there's a pitcher plant." He pointed to a mottled green thing in a swampy area. "It eats bugs. See how the insides of the pitcher are lined with little hairs pointing downward? Bugs can go down but can't come up."

Jim learned the difference between the orange patridge berries and the scarlet berries of wintergreen and chewed some of the latter's leaves. They picked a few hazel nuts and got their fingers full of prickers as they peeled them, cracked them on a rock, and tasted the delicious little kernels. "I've got two quarts of them at home for winter eating," John said. "We put them in a wet burlap bag and thresh them by pounding it on a rock." How fast the morning passed! Though their roles had been reversed, with John being the teacher, Jim had loved every moment and was anxious to learn more. Now he was not so utterly alone; he had a real friend and a warm home. Tioga wasn't so bad, after all.

He also felt that way after their dinner. "Maijuka," they called the venison stew with turnips, potatoes and other vegetables in it. Mrs. Salmi said it was her last can of deer meat, but she knew John would shoot another buck in November as he had last year. An eight pointer, it was, and very tender. John was very proud. "Yah, just one shot," he said. "Got him after school in the Buckeye swamp. I'll take you there some time."

After the meal was finished Mrs. Salmi asked John to dig the rest of the carrots and turnips, put them in the sand boxes and take them to the cellar. Jim helped him cut off the tops then hold them upright as the sand was poured around them. The cellar was an interesting place lit dimly by small widow wells. Shelves hanging from the ceiling were loaded with hundreds of jars of fruit. Five burlap bags of potatoes, a barrel of apples and a box of upended caggages sat on the dirt floor. In one corner was a bench holding crocks of pickles and some large bowls of milk covered with cheesecloth. Jim asked why the jars were on the hanging shelves.

John grinned. "We have to keep them high," he said, "because at spring breakup a lot of water comes into the cellar. One year it was up to the sixth step. By that time though we've eaten all the vegetables. We can put these on the floor for now."

Then John took Jim out to help him fire up the sauna. A tight log structure, it belonged to the Salmis and to the Laitalas next door and the two families alternated heating it each week. "We go sauna in afternoon and the Laitalas after supper," he explained as he cautiously opened the door and looked in. "Sometimes there's a big black pine snake comes in the fall. I didn't want to scare you. They're harmless. No poisonous snakes in the U.P." It was dark in the first room, the dressing and cooling room, despite some light from a small window. Two benches sat along opposite walls, one bearing a farm kerosene lantern. A large wooden water barrel was in the center of the room. "Here's where we get undressed and wash before we go into the steam room," John said, "and where we cool off and dry ourselves later. The cracks in the floor let the water out."

Opening the door into the inner room, John saw a long boxstove covered with round rocks, another water barrel, the hot water one connected to the stove, and a set of steps or benches, one above the other. "Here's where we sit," John explained. "Once we've got the rocks heated good we pour dippers of water onto the rocks, and that makes the steam. The higher up you sit on the benches, the hotter it gets. You'll like it once you get used to it. Sure cleans out your pores, right to the bones."

After John opened a vent to help the fire get started and washed the room's only window, the two of them filled the water barrels by carrying pails of water from a well outside. Then they put some birchbark and a lot of pine wood in the stove and lit it. "We'll have to fire up again about two o'clock and that should have the rocks hot enough to cook us good." Knowing that Jim was dubious about the whole thing, John was enjoying himself. He pointed to a pile of cedar switches. "We use those to beat ourselves after we've been broiled," he said. "Too bad we don't have any snow yet. In winter sometimes we roll in it and then go sauna again and again. You'll sure get clean." Remembering the sponge baths he'd been taking in Aunt Lizzie's claw-footed bathtub with only two teakettles of water, Jim knew he needed such a cleaning, but he was apprehensive.

On their way back to the house Jim saw a very pretty girl brushing her yellow hair on the steps of the neighbor's house. "Who's that?" he asked.

"That's Ruth Keski," replied John. "You know her. She's the seventh grade teacher. She rooms and boards with the Laitalas. She's a Finn too." Jim went over and his shocked surprise made the girl giggle.

"Yes, it's me Jim. You've caught me without my disguise. I don't need to wear those horrible glasses or keep my hair in a bun and am about to quit doing so." She went on to explain that when she'd started applying for teaching positions she'd been turned down three times because of her picture. "They said I looked too young to teach for them," she said. "So I bought these glasses and fixed my hair and had another picture taken, and Mr. Aronson wrote back offering me the Tioga job right away. Well, I thought I'd might as well keep looking that way at first because seventh graders need a stern looking teacher…"

Jim interrupted. "I can't believe it!" he said. "Will you take me to the Finnish church tomorrow?" She laughed at the implication but said she was glad they were neighbors. "No, I won't go to church but I'll walk to school with you Monday. I bet I'll shock my pupils too."

About four-thirty Mrs. Salmi took her sauna and then her "poikas" had their turn. Even the cooling room was steamy as they soaped and scrubbed and poured pails of very cold water over their heads. When Jim reached for his towel, John said no, that they should go in wet so the heat wouldn't be so bad at first. "You sit on the bottom bench. It's not so hot." he said.

When he opened the inner door, Jim felt as though he were in a blast furnace. The heat was incredible, overwhelming, and only his pride kept him from bolting. When John poured some dippers of hot water on the rocks a cloud of more steam filled the room. Jim sat down on the furthest corner of the lower bench only to spring up with a yell. "Oh, I forgot to tell you," John laughed. "Always sit in the middle of the bench. The hot nails are on the ends." Jim felt the sweat oozing out from every inch of his body but it didn't cool him a bit. How could John stand it up on the highest bench? It was hard to breathe and Jim could feel his heart pounding. He looked at his legs. They were beet red; even the soles of his feet were. His fingers dripped. He gasped for air. His eyes watered. But somehow he endured until John felt he'd had enough and led the way back to the cooling room. It seemed frigid there but his body didn't. As he stood there naked, a delicious tingling swept over him. Pins and needles even in his armpits. Oh what a relief and also what a wonderful sense of well-being and complete cleanliness! He felt loose all over as he dried himself with the towel and put on his clean clothing. When John went back inside for another broiling Jim was almost tempted to join him. "No, that's enough for the first time," he said to himself. "It wasn't really as bad as I'd expected. The hell it wasn't!"

That evening when Jim went up to his room to study, Mrs. Salmi soon came to get him. "No, Yimmy," she protested. "Bedroom for sleeping only. This your house too. You come down now. You read in living room if we bother you in kitchen." What a change from Aunt Lizzie's house! Most of his evenings thereafter were spent in the large kitchen at the round table or occasionally in the living room beside it. Mrs. Salmi had her loom there and often wove some of the rag rugs she made for sale as he was reading. Occasionally, when the thump, thump of the loom stopped for a moment to let her adjust a spindle, the two of them would have good conversation.

Aiti wanted to know all about college. She and her absent husband had saved for years so that their children could attend one. Neither of her other sons had been interested but

Yonny was. Did Jim think Yonny was bright enough to go? How much would it cost to go to a university to be a teacher or doctor or scientist? What courses would he study? How long would it take? Jim told her he was sure John could handle it, that he was one of the brightest students in the whole high school. When Jim described scholarships and part-time jobs, and all the possibilities that opened up when one had a higher education, she hung on every word he said.

"We Finns from old country, we know education is good," Aiti responded. "In Finland only rich people send kids to school. My husband, he now tired of diamond drilling and being away so long, so far away. Maybe this be last year on the road for him then, but if Yonny need more raha, he go again."

One other evening she explored Jim's name. "Heiken? That almost Finn name. Where your family come from?"

Jim told her that it might have been Sweden, that his father had traced their ancestry back to an ancestor who had come from Sweden in a sailing ship to his country before the Revolutionary War, to what was then called New Sweden on the banks of the Delaware River.

"Heiken no Swede name," she protested, "but lots of Heikinens in old country. One family of Heikinens here in Tioga." When Jim remembered that his father had said the name had been shortened shortly after the first Heiken came, that perhaps Heiken came from Heikenson, Aiti was certain he was a Finn. "No, Heikenson not Swede name. You were Heikinen. Back then Sweden and Finland same country. Lots of Finns work in Sweden too. You Finlander, Yimmy." From that time on, when visitors came for coffee, she always introduced Jim as Mr. Heikinen. He didn't mind a bit. Indeed he felt honored. The Finns were fine people and perhaps he really had been one once. Anyway, he sure was enjoyin the saunas now.

That whole fall season was a delight. Not just the teaching but the long hikes in the woods with Yonny as they hunted partridge and rabbits or ducks. Always there was something new to learn, and when they returned to that warm loving house Jim almost pinched himself, hardly being able to believe his good fortune.

Living in that Finn house was quite an experience. Many of the foods were completely strange to Jim but they were always good. For breakfast they often had kropsu, an oven-baked pancake, with maple syrup, and pulla, a delightful coffeecake. Sometimes dinner consisted of suola-silli, salted herring, with potatoes, and a fruit soup called hedelma. Always there was leipa, homemade bread, or occasionally nakki-leipa, hardtack, with newly churned butter on it. Jim even developed a taste for kirnu-piima, buttermilk, and drank that instead of coffee as he ate uuni-juusto, a baked soft cheese that looked like custard pie. It was no wonder that the first Finnish word he learned was kituksia, for "thank you."

As the days grew shorter and the evenings longer, there always seemed to be something interesting to do even when they sat in the kitchen. When he found that John could always beat him playing checkers, Jim sent home for his chess set and because he didn't want him to be discouraged, he occasionally invited Ruth over to learn the moves so she and John could play together. Both of them learned swiftly and soon were challenging him too. Aiti sat smilingly beside the kitchen range knitting or mending or winding a ball of rags she had cut and sewed for her loom.

One night after Jim had walked Ruth back to her house and had tried to kiss her but found she sure could dodge, Aiti said to him, "I think you like Ruth, eh Yimmy? She make you good Finn wife and give many children. Why you no ask her sometime?" When he told her that Ruth didn't seem interested, she replied. "Not so, Yimmy. She beginning love for you. Women always know." Well, that was encouraging, but why did Ruth always shake his hand loose when he just tried to hold it as they walked home from school. And why, when they had been looking at the stars through a telescope he'd built from some lenses he'd found in the physics lab and he'd put his arm around her, she'd pulled away. Always she said "No yet, Yimmy." "Not yet?" Damn her hide! Always "not yet."

Nevertheless, Ruth did seem to enjoy being with him, and once when Aiti had been ironing his shirts (she refused to take any money for doing them), Ruth had taken the iron from her and learned how to do it. And when the snows came Ruth would ski with him down Company Field to Lake Tioga and, by a little coffee fire, sit very close, closer than she needed to. There was also that stormy morning when the two of them encountered a huge drift on the way to school and he picked her up in his arms to help her through it. For just a moment he'd felt her relax and even snuggle up to him, but again when he tried to kiss her she dodged and all he got was a mouth of wet parka. "Not yet," she said again and when she laughed outrageously he threw her into a snowbank.

Ruth also, unlike most of the teachers, attended all the basketball home games that Jim coached, usually coming with John's mother, John being the star of the team. Basketball, Tioga's only organized sport, always brought big and enthusiastic crowds, perhaps because there was nothing else to do in wintertime, or because it only cost a dime admission. To his surprise Jim found his players still using both hands to shoot baskets. They'd squat with legs apart and swing the ball up from between them before throwing it in a high looping arc. Jim taught them the one-handed way of shooting he'd learned in Chicago. "Don't arch it; just get it over the front rim," he had to tell them again and again. The training paid off. They won most of their games, even the two with Michigamme. Strangers shook Jim's hand when they met him on the street. "You-sta goot coach, I tink! You come back next year too?" Yes, coaching was fun.

Just before Christmas when he was to return to his home in Chicago, Jim prowled Flynn's store hunting for presents for his aiti and Ruth but could find nothing, so he took the train for Ishpeming one Saturday, returning with a large box of Whitman's sampler candies and a dozen roses double-wrapped against the cold. He'd planned to give the chocolates to Ruth and the roses to Aiti, but when he remembered his aiti's love of sweets he gave the candy to her with half of the roses and brought the other six roses to Ruth. Both were overcome by the gifts. Aiti even wept and hugged him. Ruth didn't, but for the first time she touched his cheek affectionately as she told him how much she appreciated the present. Somehow the Christmas vacation at home seemed very long and Jim was glad to get back to Tioga.

When Valentine's Day came, Jim again brought them flowers from the Ishpeming greenhouse, and in return received a batch of his favorite saffron raisin buns from Aiti and a homemade valentine from Ruth which said: "Roses are red and violets are blue; Tioga was made for just us two." Not much love in it but he put it under his pillow that night.

Finally spring came with its usual breakup mess. Jim and Ruth couldn't walk in the woods because there was still too much wet snow, and except for the hill street all the roads were quagmires of mud. He felt the old hunger to walk and walk that all in the U.P. know at that time of year, so one Sunday afternoon he and Ruth went along the railroad track toward Red Bridge to see the river bursting its icy bonds. Unfortunately, some damned little French kids followed them for a while, chanting "Take down yer pants and give him a chance." Seeing his fury, Ruth told him just to ignore them and soon they were left behind. Oh, it was a glorious U.P. day–sunshine and warm with a few lazy white clouds drifting over a sky as blue as her eyes. Near a rock cut, they found a patch of arbutus already in bloom. Ruth lay down in it to smell the wonderful frangrance and Jim did so too, right beside her, their faces separated by only a few of the vines. Suddenly he tried again to kiss her but got just a taste of her blonde hair. "Not yet, Yimmy!" she said in a whisper. "Not yet!"

"Damn your 'not yets'" he yelled, pulling her up by the shoulders and shaking her till her hair swirled. "What the hell is wrong with you? It's spring! Spring! You drive me crazy. Haven't you got anything but icewater inside your skin?" He put her down and covered his face with his hands. They walked home without speaking to each other.

The next morning Jim walked to school early and alone, and also that afternoon he came home alone. He would put Ruth out of his mind. To hell with her! There were other girls! It would be misery being married to such a cold fish anyway. But, despite his wishes, he couldn't help thinking of her. Day and night he held her in his arms but only in his thoughts. Only once, when John took him trout fishing in the rapids, was he able to forget her. It became clear to him that he'd just have to get out of Tioga. So when Mr. Aronson offered him a contract for the following year, Jim replied that he wasn't sure he'd return but would give him his answer before the end of school.

Aiti became concerned with the change that had come over Jim. "You sick, Yimmy?" she asked when he ate only half of one of her delicious pasties. "You no happy any more. What wrong?" He couldn't tell her then but later one evening when they were together in the living room, he studying and she working her loom, he blurted out the whole story. Ruth was driving him huts, he said. He was much in love with her but she wouldn't respond. She wouldn't even let him kiss her. He would have to go away so he could forget her. He probably wouldn't be back in Tioga next year.

"You want marry her?" Aiti asked gently. When he nodded miserably she smiled. "You don't know Finn girls, good Finn girls, I guess. They save it! Why you no ask her to marry her and see?"

So one late evening in May when Jim saw Ruth going to the sauna clad in a kimono and bath towel, he waited a bit then went too. Quietly opening the outer door to the dressing room, he disrobed and hung his clothing over hers, then entered the steam room. Ruth was sitting on the lower bench, naked and beautiful as the dawn, and she squealed when she saw him. "No! No!" she screamed. "No! Not yet! Get out of here!" But when he put his arm around her there in the steam and drew her close and asked her to marry him she flung her bare arms around his neck and kissed him passionately. "Oh Yimmy, why you no ask before?"

One Day In May, 1915

4:30 A.M. I was awakened by an angry snarl at my bedroom window. It was Puuko, our black tomcat, back from a long night of fornication. Because it was the middle of May and the mosquitoes and black flies had not yet arrived, I'd open that window six inches when I went to bed so I wouldn't have to get up at dawn to let the old devil in. It was not sufficient because Puuko wouldn't stoop for man or beast. He was too proud. After all, what other tomcat had been able to change the color of all Tioga's cats from grey to black in his nine lifetimes? Groaning, I staggered over to lift the window sash, then went back to my blankets.

5:00 A.M. Louie Fachon made himself some coffee and after eating six blueberry pancakes went down to the creek to get the pail of chub minnows he'd stashed there. The big pike in Lake Tioga always bit best shortly after dawn. It was going to be a fine U.P. day, he thought. Perhaps too good.

5:30 A.M. Pierre Rousseau our Prophet, measured the level of the water in his well and examined his weather stick. "Oui," he said, "Ze weathair, she's goin' be fine zis day for sure." Never had he seen the water drop so much in one night. Never had he seen the weather stick point so high.

6:00 A.M. Wakened by the roosters, all the dogs in Tioga rose from their beds, stretched, and began to howl as the sun came up. No, not all of them. Old Pullo, the spotted hound, was sleeping outside the fence at Aunt Lizzie's house waiting for her to bring out Lulubelle to do her duty and dirty. When she and the Pekinese appeared, Pullo opened one eye and said a loud, "Galoom!"

One Day In May, 1915

By this time most of the chimneys in town wore plumes of white smoke rising straight up into the windless air, as our people made their breakfast fires. Cows mooed, insisting on being milked. The morning freight train's time whistle filled the surrounding hills with echoes. Time to get up!

7:00 A.M. Pierre Paquin limped up the long stairs to the Catholic church and ejected his cud of Redman tobacco before pulling on the bell rope that rang the Angeles. All of us in town, even the Finns, loved the sweet sound of those morning bells.

Passing through our kitchen with the rich smell of new coffee, my father greeted the fine spring day by blowing his nose as he stood on the back steps. A mighty snort to which our neighbors set their watches, it was his daily ritual. No handkerchiefs either. Dad always said that a rich man put in his pocket what a poor man threw away.

Robins bounced across the lush green lawn with their hands in their pockets, seeking a worm too lazy to have crawled back in its hole. Crows cawed in the Grove. In a hundred houses wives turned pancakes that would soon be smothered with the maple syrup boiled down just a month before. Charley Olafson unlocked the jail cage in the Town Hall to let Pete Ramos out. Making his rounds at midnight, he'd found Pete drunk and unconscious lying on the sidewalk in front of the school. Neither of the men said a word. It had happened before and would happen again.

Mrs. Hokkinen went out to her strawberry patch to enjoy the early morning sunshine and to see how the plants had made it through the winter. They looked fine. They should have! All through March she'd emptied the slop jar on them because she never knew when her husband might shoot up their outhouse.

7:30 A.M. Mrs. Waisanen who was then doing our milking, brought in a ten-quart pail of warm milk and I hastened to feed Rosie, our Jersey cow. That milk would be put into large brown bowls in the cellar so the thick yellow cream would rise to the top for skimming. Tomorrow, Saturday, was butter churning day. I also let our white horse, Billy, out into the barnyard so he could roll around a bit while I fed the chickens. Then I began pumping water up into the tank upstairs. Three hundred strokes later, mother stopped me though I knew the tank was far from being filled. "Cully," she said. "It's getting late and you'll be tardy for school. Better get going. You can finish your pumping when you come home for dinner."

8:00 A.M. Mr. Marchand drives his old horse, Maude, up our hill street, bringing the mail. Annie, our postmistress, had to read all the postcards first, but soon had it distributed in the boxes as four or five women and men waited in the anteroom in front of the partition. Not Scotty McGee. He only came to the post office once a month to get his pension check from the Oliver Mining Company. Having had his coffee and hardtack, Mr. McGee was reading the bible to his dog, Tam O'Shanter. Down in the valley, Sieur La Tour, the oldest man in the village, was sitting on his front stoop in the sunshine, remembering the days when Tioga was only a stage coach stop on the road to Fort Wilkins at the tip of the Keweenaw Peninsula. Also in the valley, Josette Bourdon was filling the big copper boiler on the kitchen range so her mother could wash the clothing the trainmen brought over, but she was happy that she would not have to do the ironing now that she was clerking at Flynn's store uptown.

9:00 A.M. Aunt Lizzie removes her wig from the teakettle that has been warming it, gets dressed and starts her daily gossip rounds. Lenna Kangas starts her spring cleaning by scrubbing the floor of her summer kitchen, glad that the old potbellied stove her husband had put outside to heat all outdoors was gone. Leif Larsen goes to Beaverdam Swamp to get cedars to support his perfect outhouse so the kids couldn't overturn it, come Halloween. My father reluctantly hitches Billy, our white horse, to the buckboard, wishing that the roads weren't still in so much of a mess. He preferred making his calls in the new 1914 Ford but the roads were too bad. He also dreaded having to give Old Lady Haitema an enema again, trying to get hold of that tapeworm of hers that had broken off last time.

9:30 A.M. It was sure hard to be in school that fine spring day. Our teacher, P.P. Polson seemed ornrier than ever, so we kids raised hell when her kidneys got the best of her and she had to leave the room for a few minutes. I plugged the peephole in the classroom door with some gum I'd been chewing furtively all morning, and when we saw that bony finger pop it open all of us were studying hard when she entered. Unfortunately, Mule Cardinal couldn't control himself and burst out laughing so all of us did too. But we stopped abruptly when Miss Polson lifted Mule out of his seat by his ears and stood him in the corner until recess.

10:00 A.M. Smoking Peerless in their corncob pipes, Eino and Emil began to play their first checker game of the day, but they got to arguing so hard about when to plant their peas and beets they forgot whose turn it was to move. In the living room of our house Grandma Van got out her knitting, thinking perhaps that those long needles would sure be good for goosing anyone who passed by her. In our kitchen Mother was baking Dad a mince pie. Uptown, Old Bridget Murphy shooed the chickens off her bedposts and Paddy, her pig out of the house and into his pen, fearing that Father Hassel might be coming up to examine her soul. Josette's mother hung the trainmen's clothes on the line as the midmorning freight chugged past the depot. A good day for drying even if there wasn't much of a breeze.

11:00 A.M. Jacques Cousteau, his wife Marie, and Willie the springer spaniel, all sitting high on the seat of their hay wagon, drove to Flynn's store singing old French songs all the way up the hill. It was spring! He would buy Marie a pretty new hat, maybe with pink ribbons on it, and buy himself a whole pail of Peerless tobacco so he'd feel rich. Higley swept out his saloon, then had to mop it too. "Why don't them bastards use the spittoon?" he asked himself for the thousandth time. Untu Heikkala sanded the share (the blade) of his one-horse plow until it shone, then tested the soil of his garden by kicking a few holes in it. No, he decided, the ground was still too wet to plow the potato patch.

Noon. At his little cabin by Mud Lake, our old hermit Eric Niemi, began to fry some salt pork in the cast-iron frying pan. No potatoes; they'd gone soft. Just a mess of sprouts. It would be trout and hardtack. Enough! He'd caught five small trout in the creek that morning, so he squeezed each one till it squeaked, put them in the pan and when they were brown he gnawed them like sweet corn, heads, tails, bones and all. Very good!

Mother had a find dinner ready for us: pot roast and mashed potatoes. Dad served me the part with the marrow-filled bone because he knew I liked that marrow with salted crackers. My little brother Joe got part of it, not that he liked marrow as I did, but just because he couldn't bear to have me have something he didn't, the wart! After Dad had his second piece of venison mincemeat pie, he patted his vest and said to mother, "A fine meal,

Madam. You have acquired merit!" Then he told us of his morning calls. "Edyth, I think I've finally found a way to convince the Finns that they shouldn't eat raw fish. I got that tapeworm out of Mrs. Haitema this morning, all eight yards of it. Brought it out of her hind end, hand over hand, like hauling in a big pike. Lord, how she squealed! I'm going to put it in a big bottle with formaldehyde and show it to any Finn I think is eating the stuff." "Oh John," Mother interrupted. "Don't tell those awful tales at dinner time, please!"

1:00 P.M. Herb Anderson, the one we called the Deacon, drove up the hill in his buggy and tied his horse to the hitching post in front of my father's hospital. "Doc," he said, "I want to buy some potassium permanganate if you got some." When Dad asked him why, he said, "Got an old horse I aim to trade one of these days. Trouble is Betsey's nigh to being seventeen years old now and shows it. Getting pretty gray, she is. I've filed her teeth but I got to get some color on her mane and hide."

"But potassium permanganate will turn her purple." my father protested. "That won't do you any good."

"Oh, I don't use it straight, Doc. I mix a spoon of it with strong hot coffee and that turns it brown. A trick my pappy taught me. Makes the brown stain indelible. Nothing'll wash it off a horse's hide."

Mrs. Bourdon takes the clothes off the line and sets up the ironing board with a sigh. Wetting her finger, she touches the bottom of one of the sad irons on the range and hears the hiss. Hot enough! She'll still be ironing until six when Josette comes home from the store.

2:00 P.M. Jules Fontaine and Matti Mattila, pumping the handcar as fast as they could to reach the side track at Clowry Siding before the afternoon freight train tore down on them, managed to do so just in time. "Jules," said Matti to his old friend, "I hear you're going to run for Township Treasurer. How'd you feel if I run too?"

Jim Fortas, Tioga's inveterate gambler and Laf Bodine, our best poacher, were sitting on a baggage cart outside the depot. They'd heard that the D.S.S.&A might be hiring temporary help to fix the red bridge over the Escanaba, but the station agent had not returned from his noon break. Meanwhile, they were watching a black and tan hound walking toward them. "Laf," said Jim, "Betcha a dollar that there hound will turn around three times before he lies down." "What odds you give me?" asked Laf. "My buck against your two bits though you're stealing me blind," said Jim although he'd watched that hound before and he knew it always turned around three times before it lay down. "OK!" But this time the hound only turned around twice.

3:00 P.M. Mrs. Saari went across the road to Mrs. Pekkari's house for afternoon coffee and they discussed their mate's competence in bed among other things.

Down at the blacksmith shop Paddy Feeney has an hour free time although Pete Himmel will be bringing over his team to be shod later. Knowing that soon school will be let out and the kids will come to watch him, Paddy heats up the forge and makes a puzzle for them out of iron, consisting of a heart, a ring, and a chain. They'd have fun trying to get the heart off the ring. Not too hard! One of them would be able to do it.

Siiri Sivola builds a fire in their sauna. John will be needing one after his long day in the woods. They would be taking the train to Ishpeming in the morning to buy her a new dress and him some axe handles and a new pitchfork.

3:30 P.M. Old Blue Balls, our tough school superintendent, catches Mullu and Toivo fighting in the schoolyard, a no no. He hauls them up to his office but feeling a bit mellow because he and my father would be going trout fishing up the West Branch next morning, he just gives Mullu *The Strap* and tells him to wallop Toivo ten times, with Toivo getting his turn later. Unfortunately, Mullu didn't hit hard enough so Old Blue Balls had to show him how to do it right. Both kids were bawling when they left.

4:00 P.M. Mrs. Hivonen goes to see Ben Tremblay, Tioga's wise man. She explains that Lempi, her teenaged daughter is pregnant but will not tell who the father was. Ben gave the matter some thought, then said, "When the egg is laid, to hell with the rooster." And that was that!

Father Hassel, our old Catholic priest, comes to our house for his weekly chess game with my father and for the glass of whiskey and cigar that always went with it. "How's the sinning going in Tioga, Father?" my Dad asked. The priest chuckled. "It's spring, Doctor," he replied. "You'll have your answer nine months from now."

Fisheye and I got some red worms out of the manure pile and went down to Beaverdam Creek. He caught a seven-inch trout but all I caught was a big redhorse sucker which I took home for Peter White, our big pig. Peter sure liked those sucker. How he squealed!

5:00 P.M. Tim O'Leary brings Molly Malone a big bunch of wild iris (blue flags, we called them) only to have her fling them in his Irish face. That wooing was sure going hard.

The cows began coming back for the evening milking, mooing lustily as they swung their big bags from side to side climbing the hill street. I let Rosy into our barnyard and got a pail of hot bran and water to put in her stall. Billy got a big pail of oats and some fresh hay from the loft. And a sugar lump!

Madam Olga, our fortuneteller, grateful for Fisheye's replenishing her woodbox, reads his palm and tells him he'll have nine children when he grows up.

6:00 P.M. Mr. Marchand brings up the evening mail. It is late because of some accident or something down the line that delayed the South Shore train. Annie, the postmistress, puts up a note on the door saying, "Having my supper. Mail will be disturbed from 7 to 8 due to late delivery."

Sylvie, Father Hassel's ugly housekeeper, burns his evening pot roast. That takes some doing but the priest forgives her, of course.

7:00 P.M. Mr. Rich, having had his supper, unlocks the front door to his combination barber shop and poolroom. Three of our men enter. It's a place to go and only costs ten cents a game per player. On a good night Mr. Rich will take in two dollars from the pool table and perhaps another half dollar in haircuts at a quarter each. Not much, but it's a living and for an ex-miner with a wooden leg it's helped him make do. As two of the men rack up their balls and chalk their cues, a stranger enters, evidently a lumberjack with a very heavy beard and shaggy hair. "Just come from Silverthorne's camp," he explained. "They kept me on after the log drive to build their new cook shanty. Haven't been out of the woods since last summer. How much you charge to get rid of this hair and beard?" Mr. Rich looked him over, then said. "Fifty cents, maybe seventy-five. There's a lot of cutting and shaving to do." "OK," said the jack and climbed up into the red plush barber chair. Mr. Rich didn't put the apron around him. Just parted his hair and looked. "No sir!" he said. "No sir! You're lousy, lousy, Mister. I wouldn't cut your hair for ten dollars. Come back when you're free of the critters." As the lumberjack left, the man who wasn't playing pool said, "Don't blame you a bit, Mr. Rich. Don't blame you a bit! Lots of them lumber camps are full of lice. Worst one I seen was A.W. Read's Camp Five on the Yellow Dog. They damn near ate us to the bone. We had a young fella there just starting out and he like to go crazy, he did. Not used to it like us old-timers. We tells the kid to go ask the cook for a lot of salt and rub it in everywhere he got hair, crotch and all. 'What good would that do?' asks the greenhorn and we tells him that after he's got hisself salted down good and plenty, to go down to the creek and soak his bare feet in it, that then the lice, thirsty after eating all that salt meat, would go to his feet and be washed off by the current. Damned if the young fool didn't do it. Gadamighty how we laughed."

The bells of the Catholic Church tolled Vespers.

Old Billy Bones pulled his little red wagon down to the depot. All of us knew that under the burlap bags that covered it were jugs of Billy Bones' extra-powerful dandelion wine to be sold to the trainmen. Three or four kids had picked bunches of arbutus that they would peddle to the passengers of the evening train from the Copper Country, if they could sneak onto the coaches without the conductor seeing them.

8:00 P.M. Some of the little kids are playing hide-and-seek; others knock-the-stick; still older ones are playing shinny, knocking a condensed milk can from one goal to another with the crooked sticks they'd gotten from the swamp. Swallows circled the tall chimney of the abandoned mine and every so often a few would plummet down into it for their night nesting. Horses clomped up the wooden sidewalk leaving piles of golden nuggets behind them.

8:30 P.M. The sun went down at the far shore of Lake Tioga tinting the water pink and gold. Men who'd been fishing off the railroad bridge for the pike and walleyes that were making their spawning run up the river picked up their minnow buckets and started the long walk home. At the depot, Maggie O'Connor, the station's cleaning woman, cleaned the spittoon and practiced a bit of spitting herself. In the back room of Callahan's store, Dinny played a hand of solitaire, wishing it were Saturday night when he and the other Regulars of the Last Man Under The Table Club would tap a new keg of beer and play poker.

9:00 P.M. Dad tells me I don't have to go to bed yet, that he wants me to pick a can of nightcrawlers so he and Mr. Donegal can fish for trout on the West Branch. I get the flashlight and look but they aren't out yet. "That's all right," Dad said. "Just hang around until they do appear." Whoops!

At Higley's saloon things aren't jumping yet but most of the usual customers are there. Pete Halfshoes sits in the corner of his booth nursing his second beer and saying nothing. He will have just one more before climbing the hill to his house where Mabel, his pet skunk and bed partner, waits for him. Laf Bodine is telling again how he outwitted the game warden by wearing his snowshoes backwards. Slimber Vester starts a long rambling lie about how he wrestled a big buck and broke its neck. Arvo Mattson began to tell his bear story. "No you don't!" yelled Higley. "The last damn time you told that story about climbing the tree to get away from that bear, you grabbed my chandelier and crashed it to the floor." "Yah," said Arvo. "Rotten branch!"

The Trevarthen boys and their father parted the swinging doors of the saloon and got an enthusiastic welcome. Twirling his black mustache, Higley was happy to see them too.

"All the beer you want for as long as you sing them old songs," he said, sliding three mugs down the polished bar. "But start with 'Turaluralura' that Irish lullaby one." The Trevarthens obliged in close harmony and even Higley had a tear in his left eye. "Nuts to that Irish stuff," yelled someone. "Give us 'A Hot Time in the Old Town Tonight'". Things were finally getting going in Higley's saloon.

10:00 P.M. One by one the kerosene lamps in the village flickered out and the yellow windows turned black. I bring in the full can of worms and let Puuko out to do his duty. As Grampa Gage used to say "England expects every man to do his duty; so does Puuko!" Those French cats down in the valley will squall tonight. After the Trevarthens sing their way up the hill under the tall maples overhanging the sidewalk, it is very quiet in Tioga.

Except in the Jensen house where Alf snores so loudly Helga has to put more cotton in her ears.

Postscript

I cannot end this book without expressing my appreciation to the many readers who have written me. Through them I have made many new friends. That's really something at the age of eighty-three when most of my old friends have passed away. The letters have come from all over, even one from Hong Kong, and from people of all ages and walks of life. A nine-year-old boy wants me to be his grampa; a teenaged girl stranded in Wisconsin writes that she can't wait to grow up so she can go back to the U.P. again; an old man thanks me for reviving memories of his own youth. All of them tell me that they share my love for that still wild country above the Straits.

I'm sure that this mail is what has kept me telling the stories of the interesting people I knew as a boy early in this century. I've tried to quit several times fearing that there may be dotage in my anecdotage, but then I get some more mail telling the tales their grandparents told them about the old days, or providing glimpses of their own lives. The fact that I can still have some impact, can make some unknown reader chuckle or share a tear with me, enriches an old man's life, so again I thank you, my friends.

Most of those letters are short but a few of them are not. I can't resist including two of the latter.

The first comes from Amy Van Ooyinen of Ironwood and describes how the people at the far end of the U.P. make the best of the long winter:

"Saima Walkonen phoned. The Grandmothers Ski Marathon would be held tomorrow at eleven. Her husband, Whitey, had made the trails through their property and put up some of his crazy signs along them. There would be six or seven grandmas curing their cabin fever.

"Lena went with me and we were the second to arrive because Sylvia Niemi was ahead of us, dressed in very classy tight stretch pants like those the pro skiers wear. She must be nearing seventy-five but isn't telling. Lena wore a man's quilted overalls with a heavy down vest. Saima's three sisters then came and we made a nice row of sliding women in front of Whitey's woodshed. That woodshed is a very patriotic one because Whitey has painted an American flag on it. Next to the flag, however, is fastened an open #3 trap with its trigger pan painted red and above that is written 'To Register Complaints, Press Here!' Standing beside another sign he had just painted, Whitey saw us off. That sign said, 'Never mind the dog. Beware of the Husband!'

"So we moved off in single file. As we entered the woods, there was another sign: 'Alpha and Omega'. Lena bumped into me. 'My skis are too slippery,' she explained. I told her to go ahead, that she was faster than I was. Besides, if she'd fallen on me in that three feet of snow, I would have been buried till spring.

"Suddenly we saw what looked like a black bear half rising out of the snow, but it was evident that he'd already eaten because all that was left was an old red cap. Whitey had sure been busy preparing for us. A bit further along the trail was posted the warning, 'Beware of Snow Snakes'. After that a grove of maple saplings waist-high in snow had to be conquered. Then around a bend was a sign saying 'Head Hunters in the Woods' with a spear bearing a doll's head on top of it. On we strode.

"But Whitey had been thoughtful of the seven grandmothers. There beside the trail was a comfort station. No outhouse, just an old metal door hung between two trees and a log to sit on. Though the Sears Roebuck catalog was a bit wet, the door was clearly labeled 'VE SA' in large letters, the Finnish word for outhouse. Beside it in smaller letters were directions. 'We aim to please you. You aim too!'' 'Radioactive Heap. Pull chain; Wash hands!'

"Much comforted, we entered a less well traveled trail with difficult gullies and hills to tackle, but we weren't lost. We found a sign and arrow that pointed north to Helsinki, Finland, only 4853 miles and one-fourth foot. When the trail went up a long hill we were getting tired. I noticed Marion leaning heavily forward on her skis, not a good position because the heaviest part of a lady comes last and so she slid backwards. There was a sign saying, 'The worst day of skiing is better than the best day of working.' Marion looked at it and said, 'Oh Shut Up!'

"Finally we came again to the section line of Whitey's property. 'All may trespass here' it said, 'If you have permission.' A bit further we found a kitchen fork fastened to a tree sign: 'Fork in the Road' and beyond that another sign saying 'Krik Krossing,' telling us also that the water in it ran to the Atlantic Ocean via Mud Creek, Montreal River, and Lakes Superior, Huron, Erie and Ontario. We were careful not ot get swept away.

"At long last we came to the Alpha Omega sign agains and then back to Saima's and Whitey's house. Potluck was waiting and did it ever taste good! Coffee, homemade bread, korpua, Spanish rice, two kinds of salad and spicy apple bars.

"Who won the Grandmother's Marathon? We all did."

Here's another. Charlie Shilling, its author, is a born storyteller and his accounts of his childhood on the farm have delighted me.

"When I was still at home we had a neighbor who had two boys a little older than me. Their Dad done blasting with dynamite, blasting stumps, drainage ditches, and stuff like that. Well, we kids became quite knowledgeable about things you could do with dynamite–like fishing. One day we were up on the hill playing in the woods back of our house and one of the boys had a stick of dynamite that he took when the old man wasn't looking. We were thinking of something we could blow up, when one of my Dad's old coon dogs come up where we were. Now that dog was a no-good old possum dog and hurting so bad Dad had talked about shooting him all fall and winter but he wasn't worth a shotgun shell. Well, we decided to do the job for Dad by tying that stick of dynamite to his tail and putting him out of his misery quick. We had not trouble catching him or tying on the dynamite with a long fuse that we lit. But that damn old dog wouldn't run away and keeps following us even when we throwed stones at him. So we did the running. Run home. We ran faster. So did that old hound. We ran up the back porch steps as the dog run under the porch. Well, in less time than it takes me to tell this we didn't have any back porch or steps. And we didn't have to dig a very big hole."

Dear Cully:

I was born in Champion (You called it Tioga), and your father delivered me. That was in 1899 and I grew up there until the mine closed when my folks moved to California. That was a good place to grow up, but I never made it back there. We lived downtown in a white-washed cabin on the road just north of the blacksmith shop. I picked spring beauties and adders tongues and bloodroot in the Grove behind your father's hospital. I climbed the steep hill often even in winter to go to school or to Mass. I slid on Sliding Rock too. Your books helped me to go back, after all.

Marie Rousseau

Dear Cully:

You write like it was when I was a boy. Write some more.

Kris Carlson

P.S. I keep your books in my outhouse and read a story every time.

Thank you again, all of you.

*Grampa Cully once taught me never to set the hook too
soon on a bass trying to swallow the minnow "or you'll
both go away hungry. But don't wait too long or the bugger
will swallow yer hook!"*

*He knows how to catch people too when he throws out a
tantalizing tale. Like the one I swallowed which for years he
played out to my folly. Then he hauled me in and cut the line
quoting from the Mikado, "No, no lie that. It's merely
corroborative detail intended to give artistic verisimilitude
to a bald and unconvincing narrative."*

*With that I offer these illustrations as merely corroborative
artistry to Cully's rich and convincing narrative.*

Andrew Amor is a graduate of The University of Michigan. He practiced as an
architect in Detroit for four years and is now in Tuscany, Italy, working as an aesthetic
inspector of granite for five months, with his wife Elizabeth and 9 month-old son Peter.

OLD BONES AND NORTHERN MEMORIES

BOOK SEVEN

Foreword

Old buggers from the U.P. are hard to kill but The Reaper has been doing his best lately to make me extinct. Nevertheless he's failed so far and I'm determined to make it through the winter and be back at my lakes in arbutus time next spring.

Not content with hitting me in my old age with arteriosclerosis, ventricular tachycardia, phlebitis and diabetes he recently took a swipe at me resulting in congestive heart failure. It wasn't a particularly pleasant experience.

Awakening one morning I found myself desperately gasping for air, coughing hard and interminably, and with my heart going crazy with fibrillation, racing so fast I could not feel a pulse. There were moments when it not only skipped beats but stopped completely. I've had heart trouble before but nothing so utterly devastating. Waves of darkness swept over me but somehow I fought them off. I now recall that I had no fear of the death that I thought was happening. Nor was there any acceptance of it either. Instead I was angry, if anything. Nothing was going to keep me from seeing the forests and streams of my Shangrila. Nothing! After all, I'd had my first heart attack twenty four years before and had survived it. I would do it again. Somehow I did!

How long did it last? I have no idea. Time stopped whenever my heart did. I do remember once in the midst of my struggling that I looked at my bedside clock and it said five minutes past six, the exact time that Milove had died six years before. I knew because I have never reset that kitchen clock of hers. What is even more eerie is that my heart failure occured on the same date that she passed away.

When, a day later, I had recovered sufficiently to see my doctor he examined me carefully then told me I'd had a "textbook" case of congestive heart failure, that my old heart muscles had become too weak and tired to pump the blood back from my lungs, hence the gasping and dry coughing. He said I'd been very lucky but that, since another similar episode could occur at any time, I should put my affairs in order immediately. After giving me some prescriptions for various drugs he also gave me a big handful of don'ts. Don't ever get out of breath! Don't lift anything heavy! Don't get excited or angry! No, of course I couldn't go deer hunting nor drive me car. When I asked him facetiously if, at the age of 85, I should also abstain from sex he didn't smile but rebuked me. "You're in grave danger," he said. "Don't make light of it. Your days are numbered." If I behaved myself, rested a lot and took it very easy perhaps, just perhaps, I might see my lilacs bloom next year again if I were very lucky. He sure didn't seem very optimistic.

The Clock That Stopped

Well, so be it! It's not easy changing one's life style even when you know you must. I had to discover that I could plant only two tulips at a time, not three, that I had to rest three times going to the mailbox and four times on the way back, that I could not bring in an armful of firewood from the barn, and especially that I had to avoid all real effort and stress. My heart was my teacher. It told me in no uncertain terms whenever I had exceeded my limits, limits that kept shrinking from day to day.

But you do what you must do. Long ago I learned that lesson and to accept the dictates of fate without undue protest. Whatever adjustment It takes I'm returning to my homeland next spring and meanwhile I'll live each day as joyously as I can.

So, my friends, I'm writing another happy little book–this one about the last days of Cully Gage

or
Hell
or
Heaven

Day One

Most happy old men and women have discovered the secret for making the last years of their lives enjoyable despite the physical troubles and other miseries. That secret is this: It is possible to live two lives simultaneously. Children live only in the present; the young and middle aged live in the present and the future with all the anxieties these entail. Without much of a future yet freed from the need to work or raise a family, old people have the time to indulge themselves by recalling the good memories of the past as they go about their daily activities. Let me illustrate how I have done so in these, my dessert years.

This morning, awakening at seven, I sat on the edge of the bed for a few minutes to prevent the blackouts that occasionally occur upon arising due to my poor circulation. As I sat there, suddenly I was a boy again, leaping out from the bottom bunk of the Old Cabin, galloping nakedly down the hill path to our wilderness lake, then launching myself into the cold water. When my joyful splashings startled a nearby loon to skittering across its surface I echoed the wild laughter, shook my tingling hide dry, then ran up the hill again to make my breakfast.

That memory was so vivid it almost erased the realization that I was tottering rather than walking down the hall to the bathroom on legs that hurt. (They always do after being inactive.) While dressing I chanted "Old bones! Old bones! Damned old bones!" but I felt much better after sliding down the bannister railing of the seventeen steps as I and my children used to do when they were very small. How they'd squeal and beg for just one more ride. I could almost hear their young voices. Old men don't have to be dignified and I felt much better having done so.

As usual, before I made the coffee, I poked my head out of the backdoor to greet a new day. "Hello, world!" I whooped. So far that world has never answered me nor have my neighbors who live on the far side of my east soybean field. Yes, it would be another fine autumn day and to celebrate I gave the old farm bell a couple of strong tugs. I love the sound of that bell early in the morning.

As I filled the filter of my automatic coffeemaker and threw in the water, again I suddenly found myself a boy. This time I was fifteen on the mossy shore of Log Lake making a birchbark pail for our morning coffee. Arvo Mattila and I had hiked up there the night before hoping to catch some of the lunker trout that always swam in the strip of dark water surrounding the central ice cake. Arriving at dusk we had made a little night fire, lay down beside it and slept until dawn.

Arvo had awakened before I did and had a good cooking fire going but had gone down the shore a ways to fish. If we were to have coffee with our bacon and korpua I had to make a birchbark pail for we had no other one. Stripping off a square of the white bark (it strips easily in early spring) I folded its corners inward, turned up the sides and fastened them in place with split pegs made from a maple branch. For a bail or handle I used a peeled spruce root. Then filling it with lake water I hung the pail over the coals from a slanted pole jabbed into the ground.

You might think that the birchbark would catch on fire but it never does. So long as you keep the bark from direct contact with the flame the heat seems to go right through the bark into the water.

To make good camp coffee you throw a good handful of coffee into the water, let it boil two minutes, take it off the fire for one minute, then let it boil one minute more. No one has ever tasted better coffee than that cooked in a birchbark pail.

I also made two birchbark cups. They're easy to construct. You just roll a strip of birchbark into a cone, fold up its bottom half and pin it together with a peg that can also serve as a handle. Try it sometime.

Arvo had no pole. Instead he had fastened a three foot length of line to a big chunk of cedar with a large hook at the other end. Another line from that bobber lay in coils at his feet. Baiting the big hook with three or four large nightcrawlers he whirled the bobber around his head then let it fly far out into the water.

Almost immediately the cedar bobber began to jiggle. "Hey, Arvo," I yelled. "You've got a bite!"

"Naw," he answered. "Those are just little trout. They always bite first. When a big one sees their activity he will come to investigate and then wham! Down goes the whole big bobber and I've got him."

I was lacing together some peeled maple branches to make a grill for our bacon when suddenly Arvo let out a yell. Hand over hand he hauled in a very big fish. "A sloib," he shouted. "I've caught a sloib!"

I'd never heard that word before although I often have in recent years. It means a whopper. It has been used to refer not only to designate a big fish but to a pancake, a buck and even to a baby in the Upper Peninsula of Michigan. When I asked Arvo where he got the word he said it had just come to him. Not many people have been present at the birth of a new word. Anyway, it's a good one. After we roasted that sloib of a trout over the coals I caught some sloibs myself but none so large as Arvo's.

Well that was the memory and back to the present. Since I can have only one slice of bacon each week I like to have it thick and fried slowly and thoroughly so I use slab bacon only. I grinned as I put the slab on the back of a heavy wooden plaque that had been presented to me long before by Governor Romney because on the other side are the words "Michigan Frontiersman of the Year: Charles Van Riper." That's Cully Gage's alias. When I wrote my first Northwoods Reader I used a pen name and changed a lot of names and places fearing I might be sued by the descendants of the zany characters I wrote about. I needn't have worried because they felt flattered instead of being upset. "Cully" came from the Finnish word Kalla for Karl or Charles and Gage is my middle name and my mother's name. Everyone called me Cully when I was a boy and so did my wife and close friends. So much for that.

I grinned because I was remembering how Jim Miller, president of our university, reacted when I told him that I wouldn't accept it, that such honors always embarrassed me, that I was small potatoes and few in the hill and that I just didn't believe in honors. "Ever hear of the man who married for honor?" I asked jestingly. "He got on 'er."

That made him mad. "Van Riper," he said, "You'll damned well accept it. No matter how you feel, the university will benefit from the publicity. Tell you what I'll do. I'll drive you over to Detroit to the Economic Club luncheon where the presentation will be made, then drive you up to the Pere Marquette River, show you the biggest brown trout you've ever seen and let you flyfish for him." So I gave in and as a result got a fine cutting board for my bacon even if I didn't catch that trout.

All through breakfast and for some time afterward I got to thinking about honors and recognition and fame and how so many people hunger for them. What folly that is. Fame is for fruitflies. No matter how great our achievements we'll soon be forgotten. The life of our universe is measured in billions of light years and our little lives wink out like the sparks from a campfire. No, I've never worked to be famous or for the applause of others. Nuts to honor.

Nor have I beat myself to acquire possessions although they have come to me incidentally. I own an eighty acre farm in the middle of the city of Portage and more land in my beloved Upper Peninsula where I have my cabins but so what? How much do these amount to when you think of the immensity of space? Specks, we are, tiny insignificant specks in time and space.

As I munched my toast I recalled how small my farm looked when I took my first hot air balloon ride at the age of eighty. From that basket floating lazily high in the sky, it was no bigger than a postage stamp. Yet there in the balloon I was the same size I'd always been. My house down there was just a tiny spot. How come I wasn't?

One of the real rewards of growing very old is that you have the time for watching your thoughts unfold and no guilt about doing so. Though you know there aren't many leaves left on your calendar, for the moment you have the feeling that you can spend your minutes any way you wish.

"Hey" I thought, "Even though you're just a point at the intersection of the two infinitely long lines of time and space, you can erect a perpendicular at that point, the perpendicular pronoun 'I' and that perpendicular can grow very tall. Yes, that's me. I'm not just a speck. I'm a perpendicular and the units of that perpendicular are the impacts for good that I have accomplished in my short lifetime. That's the measure of a man, not his possessions or fame. After a rough beginning I made my life into a shining thing by helping so many other poor devils down in the swamp of despair. Pioneering the new profession of speech pathology gave me the opportunity to grow tall and I'm lucky to have had that chance. No, I'm not insignificant. I'm no speck. I'm a perpendicular."

I found myself getting excited. I always do when I am doing some new thinking. "What is in that perpendicular?" I asked myself and the answer came immediately. It's the impact for good that we have no others. Every time we help another person, or make the world a bit more beautiful, we add a unit to our perpendicular of significance. And every time we hurt or create some ugliness we subtract from it. I've been fortunate in having had the opportunity to help a lot of poor devils who possessed tangled tongues and every time I did I grew a bit taller. No, I was no tiny speck.

Suddenly by train of thought braked to a halt. Once again my heart was going berserk, racing, and skipping. I knew it wasn't another bout of congestive heart failure because there was no gasping for air or hard coughing. It was probably another episode of ventricular tachycardia which is bad enough. Thanks to medication I have been free from it for a long time but its threat is always there and you can die from that too if fibrillation occurs. But I wasn't too worried until the condition persisted and sweat broke out all over me. Sometimes if I cough hard or bang my chest with my fist it will cease but not this time. So in desperation I took another quinidex and tucked a nitroglycerin pill under my tongue. Soon I sensed the familiar electric taste and a bit later the slower, and more regular thumping of the pulse in my forehead which usually means I'm coming out of it. Not so! The irregularity returned. Feeling that I was extremely tense and that the tension might be contributing to the tachycardia, I decided to try the deep relaxation methods I'd learned from Kima, a wise and holy man from India. Occasionally it had helped me before. The procedure is this: 1. Greatly prolong each exhalation; 2. Roll your eyeballs upward under your eyelids, and 3. Let all your body slump. After about ten minutes of this Hindu relaxation the heart was beating smoothly again but I was exhausted. Phew!

Lord, I thought, even thinking can be dangerous. I had let myself become too excited. Well, I'd again learned something new about my limits.

Knowing it would be wise to be quiet for a time but reluctant to lie down lest I start thinking again, I went to my study and got an old book I'd written years before that had a tale about Kima in it, about the man from India who had taught me his way of relaxing under stress.

This is the essence of his story.

In 1932, during the depth of the great depression I was at the University of Iowa getting my doctorate in clinical psychology. With very little money I was existing on peanut butter and day old bread from a local bakery until I finally got an assistantship helping Dr. Travis in the laboratory where he was doing pioneer work in recording brain waves. While it only paid fifty dollars a month that was quite sufficient for all my needs and I was shocked when one day he told me he was relieving me of all my duties. "No," he said when he saw my fallen face, "You're not fired. I've just got another project for you–to photograph the soul."

Grinning, he explained that his dean had told him that a very important scholar from India had arrived on campus and wanted to know more about those brain waves, that he hoped thereby to see the mind or soul in action and to have it photographed. "He's nuts of course," Dr. Travis said, "but I'm assigning the project to you. Just keep him out of my hair."

Kima was a short man of about sixty years but had the unfurrowed face of a boy. "For many years I have sought to see my soul," he told me, "and now I have heard that you of the Western world have found a way of showing the brain in action. This I must see, my son." When I was about to hook the electrodes on his head however, he said no and that I should demonstrate it on another person first.

So I hooked up a friend and showed him the action currents on the screen, the alpha and beta waves and all the jumbled rest of them. Of course they made no sense to him because all they showed was consciousness, that the brain was alive.

"I must see pure thought," Kima said. My own thoughts weren't very pure at the moment but I said I'd have to think about it. At last I came up with a possible solution. Kima had told me that the soul is most active when the person is inactive but imagining, so I built an apparatus consisting of an arm chair and a board to which a person's arm could be strapped. "We'll sit the subject in the chair," I said, "then compare the brain waves when he voluntarily lifts the board, when the board is lifted for him by this rope and pulley, and finally when he is just imagining that he's lifting the board. By seeing the difference in the brain waves when he is just imagining we should come pretty close to finding what you want." Kima agreed and was excited when I put Travis's pretty secretary in the contraption and hooked on the electrodes.

She lifted her arm, I lifted her arm (and wished it were her leg), and she just imagined lifting it as the camera rolled. Alas, when I developed the film there wasn't a damned bit of difference between any of the recordings.

"I must meditate upon this thing," said Kima.

The next day when he returned he had the solution. "We failed," he said, "because you Americans are too tense and that tension masks the pure thought of imagining. I must teach you how to relax." I gathered some other graduate students and Kima trained us for several days before attempting the experiment again.

Unfortunately, that failed too and I know why. It was Kima's third step, the one where we also had to visualize existence as a whole while contemplating our navels. All of us mastered prolonging our exhalations and rolling our eyeballs up under our eyelids but every time we contemplated our navels our eyeballs went down. Kima was disappointed and so was I. Nevertheless, I have used his first two steps often since and was usually successful. And this morning I did so again.

By the time I had finished reading about Kima I was feeling pretty good so I decided to take my usual morning walk in my park. I've always enjoyed walking and in my youth I hiked all over many of the wilderness areas of the Upper Peninsula. Not any more! My diabetes led to neuropathy in my legs and though last year I had arterial by-pass surgery on them every step I take hurts. Nevertheless I walk all I can and am happy I don't have to use a cane as I did for some months. How I hated that damned cane even though it was a beautiful shillely I'd bought in Ireland. It always made me feel old and despite my years I rarely do unless reminded.

So, with a bit of wincing, I walked down the lane behind the old barn into my park. When I bought the farm about fifty years ago there was a little four acre barren field there that had been used as a holding place for dairy cattle. Foolishly I thought that manure from years of cows would have made it fertile so I planted it to corn. Only a few straggly stalks appeared and they were as stunted as the weeds. The ground turned out to be mainly hard pan clay with only an inch of topsoil on it. How my wife snorted when I told her I would make that field into a park, into my own little bit of the U.P.

But I did! The next spring I plowed the whole field and sowed it to sweet clover with lots of fertilizer, plowed that under and sowed a crop of buckwheat, again plowed that under and in the fall I put in a cover crop of rye. After three years of that rotation the soil was soft and mellow and I could begin to plant the bushes and trees of the U.P.

First I planted hundreds of seedling spruce, balsam, and various kinds of pines, then some poplars and birch. Every summer I brought back from my cabin on the Van Riper Lakes large rocks covered with moss, ferns or groundpine. Arbutus, however refused to be transplanted. Year after year I tried but it always withered and died. I guess it didn't want to live Down Below any more than I did. Two hazelnut bushes flourished but two tamaracks did not. I did manage to bring back some U.P. flowers that have done very well: trilliums, jack in the pulpits, adder's tongues, violets and Dutchman's breeches.

As I walked through the park today I was again amazed to see how tall those trees had grown. The firs and pines were at least fifty feet tall and the ground beneath them was covered by a thick mat of brown needles. To rest my legs I lay down on them for some time listening to the wind in the branches as I'd done so often in my beloved homeland. For a few moments I was again a boy in the forest.

Then I went over to the little blue pool in the pines. Compared to my sparkling lakes north of Tioga it is just a trivial gesture but it's water and I couldn't have my bit of the U.P. without some. I fill the pool with a three hundred foot hidden hose from the barn and let the water flow over the bordering rocks just to hear the familiar sound. Often I sit hidden back from it to watch the animals come there to drink at dusk. I've seen raccoons, possum, rabbits, squirrels and occasionally deer. My farm is about the only free space where animals can live out their days, surrounded as it is by subdivisions of expensive houses.

This morning however there were no animals but a pheasant flushed from the tangle beyond the pool. I've let part of my park grow up to underbrush so my visitors can hide.

Then I followed the little path through the rest of the firs to the back gate of my park and stood there overlooking my meadows. After a disastrous experience trying to grow wheat in my back forty acres I've just let the land go fallow. The land is hilly and rolling and long grass covered all of it except for my woodlot and the wild cherry and other trees that have appeared. It's a lovely spot and for years I've walked it every day and for a moment I was tempted to do it again.

I didn't, knowing it would be enough just to walk back to the house but I promised myself I'd come back that afternoon to see if the kids from the big houses beyond the boundary trees had been building shacks again. They do so every year and sometimes build fires that have threatened my park. When I find such a shack I try to visit it when the kids are there, show them how to build a firepit, tell them tales of Pete Halfshoes, my boyhood Indian friend, and give them a handful of marshmallows to roast.

Getting back to the house yard sure wore me out so I sat for a time on the bench that encircles the biggest of my large oak trees. How often my wife and I have sat there watching the sun go down over the west fields! After some good memories I reentered the house.

There I lay down on the davenport and had almost dozed off when the phone rang. Ach! It was Patrick Mulligan from a little town in Illinois. He said that he had just preached his last sermon before retiring and wanted to thank me again for curing his stuttering. He said he was thinking of coming to see me to tell me about all the souls he had saved and perhaps to save my own. I firmly said no, that I'd had a heart failure and was seeing no visitors, I just couldn't bear the thought of seeing him on his knees before me praying for my benighted soul. Finally I convinced him or hoped I had.

I couldn't help remembering that Pat had come to me in 1953 stuttering very severely with many gasps and head jerks. For some years he had worked on an oil drilling crew in Oklahoma but had become a born again Christian with a calling to preach the gospel according to Saint Patrick. He'd had little schooling but could read and write even if he couldn't talk.

Respecting his sincerity and high motivation, although I felt the prognosis was very poor, I started to teach him how to change and modify his stuttering so he could be fluent enough to preach. To my surprise Pat progressed rapidly and within the year he was remarkably fluent. When he left on his mission I confess I felt relieved. How many hours I had spent with him reading the Bible, praying and preaching and resisting his efforts to convert me! For some years thereafter Pat visited me to report on his missionary progress and to save my bloody soul. A self ordained minister, he had built a small church of concrete blocks with his own hands in a farm community and gradually gathered a little congregation to hear his impassioned sermons. No small achievement, that! In a way I envied his simple faith in God and the hereafter.

In my long life I've seen how much strength such a faith has given others in deep trouble. One of them was my wife's Aunt Nell who spent a week with us when she was almost eighty. She had the unwrinkled face of an angel and serenity radiated from it. All of us felt it, even my children. I knew that she'd had a miserable and tragic life with a husband who was one of the nastiest, cruelest men I've ever known. For years they'd existed in abject poverty. One son had committed suicide; another was a scoundrel. And yet Aunt Nell was a saint, a very happy beautiful person. How had she been able to surmount all those difficulties and have such peace? When I finally asked her, she said, "Every morning when I wake up I ask the Lord what wonderful things He has in store for me and, you know. He has never once disappointed me." I've worked with cancer victims who had lost their tongues or vocal cords who had that same faith and always I've marveled at their courage and peace of mind.

I have long sought that faith. It would be good to have it now but I'm an agnostic like my father except that I doubt my doubts and he never did. Though he never flaunted his scepticism and agreed with my devout mother that I should go to Sunday School and church, he never attended. He said he'd lost his faith in medical school and that religion, like most of medicine, was largely humbug. Yet his best friend was Father Hassel, our old Catholic priest, with whom he played a weekly game of chess over a small glass of whiskey and a cigar. Once I heard them arguing about religion and hearing the priest say, "Doctor, you're an old fraud. You're more religious than anyone I know. You've always sacrificed yourself for others. God works his wonders in many mysterious ways and you, sir, have been his instrument whether you know it or not." Others have said the same about me.

And I've often had truly religious experiences–though not in church. I love the old hymns and the liturgy but most of the sermons have always turned me off. The forest is my temple and I've had some peak experiences therein during which I found myself caught up in a power far greater than myself. In *The Last Northwoods Reader* there is a story called *Campfires* which describes one such incident.

The Bench

When my legs finally stopped hurting I went outside to the old barn to chop some wood for the evening fire. Knowing from past experience that I had to be careful, I started on a chunk of cedar I'd brought back from the U.P. Splitting cedar is always enjoyable and easy. You "read" the end of the chunk to see just where to hit and then, by angling the blade at the last moment, the slab breaks away cleanly with one swipe. So I made an armful of kindling without any ill effects. I knew I should have quit right then but a nice clean chunk of oak was so inviting I got the heavy maul and whopped it a good one, breaking it in half. Oops! I felt the old heaviness in my chest and quit immediately, then sat on the bench in the sun humming "Lazy bones, sitting in the sun. How you gonna get your day's work done, sitting in the noonday sun?" Now my voice is only good for cooling soup but I sang anyway. Ours was always a singing family. All of us always sang at the dining table between the main meal and dessert. Sitting there on the bench I could almost hear the bright voices of my children singing Harvest Moon, Home on the Range or that one about the pufferbellies. How did it go? Oh yes, "Down by the station/ early in the morning/ see the little pufferbellies all in a row/ Hear the stationmaster blow his little whistle/ Pop Pop. Toot Toot/ Away we go." Always my wife was singing the old songs and doing little dance steps as she cooked or did the dishes and she could always harmonize wonderfully too. Oh well, that was long ago-but not too far away.

Getting up from the bench I gathered asters and chrysanthemums for the house. Milove always loved flowers and I've kept some fresh ones in her bedroom ever since she died.

Those I put in her vase were Yoshiko's mums, special ones. Yoshiko Ohashi was the stuttering daughter of a prominent Japanese government official and when she came to me for therapy she proved to be one of my most difficult patients. I just couldn't know her feelings because her body language was so different. When that oriental mask of a face smiled it was not with amusement but rather embarrassment. When she giggled, she was angry. Moreover she fought me tooth and nail, sabotaging the assignments I gave her and often just refusing to cooperate in anyway. I felt she hated me. Was she reacting to me as though I were a rejecting father figure? I didn't know but it was obvious that I was failing and would have no possible chance of helping her. Finally she stopped coming for therapy although she continued her academic studies in speech pathology at our university.

I decided that if I were to help her I just had to know more about the Japanese so for several months I immersed myself in Japanese art, literature, history and culture, reading everything in our library that I could. It was in itself a fascinating and rewarding experience and I found some important new insights. Evidently the Japanese penalized the deviant individual much more that we did. In one of their famous plays, the Domo Mata, a famous painter was urged by his wife to commit suicide because of his shameful speech. I learned that a frustrated stutterer had deliberately burned down one of their most sacred shrines, the Temple of the Golden Pavilion, much to the shock and anger of the whole nation. In one of their books I read about a man who said that every time he stuttered a hundred of his ancestors turned in their graves with revulsion. It became obvious that I had asked Yoshiko to confront her disorder before she could possibly tolerate doing so. Somehow I had to desensitize her to her stuttering before we could make any headway.

I sought her out and we began therapy again, this time with much more success and she returned to Japan fluent enough to become an instructor in speech pathology at one of their universities. Then some years later when she wrote that she was returning to see me and thank me I asked her to bring some seeds of their national flower, the chrysanthemum.

She came but not with seeds. Instead she brought some cuttings, hiding them in her bra to escape customs. I planted them by the windmill and one of them that survived has bloomed gloriously ever since. It was some of Yoshiko's mums that I put on Milove's bedside table.

It was now time to get on my exercycle (a stationary bicycle) on my daily ride to the Upper Peninsula–or so I pretend. I travel on it one or two miles each day and at present I'm a few miles north of Grand Rapids. By March I will be in Cadillac, in two months I'll be crossing The Bridge and by June I'll be at my lakes. I hope the arbutus will still be blooming on the north side of the hills.

As always, the morning had passed swiftly and it was time to take my mandatory nap. To make it more tolerable I play classical music on my big stereo and this time I chose a Beethoven Symphony. For a long time I followed the familiar music but then dozed off, not awakening until the music stopped.

Refreshed, I made myself some soup and a sandwich and after some self debate about riding down on my garden tractor I decided to walk to the mailbox. My 132 year old farmhouse sits on a little hill and there are 239 double steps that I must take to get to it, each of which will hurt me because, due to my diabetic neuropathy, I have only half the circulation in my legs that I should have. The diabetes is now under control by a strict diet and glycotrol but the neuropathy still remains. Once on the way down and twice on the way back I had to rest but the effort was worth it because there was a lot of good mail, much of it addressed to Cully Gage. I sure love those letters from my readers and answer most of them. Impact again! Back in the house I read a few of them, then saved the others until later.

Tired of sitting and reluctant to miss any of that fine day, I went to the north garden to dig a few potatoes. I did so with anticipation because for forty years I have tried to grow The Perfect Potato. Let others seek to grow the perfect rose or dahlia or orchid. My goal has been to take a lowly clod of a vegetable and make it into a shining thing as I've done with some human clods, including myself.

People have asked me how I would know if I'd grown one even if I did. I tell them that I would know. It would be unblemished, have closed or sleeping eyes and be very large. Eight years ago I grew a ten inch one that looked so perfect I almost had it bronzed. Although I kept it on my fireplace mantel until it got soft and wrinkled I knew that on its underside there was a flaw. So my quest has continued.

This year, knowing that my time was getting short, I had planted the potatoes with special care. Two wide and deep trenches had been filled with a mixture of compost, peat moss and rich earth before I laid down the cut seed tubers and covered them with bone meal and more compost. All summer I had weeded and watered the patch carefully. The vines had been thick, and heavy with flowers but now they were brown and shriveled. It was time to see if I had fulfilled my dream.

Getting a spade from the old horse stall which was now my garden room I went over to the potato patch but rested a while on a nail keg before starting to dig. Again more memories filled my head. That potato patch had once been my pigpen and had held an inverted V-shaped pig house in which my children played happily until their mother discovered them. She told me to get rid of the structure but instead I bought two month-old pigs naming them Cornelius and George after two of our university deans who had given me trouble.

How I enjoyed those little buggers! They'd see me coming with a pail of slop and race around the pen oinking to high heaven, and after they grew into huge hogs they loved the hard cider I mixed with their mash. Like me, they also loved flowers, especially those in my wife's house beds. Time after time I would have to coax them back to the pen they'd tunneled under and then try to repair the fence. Pigs are smart animals, smarter about fences than I was.

Sitting there in their old haunts I remembered the time I came home from a long speaking trip to find my wife so livid with fury she wouldn't even kiss me. "You'll have to get rid of those damned pigs or you'll be rid of me!" With fury she told about how those pigs of mine had broken out again and cleaned out all her lovely annuals, how she'd gone out in her nightgown to chase them away and they wouldn't chase. Wow! Was she mad. And beautiful too with her brown eyes flashing lightning! When I couldn't keep my face straight, visualizing that scene, she sure let me have it.

In any happy marriage there are times when a man has to do battle but this was not one of them. At first I thought of having Dean George and Dean Cornelius butchered and processed for our freezer but I knew that would create many future difficulties, that neither she nor my children would eat a bit of them. So I sold my beloved hogs and every time we had oatmeal for breakfast, or hamburger for dinner I mourned the loss of bacon and sausage and chops and roasts. Most of all I missed the chance to munch on my academic enemies but there was peace in the vale.

Still smiling at that memory I began to dig the potatoes, pausing after each hill to sit for a time on the nail keg. Oh, it was going to be a fine crop, the first hill yielding fourteen spuds, most of them big ones. They were clean, white and noble. Two of them were more than eight inches long so I dug three more hills with eagerness, but The Perfect Potato was not among them. No matter! There were thirty six hills still to be dug and surely in one of them I would find it. How I wanted to keep on digging but sensibly I did not. I hate being sensible. Laying all I'd dug on a blue tarp to dry I returned to the house.

One of the consequences of congestive heart failure, as my doctor told me, is deep fatigue after very little effort. "When you feel it, lie down whether you want to or not." So I did, remembering how in Tioga shortly after the beginning of school the boys were excused to help in the potato harvest. I remembered working on John Delongchamp's farm from six to six, going along the rows of potatoes that had been dug, sorting them and putting the good ones into burlap bags. We also put the small ones in piles and set aside the sloibs. These Jumbos were the really big ones, up to a foot long. Delongchamp saved these for the county fair or for special customers. Once he gave my father a bushel of those monsters and I recall that for one dinner meal my mother baked just one of them for the whole family. Some Jumbos had a cavity within them but this one did not. I've never seen potatoes like those since. Dad said that Delongchamp grew them in virgin sod without manure or fertilizer–just U.P. sunshine and rain from Lake Superior.

Next I read the rest of my mail and wrote some letters, one to a little boy who said his teacher had read some of my stories to his class. He liked the ones about me and Mullu and Fisheye and the tricks we played in school but his favorite was the one about the bat in the hat. Finally I wrote one to a man who said he'd been hunting for Tioga for three summers and where the hell was it anyway? Tioga was really Champion, I wrote, and Lake Tioga was Lake Michigamme. Van Riper State Park was named after my father who started it because one day when he went there to go swimming and had to change his clothes in some bushes some little Finn kids had embarrassed him by chanting "Look at Doctor's big white ass! Look at Doctor's big white ass." My father got the township to put up some dressing rooms and rake out the beach, took one more swim and never went back there again.

Noticing that the battered old copper boiler that holds my firewood was empty I went out to the bam to get the garden tractor and cart to haul the wood for the evening fire and at the same time to fetch the evening paper from the mailbox. As I rode back up the lane

I glanced at the headlines. War in the Persian Gulf, homicides, rape. I wouldn't read it till morning. Hell, I wouldn't even read it then so I rolled the sheets into cylinders, placed them on the grate, laid the apple small wood and an oak chunk on them and started the evening fire.

It was time to see if I could have whiskey for Happy Hour so I went into my study to test my blood sugar. Diabetics have to be careful about alcohol. Pricking my forefinger with the lancet, I put the drop of blood on the test tape, closed the instrument's door and waited while the display said testing, testing, until it wrote 127. Good! No Diet Cola tonight. The blood sugar was well within the 80-140 range of normality.

Old men need to pamper themselves a little so I buy good scotch, Chivas Regal or Glenn Fiddich, for my two fingers of whiskey in a tin cup I'd brought back from the old cabin. Whiskey somehow always tastes better from a tin cup. I wished I had water from my big spring up there but because I still have my own well at least I don't spoil it with the hint of chlorine that pollutes city water. Because I sip it very slowly, one cup usually lasts a long time beside the fire at Happy Hour.

I love that hour and so did Milove. We'd sit and share with each other the happenings of the day. It was always good talk, sometimes crazy talk. Even now, especially on a day when I 've heard no human voice, I converse aloud with her knowing just how she would respond to my nonsense . Though her picture is on the TV it seems as though she is sitting next to me in her blue chair. "I'm only a smile away," she wrote on an Indian slate at the cabin before she died. I smile a lot at Happy Hour.

Then it was time to make supper . Though I wasn't hungry I know I must not skip a meal because of the diabetes, so I cut one of my acorn squash in half, filled the cavity with bits of link sausage, and put it in the oven to bake. That, with milk, bread and an apple would be my evening meal. While it was cooking I thought of a tale that I had started to write but had never finished. Where the devil was it? I searched my messy study and finally found it on top of the encyclopedia. It was fun reading and the need to finish it was so strong I went to the typewriter after supper and did so. Here it is:

Aunt Lizzie's Downfall

Even roses wither and age by the clock but that didn't seem true of Aunt Lizzie Compton, Tioga's gossip and trouble maker. Daily she made her rounds down our hill street and on the side roads to Frenchtown and Finntown. Only the worst blizzards kept her inside. Physically she changed little as she aged. Her step and her voice were strong, the latter too strong because Annie, our long suffering organist, finally gave our new preacher an ultimatum.

"Mr. Jones," she said, "You've got to get Aunt Lizzie out of the choir or I'm quitting. For twenty years she has tortured my ears and those of your congregation. She fancies herself quite a soprano but she's never been able to hit the high notes fair and square; she flats them and screeches them instead. I've tried for a long time to cover them up by playing the organ louder but my feet get tired from all that pumping. What's worse is that lately she's lost the top part of the range she had. She doesn't know that, of course, but everyone else does. Her lower notes are ok but oh she murders those high ones. I feel them in my spine! I tell you it's Aunt Lizzie or me and you'll not find another organist in town." The Reverend Jones said he'd see what could be done.

So the next day he called a meeting of the church board and found that all its members agreed with Annie. It was high time that Aunt Lizzie stepped down. "But who is to grab that wildcat by the tail?" asked one board member. Most of them had felt the bite of Aunt Lizzie's tongue at one time or another. "You're the preacher," they said. "That's your job."

Feeling sorry for the preacher, Annie suggested that he circulate a petition and use it if Aunt Lizzie refused to cooperate, so that is what the preacher did. The only dissenter who refused to sign was old Andy Anderson. "Hell," he said, "The only reason I go to church is to hear the old gal screech and watch the people try to keep their fingers out of their ears."

Thinking it was just a pastoral visit. Aunt Lizzie made the preacher a cup of tea the next afternoon when he called at her house, but when he gently told her that she should let a younger singer take her place in the choir she took it away from him.

"Preacher," she said, "I'll do no such thing. I can sing as well as I ever could. I'll have you know that I started your choir thirty years ago. I bought the robes, much of the music and helped pay for the organ." She was getting madder by the moment. "Who puts a whole dollar in your collection plate each Sunday? Who makes the best cake for your cake sales? Who teaches your Sunday School when the regular teacher gets sick? Of all the nerve! No, I say. No, no, no!" When the preacher told her of Annie's ultimatum Aunt Lizzie said she'd play the organ herself and sing soprano too. Fearing that soon she'd be scratching his eyes out, the preacher handed her the petition and fled with her final words ringing in his ears: "I'll be there next Sunday, preacher, and I'll be singing soprano in the choir!"

As you can imagine, the news of Aunt Lizzie's firing traveled like wildfire throughout Tioga. As she made her daily rounds. Aunt Lizzie for the first time found herself on the defensive. "Hey, I hear they kicked you out of the choir." "You aren't going to let them do that to you, are you Aunt Lizzie, without a fight?" "I hear they've moved Thirza Lowe up from contralto to soprano and that Bill Trevarrow will be singing tenor. Funny choir, that will be, with three men and only one female voice!'

Wow! That news sure made Aunt Lizzie furious. "You mean they're picking that saloon singer in my place?" she shouted incredulously, "I won't stand for it! " Yes, they told her, Bill is going to be in the new choir and they're practicing in the preachers' house every evening.

Although it was a fine summer day the church was full that next Sunday morning. Our people knew that Aunt Lizzie would put up a battle and when they saw her going down the street wearing her choir robe they knew the fireworks would soon begin.

Their expectations were fulfilled. Up into the choir loft strode Aunt Lizzie to join the three men and Thirza. When the preacher went over to persuade her to leave she shouted NO in such a loud voice the whole congregation gasped. Annie gave the organ a big blast and left her bench to sit in the front row to see what would happen, and soon the other members of the choir followed her. There was Aunt Lizzie up there alone but undaunted.

She held up her hand for silence and sure got it. "Our first hymn this morning will be *The Old Rugged Cross*, she announced. "I shall sing the first verse while accompanying myself on the organ and you will then join in on the second which you will find on page 64." Hers was the voice of command and many people did open their hymn books to that page.

At first the congregation was stunned but by the time Aunt Lizzie had finished that first verse all hell broke loose. "No, no!" they yelled. "Step down. Lizzie! We want the new choir. This is our church, not yours. Down, down!" Nothing so exciting had happened in Tioga since Bridget Murphy's pig fell in the well.

Trying to maintain the holiness of the sanctuary in all that commotion, the preacher went over to Charlie Olafson, our town constable, and whispered something in his ear. Up got the big man from his pew and striding up to the choir loft he picked up Aunt Lizzie and carried her to a back pew despite her struggles, then sat beside her.

The new choir made its way back to the loft; Annie returned to the organ bench, and the preacher to the pulpit. "Friends," he said. "I deeply regret the disturbance and am sorry it occurred. Mrs. Compton has done many good works in this church and I'm sorry she has been hurt. The text for my sermon this morning comes from Luke 10, verse 5. It is 'Peace to this house.' But first let us listen to our new choir's first selection." Annie belted out a triumphant fanfare and the three men and Thirza sang a hymn whose title I've forgotten but it was one of those with a lot of the high notes that Aunt Liz loved.

And in that back pew Aunt Lizzie sang with them. Loud and clear, she sang and way off key on those high notes until Charlie put a fat hand over her mouth.

She bit that hand right to the bone and the words that Charlie uttered were not those usually heard in the house of the Lord. Dead silence! Charlie picked up Aunt Lizzie, slung her over his shoulder, and carried her up to the steel cage in our Town Hall that served as the jail. "You'll be here till morning, Lizzie," he said, "and then I'll decide whether to have you arraigned before the justice of the peace for assault and battery upon an officer of the law. So shut up!"

That afternoon some of us kids were peering through the windows of the town hall to enjoy her shaking her fist at us when Charlie came and let her out. She was not at all contrite and we couldn't help admiring her spirit. Nothing could conquer Aunt Lizzie.

And nothing did. Wiser heads worked out a compromise because they felt sorry for her. After all, she'd done a lot for the church for many years and didn't really know how off key she sang. So they moved Thirza up to sing soprano and asked Aunt Lizzie to be the contralto. It worked out fine. Peace in the valley and peace on the hill came to Tioga and everyone lived happily ever after. Or should have!

Well, that done I went to bed. It had been a good day.

Day Two

I awoke a bit later than usual probably because at three o'clock I'd gone downstairs to limber up my hurting legs on my exercycle. It had helped and I'd gone back to sleep swiftly but this morning they were aching again so I began to exercise them and my toes before I even got out of bed to get the circulation going. Diabetics develop a neuropathy that causes numbness in the extremities and that has happened to me. Once I stepped on a thumbtack before I went to bed and it was there next morning when I found it while taking a bath. Exercising my toes doesn't eliminate the numbness but it may prevent the severe ulcers that plagued me last year. So I wiggle my toes a lot every morning.

I've set myself a quota of thirty wiggles and was half through doing them when I got mad. I was in a rut, living my hours and days in the same way. I was a damned robot! I've always enjoyed being a bit different and unpredictable. I like to do the unexpected, to explore new experiences, to take crazy chances and here I was, just a laboratory rat, running the same maze day after day. Furious with myself, I vowed that this new day would be different.

Therefore I got out of bed on the left side rather than the right where I usually slept and I exercised those toes by dancing on them down to the bathroom to the tune of Waltzing Matilda and I put on a bright red shirt and red socks to complete a costume that was decidedly different from that which I usually wear. Felt like a bull fighter.

Instead of greeting the world with my customary hello, I rang the old bell instead to greet the day. Once again I was glad I'd not sold the farm to those beady eyed developers who pester me. I enjoy the feeling of isolation, to be able to do my Dance of the Wild Cucumber under the full moon or to ring that bell when I want to without worrying about my neighbors.

Washing out an old black jug I'd found in a lumber camp up north I filled it with cider and drank it from the jug. Now for a different breakfast, not the usual oatmeal or bran flakes, toast and coffee. Peacock tongues? There weren't any in the cupboard but I did find a string of Upper Peninsula mushrooms my wife had long before dried by hanging them from our cabin window frame. Were they still good? I didn't know but I made them into an omelet anyway. Instead of using my automatic coffee maker I made a pot of boiled coffee and suddenly thought of the best cup of coffee I've ever tasted, the one I had on the Bayou de la Fange in Louisiana many years ago.

I was in Louisiana to conduct a week-long seminar in stuttering for the speech therapists in that area. The group was a large one, perhaps a hundred or more but they were hungry to learn and the days passed swiftly. Most of them were young and attractive but I especially noticed one of them, a white haired old lady, who sat in the back row and took down every word I said. At the end of the Thursday session she came up and introduced herself.

She was not a speech therapist, she said, but had come to hear me in the hope that she could help her forty year old son, Raoul, who stuttered and who had isolated himself on their plantation since quitting high school at sixteen. She told me Raoul talked as little as possible to anyone, spent his days in his room listening to the radio or reading or wandering in the swamp. Perhaps if he saw me and heard me, another person who had stuttered and became fluent, he might get some hope and stop being such a hermit. She said she hesitated to ask, but could I, would I come to their home to see Raoul? She warned me he might refuse to come downstairs or refuse to speak to me, but would I please come. Of course I said yes.

Her chauffeur picked me up that afternoon and drove me to a landing on the Bayou de la Fange where we took a launch to the plantation. The driver explained that it was easier that way because of the muddy roads and that Mme. F. thought I would enjoy the boat ride. I certainly did. The trees hung heavy with moss, there were strange shrubs in full bloom, and birds sang everywhere.

The house was very old and very beautiful. Mme. F. welcomed me graciously and showed me a huge book of historic homes in which the house was pictured. The book said it had been built in the days of Napoleon and that the roof tiles had come from France in a sailing ship. Both she and her husband were of French descent, very proud to be Creoles. He was a consulting engineer specializing in the construction of sugar refineries and soon to retire. He would be joining us later, she said. She led me through a large drawing room into a little alcove overlooking a beautiful garden and excused herself. "I must persuade Raoul to come down if I can." I suggested that she should let us be by ourselves if he did show up and she agreed.

More than twenty minutes elapsed before Raoul appeared and sat down. A large man, very fat, he wouldn't shake hands when we were introduced. At first I did almost all the talking, telling of my own experiences as a stutterer and demonstrating that I knew his feelings about his disorder. I showed Raoul how I used to stutter and also how fluent I had become. I verbalized the joys of being freed from a tangled tongue. No hard sell, of course, just a calm, almost casual presentation of factual material.

Throughout the long soliloquy, and that is what it was because Raoul didn't say a word, I was watching his body language intently. At first it seemed to reflect complete indifference, then some flickers of attention, then some alarm, and finally some real interest. When these signals appeared, I told him I wasn't there to try to get him to undertake any therapy, that I had come only because of his mother's concern, and because he probably needed some hope. It was only then that he began to talk.

"I know," Raoul said. "My mother is worrying about what will happen to me when she and my father die and I am left here alone. They are getting old, yes." He didn't stutter frequently or severely as he said this and had only one hard blocking. He told me that he wasn't worried because he lived only one day at a time. He was never bored because his hobby was baseball. Although he had never seen a professional game, Raoul knew the batting averages of players on several baseball teams and followed them closely on the radio and in the newspapers. He made predictions and bets with himself on the outcomes of the games. Yes, it was almost an obsession but it passed the time away and when there was no baseball he hunted and fished. Why go out into the evil world and have to talk and suffer? Here he was safe and happy. "Glad to have met you." He shook hands with me, smiled and left. I lit my pipe and wiped my brow.

When his mother came in she took one look at my face and knew. "Ah, mon fils," she said, patting my arm. "It was a long chance and I know you tried. Raoul, he has lived this way too long. Now you must meet my husband and share our pleasantness." A maid came in with sweets and tiny eggshell thin cups. "These are from old France," she said, "and now you must know the coffee of that time." The maid put a bit of very black coffee in each fragile cup, then a teaspoon of boiling water over it, then another teaspoon of boiling water and so on until the tiny cup was almost full. Then brown sugar and thick cream were added. It indeed was the best coffee I've ever tasted. Raoul's father, a gay spirit, joined us and had some too. No further mention of the son - just gaiety and civility. The father told tales of the Creoles and I told about the French Canadians of the forest village where I had spent my boyhood. We even knew and sang the same old song of the voyageurs:

> *"Oh ze wind she blo from ze nort,*
> *And ze wind, she blo some more,*
> *But you won't get drown on Lac Champlain*
> *So long you stay on ze shore."*

I don't know what happened to Raoul when his parents died and he had to leave that shore.

Still remembering that wonderful coffee I poured out the boiled coffee I'd made and started anew. Getting one of my wife's fragile Haviland china cups from the china closet I put a pan of water to boil as I fixed the omelet. Then I made my coffee as the maid in Louisiana had done. It was a fine breakfast but the coffee wasn't so good. Perhaps it was because I had to use Equal instead of the brown raw sugar, or the coffee itself didn't have that slight taste of chickory or because I had to use milk instead of thick cream. Anyway it was a different breakfast.

Rather than taking my customary walk in the park I rode the John Deere down the lane and into the meadows of my back fields. Around its perimeter I went, often having to dodge a young tree or two. Under a blowdown I discovered a new fox hole complete with paw print in the sand it had dug out. On the second hill I saw the oval flattened bed where a deer had slept. Two pheasants and three rabbits were sent scurrying. Down in the south valley I got off the tractor to look over my woodlot. Yes, there were many dead elms and some old wild cherry trees that should be sawed down. Returning along the west and north boundaries I saw the hint of autumn in the rose colored leaves of sassafras. Soon those fence rows would be aflame.

When I got back to the house I found I was very tired even though all I'd done was to sit and bounce. I felt like Samson must have felt after Delilah cut his hair, but it was good to lie down, a little old man in a big old house with sunshine streaming through the tall windows.

Yet I would rather have been barreling across those back fields in my ancient truck with my chain saw because I had a touch of the U.P. fall fever for making more wood for the winter. I was pretty sure I had enough stacked in the barn to last until spring but you never know. Perhaps we'd have a winter like that of 1946 when the drifts touched the farm bell and all my firewood was gone by the first of March. Oh nuts! I had enough and if I needed more I could buy it.

In the U.P. when I was a boy some of our men started making wood early in the spring. They'd go out on snowshoes and cut down three or four big maples that they would cut up later in the summer. That way there'd be no sap in the trees and the wood could dry better. Most of us waited until July when the black flies, gnats and nosee-ums (big feel-ums) were gone. But when September came with its first hint of frost the wood fever flared again. We had to make it through the winter. "Got all yer wood made yet?" was a common greeting.

How the forest rang with the sound of crosscut saws and toppling trees in October! How vividly I recalled the sharp crack of the axe as it bit into the tree, the sight of our breath in the frosty air, the zing-zing of the saw, the smell of fresh sawdust. With a good partner on the other end of the long cross-cut saw the experience was very pleasant; with a bad one, it was not. "Dammit!" we would growl. "Don't mind yer riding the saw but quit dragging your feet!" Some real skill was involved. One had to pull hard but smoothly and without twisting the handle and on the return stroke you didn't push but merely guided the blade. Most of all, the two of us had to be in complete synchrony. With a well filed saw and sometimes a bit of kerosene on the blade the sawing could be almost effortless. Yes, it was fun making wood for the winter.

No one in Tioga ever seemed to have enough room in their barns or sheds to hold all the wood that had been cut and so each house usually had a woodpile outside. Some always stacked their wood by the outhouse in order that anyone going there to do his duty would remember to bring back a stick or two to the kitchen. Others used it for insulation, piling it around the foundations of their houses. A few made their woodpiles of split wood like igloos so the snow or rain wouldn't wet the inside of the pile. By deer season you could take the measure of a man by the looks of his woodpile.

Sometimes the fever became compulsive. Norman Bentti once had a pile of split wood higher than his two story house although his cellar and shed were full. People came from afar to admire Mount Bentti. Most of us made more wood than we really needed because it would always keep and besides it could always be given to someone in the village who might run out. We took care of each other in Tioga.

As I got off the davenport the obsession to live differently still had hold of me. How could I ride my exercycle on my way to the U.P. differently? Well, I could try to ride it backwards but, much to my surprise, that proved to be very difficult. My feet stuttered. They wanted to move in their accustomed way. When I pedaled slowly I could do it but reversals occurred at normal speeds. I managed to do only a half mile before giving up. Ruts were hard to break.

I then went out to tend my roses which had been neglected for some time because of the lush blooming of dahlias and chrysanthemums. Yes, they needed some tending but every bush was glorious with large blooms as they often are late in autumn. I grow fine roses though most visitors never see them because the rose bed is back of the old barn where many years of cow manure had been piled. They also grow well there because underneath the bed is a layer of the cinders and cobblestones that once had covered the entire barnyard. Roses need good drainage.

But I like to think there's another reason they grow so well. About twenty years ago when I was shredding cornstalks the machine jammed. Forgetting that one must always detach the sparkplug wire before cleaning out debris from the sharp blades, I looked down to see a beautiful mound of scarlet and green. The blades had started rotating and had sliced off the middle fingers of my left hand. Well, after getting them sewed up in the emergency room, I took that bloody compost and spread it on the roses. Not many men have recycled themselves to be reincarnated as a rose. Anyway they've bloomed mightily ever since. I picked a perfect red one and took it to my wife's bedstand and grinned remembering the time I put a similar red rose in the toilet bowl before she got up one morning. With the rose still dripping in her hand she came down and kissed me. "Oh Cully," she said, "You're still the crazy nut I married years ago."

The strawberry bed also needed weeding so I went out to begin that task. As I passed my thirty foot compost bed I felt very wealthy. All that careful layering of leaves, grass and horse manure would produce many loads of the crumbly black humus that had made the gardens so productive. Now the garden had been rototilled and seeded with annual rye grass and it was one lush green carpet. Not so my strawberry bed. Lord, there were so many tall weeds I could scarcely see the plants.

Cautioning myself not to overdo, I began the job but didn't quit in time. Suddenly I began to feel dizzy and the next I knew I was lying there with my nose buried in the soil. Was this the next episode of heart failure my doctor had warned me about? No, though the heart was beating rapidly it was not irregular and there was no gasping. I'd just suffered a blackout, a TIA or transient ischemic attack such as I'd often experienced some years ago. As I lay there I recalled the similar one I'd had in the U.P. when blazing a trail around Porcupine Bluff. Nothing to really worry about but I shakily returned to the house.

Why had that blackout happened now after so many years of being free from them? Perhaps it was because I'd been bending over too long as I pulled those weeds. In the past that had often made me dizzy. The thought came to me that perhaps my blood sugar was too low, that I'd had some diabetic hypoglycemia, so I checked my blood sugar level on the glucometer and the reading was only 42, far too low a level. I hadn't had such a level since I gave up shooting myself with insulin. Pulling out of my pocket the little bag of sugar lumps I always carry I chewed down two of them and drank a glass of milk. Soon I was feeling fine. No big deal!

Deciding I'd better take it easy I went to my study for a book to read. As always it was a visual mess. Books line three of the walls and above my typewriter are two short shelves holding the 37 books I've written. Most of them are textbooks but my favorites are the *Northwoods Readers* that have brought me so many new friends and fan letters.

For casual reading I like to choose a book at random and today I reached for one behind my back sight unseen. From the feel of it I knew immediately that it was Mackenzie's "Five Thousand Receipts: Practical Library". Bound in tattered leather and now held together by a rubber band, it had come from New Jersey to Michigan with my great grandparents before the Civil War by canal boat, sailing schooner and covered wagon. The book, published in 1829, is a fat one with very fine print. Designed for pioneers, it contains instructions for doing almost everything a settler might need to do in a new land. There are sections on agricultural practices, bees, brewing, engraving, metallurgy, indeed on any subject needed for living or survival. Opening the book I read:

"Utility of sheep dung. This is used in dyeing for the purpose of preparing cotton and linen to receive certain colours, particularly the red, which it performs by impregnating the stuffs with an animal mucilage of which it contains a great quantity."

As I browsed through the book I learned how to shoe an ox, make perfume, force rhubarb, know good mushrooms, manufacture glass and build a barn. A large segment of the book dealt with medicine and this is what it said about my congestive heart failure—then called dropsy of the chest: "Symptoms: Great difficulty breathing especially when lying down, oppression and weight in the chest, countenance pale, pulse irregular, dry cough and violent palpitation." Yes, that was what I had experienced. "Treatment: This is one of the diseases that mock the art of man. To say that it is incurable would be hazarding too much but as yet it has nearly always proved so. All that can be done is to use purging, emetics, diuretics and to have the patient abstain from any heavy toil." Not much medical progress in 170 years.

Because my eyes were tiring from the fine print I looked out of the wavy panes of my study window to see if the mail had come and the red flag on the mailbox showed that it had. Rather than go down the lane I walked along the east lilac hedge that borders the long front lawn picking off the spent flowers of red cannas and yellow marigolds that border it. When those lilacs bloomed next spring, would I be here to see them? Of course I would, and I'd bring great armfuls back to make the house fragrant. Disappointed to find only catalogues and circulars, I was elated when I found a package addressed to Cully Gage that had come from Laurium in the U.P.

Unwrapping it when I returned, I found a note: "Dear Cully Gage: You don't know me but after reading all your books I feel I know you and that you like saffron bread so here's a loaf from our little bakery." Saving the lady's name and address so I could thank her, I ate the end slice even before taking off my jacket. As our Cornish miners used to say, "I dearly love they saffron bread." My wife used to bake it about once a month and my daughter, Cathy, brings me a loaf on my birthday so it was a real treat. It's hard to find saffron Down Below.

Time for my mandatory nap. How could I do that differently? For one thing, I could change the music. No symphonies for me today. At first I considered playing one of the Yoopers cassettes, the one about the second week in deer camp that became a national hit, but rejected the idea. I'd never rest well listening to those crazy buggers. No, I'd get some Jamaican music and sleep in Abraham's bosom.

Abraham's bosom is one of the five bedrooms in this old house, one of four dormer rooms added by Dr. Henwood from whom we purchased the farm. It is named after the Biblical Abraham who lived happily for 175 years or so the Book of Genesis says. It is a comforting room and all who sleep there arise refreshed. I'd never slept in it.

House-Front View

Lying there with the sun streaming in through the casement windows and listening to Belafonte singing "Island in the Sun" I slept deeply but not until some more good memories had run their course.

Probably because of the music, most of them reflected our two holiday visits to Jamaica. Those visits occurred because one afternoon I was about to go fishing when a Cadillac arrived in our barnyard and a distinguished looking gentleman stepped out. "I'm Malcolm Fraser," he announced. "You may recall our correspondence about whether the term stammering should be used instead of stuttering. No, I'm not here to argue further about the matter but to seek your advice about how to spend a lot of money...."

I interrupted the bugger. "Mr. Fraser," I said. "Had I known you were coming I could have set up an appointment but the fishing fever is on me and I'm not interested in anything else."

"But you don't understand. Dr. Van Riper," he replied, stuttering a little as he did so. "I am the co-founder of NAPA and have established a tax exempt foundation dedicated to the relief of stuttering. To keep that tax exemption the Foundation must annually spend a portion of its considerable income. Perhaps we can give your speech clinic a substantial grant. In any event, I need your counsel since you are one of the most esteemed...."

Again I interrupted him. "No, dammit," I said. "I don't want any of your lousy money. I'm going fishing. Good day!"

As I climbed into my truck I saw him walk dejectedly back to the Cadillac and felt ashamed of myself. I've never liked hurting anyone. So I got out and accosted him. "Mr. Fraser," I asked. "Do you know how to row a boat?" When he nodded affirmatively I told him that if he'd go with me to Atwater Pond and row the boat and not say a damned word until I'd caught five fish with my flyrod I'd give him a glass of whiskey and listen to what he had to say.

But what has that to do with Jamaica? Well I told Malcolm that his Foundation should concentrate on producing books and pamphlets on stuttering because of the widespread ignorance about the disorder, that he should hold conferences to which the best brains in the country could be invited to share their expertise and to create the nuclei for the publications. "You'll have to hold these conferences during the Christmas holidays when they could be available and have them in exotic places to attract them. You should pay all expenses and also provide an honorarium so they can bring their wives along." Well, we've held those conferences in Puerto Rico, Florida, the Virgin Islands, Acapulco, the Bahamas, Hawaii and Jamaica. The project proved very successful and his Speech Foundation of America has done a lot of good.

As I lay there in Abraham's Bosom I was remembering the one we held in Montego Bay, Jamaica. Not the morning or afternoon sessions during which we tried to reach agreement on what should go into the proposed book but those wonderful evenings when we got together singing and drinking rum with a native band of musicians and having a high old time.

Neither my wife nor I nor the others had experienced such luxury. We lived in our own beach cottage complete with maid service and fresh flowers and fruit on the table when we awoke. We breakfasted in a patio covered with vines on ogli fruit, papayas, or anything we wished to order. Late in the evening we dined on escargo, oysters Rockefeller, roast pig or whatever with wine. We strolled the wide beaches and went swimming in the warm salt water. Often I asked myself what a bush bum from the U.P. was doing there.

Oh yes, and there was the occasion of Milove's seventieth birthday. I'd forgotten to bring along any present for her and our schedule prevented any shopping so I paid ten dollars to a handsome young beach boy to give her a loud wolf whistle every time he saw her. "She's the old gal in the red and white dotted bikini," I said, "the one with a fine figure."

"I've already noticed her, sir," he replied. "It will be a pleasure." Milady Katy had a fine birthday.

Realizing that for months I'd been lunching on soup, half a sandwich, milk and fruit I decided I'd eat the same things I did when hiking cross country to Lake Superior. I hard boiled an egg, cut off a small chunk of bologna and had some korpua, the delicious hard cinnamon toast of the Finns. I cheated a bit on the tea by not steeping it in a clean sock in the worm can. I ate that lunch under the pines of my park. Very good!

When I reentered the house I found a huge box in the shed. United Parcel Service had brought the bushel of daffodils I'd ordered last spring to naturalize them in the grassy area east of the pool. Well, I couldn't possibly plant them now. Perhaps I could get Ted Redmond, a husky high school kid who lived across the road, to do it for me. But I love to plant promises so much I just had to try. Getting the posthole digger and a pail of compost mixed with bonemeal I began to dig some holes next to the fireplace where the earliest flowers bloom in the spring. I dug just one hole and quit because I knew if I dug more I'd have some trouble. Using a posthole digger is hard work. Fighting off a bit of depression I sat on the bench round the big oak tree and smoked a pipe of Sir Walter Raleigh.

Day Two

This need to curtail one's activities and to fit them to one's limitations is one of the hardest things an old person has to accept. I've always liked to live recklessly, not carefully. That's why I once hiked cross country all the way from Lake Superior to Tioga in one day, a distance of forty miles. The thought of that trip, however, brought back some fine memories of spring in the U.P. Not of daffodils but of yellow cow slips, the early marsh marigolds. And of the white, blue and yellow violets that were everywhere in the woods, and of the arbutus, pink and white, with its fine fragrance.

On that long hike whole hardwood hillsides were carpeted by spring beauties, the tiny pink striped flowers so thick that I left footprints in them. Patches of trillium proudly wore their three large white petals under their green umbrellas; clumps of Dutchman's breeches were spaced with adder's tongues and blood root; occasionally I found a rare pink lady's slipper. We didn't need daffodils up there in the springtime.

Wanting to do something constructive that wouldn't require a lot of effort I decided to clean the cowbarn. That area is at the east end of the old barn and still contains the stanchions where the cows were milked, not that I've milked any there. As a boy I sometimes had to do the milking when Mrs. Waisenen who usually did it was sick. Old Rosey, our Jersey cow, was a cantankerous beast who liked to kick me off the stool or spill the milk pail. I got no pleasure from interminably squeezing her teats except when directing a stream of the milk into the mouth of a waiting cat. Over the years here I've had horses, pigs and chickens but no cow.

The cowbarn wasn't very dirty except for the droppings under the swallows' nests on the beams above and I had it cleaned up in short order. Then I went into the space behind the stanchions and swept that with the push broom and noticed something covered by a tarp. When I removed the latter I began to laugh until my sides ached. I had uncovered the mynah birds' cage.

All my life I've wanted a parrot I could teach to sing or cuss or stutter but once when I told my wife I was thinking of buying one she vetoed it with such vehemence that I gave up the idea. It seems that when she was a child she'd been bitten by one when she tried to feed it a peanut rather than a cracker.

When I mentioned that to a graduate course in speech development one of my students told me that his uncle, a psychologist at the University of Cincinnati, had just finished an experiment on the social behavior of mynah birds from India, birds that had been reared in complete isolation from each other. He said he might be able to get them for me. I told him to get them if he could because mynah birds can be taught to speak as well as parrots.

I was delighted when he returned from his Christmas vacation with them and, my wife being away at the time, I set up their big cage in my study. A fait accompli! When she returned and found them she was hot tongued for a bit but calmed down when I told her it was only a temporary experiment in teaching birds to talk and that mynahs weren't parrots. I said I'd do all the caretaking and she could keep the study door closed. "OK," she said, "I'll give you a month and then let in the cat."

The psychologist had told my student that trying to teach them to talk was a hopeless task, that their long isolation would make it impossible and that the age of speech readiness had long been passed. In reply, the student had told his uncle that I was the best speech therapist in the world and that I'd prove him wrong.

Old Bones And Northern Memories

When I told The Madam that my reputation was at stake, she sniffed, a most unwise thing to do if you have mynah birds in the vicinity. Like geese, they are dirty birds, producing incredible amounts of excrement with a stink that would wither the nostrils of a polecat. Though the mynahs are long gone from my study and many years have passed, I can still smell Jack and Jackie every time it rains.

According to some psychologists, birds learn to talk because the human beings who tend them speak to them as they are being fondled or fed. Then, whenever the bird happens to make a similar sound, it remembers the feeling's of comfort and relief that had been associated with those sounds and so emits more of them to get that rewarding experience. The bird must also fall in love with you or it won't talk. That means you must love it too.

Well, I tried but it's hard to love a dirty bird with a quivering and squirting hind end. Besides, Jack and Jackie were not at all loveable. They regarded me with hostile eyes and tried constantly to take a chunk out of my fingers when I sought to touch them or clean out their cage which needed it hourly. Finally I learned how to slip one newspaper in and the other one out without being pecked to the bone. I had to subscribe to the New York Times to keep even with their south ends. Lord, how they shat!

And they were mute as a stone. Not even a twitter did I hear those first days. Perhaps the psychologist was right. The birds had been reared in separate cages; now they shared one and I hoped that love or lust might give a more favorable prognosis. One trouble was that I wasn't really sure that Jack and Jackie were of different sexes. Perhaps they were mynahsexuals. They did peck at each other perfunctorily but did not ogle or preen. Why was I spoiling my life with feathered imbeciles? But I've had other resistant patients and have taught mute children and deaf ones to talk. There was always a way. All problems had solutions. I changed another newspaper.

The insight finally came. They needed a model with whom they could identify. Having never heard another bird, they had to hear birdsong. Not having any canaries I went to the piano and played "Listen to the Mocking Bird" on the highest notes of the keyboard. Immediately they began to hop around excitedly, ruffling their feathers and cocking their heads to one side. Then, as I continued to play, they began to utter sounds of great variety: gurglings, whistles, rattles, cackles and a few true vowels. I hurriedly fed them and left the study hollering "Eureka!" like Archimedes in his bathtub. The Madam surveyed me coldly. "Happy New Year," she said.

That weekend I hardly left the study except to eat. Once my wife brought me a sandwich, a birdseed sandwich, but I had found a way to get them to vocalize. I could do it every time-just play the black keys on the piano and the birds would stop crapping and start making sounds. All I had to do was to reinforce with food the human sounding vowels that they produced and then later to shape these into human utterance. My first target was to be "Hello!", then later I would teach them to say, "Hello, you damned psychologist," and send them back to him to crap in his lap. Or so I dreamed.

The training was difficult. Once I got them vocalizing to the piano I had to imitate their vowels in unison, then feed them quickly with a few sunflower seeds, their favorite food. Under this schedule the number of their vowel sounds markedly increased. A transcription of one morning's utterances yielded the following: Jack: a, (as in cat) 68 times; e (as in met) 6 times; o five times. Jackie said about the same but also combined two vowels to produce a-o and eh-o. These I recorded on a tape recorder and I could identify which one was speaking because Jack's pitch was lower than that of the other mynah. Surprisingly, they rarely spoke at the same time but took turns. So did I.

After about a week of this training. The Madam opened the study door and presented me with a care package. The birds eyed me with interest as I unwrapped it. Inside were pictures of my children and of the university, a jar of peanut butter, some crackers and a safety razor blade with a note saying, "I'm not going home to mother, no matter what!" Somehow I got the impression that she was hinting at something.

I'll have to admit that I was getting pretty sick of those dirty devils by that time. Often I had the disturbing thought that they were training me rather than I training them, making me bring them food and drink and play the piano and clean their damned cage. Often they seemed to smile!

When one day I heard Jack chuckle and Jackie produce a very human sounding laugh, I knew that I needed emancipation so I went down to the university and brought home a new recorder with a voice-activated switch that would turn on automatically whenever the birds made a sound. I then prepared a loop of tape on which I recorded my rendition of Listen to the Mocking Bird and my loving imitations of their vowels, especially the eh-o combinations, and "Hello" spoken in a high falsetto. It worked! Through the closed study door I listened and found that the birds were talking more than when I was in the room. So I kissed Milove and went ice fishing. As I knelt there, slowly congealing, watching the cork in the hole and breathing fresh air for a change, I felt a tingle of triumph. I'd outwit those birdy bastards yet. A man had more brains than a mynah.

After two days of this tape recorder therapy Jack and Jackie were producing the two target vowels profusely and saying them in sequence and even at times saying something that sounded like hello. Then I made a new tape loop that just said the hello over and over again.

Finally one morning when I opened the study door I was greeted by a very clear "Hello" from Jackie. La dee dah! I did The Dance of the Wild Cucumber and called my wife, but the damned bird wouldn't do it again. The Madam gave me one of those strange looks that had characterized her of late, held her nose, and departed without a word.

But Jackie had said hello, and said it a lot of other times that day. I turned on the other recorder and left for the university. When I returned, I played the recording with great anticipation. Yes, I'd done it. Both birds were saying hello although Jack's rendition sounded more like "Allah," A Moslem bird, no doubt, though he didn't say it at all prayerfully. No problem! I could shape his Allah into Hello. I slept well that night, though again alone. How long had it been that Milove had moved to another bedroom?

The next morning I arose before dawn, entered the dark study, changed the newspapers in the cage, filled the pellet container, set the two recorders to going and left for the university, planning to return at 9:30 for a late breakfast. At 8:30 my secretary barged into my office. "Your wife is on the phone and she's crying and swearing and told me to get you even if you're in class. I think you'd better answer it."

The Madam was almost incoherent in her fury but I got the message. I'd left the cage door open when I changed the papers in the dark and left the study door open too. Those damned birds of mine were flying all over the house, defecating everywhere and she had locked herself in the kitchen and couldn't get her coat and hat to get out of there and when

I got home and I'd better get home soon, she'd strangle me with her own hands and enjoy every gasp. There was more sobbing and terror and insult. I hung up the receiver and scratched my head. It was more than a crisis; it was a domestic catastrophe. It was a choice between Milove or two dirty birds. She was a fine woman; she had given me three fine children. She had given me love and apple pie.

So I called in the student who had brought me the birds, told him to buy a long handled net and to get the hell out to my house, catch the birds and take them to our biology department if he hoped to have his assistantship renewed. And then to go back and clean up the mess.

When I got home at noon the birds were gone and with the exception of a broken lamp and two shattered pictures all was well. For half an hour she gave me the silent treatment and then let me have it. I hunched my head down into my neck and bore it, feeling like the peasant described by the Roman poet Horace who waited for the river to run by so he could cross. Once again I was glad I'd had a classical education because I recalled the tale of Socrates who, staggering home one night after some boozy dialogues with the boys, had found the door locked. When he knocked, his wife opened the window above the door and laced into him. Like my wife, Xantippe was most eloquent when furious, and like Milove, the longer she ranted the madder she got. Finally she even got a chamber pot and dumped its contents onto the head of the philosopher. Socrates stood there and wiped his brow. "After the thunder, comes the rain," said he.

All things, good and evil, eventually end. The Madam forgave me and we lived many years in domestic tranquility ever since. Except once, when on a damp day she entered my study and I said "Ello!, Ello," in a high falsetto.

The rest of this day passed quietly but always differently. For Happy Hour I drank wine instead of scotch, ate my supper standing up, and went to bed, climbing the back stairs instead of the front ones. It had been another good day.

Day Three

This day began at two in the morning in the middle of the Manistee National Forest in southern Michigan when John Eaton and his akita dog went outdoors to relieve themselves.

But I'd better make some introductions. John Eaton came to do part time work for me shortly after my wife died six years ago. After serving four years in the Marine Corps he decided to get a college education and needed to work to supplement the meager college subsidy given to four year veterans. A short but very tough and strong man and very intelligent, he has become a fine companion, friend, almost a son. He mows my lawns, does my banking, dresses my surgical wounds, buys my groceries, rototills the gardens, and with the chainsaw has kept my barn filled with wood for the winters. Indeed, he does everything I used to do but cannot do now. I've often taken him up to my lakes deer hunting and fishing and he loves that land almost as much as I do. I've been blessed and very lucky to have found him.

The akita is John's dog of a hunting breed that served Japanese royalty for centuries. Bigger than a German shepherd, it is covered with a heavy white coat of hair except for a black face and pointed ears that stick straight up. John calls him Teddy which doesn't fit his dignity at all. He should be called Hirohito or something such. Usually very aloof, Teddy likes me and we howl at each other whenever we meet. Hunting the farm joyously, he has killed many of the woodchucks that have plagued me for years. I've always had dogs, mostly springer spaniels, but for obvious reasons do not have one now. Perhaps that is why I enjoy Teddy so much.

What were we doing up there in my little cabin on Gut Lake? I guess it was that my hunger to see the fall colors had overcome my good sense. This year many of my U.P. correspondents had written that the foliage was absolutely spectacular, the best it had ever been and they had pictures to prove it. Photos, however, are no substitute for the real thing. For many years I've made the long trip north to see them and, before the heart failure, had intended to do so again. Down here the autumn colors are dull, mainly dirty yellows or the bronze of oak, none of the little sugar maples I'd brought down had survived to burst into red flame as they do in the U.P. Why are the fall colors so much better up north? Perhaps the Lord thoroughly soaks the souls up there with gorgeous colors so they can make it through the long months of black and white.

Feeling that I needed some of that soaking if I too were to survive the winter I decided to spend the weekend at the little cabin because it is only about a three hour drive from here and because in other years I've found some fairly good colors there around our little lake. Knowing my doctor would probably say no, I didn't tell him. So one Friday evening after John had finished his work on the construction job, north we went.

Before we started I told John we'd make two stops, first at the rest stop on US-131 near Grand Rapids and the other at Half Moon Lake Park near the little town of Grant. I'd get out, walk around, and then decide whether to continue or to return. Even though the colors along the roadside were no better than those here, it was good to be heading north.

When we reached the rest area I was feeling fine and told John to drive on but by the time we reached Half Moon Lake the usual profound fatigue was present though my pulse was strong and regular. Teddy loves that park and knows every tree in it so we spent fifteen minutes there as I recuperated. By this time it was dusk and on we went through Grant, Newago and White Cloud. Crossing the Muskegon River at Newago I told John how once a friend and I had canoed down to that bridge from the headwaters, a two and a half day trip. Sure couldn't do it now. Finally, just south of Baldwin, we left M-37 and took a road to Bitely, then westward to the little dirt road that goes to our cabin in the forest, seeing in the headlights one deer and the eyes of several others.

While John took off the padlocks, removed the internal shutters from the windows and made a fire, I sat in the car before staggering in to flop myself down in the big Morris chair. I felt triumphant. Damned if I hadn't made it. While Teddy roamed in the dark woods, John fixed me a good dollop of whiskey and water which made me feel even better. Hell, I'd be able to make it back to the U.P. next spring. The exhilaration didn't last long, however, and after a sandwich and some milk I crawled into my sleeping bag and fell asleep instantly.

It must have been John banging the gong that woke me. Oh yes, I should tell you about that gong. It's really a large brass cymbal, the kind they use in a band or orchestra. It hangs about four feet from the ground from a cross bar between two trees right in front of the cabin. Camp Rule No.1 states that any man who has to take a leak must do so under the gong, then celebrate his masculinity by banging it with his dong while yelling "Ow!" So far as I know, no one has ever obeyed that rule due to shortage of courage, stature, or appendage and a convenient club also hangs from the crossbar so they can pretend to have done so. Anyway, the gong woke me but soon I was asleep again.

Shortly thereafter John was tugging at my sleeping bag. "I need some help," he said.'Teddy has tangled with a porcupine. Having once stepped on some quills, I put on my shoes to see Teddy's face covered with them.We tried rolling him in a blanket and pulling out the quills with pliers but there were just too many of them. All of us had a hard night and I slept little because Teddy kept trying to crawl in with me for comfort. Finally came the dawn and after a short breakfast I told John to take Teddy to Baldwin in search of a veterinarian, and if there were none in that town, to any other place where he might find one, even if it meant going back to Grand Rapids.

They didn't return until afternoon but a vet in Reed City had done a fine job. John said he had to remove over fifty quills while the dog was sedated.

So I had the morning to myself and it was a very good one. Venturing outside I found our little lake surrounded with scarlet and clear yellow contrasts with the green of the pines I'd planted years ago. I sat on a log for a long time just looking.

Then, needing to limber up the old legs I walked the trails, finding memories with every step.The rhododendrons I had planted were eight feet tall, the three mountain ash had berries and robins in them; the dogwoods wore that indescribable pink sheen. As far as I could see, the open woods were dotted with pines and spruce that had been only six inch seedlings when I planted them. When we first built the cabin twenty six years ago there had been no green firs at all, just poplars, soft maples and oaks. A man from the U.P. needs firs and pines in his forest so I had put in over four thousand of them. They are my children too. When a bright yellow leaf zigzagged down and settled on my head I wore it back to the cabin. I had been anointed.

Opening the cabin door I noticed that above the doorway the phoebes had left the nest they had built there year after year. How they would scold us with their name when we opened it! I also recalled the sound of whippoorwills and the gobbles of wild turkeys. Once again the magic of the forest was healing me and making me young again.

This was Milove's favorite cabin though she loved those in the U.P. too, especially the old hunting cabin where we'd honeymooned. Perhaps it was that here the forest was not so wild or threatening. Besides she had selected the site, and bought all the furnishings. Here she roamed freely without having to watch out for bears. She never forgot the time when we were trout fishing on the Tioga and a mother bear chased us away from her cub and we got back to the car just before the bear did.

How vividly I felt her presence! There on the far wall hung her red rain jacket, her sweater, and the silly little hat she'd purchased in the Bahamas. On a sunny afternoon she'd row out into the middle of Gut Lake (which she insisted was Blue Lake), lie down in the bottom and let the boat drift with the wind.

Even the log walls reminded me of her. Because of the many coats of preservative she'd put on them they seemed almost newly cut while outside they had turned grey. I found the camp log in which both of us had written much about the doings of our days there and opened it to see her handwriting. "September 7-9. Cully and I got here after dark again in the rain and someone had burned up all the firewood I'd sawed after lugging maple poles from the lakeshore. Don't you ever do that again without replacing them." "June 17, 1972. Cully was napping when I looked out the window to see four wild turkeys striding up the road, one a very big one with a wide fan tail and red wattles below its beak but by the time I roused him they were gone. He saw their big forked tracks though so he knew I hadn't been imagining."

Yet another item from the log: "I am blessed to be back here with the man I love. He had the coffee made and the pancakes too before he tickled my feet to wake me up. Luxury!"

Still feeling the effects of the trip and loss of sleep, I crawled into the bunk again and didn't awaken until John and Teddy returned. The akita seemed to be in fine shape and after a swift lunch they left to do some flyfishing though I told John it would probably be fruitless. There were no flies and at that time of the year the bass and bluegills would be deep. They went anyway though Teddy wouldn't enter the boat but just prowled the shoreline, then swam out to the boat and almost tipped it over when John hauled him into it. That ended the fishing. As they climbed the steep hill from the lake I envied them knowing I'd never be able to do that again. Yet it was very good just to be sitting on the steps surrounded by beauty.

Just west of Gut Lake lies another little lake. Bass Lake, a shallow one surrounded by muskeg. I think I told about it once in one of my *Northwoods Readers* because I almost drowned in it. I'd shot a goose and trying to reach it with a long pole by going out on that floating muskeg I almost drowned but I had survived. I would survive this heart trouble too. Along the northwest shore of Bass Lake there often are cranberries in the muskeg moss and for years my wife and I had gathered our Thanksgiving cranberries there so I asked John to see if he couldn't find some. To show him the old logging road that went to the lake I walked part way with him and the akita and was bushed when I returned. It's hard to grow old. Taking a folding camp chair I brought it out to the firepit where we do most of our summer cooking. A little breeze had sprung up and the tall poplars waved their tall tops slowly back and forth shedding a few yellow leaves with each swing. As I sat there I remembered how Ken Frielink and I had tried to dig a well there. One of the few bad features of this little cabin is that we have to bring up our drinking water in jugs because the lake water is too full of sediment except for use in cooking.

When I was a boy in the U.P. there was an old man named Nels Peterson who was the town's dowser. Everyone said that he could always find good water and called on him before they dug their open wells. The story was that a man who thought dowsing was all nonsense once dug a hole five feet down and planted a jug of water in it, then after the field had been plowed and planted to oats, he challenged Nels to find the jug. It took Nels only ten minutes to find it or so the tale went. I, myself, watched the old man picking a well site for the Plankeys who lived three doors down from us. With a forked branch that had a substantial stub, Nels curled his fingers over each branch, held it horizontally before him and walked around the yard. Suddenly the stub went down as though some hidden force had hold of it. I could see the tension in his arms as he resisted the pull. "Dig yer well here," he told the Plankeys and when they did they found fine water only nine feet down. Nels said that the best dowsing sticks came from willow or applewood but that many people didn't have the feel for deep water that he did. He also said he had so much of it he'd even found water with a wire coat hanger.

Ken borrowed a drilling rig from a friend and we loaded it onto my truck with four sections of pipe, a perforated well point and some big monkey wrenches. I brought along a dowsing stick I'd cut from our apple orchard and when we got to the cabin we took turns exploring the area on top of the hill. There was only one spot where the stick dipped a little and that was near the gong so we tried there.

Phew! That drilling was hard work. The drilling rig looked like a guillotine except that instead of a sharp blade there was a very heavy steel bar that slid up and down in the tower's grooves. We first had to crank up the bar so it was above the pipe bearing the drill bit, lock it in place, disengage the chain, then unlock the catch and bam! down it went. Sometimes the blow would pound the pipe down a foot; at other times only a few inches. When the first pipe had been driven, we pulled it up and examined the point. It was dry as a bone with not a hint of water on it. So we added another length of pipe, drove that down too. Nothing! Before giving up we had gone down twenty five feet without finding water. So we drank the rest of the beer, had supper, and went to bed exhausted.

The next morning I was ready to call it quits but Ken suggested that we move the rig down near the lake. "We'll drive down just one length of pipe," he said. "We're bound to find water so close to the lake. Even if it's lake water, it will be filtered enough for drinking."

He was wrong. After all that tough work of dragging the rig down the hill, we again got only a dry hole. Incredible! Why, we'd drilled it not six feet from the water's edge.

I found out later that our lake was what was called a pot hole or fault lake, that when the glacier retreated a great mountain of ice had broken off and settled there compressing the clay beneath it into an impermeable basin.So that is why we bring up our water in jugs.

John and the akita had returned. The dog had chased a raccoon up into a hollow tree and John had found a big handful of cranberries. Remembering The Madam's admonition in the log book and because it was getting much cooler I asked him to get some dry maple poles and cut them with the chainsaw into stove lengths and also to saw and split that big oak limb by the outhouse so we could have good coals for our steaks.

While he did so I took another little walk down the road and on my return I noticed a large oval patch of moss near where we park our car. I blew Milove a kiss. That moss was all that remained of the nine by twelve braided rug that she had made for our living room floor. How hard she had worked on that rug all one winter, cutting and sewing strips, winding them into balls,then doing the hard work of braiding them together. Once I caught her weeping because of the bursitis it gave her but when the rug was finished it was beautiful. Mainly blue and tan, it contained rags made of wool clothing, some of it donated by friends who used to enjoy coming out to identify their old coats and pants. After many years of having dogs and children romping on it or lying on it to watch the fire, the rug began to disintegrate a little. I couldn't bear to throw it away so brought it up to the little cabin for several more years. Finally, when she suggested I take it to the Bitely dump, I spread it out by our parking spot. Now it was moss, beautiful moss. Perhaps I would be moss too someday.

I sat outside for a time by the firepit watching the fire burn down into coals until the trees lost their color, then went inside to build a fire in the stove, light the kerosene lamps and candles, and set the table. Very snug and cozy as always, the radiating warmth felt good. Old bones appreciate warmth and young ones do too on a cool evening.

How beautiful Milove always looked by candlelight, even when she was in her seventies.

The steaks and mashed potatoes were excellent. "Pierre," I said. "You have acquired merit." Full fed, I dozed in my chair while John did the dishes and Teddy munched the steak bones. Then, when John announced that he and Teddy were going for their evening walk by flashlight, I crawled into my sleeping bag and never heard them return.

The next morning I roused when I smelled the coffee and bacon and heard John cooking. He'd made cranberry pancakes, the first I'd ever eaten. They were delicious. Outside it was raining hard so we packed, cleaned up the place, and left for home.

The miles sped by swiftly after I got John to telling about his boot camp experiences in the Marines. He described the "Slide for Life" where he had to climb sixty feet to a platform, then slide down a plastic coated wire over water while the damned drill sergeant tried to shake him off. He told how in the gas chamber he had to take off the gas mask, give his name, rank and serial number, and put the gas mask on again before he could open the door. He described the Stairway to Heaven which consisted of two tall telephone poles with cross pieces increasing spaced so that for the last one he had to jump to reach it. Oh, he had a lot of good tales.

John even began to sing some Marine songs, one of them which went: "I put my hand upon her toe/Yo ho,Yo Ho/ I put my hand upon her toe/ She said. Marine, you're mighty slow/ Yo Ho, Yo ho." The rest of it is unprintable. Then, when we passed through Newago I saw a handprinted sign in a store window advertising an auction bake social. That reminded me of a similar social in Tioga seventy years ago so I told it to John. Here is the tale:

In the Upper Peninsula of Michigan, the U.P., February was the cruelest month of the year. Great drifts of snow confined our people to their homes and each week brought a new blizzard. Spring was just an impossible dream.

However, there was one year when I was a senior in high school that the Methodist church decided to ease our depression by holding an auction box social in the town hall. Hand printed notices were put up in the postoffice and stores: "Free admittance! Dancing! Ice Cream! Auction of baked goods made by pretty girls! Nuts to winter!"

The preparations for the event took a lot of work. Girls and women baked cakes and cookies and pies and put them in gaily decorated boxes. The Town Hall's two big pot bellied stoves had to be fired up for two days and nights. Because my mother had volunteered my services in setting up the tables and chairs and streamers, I was there when the girls brought in their boxes to be placed on the long auction table. I especially noticed the one brought in by Amy Erickson, the prettiest girl in Tioga, thinking I might bid on it myself. No, she was Mullu's girl and I was his friend. I'd tell him that her box was the one with the yellow and red ribbons. There was one other box, the biggest one, almost two feet square and bearing an artificial rose on its top. When Billy Simons, our Sunday School Superintendent, saw who brought it I was shocked to hear that pious man swear for five minutes. Aunt Lizzie had brought it. 'Oh, that damned old fool," he roared. "She'll put the kibosh on the bidding, she will that!" Aunt Lizzie had buried three husbands but she was still looking, and still thought of herself as a girl though she was in her late sixties.

By suppertime everything was ready. Twenty chairs were set along the west wall where the girls who brought boxes would sit; three more by one stove for the accordion players, and the table for the cookie and ice cream server was by the other. A big blue enamel coffee pot was kept warm on that one too.

Near the stage was the auctioneer's table and change box. Behind the stage were bleachers for those who didn't want to bid but wanted to see the fun.

We usually eat supper early in winter time so the doors opened at seven and soon quite a crowd had assembled. Most of them just bought an ice cream cone and cookie and sat in the bleachers to watch the doings. Then the girls filed in to sit on the chairs and among them was Aunt Lizzie wearing one of her wedding dresses and with a little blue bow in her wig. Then men and boys went over to the auction table to examine the boxes, shaking and sniffing, before forming a cluster by a stove to wait for the auction to begin.

Billy Simons, the auctioneer, laid down the rules. The first bid must be at least twenty five cents and increments of no less than ten cents would be allowed. The men should step forward before bidding to identify themselves. When he banged his gavel, the bidding was over and the last bidder got the box. He would then open the box and show its contents to everyone before picking up the card that said, "Congratulations. Your partner for the evening is so and so. Take the box to her and then dance. After the auction is over there will be free dancing for everyone."

Although I had no intention of bidding I was there with my friends Mullu and Fisheye among the men when I had a brilliant idea. I'd tell Mullu, who was nuts about Amy, which box was hers but I'd tell Toivo Maki who had bullied us for years and who also had a crush on Amy that Aunt Lizzie's big box was really Amy's. A dirty trick but I had a lot to get even for. Wait a minute! I'd better not tell Toivo that or he'd kill me! So I called Mullu and Fisheye aside and told them my plan. We'd go over by Toivo and let him overhear me telling Mullu that the big box was Amy's, and Mullu should make the first bid on it. Then he should drop out after Toivo started bidding and Mullu could really bid on the real box of Amy's which I described. Mullu protested at first.

"But what if Toivo doesn't fall for it?" he asked, "and I'm stuck with Aunt Lizzie? Hell, they'll laugh me out of town." We assured him that someone was sure to bid for that big box so he agreed. And the deed was almost done.

After the band played its first number the auction began and at first it looked as though it would be a disaster. When Billy picked up the first box at random and held it in the air nobody bid. Nobody! He picked up another and the silence was deafening. We knew why. All the men were looking at Aunt Lizzie and anticipating the outrageous kidding they'd suffer for months if the box they got was Aunt Lizzie's. They weren't playing any Russian roulette, no sir!

Finally when Billy held up a third box Pipu Verlaine bid fifty cents because Marie, his girlfriend, had tipped him off. That broke the ice somewhat. A few other men upped the bid and it finally sold for Pipu's ninety cents. Another box brought a dollar from Eino Hyry who showed all of us the delectable angel food cake before taking it to Lempi Salo, his long time girlfriend. The band played a waltz and Pipu and Eino and their girls danced. After two more boxes went without any bids. Billy Simons got mad and gave the men hell. He shamed them; he cajoled them; he reminded them how hard so many pretty girls had worked. Then he held up the big box. "Now which of you boogers has the guts to bid a quarter for this lovely one. In it must be a big cake, and cookies, even a pie? Who'll pay a lousy quarter for all this and a pretty girl too?"

Mullu gulped his bid of fifty cents and Toivo countered with seventy five. Other men joined in. Great excitement! Even when the bidding hit a dollar, Toivo wouldn't give in. "One fifty!" yelled another man and you could see Toivo sweating. When you earned only five cents for felling and limbing a big spruce tree, that was big money, but when Amy smiled at him, up he went. Finally, at two fifty the auctioneer yelled sold and banged his gavel. Toivo forked over the money to Billy and opened the box. Yes, there was a huge chocolate cake inside and some peanut butter cookies and other stuff too. The crowd ooh'd and ah'd. "Who's yer partner, Toivo?" they yelled.

Toivo reached for the card and stood there stunned, then bolted from the hall with Aunt Lizzie after him though not before she'd snatched up her box. "Bet she catches him," one man yelled. "Naw, Toivo can run like a deer," shouted another.

After things quieted down, the auction went very well and all of the boxes were sold and lots of people had a high old time doing the polka for the rest of the evening. The church gained over fifty dollars and Tioga had a break in the middle of winter.

We got back to the farm and after a bite to eat I slept until evening. It had been a fine weekend and I hadn't had a bit of heart trouble. I'd be back, Old Cabin.

Day Four

As I opened the back door and saluted the new morning I saw that it would be another fine Indian summer day, most surprising because November rarely had them. We'd had two light frosts, enough to wither most of the flowers, though some of the more sheltered ones were still blooming, but very low temperatures had been predicted and probably would soon be forthcoming. I decided to have breakfast in my Secret Garden.

I wish you could see that Secret Garden in all of its spring or summer glory although even now just before winter begins it is still a beautiful spot. Located against the west wall of the garage and encircled by dense flowering shrubs and a fence covered with vines, visitors would never know it was there unless I showed them.

Secret Garden

In its center stands a crabapple tree and about it are circles of red and white impatiens, begonias and red salvias creating one huge bouquet. These in turn are surrounded by a circular path and outside it grow lilies, cardinal flowers, astilbe and many annuals. Springtime brings a riot of crocus, daffodils and tulips. Now, in November just the flowers around the crabapple tree were still blooming.

I had my breakfast, a modest one, sitting within an arbor covered by clematis and wild cucumber vines. Across from me a fountain leaped in a large cast iron kettle once used for scalding hogs in the fall or for boiling down maple syrup in the spring. Watching that fountain flinging its droplets about in wild abandon almost hypnotizes me. For both Milove and me the Secret Garden has been a sanctuary within a sanctuary.

It certainly wasn't a very beautiful area when we bought the farm in 1945 but just a garbage dump full of junk, rusty cans, and broken bottles. For a few years after I cleaned it out we used the space as a chicken yard with the coop being in the north section of the garage. Behind the arbor where we sit is a hole in the garage covered by a plaque which reads: "And they shall sit, every man under his own vine and under his fig tree: Micah 4:4". Through that hole the chickens entered their yard until the foxes entered it too and made way with them. Though I still sit under the vine our hard winters made it necessary to bring the fig tree into the house where it has flourished for decades, yielding just one fig in all that time and that was inedible.

The breakfast I brought out to the arbor was a sparse one, just an orange, two pieces of toast and a chunk of Havarti cheese. I guess I was just too anxious to get out into the Secret Garden. But as I ate it I tried to recall the best breakfasts I'd ever had. Two of them came to mind immediately, the first one in a quaint little hotel in Ireland and the other on top of Donegal's Bluff in the U.P.

Having had an Irish ancestress, my wife had always wanted to go to Ireland so when Dr. Damste of the University of Utrecht in the Netherlands asked me to come there to help dedicate his new speech clinic I told her she could have two weeks in the Emerald Isle. Once there, we hired a driver, Malachi McMullen, to help us explore the back roads in the southeast corner of the country along the River Shannon and the coast. It was a wonderful trip. I caught some trout in a lake below an old castle; we had tea beside a peat fire in an ancient stone cottage; we met a caravan of gypsies on a little winding road lined with great mossy stones. And we had that breakfast.

It wasn't anything fancy, just oranges, coffee, scones with marmalade and an omelet. But what an omelet! Milove always was proud of her omelets with good reason. She baked them in the oven and insisted we eat them immediately before they fell because they were two inches tall.

But the one we had in Killarney, a ham omelet, surpassed even the best ones of Milove. Fully three inches tall and with a light brown crust, it so impressed my wife that she went to the kitchen to ask the chef how he'd made it. "My husband says I make the best omelet in America," she told the little red haired cook, "but yours is much better. Please tell me your secret."

He grinned. "Ah, ma'am," he replied. "'Tis no secret. I just use a bicycle pump to aerate the whipped eggs." When we got home and I offered to buy her a bicycle pump she said no, that from his grin she knew he'd just been kidding.

The only other breakfast that could compare with that Irish one I ate on top of Donegal's Bluff which is the first one north of the fourth bridge on the Huron Bay Grade road near Tioga. That very tall bluff rising alone from the plain was named after Old Blue Balls, Tioga's tough school superintendent, because he had tented on top of it for a week in June one year when the mosquitoes and black flies were so fierce camping down on the river bank was not bearable. I was there to escape them too.

Arising at dawn from the balsam bed I'd made the evening before I cooked coffee and six small brook trout, frying them with bacon until they were almost crisp, then eating them as I would sweet corn. These with korpua and a pint of wild strawberries comprised that wonderful breakfast. Perhaps it was my surroundings that made the meal so memorable. High up on that great granite hill I could see the Tioga winding for a mile or more, a curving ribbon of white fog tinted a delicate pink by a rising sun.

There in the Secret Garden as I was smoking my pipe after a lesser breakfast John Eaton and his akita dog, Teddy, appeared. As he always does, the dog ran right to the fountain to drink from it as John said, "Don't you think we'd better get rid of some of these early fallen leaves?"

I told him to do so but to shred them first with the big tractor and to put them in the old horse drinking trough or the holding cage by the compost heap. As he left to get the tractor I envied him. I've always loved putting the farm to bed for the winter, always enjoyed playing in the leaves. While doing the breakfast dishes and tidying up the house I thought about how we got ready for winter in the U.P. When leaves had fallen a flurry of activity spread all over Tioga. The chicken coop behind my father's hospital had to be filled a foot deep with leaves, the old sawdust from the ice house shoveled out to make room for the new ice we'd get from the lake, the collapsible storm shed for the front door had to be reassembled. Inside our house the big radiant coal stove with its isinglass windows had to be brought from the woodshed into the living room by Charlie Olafson, the only man in town strong enough to handle it. Stove pipes were taken down and cleaned and chains lowered down the chimneys to scrape off the creosote. All the house windows were washed before putting on the storm windows.

Our clotheslines were full of woolen clothing and my father's beaverskin coat and hat to eliminate the smell of moth balls. Dad's 1914 Model-T Ford needed to be jacked up and put on blocks. Not until after the spring break-up made the two-rut roads passable again would it be used.

One of my jobs was to sandpaper the runners of the cutter (sleigh) until they gleamed because it was in it that my father made his house calls. I also rubbed neatsfoot oil on all the harness of Old Billy, the horse that pulled the cutter. Also, since he often made calls on snowshoes I revarnished the webbing.

At this time of year it was always fun to go down into our cellar. From long hanging shelves, filled with jars of fruit and jellies, hung cabbages, braided onions and the like. In one corner sat a big barrel of apples; in another were crocks of sauerkraut or pickles. Three large bags of potatoes lay against one wall, a crate of rutabagas near them. On the dirt floor mouse traps and rat traps held their cheeses. We were ready for winter. Let it come!

Hearing John on the big tractor I just couldn't stay inside on such a fine day so I began to rake the leaves from the flower beds by the house out onto the lawn so he could shred them. It went very well at first but when I got under the big black walnut tree the leaves were hard to handle because too many twigs clogged the rake. That tree, by the way, is the largest black walnut I've ever seen. It towers above the house and has a circumference of eleven feet. A man once offered me a thousand dollars for it but no deal! Anyway it produces a lot of leaves as well as bushels of nuts, so many I burn them in the fireplace. When I became aware that I was getting out of breath I quit immediately.

As I entered the house the phone rang. After introducing herself, a woman said that she was a newly appointed board member of the Portage Historical Commission and would appreciate being able to tour the old house and hear something of its history. Some of the other members of the board would like to come too. I told her I could see them any time after three that afternoon.

After the phone call I went through the house trying to see it through their eyes. It was clean enough and all I had to do was put away some clothes lying on chairs in my bedroom and to carry some empty fruit jars to the cellar. I've improved a lot in neatness since my wife died, not wanting to become a dirty old man. I do my dishes after each meal and make my bed when I leave it.

Old House - Rear View

The rest of the morning was spent writing my first Christmas cards because I felt I'd better get an early start on them lest my condition deteriorated. Once again I missed Milove who always did that job. After my daily nap and lunch I got the mail and was sitting on the circular bench when my visitors arrived. Strangers sometimes gasp when they enter the house because it is not only very old but very beautiful. These ladies did too. They marveled at the nine foot doors and eleven foot walls and the spaciousness. When I told them the inner walls were also of double brick, they then thumped them to make sure. They noticed the wavy window panes and the heavy white woodwork.

"Please tell us what you know about the history of this lovely old house," they begged.

"Oh, there's too much to tell," I answered. "You can find most of what I know in a book I wrote called 'Our House' which is in the Portage Library. But briefly, it was built before the Civil War in 1859 by Steven Howard who was one of our first settlers to come to this region. Led by his father John Howard who had hauled cannonballs to George Washington's army and who had witnessed the surrender of Cornwallis, the Howards came here in 1831 to build the first log cabin on Dry Prairie across the street from this house. Old John lived long enough to have been in this house many times and to sit by a fire similar to the one you're watching now. In the early years the house was heated by three fireplaces and a cookstove. The one in the dining room has been covered with plaster and wallpaper but you can see the one in my study hidden behind my desk."

When I led them to it they exclaimed over the stuff that clutters my study, the arrowheads I found on the farm, the case of stuffed birds which includes a passenger pigeon shot by my grandmother. The species died out in 1913 so it's a rare item.

One of the women noticed the four foot slab above my desk bearing my carved signature: "Cully Gage" so I had to tell them about my alter ego and show them the *Northwoods Readers* I'd written under that pen name. I have a set of them with the many textbooks I've written on the double shelf above my typewriter so they soon were exploring. One lady pulled down a copy of the Korean translation of one of them and asked if any of my books had been published in other languages. Questions like that always bug me but I managed to say a polite yes without elaborating.

When they returned to the living room I asked them if they'd like some coffee or tea and when they said they'd prefer the latter I told them they'd have to make it but could use the fragile fluted china cups that had come to Michigan by canal boat, sailing schooner and covered wagon. As they busied themselves in the kitchen I rested in my big armchair and smoked a pipe. I was tiring.

As they sat in the living room sipping their tea and eating the korpua I gave them, I told them some more about the first brick house in Portage. The Howards had held parties here to buy uniforms for the soldiers during the Civil War, according to Steven's granddaughter whom we had interviewed at the age of ninety-three when she was in a nursing home. Steven was a short, jolly man with a useless right arm caused when on a very windy day he had gone to the loft of the barn to close the upper door. A strong gust had blown open that door carrying Steven with it and he'd fallen twenty feet to the ground. Despite that bad arm I discovered in the Agricultural Reports for 1870 that he had nine horses, seven pigs, four cows and two hundred sheep; that the farm had produced 700 bushels of corn, 300 bushels of wheat, 400 bushels of oats, thirty tons of hay and six hundred pounds of wool. Not bad for a man with only one good arm. I suppose he had hired help. After Steven and his wife Catharine died, his two sons worked the farm but did not live here. His daughter, Amanda, and her aunt Belda did and when Belda died, Amanda lived here alone until she went insane, tearing off her clothes and dancing nakedly in the fields before they put her in the State Hospital. Sometimes at night I hear her screaming.

The next people to live in the house were the Henwoods. Dr. Henwood, a highly respected physician, ran a dairy farm here and made numerous improvements to the house including a sunporch and four dormer rooms above its west wing. He also installed a steam furnace and radiators and modernized all the wiring. Dr. Henwood used my study as his dispensary and office. On a warm rainy evening I can smell some of his medicines. After he retired. Dr. Henwood and his wife ran the dairy farm with their son Jim before moving to Florida and selling the house to us. It was Jim Henwood who had planted the two rows of lilacs on each side of our long front lawn. Full of Ho Hum, I suggested that the women might like to see the upstairs. "There are five bedrooms and a bath and a sewing room up there," I told them. "You'll find some interesting old furniture and a picture of the house taken shortly after it was built. Take your time and when you come down the back stairs I'll show you the basement."

They were gone a long time for which I was grateful and when they came down I showed them the basement with its hand hewn beams and fieldstone foundation walls. As they passed the big white door to the furnace room they giggled to see the names of my grandchildren scrawled on it. Finally, I took them into the fruit cellar with its shelves full of the wine I'd made long ago and the fruit Milove had canned. I gave each of them a dusty bottle hoping that it had not turned to vinegar. Having learned to drink whiskey, I hadn't opened a bottle of that wine for thirty years.

Before we left the fruit cellar when I asked one of the women to open the cupboard she let out a shriek. "All old houses should have a skeleton in a closet," I said, "and this skull is one I found when I was a youth in the U.P."

"If you'll look closely you'll see that the person was probably killed by a hard blow to the side of the head or perhaps by a mastoid infection. See the hole behind the ear?" Well, that was enough and they soon left. I bet they gobbled all the way home.

As for me, it was Happy Hour and I had another imaginary conversation with Milove who gave me the devil for letting those women see her upstairs. "Oh Cully, don't do that again. It's like showing strangers your underpants. I hope they didn't see my sewing room."

Supper consisted of beef hash from the freezer and a salad because I was too tired to cook a real meal. I did light a candle to make amends to Milove. The two of us always had our evening meal by candlelight.

After supper I put Haydn's Fourth Symphony on the stereo and opened the day's mail, There were a lot of good letters. Here's an excerpt from one of them:

"We lived through a tornado on Palm Sunday in 1965 which took the roof of the house right off us while we were in the basement. We lost all our buildings, barn and all. What a hell of a mess! I don't know if fire is any worse but I sure hope I never have to go through another tornado.

"Tornados do some very strange things - almost beyond the imagination. The wind drove straws into a maple tree next to where our barn was. They were sticking out of that tree as though it were a straw bush and we have pictures to prove it. I had a white straw cowboy hat sitting on the TV next to the west wall of our house. When we came up out of the basement after the storm our house was in bad shape, half on and half off the foundation and both ends were gone. The TV was now in the kitchen area at the opposite end of the house, yet that hat was still on the TV and looked as if it hadn't been moved at all.

"I had bought a set of steel doors, big doors, twelve feet high and ten feet wide, so heavy it took four strong men to lift them and they were blown away so far we never found them. Yet I had a large oval glass picture of my great great grandparents stored in our grainary. After the storm, the building was all gone. The tornado just picked it up and took it away. Nothing was left of it except for the floor and that picture, and the glass on the picture wasn't even broken.

It also blew the feathers off a half dozen chickens we had, some more bare than others. One was a little bantam rooster who was completely naked. Well, come fall, he hadn't grown back any feathers. My wife was feeling sorry for him so she made a pair of little bib overalls and put him in them. Sure looked comical in those britches. One day soon after she made them, a salesman stopped at the house and when he saw him said, "'That's the funniest thing I ever seen.' 'You think that's funny?' said my wife. 'You should see him catch one of the hens, hold her down with one claw and try to get those suspenders down with the other.'"

It was time for bed and I climbed the steps without having to pause for rest. Once again I'd had a good day.

Day Five

About three in the morning I awoke from a dream in which I was crossing a turbulent stream on a springy birch log while burdened by a heavy pack sack. It was a precarious business and I was relieved to find myself safe in bed. Not too safe at that because my heart was acting up again. I suppose it was one of those sleep protective dreams such as the one, when the alarm clock is ringing, that you dream you are hearing church bells which means it's Sunday and you don't have to go to work and can continue sleeping. But I couldn't go back to sleep. The irregularity prevented my doing so and I went downstairs to sit in my big chair by a fire still blazing. Sitting up often seems to stabilize the pulse and I took a nitroglycerin pill to help calm it. After some time the heart had slowed down but I slept the rest of the night on the davenport rather than climb the stairs, an act that might have set the heart going haywire again. When again I woke I was feeling fine.

While making my breakfast I thought of the worst cup of coffee I'd ever had. It was in a hotel in Sydney, Australia. Weak, stale, cold and insipid, it was no way to start what was to be a tough day.

I should explain why I was there so far away from home. It happened because of a decision I'd made in 1932 when at last I had conquered my stuttering sufficiently to be able to speak fluently. I decided to plan the rest of my life. I would dedicate my thirties to exploring all the things I'd missed, my forties to creativity, my fifties to becoming wise, my sixties to folly and the rest of my existence to resignation.

I'd followed that plan pretty consistently, getting married and having my first child during my thirties, writing a lot of books and learning to paint, sculp, compose music in my forties. However, when in my fifties, I began to devote my energies to becoming wise, the first bit of wisdom that came to me was that if I postponed my follies to my sixties I would probably be too old to enjoy them. So I switched and made my fifties my foolish years. I also came to realize that the key formula for being foolish was to say "Yes" and that for wisdom was to say "No."

So that is why, in my late fifties, when I got a phone call from Washington asking me if I would serve as this country's representative in speech pathology at the Pan-Pacific Conference on the Disabled to be held in Sydney, Australia, with all expenses paid, I said my automatic Yes. After hanging up the phone, I was appalled. I didn't want to go to Australia. Hell, I couldn't go. It was October; I was teaching four courses, doing research and therapy, and running my farm.

But I went, thanks to my wife who took over all my duties. She had been an instructor in speech pathology at the University of Minnesota before I married her.

Two weeks later, after a long trip by propeller plane via San Francisco, Hawaii, and the Fiji Islands, we soared in over Sydney harbor, a lovely sight.

Wearied to the bone, I went immediately to my hotel, a very ancient but luxurious one, took a bath in a tub so long I could lie down full length in it, then lay down on that great bed. The moment I got to sleep, however, the phone rang. It was Miss Grace Ellis, the queen of Australian speech therapy. She was to be my hostess, she said, and she would call for me at seven-thirty to take me to the reception at the Governor's palace. It would be a black tie affair, she added. I told her I would come as I was, with a tie but not a black one and assured her I would also be wearing my coat and pants when I met her in the lobby. That produced a slight giggle.

A nice, very upper class and very British lady, we got along well throughout my stay but that reception for the delegates was tough on me. We milled around a big ballroom, holding champagne glasses, eating various delicacies including squid, making faces and small talk with strangers from many lands. By the end of an hour I felt as though I'd been inside a bass drum pounded by a hundred left handed drummers. It was no place for a man from Tioga and the forest. By the end of two hours I knew I'd have to get out of there or be a basket case so I told Miss Ellis I was leaving. "Oh, Dr. Van Riper," she said, "You can't possibly do that. We haven't even been through the reception line."

"The hell I can't," I replied, gave her my glass and bolted out of the front door of the palace into the night.

Fortunately there were some taxis there so I got into one and gave the driver a wad of Australian bills."Get me out of here fast and show me the town," I said.

"'You want girls, guv'nor?" he asked.

"Gad, no," I answered. "I just don't belong with those posh fancy pants. Take me to some of your pubs where I can see real people, real Australians, not British snobs. I'm an American and don't call me governor."

He laughed appreciatively. "Ok, matey, I'll show you the town and how the rest of us blokes have fun." After the first pub where we had some excellent ale and a waitress tried to sit on my lap, I was riding in the front seat with the cabbie, Joe, and we were boozum pals. Oh, what a fine night that was and I'm sorry I can't remember the details.

In one pub filled with sinister looking characters Joe told me how, during the war, he'd been with the Anzacs fighting the Germans all across Africa, and how, after they'd won, Winston Churchill came to review the troops as they marched past him still dirty and bloodied from the battle. And that,when old Winnie held up two fingers in the victory salute, all the Australian soldiers yelled, "Stick em up yer arse, Winnie; stick them up yer arse!"

Joe was a marvelous companion and I got a real education that night. He took me down to their long beaches where we waded, singing bawdy ballads. He liked my song about "Sammy Hall, Damn yer hide!" and joined me in the chorus. Once we got stopped by a policeman but Joe jollied him and invited him to join us as he showed this Yank the real Australia. I think the cop was tempted but he just grinned and waved us on.

I also vaguely recall Joe phoning the Minister of Fisheries at three in the morning asking him where I could catch a black marlin. Finally, he poured me back into my hotel and I slept until noon–or tried to.

I said tried to because every damned morning at precisely seven-thirty a red haired maid, dressed in black with a white apron and a doily on her head, knocked on the door and opened it to bring me that awful coffee and cold toast and marmalade. Day after day I tried to dissuade her, once even getting on my knees to beg, but she said it was the custom of the house and that was that. I suspected that she might have had another occupation too because once, with a lewd wink, she told me I could have anything I wanted.

All I wanted was more sleep. Those Australians sure worked me hard the three weeks I was with them but I couldn't resent it because their therapists were so hungry to learn about our methods for treating all the speech disorders. After every talk I gave, and I gave many of them, they would bombard me for hours. They followed me back to the hotel, bought me drinks at the bar, and continued their probing. Lord, how they wanted to talk shop! But they were also very kind to me, drove me up into the gum forests of the Blue Mountains, and in Melbourne to a rain forest. They showed me cricket matches, jacaranda trees, kookaburra birds and kangaroos and in return I served as a consultant in their hospitals and clinics. They brought me their most difficult cases and asked for advice as to treatment. All in all, it was a fine experience but I was sure glad to get home.

When I went outside to feed the birds the contrast between what I was seeing and the memory of sunny Australia was almost overwhelming. A blizzard was upon us and it looked as though it would be a bad one. In recent years we have had very mild winters compared to those we'd known in the past when great drifts of snow almost covered the farm bell. Driven by a very strong wind similar drifts were already forming. I thanked heaven for my snowblower and the plow on the John Deere and for John Eaton who would assuredly show up after work to open up the lane. Let it snow! I didn't have to go anywhere and the cupboards were full of food and whiskey. Time to play groundhog and hibernate. I spent the morning cooking and cleaning, even organizing my study which sure needed it, and as I did so I kept thinking of how we spent the winters in Tioga when I was a boy.

Although they were hard on my mother who hated our long winters with a passion and who, sometimes, would desperately scratch the windowpanes with her fingernails to remove the hoarfrost to see the pale sun, I always enjoyed that time of year. Just going to the barn to feed the horse and cow and to bring back an armload of wood was a challenge. I loved hearing the telephone lines singing in the wind, the squeak of my footsteps, the sparkling brilliant white that covered the land. Always carefully dressed for it with layers of woolen clothing, I do not recall ever being really cold though I suppose I was occasionally. When it got to thirty and forty below zero we rarely stayed outside long but I recall spitting through the mouth hole of my mask and seeing it explode in the icy air.

On milder days when the temperature remained at a minus ten or twenty for weeks at a time we had fun making caves and tunnels in the big drifts or even igloos when the snow was so packed you could cut blocks from it. Inside those caves it was always warm enough to have to shed a sweater or two. I recall once playing Eskimo and building a little fire in a can to roast my pretended whale blubber.

Of course we did a lot of skiing and sledding on our long steep hill street. When I was a small boy that street was never plowed. Instead, with two teams of horses, a huge log roller just packed down the snow. On the way down, one team with its driver would be behind the roller to keep it from running into the team ahead but returning up the hill both teams were in front. Because the roller was so large it made a hard surface where two vehicles could pass. No one shoveled the sidewalks except those to the houses and all of us walked in the roadway. I guess they still do.

But that fine hard surface was ideal for sledding. We kids could start at the crest of the hill near my father's hospital and whiz down to the railroad depot without ever having to push. Dragging the sled back up however was a chore unless we could hitch a ride on one of the big lumber sleighs. Someone in town had a long bobsled that would hold eight or ten kids and how we whooped all the way down.

We also did a lot of skiing, mainly cross country, though we always made a ski jump by Mt. Baldy or in the Company Field back of the grove. The latter also had one trail that went down through a large woods weaving through the trees and near its lower end to escape some big rocks you had to grab a certain sapling so you could make a right angled turn. I still carry in my groin a bit of dry fir branch that pierced it when I hung on a bit too long and straddled a dry spruce. It's a wonder any of us kids survived, the nutty things we did.

None of us ever learned to skate however, the snows were just too deep. One Christmas my grandparents sent me a pair of clip-on skates and I persuaded Fisheye and Mullu to help me clear a rink on Beaver Dam Pond. By the time we finished shoveling it was too dark to try and by the next morning it was covered by sixteen inches of new snow.

I remembered a lot of other things about my winters in the U.P. and only one of them was bad. It happened when I was perhaps seven years old. Surrounding our schoolyard was a fence built of iron pipes that had been discarded from the boilers up at the iron mine and one day an older kid persuaded me to lick one of those pipes. Of course my tongue froze to it instantly and I remained there stuck to it until a neighbor lady brought a kettle of hot water to release me. I still recall the pain of that skinned tongue and how I had only liquids for some days afterwards.

Yes, those winters were long but they were very happy ones and when spring came our joy was indescribable. "The crows are back! The crows are back! No, not ravens, crows I tell you!"

It sure had been a fine morning and a productive one. The house was clean, the pot roast was bubbling in the crockpot, and I even did a washing. Four miles had been put on my exercycle and soon I would be in Mancelona en route to the U.P. If I could make it past this February I really would get there.

I slept well and after a quick lunch went after my mail plowing the drive with the John Deere as I did so. It was just too cold and blustery to walk though I felt guilty because I didn't. Two letters addressed to Cully Gage were in the box, one from a soldier in Saudi Arabia who was very homesick and said he'd brought along a copy of my Love Affair book to make his ordeal bearable. I wrote him a good long letter immediately telling him I was homesick too and that we'd both be back there eventually. Then I opened the other letter. It was from a woman in Marquette who wanted some advice about how to write. "I can tell some good stories," she said, "but every time I try to put them down on paper I stall and they look terrible. How do you manage to write so easily and prolifically? What's the secret?"

I answered that letter right away too saying that being an author was never easy, that I labored hard in telling my tales, that I always had to revise and rewrite them before they satisfied me. My secret? I had no secret but over the years I had discovered a sort of procedure that helped me. It was this: First, I spent hours in mulling over the general features of the story while lying down. Oddly I've never been able to let my mind roam freely in any other position. Then, when I've got a vague outline of what I want to say and have some idea of how it would begin and end, I go to my typewriter and start pecking away, letting the tale just flow wherever it wants to go. I told her that I never looked at what I was writing or what I had written until it was, like peas porridge, nine days old. I've found that if I read it when writing it I become so critical I can't continue. I told her I bet that might be part of her trouble, that she had to rid herself of her Censor. "You can always change the stuff you write later," I told her and said that she always should keep a certain person in mind as a prospective reader. I have several such people to whom I always tell my tales, one of them is young, the other an old gaffer like me but both are life long residents of the U.P.

Since she had said she never had enough free time without constantly being interrupted I told her I'd never had any either but I'd discovered how to solve that problem. I set myself a minimum quota of just one word a day. I could write many more of course and usually did but I demanded that one word to keep the writing going. Moreover, I never stopped my writing at a period but always left the sentence uncompleted. That way, the need for closure would enable me to return to the writing easily when I could get back to it again because I always knew what I had to say next. Well, that was the gist of what I wrote her before wishing her good luck and enclosing a little story that had taken me two days to write. Here's the tale:

Infidelity

In the tight little village of Tioga there was very little marital cheating mainly because everyone knew everything about everybody. There were no secrets in our town. Any hanky panky was certain to be discovered and spread all over town. For example, when old Mr. Belanger innocently had the gallantry to help Mrs. Deroche carry a heavy bag of groceries back to her house, the tongues wagged with speculation. Nevertheless, human frailty being pretty universal, some cheating must have occurred.

At the top of the long hill street in Tioga there's a gravel road that winds westward south of the old iron mine and when I was a boy we called that area Finntown. The last two houses on that road were owned by the Saari's and the Pikkunens. They were neat whitewashed log cabins and behind each of them was a cowbarn and a chicken coop. Between the barns sat a single log sauna which both families shared.

The couples were very good friends. In their late forties with their children long gone Down Below to make a living, they lived the good life of the U.P. Seppo Pikkonen worked on the railroad and Oscar Saari cut pulp for a living. With a cow and chickens, fish and venison, a big garden and enough biting money they never had any trouble making it through the winter. The two men hunted and fished together, helped each other make winter wood, and do other things while their wives sewed and canned and had coffee together every morning and afternoon. Yes, they were good friends, all four of them.

Curiously, the man and wife in each couple were unlike in personality, Oscar Saari being always happy and outgoing while his wife, Lempi, was more quiet and serious. The other man, Seppo Pikkonen, was very reserved but his wife certainly was not. A tall woman, still very attractive with long blonde hair and a merry eye, Thelma was always out for a good time, even occasionally being a bit flirtatious. Perhaps it was because opposites attract each other that the two couples enjoyed being together so much.

But things change. As many happily married men approach their fiftieth year a strange sexual restlessness comes over them and they start looking. Is it because they suddenly realize that they are getting old and want to recapture their fast fading youth? Now, such men start having affairs–or get divorced and marry some young girl in her twenties.

Not so in Tioga! Divorce was unthinkable and only the ugliest of young women would accept any wooing from an old geezer, then the word for any man over fifty.

When the folie de vieux. as our French Canadians called it, hit Oscar it hit him hard. No, he didn't look for a young girl; he knew better. Besides there was Thelma, right next door. Still possessing a fine figure and full of fun, he bet she'd be very lively in bed or haymow. Such thoughts made him feel very guilty and he tried to reject them but couldn't. Even when tamping down a tie on the railroad tracks the thought of her kept persisting. At night, with Lempi in his arms, he fantasized that she was Thelma and sex became exciting again. One evening the two couples attended one of the rare polka dances in the Town Hall and for weeks afterward Oscar kept feeling the thrust of Thelma's breasts against his chest. When she hung up the clothes on the line, he couldn't help ogling her. Yes, he had it bad. Then came a day when, as he went to fire up their joint sauna, he found Thelma inside scrubbing the benches. She teased him a little. "Oscar," she said, "You're supposed to hang up your clothes in the dressing room before coming in here." Unable to resist the impulse, he grabbed her and kissed her. Of course she slapped his face but not too hard and for a moment he thought she had kissed him back. Wahoo! Remembering the encounter, Oscar had hot pants for many days.

His ardor might not have been so strong had he known that over their morning coffee Thelma had told Lempi what had happened. Lempi was both shocked and furious. "Tonight I'll brain the old fool with a stick of stovewood!"

"No, no," replied Thelma. "You do that and he'd just beat you up. He'll come to his senses once he realizes he's not going to get anywhere with me. He's not my type, Lempi, and besides I love my quiet Seppo too much."

Having convinced himself that all he had to do was to proposition Thelma and make the necessary arrangements, Oscar did a lot of scheming in the days that followed. Somehow he'd have to get Seppo out of the way and Lempi too. Where would they go to bed and when? Sometimes his head ached from all the planning.

Finally he figured it out. It would have to be on Saturday night when both men usually went down to Higley's saloon for a few beers and to play cards with Laf Bodine and some of the other regulars. Pretending to get sick, he'd leave about eight o'clock and when he got home he'd tell Lempi he had the runs and would have to spend some time in the outhouse until they quit. Yah, that sounded reasonable.

He'd put some blankets on the loose hay and persuade Thelma to be there at exactly eight thirty. Yep, that should work. Half an hour would be long enough and no one would ever know.

To his delight, when he caught Thelma alone and outlined the scheme, she laughed and said sure, that she'd show him how to have some real fun in the haymow, that it was about time she had some variety.

And that next morning she told Lempi all about it!

Oscar found it hard to work the morning of the rendezvous because he couldn't bend over without hurting himself. Even that afternoon when he took a hot sauna there wasn't any wilting.

After the hours finally passed the two men walked down the hill street to Higley's. Then, after a few beers, Oscar told Seppo he was feeling sick and thought he'd go home to bed. Seppo hardly noticed because he was winning big.

Looking at his watch when he got to his house, Oscar saw that it was exactly eight thirty so he went directly to the barn. He'd explain to Lempi later. Was she there? Yes, there was a big hump in the blankets. "You there?" he whispered hoarsely.

"Yah, I here," came the whispered reply. Tearing off his clothes, Oscar flung back the blankets. And there was his wife Lempi grinning at him.

At Happy Hour I read that tale to my deceased wife and she liked it. "It's a good yarn. Cully," she said. "I like that ending." So did I.

I didn't even go after the paper because it was still blowing and snowing so nastily. I was quite content just to sit by the fire. When it was time for supper I wished I had someone to share the pot roast with because it was excellent. I had cooked it with Golden Mushroom soup, a tomato, an onion, and some carrots. Oh well, I could eat it another day or days and then make hash of it for the freezer. Perhaps John might come to help me get rid of it.

That evening I watched some nature programs on the TV and went to bed early. It had been another happy day. Poor Oscar!

Day Six

A lot of people have expressed surprise and shock when they find, that I live alone at the age of 85. They ask, "What if something happens to you?" "What if you have burglars?" Most frequently they ask me if I'm not terribly lonely. "Not at all," I tell them. "I have much company."

My first companion was my beloved Grampa Gage who joined me for breakfast even though he died seventy years ago. When he lived with us in Tioga I was only ten and he was my mentor and adult playmate. Every morning he would get me up early, shave himself and pretend to shave me, then make our breakfast before we set out on one of our crazy expeditions.

This morning I recalled one of those breakfasts. "Now, Mister O'Hare," Grampa said. (He always called me Boy or by some special name of the day.) "The common way to break an egg is to hit it with a knife or crack it against the edge of the frying pan like this." He demonstrated. "But life. Mister O'Hare, should be lived dangerously if it is to be at all interesting. Observe me carefully!" He picked up my egg, banged it hard against his long forehead, then emptied it into the pan. Not a trace of the egg was on his old noggin. "Well, Boy, that time I carried it off without getting a faceful and I'm proud I've begun the day this way. A bit of danger is the pepper in the stew of life. Not too much, just a little. Today you and I will explore the use of that condiment as we go about our business. Shall we play billy goat on Mount Baldy?"

Many years later, Grampa was with me again, this morning as I carved a thick slice of bacon. "Now cut it exactly a quarter of an inch thick. Boy, no less and no more. Them store bought bacon slices are always too skinny to cook right. Now sear both sides in high heat, then turn it down so it will cook slowly. Life and bacon are too precious to spoil them with hurry." Then when I was about to break this morning's egg, he spoke again. "Well, Boy, how about it?" I knew he was referring to living dangerously so I cracked the egg on my forehead after knicking it with my thumbnail as he had done so long ago. Eureka! There were only two little bits of egg shell in the pan and not a speck on my face. It would be a good day!

It was fun having Grampa with me as I fed the birds. I asked him how I could keep the varmints from eating all the sunflower seeds I'd put in the feeder. There was a big raccoon that had been swarming up the bird feeder pole every evening about dusk to tear off the top board of the bird feeder and gorge himself on the sunflower seeds. Night after night I'd watched him outwit all my efforts to thwart him. I'd greased the pole with vasoline; I'd put a latch on the cover which he soon learned how to unhook; I'd tied the cover on with rope which he immediately bit in two. In my desperation, I'd emptied the feeder and set a Havahart live trap baited with sunflower seeds and corn but the next morning, though the trap had been sprung there was no raccoon in it. Moreover it had been turned upside down and the seeds had fallen through the mesh and were all gone.

"Have you ever caught anything in that contraption?" Grampa asked skeptically. I told him I'd caught possums, skunks, woodchucks, birds, squirrels and rabbits galore, and even other raccoons but not this big one. I said I usually took them to the woods by the Boy Scout Camp down the road so the kids could hear things that went thump in the night.

"Ever get sprayed by a skunk?" Grampa asked. "No, but John Eaton did and sure got polluted. He made the mistake of taking off the blanket covering the trap before opening the doors and the skunk came out with both cannons shooting. But Grampa, how come this coon springs the trap and gets away when the others don't?"

As always he gave the question some serious thought before replying. "I reckon he's such a big one the door falls on his rump and he just backs out." he said. "Coons are smart and you'll never get him to enter it again. Why don't you string a bit of the electric fence around the feeder pole, the fence you use around your garden to keep the varmints out?"

Of course," I exclaimed. For some years that fence had kept the woodchucks and coons and deer from eating my corn and melons. I hated to destroy it and the work might be hard. I'd have to dig up the posts, cut the wire netting, haul the battery and charger and use a heavy sledge to pound the rods into the frozen ground. That would be living dangerously indeed.

Nevertheless, with Grampa's help and counsel the project was completed. I found some extra rods, insulators, and wire in the horse stall and hauled the battery and charger in the cart behind the garden tractor. Lifting that battery was the hardest job and I had to sit down a spell but the ground wasn't frozen so deep I had to use the heavy sledge. Throughout all this activity Grampa was with me, advising, suggesting and offering bits of wisdom but all I can remember of the latter was "Slow and easy and never grunt!"

He also made the wise suggestion that I put a coil of wire right next to the feeder pole and laughed when I touched the completed contraption and yelped. I sure got a good jolt.

When the job was done I felt so tired and shaky I fell asleep on the davenport and when I awakened Grampa was gone. Still too tired, I decided to postpone my bicycle trip to the U.P. and to read while I had another "cup of jav" which is what we call coffee in the U.P. Selecting a book at random from the bookshelves in my study I came up with Sergeant's biography of Robert Frost which I hadn't read for years. Just inside the cover I found a message from Milove: "To Cul-ly a Merry Christmas for adding immeasurable poetry to my life for twenty six years. X X X K-Katy." I almost wept. She had spelled my name Cul-ly as my boyhood friends had pronounced it, not Cully, just as they always said win-ter instead of winter. She had also signed herself as K-Katy, a term I used when teasing her affectionately. Suddenly she seemed very near.

When I was a senior at the University of Michigan, Robert Frost was the "Poet in Residence", a position which gave him leisure to write. His only duties were to conduct one seminar in poetry each semester and I was one of the few students chosen to be in it. An unforgettable experience! Each student had to submit anonymously one poem a week and of them. Frost selected one or two he read aloud with his comments. Rarely did any of them get a favorable response and a few just made him mad. I recall how furious he became while reading the lines "The violin bow sucks music from the burnished wood." "Sucks," he roared. "Sucks, Sucks, Sucks!" and then he went on to provide a wonderful account of the nature and appropriateness of words in poetic discourse, their sounds and rhythms. He told us of his own struggles to find the perfect word or phrase and how often he had chucked a morning's work into the wastebasket. Actually, Robert Frost used the seminar not for teaching nor for criticism but just to hear his own thoughts as he rambled on about anything that hit his momentary fancy. Privileged to watch and hear that wonderful mind at work, I often left the class dazed with exhilaration that lasted for hours.

About the middle of the semester a poetry contest was held with Robert Frost as the judge and after some self debate I entered it with this little poem:

Five of the Dryads were Foolish

(The aged Pan grew much weary of pipes and dancing and begged Zeus to grant him peace and quietness. Whereupon he was changed into a hidden pool in the forest. Aulus Gellius.)

> Long years ago in lost Atlantis,
> When Dryads danced in the woods,
> A hidden pool in the orchard lay,
> An ancient mulberry tree there stood
> Gnarled and twisted, a grim old brute
> Of the sylvan world, it shook its head
> In grim defiance of all the dead
> And every year dropped purple fruit
> Into the pool that once was Pan.
>
> Three great roots swam out and dived,
> And in their bays great lilies grew.
> White lilies, steeped in purple stain
> Laughed in their cups and laughed again,
> For once, long before, when the pool was new,
> A band of dryads had stopped to drink
> By the brink of the pool that once was Pan.
> And the tree still grins a knotted old grin,
> And laughs in the wind of evening skies,
> For five of the dryads were foolish
> But all of the lilies were wise.

Why Robert Frost picked that to win the poetry prize I don't know. I hadn't thought it was very good. Perhaps it was that the other entries were imitations of his work and mine was not. It did look better when it was printed in the *Inlander*, the University magazine, and brought me twenty five dollars and a roll of toilet paper inscribed "Poetic License" from my friend, John Voelker, who later became a Supreme Court Justice and the author of *An*

Anatomy of a Murder. John and I drank the proceeds in bootleg whiskey and sang bawdy songs until dawn.

Anyway, Frost stopped me after class one day and asked to see other poems I'd written. Shy and overwhelmed by his interest I gave him only two, one of which "The Old Tailor" I later published in my book *Tales of the Old U .P.* He liked them too and said that if I could write enough others of the same quality he would help find a publisher. I had no other poems.

Moreover, several times that year Frost invited me to his home for a Sunday night supper of brown bread, beans and applesauce cooked by his wife Elinore, a lovely warm woman. The supper was always very good but the conversation was superb. Frost loved to talk and I don't think he ever said a dull word. He didn't like to be interrupted though, or to be asked questions. He preferred the monologue and, because of my stuttering, I was a very good and appreciative listener.

As I write this I'm tempted to insert the other poem of mine that Frost liked and felt should be published. Oscar Wilde once said that the only way to get rid of a temptation was to yield to it so here it is:

Old Man Pone

Old Man Pon? That's me!
Pone's Dam" That's yonder.
Not a trickle snaking through.
Yeah, the sluice gate's been drawn up,
Just drawn her.
Dam full, say you?
That's my business too.
I don't squander
Water. Water don't come back.
When life and water leak away
They wander.

Looking sickly?
Ought to.
Not a bite inside my sack
For two days. Naw, got plenty food.
Belly's old and water logged.

See that crack?
Yeah, it's big but it's cemented good.
That's where my old pap, he stood
Keeping back
And sousing under dynamite
That farmers floated down on rafts
Things was black
That year–thirst and drought
Cattle died. They might

Have asked for water. Not them. No!
Bust your dam or we will!
Sure, a fight.

My pap, just a little slow...
Shocked him crazy. Shakes, you know.
Dirty sight!
Also made that crack you see
But Pone's Dam it held, you bet.
Been built right.

What's that tin case in the wall?
Case of fate, maybe.
You've good eyes to see that wire.
7You get going, stranger. Quick!
You aint wanted. Git!

He'd better go. I'm no good liar.
Thirty feet of water creeping higher.
Soon I'll press upon this key
Before my own blood leaks away.
They'll get their water-valleys full.
Old God Pone. That's me!

Old Barn

I was so full of memories of the famous poet that he became my companion as I walked out to the back of my park. When I showed him the interior of the old barn he admired the great oak hand-hewed beams that supported the roof. He admired the adz marks. "The man who hewed those beams knew his craft," he said. "See how far apart those adz marks are. When I was a boy I made timbers too. Very satisfying, almost as good as creating a fine sentence."

Because I've painted it three times that old barn has held its color well on the front and sides but the back needs another coat because most of the paint is flaking off. I know I won't be able to paint it again. Frost looked at it a long time. "Reminds me of the face of an old apple farmer I knew in Vermont," he said." "Apple red spots of health on skin grey with age."

Frost talked continuously as we walked down the lane to the pines and I wish I could remember all he said. Seeing tracks of rabbits and fox and raccoons in the new snow, he mentioned something about how all of us left tracks behind us and perhaps it was just as well that rain and snow would soon obliterate them. "Poems are tracks, too," he said,a bit sadly.

On our return I pretended to meet myself and said "Good morning, sir. It's a fine day." That made him chuckle. And when we came back to the house I was feeling so happy I just had to ring the old farm bell. When I did so. Frost said to me:

> *"Something there is in arms that wants to ring a bell,*
> *To send a clang across the fields to hungry men*
> *Or just to greet the stars or sun*
> *Or just to say, 'I am!'"*

No one can be alone with Robert Frost as a companion.

It was almost noon when I entered the house and sat for a time in the big chair with the sun streaming through the big windows on my head. Old men should sit in the sun a lot. It warms the cockles of the soul. And the heart too. I'd worked too hard and was paying for it with some angina which went away after I took my little pill of dynamite, the nitroglycerin I always carry in my pocket. Soon the ache in my upper chest was gone so I took my nap. Usually when I do so I just rest but this day I slept deeply and felt refreshed when I awakened.

I ate my small lunch alone and enjoyed it.There are many times when I need no real or imaginary companions. Being alone means freedom, no demands upon you, no need to respond to the presence of others. It permits serenity.

Somehow I get the same feeling I knew as a boy in the forest. For some people solitude is unsettling. Once I brought a college friend up to the Old Cabin and when I left him there for a few hours he was almost frantic when I returned. "I can't bear the awful silence," he said. "I need people." Well, I like people too but I don't need them around me all the time.

Remembering the angina I rode down to the mailbox on the garden tractor, distributing some ears of corn for the pheasants whose tracks I'd seen there. Not much mail this time but at least there were two letters addressed to Cully Gage. I'd read them later.

That afternoon I had a series of imaginary companions, all of them from Tioga and my boyhood. The first one was Pete Half Shoes, the village's only pure blooded Chippewa

Indian, who had meant so much to me at that time. He returned because I decided to make some rice pudding, being hungry for a sweet dessert that I hadn't had for weeks. Diabetics get these sudden hungers and the only way I've found to handle mine is by making applesauce or rice pudding heavily laced with some sugar substitute such as Sweet and Low. As I poured the rice out of the box I found myself wishing it were wild rice rather than the common variety. Long grained and much more tasty as well as more nutritious, it makes the best pudding but it's hard to find Down Below, at least in the stores John has searched. It was also hard to find in the U.P. but Pete Half Shoes knew of a little bay in Lake Tioga where it flourished. Once he let me go with him to get his winter's supply. After a long hike he found an old boat hidden in the brush and he laid an old blanket in its bottom. "Canoe better," Pete said as he peeled two long sticks. "You pole and I show you."

As the boat plowed through the tall reeds and stalks it left a watery path behind us. With a stick in each hand, Pete, who was in the front of the boat, used one of them to bend the rice over its edge, then with the other stick tapped the stalks so the ripe grain fell onto the blanket.He sure was skillful as he alternately banged the grain first from one side of the boat, then from the other. There was a rhythm to it that when I tried I couldn't master. Pete didn't complain about my awkwardness, just patiently showed me again and again until I began to get the hang of it. Altogether we must have had about three quarts of rice in the blanket before we quit. That fine afternoon was seventy years ago but I recalled vividly the swish and flash of those shining sticks as we harvested that wild rice.

Another person with whom I spent some time that afternoon was Mr. Donegal, Old Blue Balls, the tough school superintendent who ruled us with an iron hand, ruler and strap. The memory of him had come with a fan letter from an old lady in the U.P. "I enjoy your stories very much," she said, "and especially those about Blueballs because we had a principal just like him who terrorized us. But you always describe him as being so hard and ferocious. Didn't he have a softer side? In your story about playing hooky, you told of how tenderly he cared for your friend that he rescued from drowning. He couldn't have been all bad."

Thinking to answer her, I had a hard time at first but then remembered the rainy afternoon when I was playing with his son, Halstead, in their attic. There were a lot of books up there and we had found one on the Vikings and their early settlements in America. It had some fine pictures of those Vikings and also of the Skelling, the Indians who eventually wiped out those who tried to live there.

Suddenly Halstead's father came up the stairs to join us and for almost an hour he told us tales of those early explorers, the runic stones that had been found as far west as Minnesota, the Viking artifacts that had been discovered in Massachusetts. And then he held us enthralled with an account of the glaciers that had shaped our land, lakes and streams long before the Indians arrived. Not once did he roar or seem formidable. He wasn't being a teacher; he was just having fun up there in the attic with us as the raindrops peppered the roof above. And when he left, he actually touseled our hair affectionately. Yes, I guess Old Blue Balls did have a soft side.

I made a cup of new coffee and wished I had some korpua to go with it but that was long gone. OK, I'd make some if I could recall how Rudi's mother, our common aiti, had done it years ago. She had cut thick slices of home made bread in half, lightly buttered both sides, sprinkled them with sugar and cinnamon, then baked them in the oven until they were very brown and dry. I didn't have any homemade bread and had to use Sweet and Low but they turned out fine. I felt proud of myself but the best part was remembering that warm wonderful woman, my second mother, my aiti.

But my best companion of the day was of course Milove. Our Happy Hour lasted for two hours as we reminisced about the fine experiences we'd had together before the cancer hit her.

All in all it had been another almost perfect day even though I hadn't seen another person nor heard a human voice. No, I'm not a lonely old man. I'm a happy one.

Day Seven

This day began with a phone call from Andy Amor, the husband of Elizabeth, my eldest granddaughter. "Sir," he said formally, "You are now a great grandfather." It didn't take long before he lost his cool as he excitedly told me that the baby's name was Peter and he weighed eight pounds and was beautiful and healthy and that Elizabeth was fine too and, and, and. "I'm a father" he exclaimed incredulously. "I can't believe it. What do I do now?"

I don't know what I told him but I went outside and shouted, "Hear ye! Hear ye! I hereby proclaim that this is Grandfather's Day, Great Grandfather's Day" and I rang the farm bell for five minutes before doing the Dance of the Wild Cucumber.

Of all the roles I've played in my long life, being a grandfather has been the most rewarding. Nine grandchildren have blessed that life, one after another, and in recent years after they grew into adults I've sorely missed the fine relationship I've always had with them. Oh, of course we're still close and I see them often but the best years of grandfatherhood are those when they're growing up. Now I could be a grampa again.

After that first fine exhilaration ebbed, I had the sobering thought that I probably wouldn't live long enough to be that Grampa to Peter, Peter the Great. The hell I wouldn't! Now I had another reason to survive despite the odds. I'd not only get back to the U.P. but I'd also play with a great grandson, no matter what!

So many memories flooded me that I found no interest in doing anything else. Nuts with doing the washing I'd planned! No, I wouldn't get a much needed haircut or my beard trimmed. The letters I'd planned to write could wait. For once I regretted living alone and not being able to share the good news. It would be silly to phone a friend and announce that I had become a great grandfather. They wouldn't understand what it meant to me. Ah, finally I found a solution to my dilemma. I'd write my son-in-law, Ben Krill, Elizabeth's father, and tell him about the joys of being a Grampa. I spent the whole day writing it and here it is:

To A New Grandfather

So you've just become a new grandfather. Welcome to the clan! Being a father was fun but being a grandfather is even better mainly because you and your grandchild share a common enemy, the generation in between. Now you can have all the pleasures without any responsibility. Now you can be a child again.

Old Bones And Northern Memories

Some say that all newly born infants are just blobs or that they all look like Winston Churchill, that until they learn to bang a cup or walk or talk they just aren't very interesting. I have not found it so. Each of the nine grandchildren with whom I've been blessed has fascinated me even in that first year more than my own children ever did. No two of them were alike. One would gurgle in contentment when I held it in my arms; another would burp or yawn; still another would wail or wet his pants. All of them would curl their tiny fingers around my thumb and not let go. You'll like that.

Many new grandchildren stare at you and their confusing world with a rather dazed expression as if to say, "What the hell is all this, Grampa?" When they do, you must say, "Child, what you're seeing doesn't make much sense, does it? It never will, but that beautiful woman over there is your mother; that man making silly faces is your father, and I, with the white whiskers, am your loving Grampa. Now that the formal introductions are over, you may go to sleep." The baby never does. It just lets out a wail and its mother hurriedly grabs it away from you. That's all right too.

As a grandfather you may occasionally be privileged to feed the baby–from the bottle, not the breast. You won't be as awkward as you were when your own children were little and if your arthritic elbow makes you call for Grandma after ten minutes, so be it. Fortunately you won't be able to see the fatuous expression on your face. Grandfathers always look a bit silly when feeding babies their bottles. Grandmothers don't. Remembering, they look beautiful.

When I was a boy in Tioga, I often visited the home of one of my Finn friends, Ted Koski. His ancient grandmother, a tiny and very ugly old woman was always rocking herself in a chair next to their kitchen range as she smoked a blackened corncob pipe or sipped coffee through a sugarlump held between her toothless gums. Her face had wrinkles on its wrinkles and resembled a withered dry apple. Yet once I saw the old lady holding her eleventh grandchild against the nipple of a bottle and her face held a beautiful, most ethereal expression. I've never forgotten it. We men can never look like that.

I hope you'll be better at burping babies than I have been. Oh, I could sling them over my shoulder correctly but I couldn't bear to thump the bonnie little bugger hard enough to evoke the belch that was needed. I've read that in Arabia the dinner guests must express their appreciation of the meal by loud and frequent belchings and burpings. When they were six months old, all my grandchildren were Arabs. I hope you'll be a better baby burper than I was.

Once your grandchild begins to explore the delights of solid food, including its use as a shampoo, you can witness again the wonderful achievements of learning to talk and walk. One of my nine crawled backwards; another crawled only in circles; another didn't crawl at all–just stood up one day and walked. Now you can witness again what our prehistoric ancestors discovered when they realized they didn't have to go on all fours. Homo erectus! No wonder the baby squeals triumphantly when he pulls himself up vertically, sidles along the davenport, and toddles into your waiting knees. Wahoo! I hope you'll yell in triumph too. I did–nine times!

Similarly you can again watch homo erectus become homo sapiens as your grandchild learns to talk, the greatest achievement of mankind. When your own children were babies you probably missed that miracle. Now you can witness each phase of the learning.

Most mothers insist that their children learned to talk about the time of their first birthdays or shortly thereafter, but that's not true. Throughout all that first year they are mastering the basic skills necessary for speech, yes, even when crying. As a father you probably disliked, perhaps even resented, that squalling especially in the wee hours of the night but to have speech you have to learn how to make sounds. As a grandfather, you'll find it interesting rather than unbearable. You'll observe him crying both on inhalation and exhalation, then settling on the latter. You'll watch him crying with his legs keeping time to his wails, and that most of the latter are nasalized vowels. Kipling claimed that he could distinguish an Oriental from an Occidental cry of pain, that we of the western world cry "Ow!" whereas the Oriental wails "Ai, ai, ai." Listening, the thought may come to you that your grandchild must have a Chinese ancestor on his mother's family tree. But don't try to figure out why he's crying. That's for mothers or grandmothers. Buhler, a famous researcher in child development, once listed ten different conditions that made a baby cry, among them hunger, wetness and uncomfortable postures, but there's an eleventh cause too. Sometimes a baby just cries for the hell of it. So enjoy and call Grandma.

Watch for the comfort sounds, Grampa, because they are the real beginnings of speech. Out of them will come the repeated syllables of babbling when he plays with his mouth much as he does with his toes. He's practicing so don't interrupt or he'll quit. Just enjoy that fairy music while it lasts for soon he will be stringing syllables that almost seem as though he's trying to tell you something. "Gobba me ma ma?" he may seem to be asking as he experiments with the inflections of questioning or of command. One of my grandchildren demanded "Bahba bahba bahba" when she didn't have enough hair to ruffle a brush. It's fun watching your grandchild learning how to speak.

And it's even better when do they start using meaningful words. Alas, I'm afraid they won't be saying "Grampa" for some time. That "Gr" blend involves too many tough coordinations, they'll use the easy sounds like those made with the lips or tongue tip, the m,p,b,w, and t and d sounds, along with various vowels to say such early words as "Mama", "Dada," or "wa-wa" for water. Yet, one of my granddaughters first words was "pitty" (pretty) a comment on a flower I'd given her. Don't insist that they imitate you. Just provide the word as a model when it is needed. And make it easy for them by speaking simply and in short phrases or sentences.

The best years of grandparenthood start when they are half past three or four years of age, when you can assume the role of an adult playmate. These are the lap years, the hugging years, the years of unconditional love. You may have forgotten how good it is to have a child squeal with delight when you come through the door, to have him grab your legs and beg to be held instantly. "Gampa, Gampa," he'll whisper in your ear. "I lub you."

Soon will come the years when the child will want to walk hand in hand with you in exploring the wonders of the outside world, so take little steps. Holes in the ground, bugs, big and small, the feel of tree bark, the sound of birds, all these are new experiences to be shared by both of you. To see these things is to be reborn, to be a child again. I hope both of you can find a Secret Place to have as your very own–even if it's only a spot behind a special tree. There you can answer his questions: "Gampa, why do I have only two fumhs?" "Gampa, will I be as big as you someday?" "Kin I see in your gwasses?"

There in your Secret Place you can invite him to find the Secret Pleasure of the day, the two mints you've hidden in your pocket. As he swarms over you, you'll hear that wonderful giggle of discovery and you may find yourself giggling too. And, as you eat your mints, you can sing, "Oh a little bit of candy makes the medicine go down/the medicine go down/the medicine go down/Oh, a little bit of candy makes the medicine go down/in a most delightful way." Children love to have you sing to them and don't mind a bit if your old voice crackles. He'll also squeal with delight if you do some rhyming. When his shoe falls off, as boy's shoes always do, you can chant, "Johnny lost his shoe/Boo hoo hoo." Then, of course, you must take off your own shoe and throw it for him to retrieve as you both chant, "Gampa lost his shoe/Boo hoo..."

Feel Grampa's Beard

Beneath your dignity? Oh, come on! It's about time you lost the barnacles of inhibition that have covered your keel. It's time you learned how to play again. Let that grandchild of yours teach you how to enjoy the present moment to the hilt and nuts to the past or future. You're a grampa now, with a licence to be foolish.

How many fine memories I have of those days with my own grandchildren! Even the furniture of this old house reminds me of them. This big recliner chair with the wooden arms was the focus of many good moments. It was my chair, Grampa's chair, and woe to any little kid who tried to preempt it, as they well knew. So, of course, whenever I entered the room there was sure to be a giggling little scamp sitting in it, eyes sparkling with anticipation. "Who's in my chair?" I'd roar and then, snorting ferociously, chase the kid around the davenport. Or I'd pretend I hadn't seen him and sit down carefully, jump up startled and chase him around again. Because I couldn't bear to throw it away, I still have a wide rubber band on the arm of that chair which we used to play "Snap Grampa." The grandchild would lift up the band while I inserted my forefinger under it, then the kid would chant "M.B.G. One, two, three" and let the rubber band snap down on my finger as I tried to pull it out of danger. Often I didn't and then I'd howl in mock anguish and chase the merry little devil around the dining room table. That M.B.G. means Monkey Business Grampa and even now when they are thoroughly mature their letters always begin with the salutation: "Dear M.B.G." Another honorary degree!

Grandchildren love magic in any form. I have a few tricks such as being able to make a coin disappear up my sleeve but the one they loved best was when I'd say the magic word, then pull out my upper denture and pretend to bite them with it when they fled. Then I'd tell them that if they could say that magic word, they could pull out their teeth and bite me too. Oddly enough. though they tried hard, they were never able to say it correctly, perhaps because it's just a jumble of connected sounds like "eeligochamasikaveronaput."

When the holidays come and all of your grandchildren are assembled I suggest that you get them all worked up and rowdy by playing "Follow Grampa." Line them up in a row and lead them all over the house doing nutty things like crawling on all fours, waving your arms, hopping on one foot, putting your head between your legs, or doing my Dance of the Wild Cucumber. When they're really war-whooping and climbing the walls, you discreetly get the hell out and let their parents calm them down.

They will want to sit beside you at the dining room table, of course, and if they happen to drop a spoon you must also drop yours, and perhaps your knife and fork as well. Great hilarity! Once when my granddaughter Julie spilled her whole mug of milk on the floor, I spilled mine too much to the irritation of her grandmother who had to clean up the mess. "You've gone too far, Cully," she said disapprovingly but Grampas can never go too far.

But there are also the quiet times when your grandson will crawl up into your lap and say, "Grampa, read me a book or tell me a story." I suggest that you do the latter because most children's books are pretty terrible. What I usually did was to pretend to read from The Upside Down Book, making up a wild tale in which the child plays an important role. Using their own names seems to intrigue them as they hear about what they did to the crocodile on the River Nile or something such. Even as adults they still recall some of their adventures that came from the Upside Down Book. Never shush them when they interrupt or ask questions but answer them very seriously after due thought. About the only problem you may encounter comes when they demand you tell the same story again because they want it told in exactly the same way. "No, Grampa. That's not right. My froggy jumped on the table first and then he jumped up into the tree." You won't find it hard to make up these tales if you're still a child at heart. Grampas are! Alas, this wonderful period does not last forever. Like you, your grandchildren will be growing older. They find other interests, other playmates. Then what they want is not a playmate but a companion or a teacher though not like those they have in school. They hunger to learn the things big people do, especially those that their own parents can't or don't teach them.

At the crucial ages of from nine to eleven I was very fortunate to have my Grampa Gage living with us and in my *Northwoods Readers* I've written much about our companionship. After we'd had our early breakfast and were sitting on the back steps in the sun he'd say, "Mister McGillicuddy, what, sir, do you suggest we do this fine morning?" Grampa never talked down to me; he always listened gravely to what I said; he never preached. Often he'd ask me to help him on some little job such as hoeing the beets or picking strawberries and always thanked me for my valuable assistance. He made me feel grown up, an equal, a cherished companion. My own father had neither the time nor the inclination to play such a role but Grampa seemed to know what I needed–the opportunity to identify with a real man.

I cannot number the things he taught me. Indeed, he never seemed to be teaching but rather just watching me learn. For example when I was learning how to fly fish and my line kept falling in coils at my feet to my utter frustration, he put an apple on a stick and bade me fling it off. That was all. No instruction, no demonstrating, but I got the idea and soon was casting my trout fly with ease. A good woodsman, he taught me much about nature without ever seeming to teach. He sought my aid in making his collections of rocks, tree bark, flowers, animal tracks, and even smells. We roamed the forest and streams exploring their delights together and almost incidently I learned that we Gages didn't lie or cheat and that we coped with adversity or disappointment with grace. And, most of all, to have the gay spirit, and enjoy every moment. I have an unbounded imagination and Grampa had one too. "Sir," he'd say to me on Mount Baldy, "We're badly outnumbered. We've got to retreat before those Philistines kill us. Get on your horse and we'll escape them." Then both of us would mount our sticks and gallop down the hill to fight another day. At various times we'd be chickens laying eggs, Bushmen hunting lions in Africa or a bird flying over our town and lakes. Last summer I visited Our Elephant, a huge granite boulder that we tamed and rode more than seventy years ago. Grampa knew my need for fantasy and encouraged it. I have done so too with my grandchildren as I hope you will with yours.

During this preadolescent period your grandson will also need you as a confidant. I told my Grampa Gage things I'd never tell my parents. As a grandfather, I've been honored to share the private thoughts and feelings of all nine grandchildren. Sometimes I've almost felt like a priest hearing confession though the sins are small, small sins. Always I gave immediate and absolute absolution–but no penances. And I never told!

The situation with your granddaughters will be different. Unlike the boys, they cannot and do not want to identify with you. They need grandmothers to be their companions and confidants, grandmothers who need their help in baking cookies and going shopping. There's no need to feel jealous. That's just the way things are.

Having found that granddaughters love to get mail, I've maintained a close relationship with them by correspondence (with each letter of course addressed to Miss). The crazier the letter, the more they like it! Often all I sent them was a bit of mildly bawdy doggerel: "Dear Miss Jennifer Ann Squires: I have a poem for you today. 'Jennifer Ann/Jennifer Ann/Did a big dirty in the frying pan/Did it twice That wasn't nice/Jennifer Ann, Jennifer Ann, Your loving Grampa."

A few years later, when they've discovered that boys have legs, I write them wild love letters from imaginary admirers. Occasionally they may answer: "Dear MBG: My dog has fleas and bites herself. School is OK, I love you."

It's always a bit hard when in their adolescence they leave you for a time. You'll go to their high school programs and plays and watch them parade in the band or compete in sports and feel good if they wink or wave at you but the old intimate relationship will be gone. They won't need you but you can enjoy watching them grow. And if you're as lucky as I am, there will come a time when their husbands or wives will phone you and say "Hello, Great Grandfather."

Well, that's what I wrote to Elizabeth's father–and perhaps for all grandfathers. With breaks for lunch, my nap, the mail and some walks it took me all day. I was very tired by Happy Hour until a good fire on the hearth restored me. Yet I couldn't get my own grandfather out of my head and thought of my disappointment when the Averys, my publishers, rejected a tale I wrote for the most recent *Northwoods Reader*, "And Still Another." The story was called "Grampa Tells Me About Sex". I thought I had handled the touchy subject with some delicacy but they sure didn't. They said it would offend too many readers.

After some search I found a copy of the tale and read it again. Yes, they were right and Milove would have agreed with them. Yet it was a good tale and a true one. Perhaps I could delete the objectionable material. After a lousy frozen fish dinner I tried revising it and here it is:

Grampa Tells Me About Sex

For some reason I had overslept that morning and as I went down the back stairs to the kitchen I heard Mother talking about me to Grampa so I listened. "Cully's almost eleven, Father," she said, "and soon he'll be adolescing. He needs to have some good information about his sexual urges but when I asked his father to do so, he refused. I don't know why. You and Cully have such a close relationship I know he'd listen to you. Please!"

"Aw, Edith," Grampa replied. "That's a crazy idea. Why don't you tell him yourself?"

"Please, Father! Please!" She knew he'd do anything for her.

"Well, I'll think about it," he replied. I could tell he wasn't enthusiastic. Behind the door I was grinning, thinking it should be an interesting morning.

After I'd had my belated breakfast, Grampa and I sat on the back steps for a spell making our plans for the day. "Mr. McGinty," he said. "I would appreciate your reaction to my proposal that we go up to make a cave on Mount Baldy. You know those two big slabs of rock on top of the east slope. By putting a roof of branches across them we can have our cave. We need one up there. Those sabre toothed tigers are always prowling around and a little coffee fire at the entrance will keep us safe. What do you say to that, Mr. McGinty?" I joyfully agreed.

As we passed Sliding Rock Grampa began telling me about Pre-his-toric Man. (He always sounded out the big words for me.) From what he told me those early ancestors of ours must have had a rough time surviving. They didn't even have bows and arrows, Grampa said, just spears and stone axes. They were always hungry and ate grubs and worms when they couldn't kill any game. They had no real clothing, just animal skins. Dangers lurked everywhere. "No point to trying to climb a tree when a sabre toothed tiger comes after you," Grampa said. "Hell, them varmints can climb a tree quicker than you can spit. Hey! What's this?" He pointed to an indentation in the path. "Danged if that aint a tiger track. Boy! We'd better be making our cave in a hurry so we can make a fire in the opening and be safe. The one thing those sabre toothed tigers is scared of is fire."

We climbed the bluff and frantically began covering the space between the two big rocks with branches. They looked a bit flimsy. I was beginning to believe some tiger would soon be getting our scent and so I was relieved when the job was done and we had a little fire at its entrance. Grampa pulled out his pipe and we sat there safe but listening intently. Then he broke the silence. "Boy," he said, "before we go outside to make ourselves some spears and stone axes I want to ask you some questions. First, let me say to you a little poem. 'The flea is wee and mercy me/ You cannot tell the he from she/ But she knows well/ And so does he.' Now my question is this: What's the difference between a male and a female, between a boy and a girl?"

I wanted to say that boys had peckers and girls did not but, hating to use that term, I used my mother's word. "Boys have wee wees and girl's don't," I replied.

Grampa was both shocked and outraged. "Don't you ever say that baby word again!" he roared. "A male has a penis, a dong. A ding dang dong is what makes a man a man. It's his proudest possession. Boy!"

Grampa lit his pipe again. "I presume. Boy, that you know why you have a penis?"

"Yes sir," I answered, "to pee with."

"That's true, Grampa said gravely," but it's also used for fornication. Do you know what that means?"

"Yes," I replied. "You taught me that word last year when Puuko, our cat, was going out screwing every night. I began to recite his poem that had the word in it: "Cats on the housetops/Cats on the tiles/Cats with syphilis…""

Grampa hurriedly interrupted me. "Oh dear me," he said. "I'm a dirty old man corrupting the youth of the land." He puffed on his pipe a long time before he continued. "I presume also that you have occasionally witnessed the act?"

"Yes, sir," I said. "Roosters do it; dogs do it; so do chipmunks. I've even seen squirrels do it upside down on trees. And last year Dad asked me to lead Rosie, our cow, over to the Salos so their big bull could service her. Wow! Was that something! She bellered all the way home. "Grampa, how do birds do it?"

"Damned if I know," he replied. "I suppose they do it with their feet on the ground or on a branch. Seems like it might be difficult to do on the wing." "But dragon flies do it when flying," I protested. "I've seen them, one on top of each other in the air."

"Mebbe so, mebbe so. Seems like you know more about fornication than I do. How the hell did I get into this anyway?" Grampa lit his pipe again.

I told him how Fisheye and I had once seen Mr. Hummel's stallion on top of a mare in their barnyard. "It was scary, Grampa," I said. "He was snorting like crazy and when he mounted the mare he bit her on the neck too."

"How about fish?" Grampa asked.

"Oh, I know all about that," I replied. "Mullu and I spent a whole Saturday afternoon watching a gravel bed in Beaver Dam creek where a big female trout scooped out a hole in the sand with its tail and laid some yellow eggs in it. And then a smaller trout came by and squirted some white stuff over the nest. Then she chased him away and started fanning the eggs with her tail. Interesting!"

"So you know all about sperm and eggs." Grampa seemed impressed.

"Oh yeah," I answered. "All females have eggs in them just like hens do but the eggs don't have any shells on them while they're still inside. I cleaned a chicken once and the eggs were soft and yellow. Boys don't have eggs in them, do we?" Grampa shook his head.

"Grampa, why do some of the eggs turn out to be boys and other eggs girls? I tried to find out by looking in Dad's medical books when he was out on a house call but it was too full of big words. They had some interesting pictures, though."

"Lord, I don't know why some eggs become male and others don't,'" he replied. "What kind of pictures have you seen?"

"Oh, there's one book that shows how babies grow from the very first when they're inside the mother.There's a picture of something looking like a tiny tadpole entering the egg. Then the egg splits in two, then it becomes an embyro."

"No, not embyro. It's embryo, em-bree-o." Grampa seemed happy to contribute to my fund of knowledge.

"OK, embryo. Anyway, they're sure ugly at first, all big head and belly and with tiny arms and legs all curled up. I think it said that at eight weeks it was only about an inch long. Is that true?"

Grampa didn't answer.

"I saw a baby being born once," I continued. "Right on our front porch. Surprised everybody, I guess. No one noticed I was watching as Dad pulled it out until after he had cut the cord.Then he saw me and asked me to go fetch a pail from the shed so he could put the afterbirth in it. And then he told me to bury it in the rhubarb patch. Some kids think that babies are brought by the stork or come in the doctor's satchel. They're nuts!"

"That rhubarb pie we had yesterday was the best one I ever ate," mused Grampa. "Let's go home. Boy. Let's go home."

As we again passed Sliding Rock I thought of something else. "What's the missionary position, Grampa?"

Again he just shook his head and didn't answer.

Well, with that expurgated version of a better tale I called it quits. It had been a great grandfather's day indeed.

Day Eight

It was another nasty day when I stuck my head outside the back door. Sleet and a very hard wind would keep me confined to the house. Where was the spring that the calendar said should be here? Refusing to yield to negative or depressive thoughts, I vowed that I would make the day a good one. "Enjoy! Enjoy!" Grampa had commanded. So I enjoyed my grapefruit-mit-bananas, the cinnamon toast and coffee and the smoke rings circling upward from my pipe. What should I tackle on this, another fine day in the life of Cully Gage?

Well, I could start by mending Mullu whose stem I had broken yesterday. All of my pipes are named after friends and Mullu is a long time favorite. Somewhere in my study is a box containing bowls and stems of broken pipes that I've gathered over the years because I've always found it difficult to discard an old friend. Perhaps in the box I could find a stem that would fit Mullu.

I never did find that particular box but I found another that had once held typing paper. It was labeled "The Impossible Dream." I laughed aloud when I saw it because I knew it contained the last remains of my crazy attempt to become a composer of Flame Symphonies. I was still grinning at the memory of my wife's reaction when, at a Happy Hour fire, I told her what I was intending to do.

"Madam, Milove," I said. "Your loving husband is about to embark on a new project. I am…"

She interrupted. "Oh no" she wailed in alarm. "No more mynah birds. No more pigs to eat my flowers."

"No, nothing like those," I answered. "I've had this idea for years and it first came to me when I was sitting by a campfire up at the Hayshed Dam. I'm going to try to become a composer, the first composer of symphonies using flames rather than musical notes."

She giggled a little. "Cully, you're having your midlife crisis a bit early but it sounds harmless enough. At least you aren't planning to chase some younger woman."

"Lord, no," I replied. "One woman like you is enough for any man but listen to me. I know it sounds crazy but think of the possibilities.There hasn't been a new art form in ten thousand years. It will be the poor man's art form. With some wood, a match and my directions he could build a fire that would have a prelude, a theme with variations and a grand finale."

Watching our own fire burning on the hearth she tried to keep a straight face. "Cully, the Mozart of the Flame. You promised me that I might have a rough time after I married you but that I would never be bored. You were correct. Milord."

"Oh, but there's much more to it," I said. "This new art form will not only have the sounds of the fire but also the colors and shapes and movements of the flames. It will combine music and painting and sculpture and even the dance because flames are never still."

Not trying to suppress her mirth any longer she said, "Excuse me but I'd better start supper. Picasso, Rodin, John Sebastian Bach and Fred Astaire will be eating my meatloaf tonight." As she left for the kitchen there was a strange smile on her face. Even now, forty years later, I can still see that smile.

In the box that contained the notes of this project I found some of the cards on which I had identified the colors of the flames. I remembered thinking that to go about the project systematically I should begin with something easy like identifying the colors and finding words or symbols to represent them but this proved very difficult. There were blue flames, yellow flames, grey flames, orange flames, even green ones but most flames were none of these. They were flame colored and no other term could describe them any better than that. OK, I'd use the letter F as their symbol and perhaps find a better one later.

Composing Flame Symphony

As I sat there on the stool by the fireplace recording the flame colors I asked my wife to help me. "What would you say is the color of that flame on the extreme right?" I'd ask and she'd answer "oriental poppy" or "custard pie." Not much help, terms like that. And one time when I was in the bathroom I heard her calling me, "Cully, come quick. There's a black flame." A black flame? I'd never seen one, nor ever a pink or purple flame either. Tugging up my pants I tore into the living room.

"Sorry, it's gone," she said. "Do you know what the date is today?" It was the first of April. Somehow I began to have the impression that she wasn't taking my project very seriously.

Another unexpected problem was that the color of the flame often depended on the kind of wood that was burning and varied with the position of the wood and the duration of the fire. For example, wild cherry yielded more blue flames than any other wood; horizontal logs had more blue flames than slanting ones; more blue appeared as the logs were just beginning to burn, then turned to yellow or flame color later. Grey flames were ghost flames, disembodied from their source and floating unattached. Green ones were rare and tended to occur in the transition between the blue and yellow. Things were getting complicated but the more I watched my fires the more intrigued I became. I had watched a thousand hearth and campfires in my time but now I was seeing things I'd never seen before.

Finally I felt I had pretty well mastered the problem of color and to test that belief I got up early one morning and laid a fire on the hearth consisting of a lot of different kinds of wood: pine, cedar, pale oak, hickory and even sassafras, arranging them carefully and writing down in my notes a prediction of the colors that would ensue when I lit it that evening.

When I did so I was met with the damndest display I'd ever seen. All the colors of the rainbow flared. I looked accusingly at my wife. "You've sprinkled some of those powders," I said angrily.

"Yes," she said. "Since you're more interested in those flame colors than you are in me I thought I'd give you a real dose of them. Cully, you worry me. You're becoming obsessed. I'm getting so I dread Happy Hour. You never talk to me but just sit on that stool watching the fire and taking notes." Of course she was right so I took a few weeks off and gave her a lot of loving attention.

Later that month, however, I was at it again, this time listening and analyzing the music of the flames. The variety of sounds I began to hear almost overwhelmed me. There were crackles, pops, ticks and tocks. There were spluts from a flatulent fire. Occasionally I heard a loud report similar to that produced by a rifle shot so loud it almost jumped me off my stool. If I had a piece of wood that wasn't thoroughly dried it would whistle or hiss, sometimes so high in pitch it was barely discernible. The best of this fire music tended to occur early as the kindling and small wood caught fire. When the fire died down there were rustles and sizzles and periods of complete silence.

Some woods produced more sounds than others, especially dried spruce and cedar. Again I had great difficulty finding symbols for these sounds and finally just used descriptive words. Once, when I was trying to imitate some of these sounds, Milove said to me "Pop pop, tick, crackle, ssss, and splut, splut, splut," so I quit building fires for three months in the interest of my domestic tranquility.

When I began again it was with sparks and they almost made me despair. There were single sparks, usually following a loud pop, that zigzagged their way up the flue. There were doubles and twins and when a log shifted a shower of them would always appear. Some sparks died almost instantly; others found a short resting place on the back wall of the hearth, often creating patterns. Once, when a shower created a pattern that resembled the profile of a human head, I asked my wife if she saw it too.

"No," she replied. "All I see is the profile of a man I used to know - my husband."

I realized that a composer of flame symphonies must not only be a painter and use colors, or a musician and compose with tones. He also had to be a sculptor because he had to deal with the varying shapes and contours of the flames. Could it be done? Calder's mobiles came to mind. They too constantly changed. Were there any words to describe these shapes and contours? Yes, there were sheets of flame, flames that curled, single flames that bounced. Often at the base of a log a long series of short flames lined the lower surface looking like yellow teeth. OK, I'll call them <u>teeth</u>. Some flames merely <u>flickered</u>: others <u>flowed</u> continuously. There were <u>flares</u> and <u>bursts</u> of flame. Some flames were <u>forked</u>: some had a single apex. We kept horses back then and often to relieve my frustration I'd go out to clean their stalls.

When I started on the final phase of my project, the recording of the movements of flames, I was beginning to get a bit tired of the whole damned thing. It meant that I would have to learn the choreography of the dance, something I knew absolutely nothing about. Flames did dance; they were rarely still. How could I possibly record them? When I asked my wife to find a book on choreography at the library she flatly refused.

"But won't you be glad to be able to say that you're the wife of the inventor of flame symphonies?" I asked teasingly.

"Perhaps," she answered, "but then the attendant at the State Hospital will say that you are in the third cell on the left, the one with the barred windows. And that when he gets the keys he'll let me see you for a few minutes."

So I never did manage to orchestrate my flames. Instead I decided to try to put together all that I'd learned and seek to create my first flame symphony. With great care I prepared the series of sheets on which I recorded the colors and sounds and shapes of what I would find once I set fire to the carefully placed kindling and logs. There was a sheet for each ten minutes and it was covered with symbols and words that would make no sense to anyone else but me.

Before I lit my masterpiece, and following the scores frame by frame, I told my wife exactly what would happen, how the prelude produced by my kindling would look and sound. I described the shapes and contours she should look for in the major theme and its variations. I presented a word picture of my grand finale. Then with a flourish I lit the match.

Ach du lieber Augustine! Gage Flame Symphony Number One was an utter flop, a disaster. Nothing I'd predicted came true. Indeed only half of my kindling caught fire at all. No blue flames appeared on the lower surface of my cherrywood triangle. The forked flames did not lick upward along the short upright chunk of oak but spread sideways instead. The osage orange slab that was supposed to create a great shower of sparks for the finale caught fire instantly and fell off to one side. My back log of maple never did flame, not even when I dumped all the sheets of my symphony on top of it. There were few embers.

And Milove laughed and laughed. So did I.

Back to the drawing board? No! I'd done my damndest; angels could do no more. I packed up my notes and hid them in the study. I've built a thousand fires since but never attempted another flame symphony. Was it worth it? Of course. It's the seeking, not the attaining of an impossible goal that counts. I now know how to watch a fire and my pleasure in doing so is much greater than it ever was before.

Like old buggers from the U.P., impossible dreams are hard to kill and when at last they do die, new dreams arise from their humus. That happened this afternoon.

No, I'd never try to compose another flame symphony but why not try to make a videotape of a fire from start to finish. Now we had color photography. Now we had a way to preserve a fire and enjoy it time and time again. I have two cherished video cassettes, one of wolf music and the other of ocean waves that I treasure and replay often. Each has some commentary which interprets what I am seeing and hearing. Why not try to do the same for a hearth fire?

I borrowed a Camcorder from a friend, built a good fire, photographed part of it, then played it back on my TV while adding my commentary. I felt the old excitement welling up inside me. Yes, it could be done and I could do it. Now all those poor souls who had no fireplace in their homes or apartments could have the joys of fire watching. What a market! If the first video cassette sold well, I could follow it with another and even better one. Oh, I'd have to learn how to edit my shots and commentary to keep them within the necessary time limits but that could be done. Now I'd have a new project for my old age and have some further impact on others I would never know in person.

When I told Milove about it at Happy Hour she laughed outrageously and told me to look up the story "Flame Symphonies" in my first *Northwoods Reader* to see how my father had reacted.

I'd forgotten all about that tale in which I told about Carl Anters, Tioga's strange young man. In it I had used my own experience in trying to compose fire symphonies. Here is the passage to which Milove referred:

"It was several years before we saw Carl again, and again he came to our house.

"Doctor, sir," he said to my father, "Please may I have an opportunity to discuss with you an insight which has come to me? I desperately need to present it to someone with some educational and cultural background. Please, sir?"

Dad was not one to suffer fools gladly but he'd just eaten a fine meal with apple pie. "All right, Carl. Come into the living room and tell me what's on your mind."

I remember some of what Carl said though it didn't make much sense. In essence, he claimed to have discovered a brand new art form, one that combined painting and sculpture and music and much more besides. He told us he'd learned how to build fires so he could predict every color and contour of the flames from one moment to another.

"I arrange my kindling so it will produce a prelude, shaping the main theme of my composition. I've even learned how to create a counterpoint effect. I've composed three flame symphonies already and I can do them every time if I have the same wood. That's the hard part, and also trying to invent a notation that is adequate. I've just started, but look here, Doctor."

Carl pulled out a large sheet that looked like a musical score except that there were no musical notes on it, just a complicated set of squiggles so far as I could see. He excitedly explained what they meant.

"This one refers to a forked flame, that one to a flame having a single apex; this symbol represents the color and duration of the flame, and that one's for the sound."

He also had symbols for tempo. It was far too complicated for me to follow, even though he quit using those big words as he became more excited.

"And these little dots on the score are sparks. Doctor. By using osage orange or sumac wood I can create a wonderful fanfare of sparks at just the right time. Just think. Doctor, here is the poor man's art form. All he needs is a match…"

Carl suddenly stopped talking and looked my father straight in the eye. "Am I crazy. Doctor?"

My father was polite, but after he ushered Carl out the front door, he made his diagnosis. "Nutty as a hoot owl," he said."

As the day came to its close I wasn't very happy so I did what I often do to make myself a better mood. I wrote another little U.P. tale, felt good, and went to bed. Here it is:

Drumsticks

People used to say that there were more liars to the square yard in the U.P. than anywhere else in the country. I don't know that this is true but I do know that Tioga, the little forest village where I was born, had the biggest one. His name was Slimber Vester, a saintly looking old scoundrel with a fine white beard, who used to tell his tales in Higley's saloon every Saturday evening when he had a beer or two or three. Here is another of his milder lies.

"I've always liked the drumsticks of a chicken better than any other part," he said, "and I never have yet had my fill of them. Trouble is that a chicken usually has only two legs."

One of the other men at the bar took the bait. "Usually?" he asked. "What you mean, usually. Never was a chicken had any more than two."

"That's what you say. That's what you say, but I know different." Slimber was not offended. He'd had many others who doubted his honesty.

"I learned better one time I guided a feller from Chicago trout fishing on the Paint River near Republic. He was one of these here fly fisherman. Wouldn't use worms and he tells me he wanted not too big a stream nor any with brush on the banks, one with a lot of meadows and a lot of trout. That's asking a lot but I figured the Paint River with its beaver meadows might be what he wanted."

"Yeah," said one of the men at the bar, "but that's a long way from Tioga. How'd you get there?"

"Well, the dude had plenty of money so we rented a horse and buggy from Marchand's Livery Stable. No, not Maude, that pokey old broken down mare. If we'd had her the trip would have taken a whole day. Marchand gave us Celeste who can step along pretty lively if you give her a little taste of the whip "

The men were getting impatient. "But what about those chickens. Slimber? Tell us about them chickens."

"I'm a-coming to it," replied Slimber, lighting his old corncob pipe. "I'm a-coming to it. Anyone feel like buying me another beer?"

Refueled, he continued. "Yep, it's a long way and I could see the man from Chicago was getting restless so I slapped Celeste hard with the reins and she was really galloping when we see a big chicken trotting along beside the buggy and then passing us."

"You're crazy," said a man. "No chicken can run fast as a horse."

"That's what we thought," said Slimber. "The man I was guiding almost lost his eyeballs looking at that chicken".

"Do you see what I see?" he asked me. "That damned chicken has three legs. Do you see three legs?"

"So help me it was true. It had one leg in front and two behind and they were big legs, bigger than you ever seen. And that was why he could run so fast. He'd reach out with the one leg then straddle it with the hind ones and gallop like a bear going up hill. Celeste she was going plenty fast and that chicken passed her like she was standing still."

"That's hard to believe," said Higley, the bartender.

"Yep, I know it is," replied Slimber, "but harder yet is that pretty soon along came three or four more chickens that passed us and all of them had three legs too. I tried to run into one of them, thinking of the fine drumsticks, but it dodged and passed us easily."

"'Well,' the man beside me said, I can't believe it. Whip the horse so I can get a better look.' Just then the road turned and there was a straight stretch ahead so we could see all them three legged chickens up ahead of us and then they turned off up a farmer's lane to the right."

"'Follow them,'" he ordered and soon we came to a farmhouse to see a woman feeding corn to a whole flock of them, all three legged."

"The man steps out and says politely , "Maam, are these three legged chickens yours? I never see their like before.'

'Guess there aren't any others like them,' she answered. 'We got them from my brother who does research on chicken breeding at the State College and he sent them up here so we could breed them for their drumsticks.'

'Wow!'" said the man. 'One of them drumsticks would be a full meal.. Are they too tough?"

'Dunno,' she said. 'We've never been able to catch one."

Day Nine

My morning greeting to the world had little fervor in it when I poked my head out of the back door. It would be another gray miserable day. Would spring ever come? Knowing I'd have to make sure that depression and negative thoughts would not add to it I made myself some french toast. Alas, it turned out to be soggy and the sugarless maple syrup didn't help any either. What could I do this day to make it enjoyable and significant? I couldn't think of a single thing.

Well then I'd do something that should be done, something I'd put off doing too long. How about putting some new washers in the faucets that had been leaking? No, I was all out of washers and John wouldn't be able to get them until the weekend. Or I could empty the fireplace ashes and put them on the lilacs. Nuts to that. There weren't enough of them. I could dust the upstairs hallway and bedrooms. No, they weren't really dirty.

While I was considering these self suggestions I knew all the time what I should really do: clean and organize my study. Heaven knows it needed it. The project was so unattractive it took an extra cup of coffee and a pipe of Sir Walter Raleigh before I could make myself get out of the comfortable chair. Like Lord Nelson at the naval battle of Trafalgar, I shouted, "England expects every man to do his duty!" OK, study, here I come."

But where to begin? As I looked it over I felt sorry for my children who would have to get rid of the stuff after I died. I knew none of them would live here in the old house; they had their own. They wouldn't want that ancient bronze spear point given me by that stutterer from Iran or the little bust of Nephrite by the one from Egypt nor the stein from Germany nor the wooden fishhook from the Fiji Islands. My son might want to have the ten pound family Bible but would he desire the black jug I found in an abandoned lumber camp? Perhaps Cathy might like to keep the brass spittoon her mother had rescued from my father's hospital and after much polishing had turned it into a lovely vase for our flowers. Would Sue want the glass cage of stuffed birds including the extinct passenger pigeon or should I give it to our museum? And all my treasured books, shell collection and tobacco pipes? Perhaps I should make the bonfire of bonfires out behind the barn? No that would be too hard work and spoil the nest in which I'd laid so many literary eggs.

Under my east bookcase is a space full of boxes of manila folders which I had put there when I last cleaned my study some years ago. Surely some of those could be discarded. I opened one and found it full of drawings my children had made when they were very young. One was of me, a monkey smoking a pipe. Another folder held all the materials I'd assembled in tracing my family tree back to Jurien Tomasson Van Riper who came to this country from Holland in the sailing ship the Spotted Cow in 1640. I put it in the wastebasket, then took it out again. My son might like to have the information when he too grew old. Let him throw it away if he didn't.

When I opened the third big envelope it was the end of my cleaning spree. In it were notes for more tales about the old U.P., unfinished manuscripts and stories that were completed but had never been published. Though I knew I would never write another *Northwoods Reader* it was so much fun reading them that I spent the whole day doing so with breaks only for getting the mail and meals and wood for my Happy Hour.

The first tale I read was about an old self taught fiddler named Waino Ohala. a very shy man, whose whole life revolved around his violin. I described how he got his first instrument, how he learned to play it, how it cured his shyness and gave him a lovelife. It told about the barn dances of the time, his battle with the drunk who smashed it. It ended with his final concert out in the woods when unable to play very long because of the arthritic pain that prevented his pressing the strings, he'd shot himself. I'd written it much better than it sounds here. Why hadn't I included it in one of my books? Too tragic? I'd written other sad tales that my readers had loved. Should I dump it in the wastebasket? No, I might want to read it again some day.

The next manuscript I found was a completed story about a morning that my beloved Grampa Gage and I spent collecting holes, mouse holes, fox holes, key holes, holes in the water produced by paddles, caves. It ended with our exploration of the huge one up at the mine that had resulted from a great cave-in that had engulfed two houses and two sleeping men. Throughout the story I had tried to express the fascination that holes hold for men and hounds alike. Grampa had some very funny and enlightening comments. But somehow the tale never really jelled nor could I find a good ending for it.

Next I found a narrative about the trip our family made from Tioga to Iron Mountain in Dad's new 1914 Model-T Ford. Now we can drive it in just an hour but then it took us a whole day each way. The road consisted of just two ruts through a deep hardwood wilderness so thick we often had to use the one man cross cut saw to open the road or to cut some logs to replace those of the corduroy in a swamp. Several times we forded a little stream. I counted forty-three deer en route. The story had a lot about that car and its problems and characteristics, the many flat tires that had to be patched on the spot, how it scared the horses of farmers and so on. I never finished that tale because I felt few readers would be interested. I can never bear the thought that some reader might say Ho-Hum.

Another unfinished tale was about how Eino and Emil celebrated a New Year's Day with a two moon toot. (In the U.P. that means you're so intoxicated you see, not one moon, but two.) It was a hilarious tale so far as it went but I couldn't find a good ending that was at all plausible.

One of the best tales was about how Old Man McGee had a fine Christmas after all. I've always enjoyed writing about him and the Easter story I published in one of my Northwoods Readers is a favorite of mine. That's the one about how he celebrated by preaching a sunrise service to the tombstones.

In the folder were a lot of my mulling cards, those on which I'd jotted down items I might use when I did write a new tale. I'll just list the titles because you could make no sense of the stuff I scribbled on them. Here are a few: The Big Fight, The Flu Epidemic, Dad's Toughest Confinement Case, Stealing Apples, Charon Wrestles the Buck, Our Little Orchestra, Sir Launcelot, Our Rooster, The Code, Our Childhood Games, Trapping, The Last Deer Camp, Memorial Day in Tioga. Mullu, Fisheye and the Billygoat, Miss Poison's Battle with Old Blue Balls. And there were a lot more.

Again I wondered where all of them came from. I was a forest spring; the more water that left it, the more came in. Too bad I wouldn't be able to write another book but perhaps I could include one of the tales in this book, a short one. It would have to be an amusing one. I didn't want to end this book tragically. In the folder was a letter from Charlie Shilling that had a good Halloween story. I'd rewrite it for all the readers of my book who have shared bits of their lives with me. Here it is:

A few years back, two of my neighbors. Bill and Emily Smith, were going to a Halloween party at the Legion Hall. Emily is quite a character, always out for a good time. Bill is slow and serious but has a good sense of humor. They decided to dress up in costumes. Bill as the devil and Emily as an angel so she made the costumes for both of them.

The afternoon of the party however Emily came down with one of her bad migraine headaches and when Bill came home she told him she was too sick and that he should go without her. Bill replied that he'd just as soon stay home but Emily told him she'd done a lot of work making that devil costume and wished he'd go without her. She didn't feel like making him any supper and they'd have food at the hall. Bill finally agreed and off he went in the big red suit, horns, tail and all. Emily had done a good job. He really looked like the devil with his mask on.

When he left Emily took a couple of aspirins and lay down to take a nap. After about an hour she woke up feeling fine. After another half hour she was feeling better yet so she decided to go to the party after all. Then she got to thinking that it might be a good time to check up on Bill and to see how he acted around women when she wasn't around. You never knew about these men when they're let loose. When she went to the closet to get her angel costume the thought hit her like lightning that he'd recognize her but if she used the old witch's costume she'd worn many years ago he wouldn't. She found it in the attic along with a pointed hat and ugly mask. Yeah, that would do it. Bill would never know if she disguised her voice.

When she got to the Legion party she saw her big red devil standing at the bar talking sweet stuff with a female, the dirty dog. She went over to them and using a high pitched voice she asked him if he would buy a hot witch a drink too. The devil said sure, she could have anything she wanted.

"What I want, we can't do here," she said, "but buy me a drink and we'll talk about it."

By the time they finished the drink she could have killed that big devil of a husband of hers. He sure was full of the devil inside as well as outside. To test him a bit further, she told him she'd like to know just how long his tail really was and he said, "Fine! Let's go outside and I'll show you under the big pine tree."

Outside they went but she broke away and fled home. She'd wait up for that two-timing skunk, and see what kind of a lie he would tell. She had him this time and she'd let him have it good. She'd never trust him again. The longer she waited up for Bill to come home, the madder she got. He could fry in hell. She'd make him sweat.

When Bill did come home about one-thirty Emily had calmed down some. She would be nice and cool and let him hang himself. "Did you have a nice time at the party?" she asked sweetly. "Did you have any fun?"

"Not really," Bill replied." I had a bite to eat, drank a few beers and sat out in the back room playing cards all evening with Fred and Ed."

"You didn't dance or have fun with some woman?" she inquired.

"No," he answered. "I loaned my costume to Frank and I guess he had a hot time with some old witch."

When I finished typing that tale it was bedtime. I'd been inside almost all that day but it had been another good one.

The Day That Will Be
Or Might Have Been

It is mid-winter Down Below. A foot of snow covers my farm and it is very cold. Unlike the dry cold of the U.P. this is piercingly damp and one feels it more intensely or at least in my old age I do. Old bones! Old bones! Damned old bones! Up there in my homeland the sun shines; here it does not. Most of our days are spent beneath gray, cloudy skies. What the hell am I doing down here anyway? Will spring ever come?

I'm not as sure as I once was that I would make it through the winter because lately I've been having a rough time. Twice this month I thought I was going to die, the last episode occurring just two days ago. I won't go into the morbid details but the Old Reaper sure took a good swipe at me with his scythe.

And that is the reason I'm writing about a day that perhaps might be or might have been. I hate to leave this book unfinished and although I had planned to include some other days of my life down here in Portage I'll just pretend that I did survive and tell you what might have occurred when I found myself back in Shangri la.

When I awakened John was gone but a fine fire blazed in the fireplace of the big cabin and the smell of coffee made it hard to lie there much longer. On the boards of the bunk above me were the words "Good Morning, Grampa" printed in a childish hand by one of my grandchildren. Ah, it would indeed be a great morning. Despite my bum prognosis I was back in my homeland again, back in my cabin on our lovely wilderness lakes. How the devil had I managed it?

Actually the long trip hadn't been bad at all because in the rented conversion van I had been able to lie down most of the way while John did all the driving except for the long Seney stretch where I took the wheel. Arriving at dusk, I had a snort of scotch while John unpacked and built a fine fire. Then after eating half of one of the pasties we'd picked up en route I hit the sack. Watching the flame shadows flickering on the burnished log walls, I was soon asleep with a smile on my face. It was still there the next morning.

I lay there a bit savoring the moment until the smell of the coffee John had made and the sight of the fire he had started got me out of bed. Opening the door to go to the outhouse in the woods I found myself deeply inhaling that wonderful U.P. air fresh from the waves of Lake Superior. In it were traces of cedar and balsam and the musky smell of deep woods. Fog devils swirled on the lake's surface chasing each other. From beyond Birch Point came the long lorn call of a loon. I almost hugged myself. I was home again!

For just a moment I was tempted to strip off my clothes and plunge nakedly into the lake as so often I'd done as a boy but instead scooped up water in my cupped hands to wash my old face. Cold water! Clean water! Spluttering, I shook the drops off my white beard and let the spring sun tingle it dry before entering the cabin. Lord, I was feeling good.

The years fell from me like those water drops.

Not knowing when John might return for breakfast I poured a cup of coffee to go with some Korpua and a chunk of the smoked whitefish we'd picked up at Naubinway and sat in the big chair before the fire. My wife had bought that chair for me because I'd purchased one for her of the same kind. Hers was sitting by the north window overlooking part of the West Bay and Birch Point. How many hours we'd spent together in those chairs watching the chipmunks and seeing the many changes in the lake's surface. There were times when the lake looked like frosted glass; at others like a dark black mirror. This morning it was very blue with waves bearing white caps surging toward the east and crashing against Herman's Rock where we always put the fish entrails so the bears wouldn't bother us. Herman, our seagull, hadn't found us yet but he will. I chuckled remembering how he had tried to defend that white rock from a tall blue heron last summer. One sharp peck from the heron's bill sent him away squawking. And the time when a bald eagle drove Herman away and ate his food.

To get the smell of the smoked fish off my hands I went to the pump and sink. Ach! The pump had lost its prime as it usually does over the winter when the leathers dry out. Getting a jug of lake water I poured it down the top as I pumped the handle with my other hand, soon felt the pressure building resistance, and out came a rush of water from the spout. It's good water but I hoped John had filled another jug from our big spring on the far bay. I like spring water for my evening whiskey. In deer camp we use the icicles that hang from the roof.

Finally rousing myself I looked out of the other window to see where John might be. Our big cabin sits on a point and from each window you can see a different section of the lake. Perhaps John's boat was in the south bay or the outlet. Looking through the big south window I felt that there was something wrong. Oh yes, we hadn't put up the flag yet on the tall pole by the dock. Milove always hoisted it the moment she arrived. After finding it in the long cupboard bench I soon had the flag waving and saluted both it and her. Cully was back in camp.

The other thing that my wife always did upon arriving was to feed the chipmunks so I took some sunflower seeds to the little tables and ladders that my daughter Sue had constructed when she was in the third grade. Though a little rickety after so many years they were still serviceable. Soon the chipmunk word would get out and we'd have a lot of them scurrying around. The big one, Manchester, (we've had a long series of Manchesters) would be spending so much of his chippie time chasing the others off he'd hardly have time to eat anything himself. I noticed the pancake nail on one of the big cedars where we always hung the extra one or the burned one. I heard a red squirrel unwinding his ratchet and knew he'd be waiting for that first pancake. I remembered the time a huge osprey swooped down on immense but silent wings to snatch a chippie off the feeder. The place was so full of memories they tumbled all over my mind, each one leading to another.

The Day That Will Be Or Might Have Been

Returning around the comer of the cabin I saw the silly little brass bell and pulled its string. It's tinkle was never loud enough to serve its original purpose which was to call the children to a meal. Instead, it was the Chase-me-Grampa bell. Whenever a grandchild rang it Grampa had to leave whatever he was doing and chase the kid around the cabin. I never failed to respond because I could get my three hugs if I caught him or her. Behind the south east comer of the cabin is a little hummock called Toad Hill on which sits a big chunk of wood. This was their sanctuary because if they could reach it before I caught them they were safe and I got no hugs. Oh, the joyful squealing. Toad Hill was called that because often under the chunk we often found a toad and then had to kiss it.

Just beyond Mr. Toad's hill is our woodshed and wondering about the wood supply I went to it. Rich Waisanen, my caretaker, had filled it with big chunks. John would have to split some for small wood and some cedar for kindling. At the corners of the shed I'd transplanted several sprigs of Virginia Creeper ivy from home some years ago. Had they survived another winter? Yes, there they were. I laid some branches up against the logs so the vines could climb, hoping that eventually they would cover the structure.

The hunger to see the Old Cabin was hard upon me. Would I be able to walk the fourth of a mile to see it? To find out I started up the road, my legs hurting with each step. When I got to the Little Bear's Hole I looked inside the hollow tree to see if there was a message. For years, ever since she was seven, my granddaughter, Jennifer, and I have used it as a postoffice. I pretend to be Little Bear and write notes to her on birch bark and she responds in the same way. Jennifer had been up at the cabin last summer after I had but she was very adult now and I wondered if she had forgotten. Yes, there it was: "Dear Little Bear: I hope you haven't forgotten me for a girlfriend in the Porcupineapple Mountains. Please leave me a note. Yours, Jen." Sure made me feel good.

I walked a bit further up the road to where the Upper Lake Trail starts its long way around our lake. Surprisingly it seemed clear and open though I knew that there would be new windfalls along its route for John to cut with the chainsaw. Tempted to follow it to Porcupine Bluff I rested on a log, then decided not to push things. Getting back to the Big Cabin would be all the limping I could handle.

For once I had been wise. Going down the hill was harder than climbing it and I was so exhausted I lay down in the bunk until I heard the outboard motor.

I was down at the dock when John expertly coasted the boat to the sand. A big grin ran around his face as he held up a stringer holding three big bass. "Caught a lot of smaller ones too," he said, "and had a big pike that got tangled in the motor and got away. I always forget to pull it up. I will remember next time. Anyway we've got fish for supper." Stripping off his pants and shoes, he wrestled the old fish cage into the water and dumped the bass into it. Lord, that cage was almost as old as he was. I remember building it after some varmint, probably a mink, had stolen my supper off the fish stringer.

"I'm hungry," John said, looking at his watch. "Hey, it's quarter after eleven. How about pancakes and bacon for an early lunch? Wish we had some cranberries or blueberries to put in the pancakes." I nodded. At home in Portage I rarely have any real appetite but up in the north country I always do. Something about the air, no doubt.

As he mixed the batter and put the bacon in the old cast iron skillet I remembered that once, as a youth, I'd eaten seventeen big pancakes in one sitting. "Make just two for me, Pierre," I said, "and see if you can find the bottle of ersatz maple syrup I brought up. I hate the stuff but it's better than nothing. I'm sure you can find some good maple syrup in the cupboards."

When he opened one of them to look he exclaimed. "Mice! They've sure raised hell over the winter and probably have some young too. I thought I heard some scampering around last night. Oh what a mess! I'll clean it up this afternoon. Look what they did to the spaghetti!"

"Yeah," I said, "Save some of the bacon grease to mix with the peanut butter for baiting the traps. We'll clean them out of here. I bet they've got a hole in the flashing along the chimney that we'll have to caulk again."

I grinned when he took down the long griddle from the wall and wiped the dust off it. That cast iron has never been washed. It's against the camp law ever since my father brought it to the Old Cabin in 1917 yet it always makes the best pancakes you ever tasted. "Be sure to make enough for the red squirrel and chippies," I said.

John, or Pierre as I call him when he cooks, has come a long way since I first brought him up here five years ago. The pancakes were perfect and I ate three of them. After wiping the dishes I asked John to drive me up to the Old Cabin for my nap. "I may walk back on the trail behind the outhouse," I said, " but if I'm not here by two-thirty, come after me."

"I've got to set the minnow traps in the Beaver Dam." he replied. "Why don't you come with me and I'll let you off on the way back? You always liked that spot." When we reached the dam it was obvious that the beavers were still there because the water had backed up almost to the road. I got out of the car to enjoy that beautiful spot again, one that I had seen in my dreams for months. Oh to see it when the fall colors were at their peak. It's breathtaking. As John put some bread in the traps and flung them into the water I felt the new silky green tamarack needles, always a miracle, and soft as a baby's cheek. And there on a sandy spot at the edge of the road I found moose tracks, huge ones, bigger than a cow could make. Perhaps we'll see them again this time, possibly in the marsh near the outlet. I must remember to get out the binoculars. What huge monsters they are, those kings of the wilderness. As we came back from the beaver dam I found myself getting excited. I've felt that way every time since I was a boy, and I could hardly wait to get out of the car at the turnaround. I'm back. Old Cabin. I'm back! That was what Milove always said, and perhaps some of my grandchildren will say it too.

This time I had an added incentive because last summer I saw that its three lower south logs were rotting and I'd asked Rich, my caretaker, to replace them. He and a friend had spent two days doing so and he'd sent me a photo but I wanted to see for myself. A fine job. It would need some additional chinking but now the Old Cabin would last another seventy years for my grandchildren and great grandchildren to enjoy.

As John unlocked the door, I asked him to open the windows and build a little fire in the box stove to get rid of the camp damp that always shows up over winter. After he left, I sat in the big chair for a long time remembering the good times I'd had there as a boy, as a youth, and when I brought Milove there on our honeymoon to find a huge log my friends had wedged in the middle of the upper bunk. I'd made a balsam bed there for us. Now she was gone and I was alone but her ashes had been scattered about the little clearing as mine would also be. She had come back as she had requested, and I too was back with her.

The Day That Will Be Or Might Have Been

The fire John had built soon warmed the cabin so I got some blankets from the hamper and laid down on them to have my nap. But before I did I found the big nickel watch The Regulars had left when their deer hunting days were over. Once again, after I wound it, the second hand started moving. How often it had ticked on the ledge beside the bunk! Nothing had changed. Not even I. I closed my eyes.

As I lay there a host of memories came back to me, some about The Regulars, Dad's old hunting cronies, when they spent their annual two weeks hunting deer from this old cabin. What fun they had. Big men freed from the responsibilities of work and family, up here they were boys again.

I thought of my own fine summers up here alone learning the ways of the forest creatures, becoming one myself. How I had roamed those deep woods until I knew every foot of them, almost every moss covered rock, the inner sanctuaries of every swamp or clump of huge hemlocks on the hills.

And I thought of Milove and wished she were here beside me. She always wanted to sleep next to the window so she could feel herself a part of the forest and hear the night sounds. I reminded myself that I must tend the little terrace garden I'd made for her near the Big Cabin. Had the arbutus and blue gentians and star flowers she'd transplanted there survived another year? It would need some weeding.

Suddenly I awakened. It was two o'clock on the old watch beside me.

After I went outside I sat for a time on the bench looking at the little clearing where so many good experiences had taken place. Even now I could see remnants of the night fires we'd had when my children were young. How excited they were as night came and the sparks drifted upward. Wide eyed, they would sit there with our arms around them until the night noises made them flee to the safety of the bunks.

And there in the ferns on a warm moonlit night Milove and I had lain once on the second of August. I know the date because our Susan's birthday is May the second.

I returned to the Big Cabin, not on the road, but on the short cut path that I'd made for my wife so she wouldn't have to walk so far to get to the outhouse. She never could get used to sitting on the log I'd nailed between two trees. "The chipmunks look at me," she protested.

That path is mostly down hill and I had no trouble mainly because I rested often, the first time beside the huge flat topped boulder where I found my son, a little lost boy, trying to climb it. Now he is almost fifty years old but I can still see him after I hoisted him on top of it and called him King of the Woods.

From there the path descends westward. I know every foot of it and could walk it with my eyes shut as I often do in my dreams Down Below. My next resting place was by my Healing Rock, a pyramidal boulder covered with lush moss that for years has given me peace and comfort. I laid my old face against it hoping it would heal me again but when I started walking I knew I had asked too much.

Still descending the hill I found that a big birch tree had fallen across the path. A yellow birch, a tough old giant, it had bested many storms to have grown so tall. As I sat upon its huge trunk I noticed that just beyond it was a row of seven or eight pink lady slippers. That surprised me because they are solitary flowers. Then I saw that they were following a depression filled with rich humus that had once been another fallen tree. And there below me was the shimmering lake....

John's Hock

At this point I will leave this special day unfinished although I know that books should have a tidy ending. Lives are not like that and surprisingly as of this writing my own is unfinished too. As I walk through the shadows of the Valley, may my remaining steps be happy ones. I am determined that they shall be. And may all your steps be happy ones too.

Lady Slipper

Afterword

FROM THE PUBLISHERS: We lost a good friend in the fall of 1994. On September 26, 1994, Charles Van Riper–known to Avery readers as Cully Gage–died in Kalamazoo at age 88. He wrote a final farewell to his readers:

Well, I guess this is about the last of our many communications, all good ones. Don't think I'd better try to prepare another. I thank you for the good company of ordinary times and for the ease you brought me in times of trial. Good connections. Good bye.

What shall you say about me when I'm gone? Say:

- *That vicariously I lived a thousand lives in the people I served.*
- *That those I touched were never quite the same.*
- *That through my works and texts I helped pioneer a new helping profession.*
- *That I loved to see the flowers bloom, especially those human flowers, my students.*
- *That through my Northwoods Readers I made many smile.*
- *That out of a barren field I made a park with tall trees, a pool, and many flowers.*
- *That I never quite managed to grow The Perfect Potato.*
- *That in my old age I again danced in the moonlight.*
- *That the deep forests and lakes were a part of all my days.*
- *That I was blessed to have lived with a strong lovely woman for many years.*
- *That we raised three fine children and they in turn nine grandchildren, all of whom loved me.*
- *That I fought myself out of the swamp of despair to make of my life a shining thing.*
- *That a bit of my tiny impact has been felt all over the world.*

Charles (Cully) Gage Van Riper

THE NORTHWOODS READER
Volume 1
Northern Wit & Wisdom

Book 3 *(Heads & Tales)* and book 5 *(What? Another Northwoods Reader?)* are back. They have been combined with book 1 (the original *Northwoods Reader)* to make the first volume.

ISBN 1-892384-02-7

THE NORTHWOODS READER
Volume 2
Northern Love Affair

Volume two of the Northwoods Reader set combines book 4 *(The Last Northwoods Reader)*, book 8 *(Tioga Tales)* and *A Love Affair with the UP.*

ISBN 1-892384-08-6

Avery Color Studios, Inc. has a full line of Great Lakes oriented books, puzzles, cookbooks, shipwreck and lighthouse maps, lighthouse posters and Fresnel lens model.

For a full color catalog call:
1-800-722-9925

Avery Color Studios, Inc. products are available at gift shops and bookstores throughout the Great Lakes region.